REVELATION

ADVENTURES IN THE GLADE | BOOK 3

MARTHA JANE ORLANDO

Jan-Carol
Publishing, Inc

REVELATION
ADVENTURES IN THE GLADE | BOOK 3
Martha Jane Orlando

Published November 2015
Little Creek Books
Imprint of Jan-Carol Publishing, Inc.
All rights reserved
Copyright © Martha Jane Orlando

ISBN: 9781939289803
Library of Congress Control Number: 2015957087

You may contact the publisher:
Jan-Carol Publishing, Inc.
PO Box 701
Johnson City, TN 37605
publisher@jancarolpublishing.com
jancarolpublishing.com

"Davy and the Old Ones, creatures that no one else can see or hear, embark on their mission to stop the encroachment of people in the form of tourists into their special world. Martha Jane Orlando, once again, leads you into the worlds of fantasy and intrigue where your imagination is always the winner."

—Linda Hudson Hoagland, author,
The Best Dam Secret

"In *Revelation*, Reverend and all the Old Ones are determined to discover what is going on with Ronnie Carson. When they discover the truth and confront him, will he listen to reason? Or will their most beloved person suffer as the result? Martha Jane Orlando weaves a wonderful story, keeping the reader glued to the page with the twists and turns of life in The Glade. She teaches valuable lessons of integrity, love for one another, and relying on God for the strength needed in this adventure we call Life."

—Jennifer Barker, author,
Walking in the Spirit, The Key to Producing His Fruit

"Once again Martha Jane Orlando draws in her readers for a thrilling ride along with Davy, Racer, Reverend and a host of other interesting characters. Readers of all ages will enjoy the *Adventures in the Glade*."

—Tammy Robinson Smith, author,
Emmybeth Speaks

ALSO BY MARTHA JANE ORLANDO

THE GLADE SERIES:
A Trip, A Tryst and a Terror
Children in the Garden
The Moment of Truth

ADVENTURES IN THE GLADE SERIES:
Revenge!
Redemption

Revelation is dedicated with love to my three granddaughters:
Virginia Rose, Savannah Jane and Alexandra Nancy.
All of you are and will ever be my dear Chosen Ones.

ACKNOWLEDGMENTS

My journey in writing *The Glade Series* and *Adventures in The Glade* has been nothing less than miraculous. I've been given so much encouragement and help along the way; I am honored to thank the following:

My Father in Heaven who blessed me with the talent for writing and who inspired my stories;

My publisher, Janie C. Jessee, and all the talented folks at Jan-Carol Publishing, Inc. who patiently worked with me and helped me to realize my dream of being a real author;

The good people at the Nantahala Outdoor Center and River's End restaurant who gladly answered my questions;

My associate pastor, Lindsey Solomon, who gave me some timely advice with regards to the character of Pastor Mike Russell;

Matt Schuurman for his input regarding real estate deeds;

Fellow authors, Jennifer Barker, Glynn Young, Linda Hudson Hoagland and Tammy Robinson Smith, for taking the time to preview *Revelation* and for providing concise reviews for the book;

My immediate family for their love and support of my writing endeavors;

My Kennesaw United Methodist Church family for all your uplifted prayers for my novels' success;

Facebook friends and fellow bloggers who spread the word about The Glade Series and Adventures in The Glade on social media and gave me those reassuring words when I needed them the most;

And last, but never least, my husband, Danny. You have been my rock and my biggest fan through it all. Your faith in me never wavered. I love you with all my heart!

LETTER TO THE READER

Revelation is the third book in the Adventures in The Glade series. As I've previously cautioned prospective readers, this novel will make much more sense to you if you've already read the three books in the original Glade Series—a Trip, a Tryst, and a Terror, Children in the Garden and The Moment of Truth, along with the first and second books in Adventures in The Glade—Revenge! and Redemption. You can find all these titles at my website: gladetrilogy.wix.com/theglade. You can also contact me personally there. I love to hear from my readers, so please don't be shy!

Many fans have asked if I will write a fourth book for Adventures in The Glade. It is quite possible that I will, but for right now, I'm resting and praying God's hand will guide me in the direction He wants me to take. I must admit, it's difficult to leave The Glade and all the friends I've made there (yes, my characters do become my friends as I write about them), but I will try to patient in the interim.

So, my friends, it is my hope that Revelation will be a story you will savor as the adventures of Davy, Racer, Reverend, and the whole gang unfold. I assure you, like all the other novels, this, too, is a page-turner. Those who have read it in advance assure me it won't let any of you down!

I wish each one of you reading this God's love and blessings always.

With a grateful heart,
Martha Jane Orlando

PROLOGUE

Ten-year-old Davy Murray detests the idea of spending the summer with his mother, Kate, step-father, Jim, and pesky sister, Anna at Grandpa Will's farm in the mountains. There is no television, no pool, no friends, and >gasp< no computer! Davy thinks his summer is ruined until he meets Grey (later known as Racer), the True Squirrel of the Old Ones, ancient creatures who reside in The Glade; creatures which only Davy can see and hear.

Through their adventures together, Davy grows close to the Old Ones and miraculously, begins to appreciate his own family in a new and refreshing light. Kate and Jim are delighted with the boy's transformation, and prayerfully hope this kinder, gentler Davy will stay for good.

When it is discovered that Jim's devious cousin, Ronnie, is plotting to steal part of Grandpa Will's acreage in order to construct tourist cabins, the Old Ones are mortified. Ronnie is building on their mountain! If he succeeds, it will be the end of their lives in The Glade!

The Old Ones, with Davy's help, devise a plan to save their home. The Tomato Plan, as they call it, is a rousing success. Cousin Ronnie's plans are thwarted, and the Old Ones hold a special celebration in The Glade for Davy, his family, and their neighbors, Mr. and Mrs. Fairchild.

But Ronnie refuses to give up on his dream to snag Grandpa Will's land. The Old Ones soon discover their nemesis is up to no good and must now rely upon their invisibility to spy on Ronnie's activities. Will what they learn be enough to put a stop to Ronnie's shenanigans once and for all? Will the Old Ones, as Reverend, True Owl of the Old Ones, warns, have to risk all to save all?

Find out in the third book in the Adventures in The Glade Series, *Revelation!*

CHAPTER 1

RAFTING DAY

Jim and Kate had tucked Anna and Davy in for the night and were now preparing to turn in themselves. They were confident the whole family would enjoy the rafting trip tomorrow, and knew a good night's sleep was in order. They had just gotten comfortable on the ancient, oversized bed when Jim had a disturbing thought. *Why didn't Eric call me today about what he found out down at the courthouse? I wonder if something happened today that prevented him from following through. Surely that must be it. I just hope that 'something' isn't bad news. I'll call him tomorrow when we get back from the river.*

Jim eased himself carefully onto his side and draped an arm around Kate's waist. He could tell by her even breathing that she was already asleep. Jim nestled into the warmth of her back, and soon he too entered the land of dreams.

***

All was dark and quiet at the Carson household. Even Buddy and Sammy, who regularly defied any bedtime limit during summer break, had retired earlier than usual. Reverend and Sharp-eyes along with Mrs. Sharp-eyes, who had been waiting on Ronnie's roof for the return of his truck so she could swoop onto its bed and into the house, sat together on the overstuffed sofa, the same one Sheriff Peabody had sat upon mere days ago. To the delight of the worn-out owl and hawk, Mrs. Sharp-eyes had brought a sack full of delectable treats from The Glade. All three had savored plenteous and much-needed helpings, but were careful to save enough to serve as breakfast the following morning. Full and quite content, the three Old Ones were tempted to fall asleep then and there on the inviting sofa, but Reverend thought it wise to rest in shifts.

"I'll take first watch," he volunteered.

"Oh, no, dear Reverend, I won't hear of it," Mrs. Sharp-eyes insisted. "You two have had a most harrowing day and are in dire need of rest."

"You can say that again," Sharp-eyes declared, and added with a wry smile, "and oh, my dear, the expression on your face when you saw we were actually *inside* the cab of Ronnie's truck, not in the bed, was priceless!"

"Priceless? I was worried sick about how and why you two decided it was a good idea to even enter the cab, when you had no idea if Ronnie would hold the door open long enough for you to make your escape once you reached your destination."

"And as close a call as we *did* have, squeezing out of there without Ronnie slamming the door on us, you had every right to be worried," said Reverend. "I know for a fact that my wing brushed up against his arm. If I had to use the word priceless to describe an expression, it would have to be the one on Ronnie's face after that transpired!"

All three Old Ones chuckled as they replayed the moment in their minds.

"Certainly, that was amusing in the moment," Sharp-eyes noted, "but won't this make Ronnie even more suspicious about us? What if he figures out we're doing some invisible snooping? Then what?"

"Then what?" Reverend repeated, blinking his round eyes at the hawks. "Why, all the better, I say. Because, my Old Ones, I think I have the beginnings of a plan."

***

"Davy, wake up. It's rafting day," Jim said as he gently nudged the boy's shoulder. Davy's eyes fluttered open, the fog of sleep falling from him instantaneously.

"Rafting! Yes! Yes!" he exclaimed, throwing off his covers and bouncing off his cot. "I can't wait!" He raced ahead of Jim toward the kitchen and made a sharp right in the hall to use the bathroom. The door was closed.

Davy knocked hard. "Anna? Are you in there? I need to go!" He heard the toilet flush. Moments later, the door opened and there was Mom, looking like death warmed over. Her skin was a ghastly white and there were dark circles under her eyes. She put on a brave smile for her son, but he knew immediately something was sorely amiss. "Mom, are you sick?" Davy asked her in alarm. "Does this mean you can't go rafting today?"

Mom patted his cropped head reassuringly. "I'm afraid I'll have to miss out today," she told him. "I've got some kind of stomach bug."

"But it won't be the same without you," Davy insisted adamantly. "Can't you try, Mom? Please?"

In answer, Mom's hand flew to her mouth; she rushed back to the toilet to endure another spell of retching. Jim heard her and ran to the bathroom as fast as he could. "Kate! Kate, why didn't you tell me you didn't feel well? Here, let me help you up and get you back to bed for a spell." Kate, feeling drained and unsteady on her feet, didn't have the energy to protest and allowed Jim to escort her back to the bedroom. As he did what needed doing in the bathroom, Davy couldn't help but feel worried about his mother. Just yesterday she was the picture of health, but now? *Why does Mom have to be sick today of all days? She was looking forward to this as much as I was! Since she's sick, will Jim cancel our trip to stay with her?* Davy loathed that thought, but knew in his heart that it would be the right thing to do. He hoped his disappointment wouldn't show too much.

When Davy returned to the kitchen, he found Jim at the phone dialing a number. "Who are you calling, Jim?" he asked.

"Your Nana and Bampa," Jim answered. "I'm going to see if Susie can keep an eye on your mother while we're on our rafting trip."

"So you're not going to cancel it after all?" Davy was amazed and delighted.

"Your mother insisted we not change our plans because of her condition this morning. She said she'd feel guilty for making us miss all the fun," Jim said. "If Nana can stay, how about we ask Bampa to come along with us today in your Mom's place?"

"Yippee!" Davy shouted, dancing around the kitchen table like a wild man. This made Maggie look up from devouring her morning meal. Sensing Davy's joy, she added her resounding bark to the celebration. Frisky, alarmed by the entire ruckus, cowed in a corner, mewing patheti-

3

cally. Anna, who was just descending the ladder from her loft, spotted her petrified kitten and ran to scoop him up in her arms.

"Davy!" Jim hollered over the din. "I know you're excited, but let's have some quiet here. I can't hear a word Bob is saying."

"Sorry, Jim!" Davy answered. Now breathless, he forced himself to stop cavorting around the room and to pat Maggie until she calmed down.

Anna stood for several moments in the corner with Frisky until the kitten regained his composure. She then walked over to where Davy was crouched next to Maggie and asked, "Where's Mom? Why isn't she up yet?"

Davy, still stroking the dog's head, replied, "Mom woke up sick this morning, so she went back to bed."

Anna's eyes widened. "Is she going to be all right? I mean, is she still planning to come with us?"

"No, Anna, she won't be able to make it," said Jim as he hung up the phone, "but your Bampa will go with us in her place and Nana will come stay with your mother until she is feeling better. How does that sound?"

"Okay, I guess," Anna said. "I'm just sorry Mom isn't feeling good."

"Let's hope she's right as rain by the time we get back from the rafting trip. She'll certainly be in good hands with Nana, so there are no worries there. Okay, kids, what do you say we eat breakfast and get ready to go? Bampa and Nana will be over here in thirty minutes."

Davy and Anna scurried for the pantry as fast as they could go while Jim filled water bottles for all of them. As Davy popped a bagel into the toaster, he glanced out the window to see Racer hopping up and down excitedly, gesturing to the boy that he wanted in. Davy ran to the kitchen door and flung it open.

"Are you coming with us, Racer?" Davy asked excitedly.

"What? Not even a 'good morning' or a 'howdy-do?'" Racer teased. "Of course I'm coming with you! I never miss a chance to go rafting, and neither do the otters."

"Really?" Davy exclaimed. "You mean Silky and Mrs. Silky are coming, too? But how will we all fit in the raft?"

At this, Racer threw back his head and laughed heartily. "Oh, my dear child," he said once he caught his breath, "the otters won't be in the raft. They'll be in the river, swimming along merrily beside us. Yes, yes, indeed! I do believe this will be a glorious day!"

4

**

When Kate finally roused from what was an unexpectedly refreshing nap, she was surprised to see Susie at the kitchen counter dicing ripe tomatoes. "Hi, Susie," she said, "what's all this?"

"Good morning, dear," Susie replied. "Remember I promised to teach you how to can tomatoes? Even if you're not feeling up to it at the moment you can simply watch, but I really had to get to them before they go bad on us. Are you feeling better now? Jim said you were having a time of it this morning and asked me to come look after you while they went rafting. Bob went with them, so it's just you and me today."

"Yes, Susie, I do feel remarkably better, Kate said. "I'm actually thinking of having something to eat, too. You wouldn't have heard me say that an hour ago. I'm happy Bob was able to go; Davy and Anna will love having him there."

"Yes, as much as he will love being there," Susie assured her. "Now go ahead and get yourself some breakfast and, if you're up to it, we can begin the canning lessons whenever you're ready."

"I'll do just that," Kate replied, "but after a quick shower. After being ill this morning, I really need to freshen up."

"Take your time," said Susie. "These tomatoes aren't going anywhere and I have lots left to chop." As she returned to the task at hand, Susie reflected upon how quickly Kate seemed to have recovered from this morning's illness. Jim had described her state of health as being mighty puny, and said he'd feel much better about leaving Kate today if she was in Susie's competent hands. Just to be on the safe side, Susie decided she would take Kate's temperature and make her drink a glass of water to see if that stayed down before allowing her to eat anything substantial. Susie reached for another tomato, placed it on the cutting board, and set the knife against the deep-red skin. Just as the blade pierced into the juicy pulp, an unexpected and startling thought sliced through her mind. *What if Kate's not sick with something contagious? What if? Could she possibly be? Wait! She said Jim and his first wife couldn't have children. She blamed Jim. What if the one with the problem wasn't Jim after all?*

At that moment, Kate strode energetically into the kitchen. "I'm famished!" she announced. "Think I'll make some scrambled eggs this morning with a bit of toast. Would you like some, Susie? Susie? Are you all right?" Kate observed, not without a sense of alarm, Susie standing stock still at the counter. Her eyes were staring off into space, as though she were deep in thought. When Kate asked if she was all right, Susie hastily shook herself free from her reverie to assure her young friend that, yes, she was perfectly fine. "That's good," Kate said with a relief she truly felt. "You looked like you were somewhere far, far away. Penny for your thoughts?"

Susie froze again. Should she even breathe her suspicions to Kate? *What if I'm wrong about this? How will she feel if I get her hopes up, and it turns out she's not pregnant after all? Oh, but I feel deep down that she is! What if she knows, too, but hasn't said anything because she's not far enough along?* It was when Susie saw Kate pouring herself a cup of coffee, she knew she had to come clean .

"Kate," Susie began, "I *was* deep in thought when you came in just now. I was thinking about you and what happened this morning."

"What do you mean, Susie?" Kate asked as she began whisking an egg with a touch of milk in a small bowl. "I either had a stomach bug or was reacting to something I ate yesterday that obviously didn't agree with me. If you're worried about getting sick, too, I'll make sure to keep my distance."

"No need for that, dear," Susie smiled and patted Kate on the shoulder. "I can't catch what you have."

Kate stopped beating the eggs. "You can't? I know you were a nurse for years, Susie, but how can you be so sure?"

Susie looked Kate steadily in the eyes and said quietly, "You don't have a stomach bug. It isn't anything you ate yesterday. But I do think you need to go easy on the coffee."

Now it was Kate's turn to freeze in place. The only time her doctor had her cut down on caffeine in the past was when she was...*When I was...* "You think I'm pregnant?" she managed to whisper, tears welling up in her eyes. "How can that possibly be? Jim said..."

"Never mind what Jim said," Susie said reassuringly. "He was only telling you what his former wife had convinced him to believe. What if the problem was never Jim's at all?"

Kate was dumbfounded. After all this time thinking she and Jim would never have a child of their own, she found Susie's theory all too overwhelming. Suddenly, feeling weak in the knees, Kate knew she had to sit down. "Susie, will you help me over to the table? I'm afraid I'm a bit woozy."

"Certainly, dear," Susie said comfortingly, and taking Kate by the elbow, gently steered her to the kitchen table and helped her to sit down. "You stay right here and I'll get your breakfast for you. More reason now than ever to keep your strength up, wouldn't you agree?"

***

Pastor Mike Russell rolled out of bed bright and early, looking forward to his morning run with more enthusiasm than he'd had in quite some time. Even though the day before him would be busier than the last, his heart was light and his soul was singing. He knew nothing could dampen his spirits today, and he had Abby McGuire to thank for it. Mike had anticipated a pleasant visit with this family who expressed interest in joining Nantahala United Methodist, but in his wildest dreams he couldn't have imagined the deep and lively conversation he'd shared that evening with Abby. They talked about everything, from school to church to current events. She had a quick wit, a lively sense of humor, and the sweetest smile he had ever seen. Because of her, he had stayed much later in the evening than he would normally have done.

Now as Mike ran his usual route, memories of his time with Abby refused to vacate his mind. She was all he could think about. He knew she was in her last year of college, and there was an age gap between them that Mike hoped her parents wouldn't deem inappropriate, should he ask her on a date. *On a date? When was the last time you went on a date with anyone? What are you thinking, man? Get a grip!* But the more Mike tried to get a grip on himself, the tighter the image of Abby gripped him. He simply couldn't shake it, nor did he desire to. More than anything, he wanted to see her again. Abby had told him that she had a summer job at the Nantahala Outdoor Center. He wondered if she was working today. His visitation run took him right past there, but he was uncertain as to whether he would even have time to stop in. Pastor Mike said a silent prayer: *If it's Your will, Father, give me a chance to see Abby today. Yes, I confess, I'm really taken with her. I can't wait to see her again. I liked everything about her, Lord, and I want to get to know her better. I pray this is in Your plan for both Abby and me. Thank you, Father, for listening to Your child as You so faithfully do. Amen.*

***

Jim, Bob, Davy, and Anna arrived at the Nantahala Outdoor Center at the stroke of nine. Zach, with his grandchildren in tow, pulled in only seconds after. Davy's eyes lit up when he saw the inflated raft in the bed of Zach's pickup, as he knew it wouldn't be long before they would be joyously gliding down the river. Jim rolled down his window to hail Zach.

"Right on time!" Zach exclaimed. "I like that. Just follow me down the road a piece to the launching site. I'll have one of my crew tote us back to get our vehicles, once we've landed here."

"Sounds great," Jim said, giving Zach a thumbs-up. "See you in a few." Turning to Davy and Anna, he said, "It won't be long now, kids. Hope you're ready for the ride of a lifetime."

"I second that," said Bob. "There's nothing like cruising down the Nantahala! Better than a ride in my pickup any old day."

Davy and Anna gave a cheer, and Racer hopped up and down enthusiastically as Jim's car pulled out to follow Zach's down the road. "The river's flowing fast! The river's flowing fast! It's going to be a blast! It's going to be a blast!" the squirrel chanted. Davy couldn't help but throw his head back with vigorous laughter.

Bob turned to Jim. "Was it something I said?"

"Not to deflate your ego, Bob," Jim replied with a grin, "but I'm willing to venture it's something Racer is saying or doing right now. I do hope you behave yourself on this trip, Racer!" Jim admonished him cheerfully. "If Davy has too many outbursts on this adventure, we might not get a second invitation."

Racer volleyed back. "Jim, the very thought I wouldn't behave cuts me to the quick! Of course I'll be good—when I feel like it."

The squirrel's answer made Davy laugh all over again. When he finally calmed down, he said to Jim, "Racer can't be anything other than who he is. It's up to me to control myself the best I can."

Jim smiled and said, "Glad to see you're owning up to your responsibility, son. You're sounding more like a man every day."

***

Sheriff Eric Peabody awoke to see slender beams of light peeking through the blinds, closed against the morning sun. Their cheerful presence made the dimly-lit hospital room seem even more gloomy and oppressive. He had slept, if one could call it that, fitfully during the night. It had been nigh impossible to get comfortable in the stiff-cushioned chair, and the nurses arriving hourly to check Elly's vital signs woke him up each time they entered, even though they tried their best to be discreet. Eric stretched his arms above his head as a yawn escaped his mouth, and realized immediately he had an unforgiving crick in his neck from trying to sleep sitting up. As he attempted to massage away the discomfort, he thought of all the times Elly had rubbed his neck and shoulders at the end of a long day, helping his tension and stiffness to melt away. Eric looked at his wife now; she was sleeping peacefully, as if yesterday's trauma had never happened. He knew that it would be another story when she awakened, and reality hit her with the force of a wrecking ball.

Eric glanced at his wristwatch. It was just after seven. He stood up stiffly and headed for the bathroom to splash some cold water on his face, hoping it would revive him. When he flipped on the light and met his reflection in the mirror, Eric almost didn't recognize himself. His hair was disheveled, his five-o'clock shadow made it appear he was growing a beard, and the puffiness of his eyelids betrayed the torrent of tears Elly and he had shared yesterday. He knew there would be more today, and tomorrow, and for many days to come. Broken hearts take time to heal, and theirs were not just broken, they were shattered.

"Eric? Where are you?" Elly's voice sounded faint and tired.

"Right here," he answered, popping his head around the corner. He headed for her bedside as he dried his face with a towel.

Elly offered Eric her hand, which he gladly cradled in both of his. She was smiling at him; there was an unmistakable sadness in her eyes, which were as swollen as his. "Were you able to get any sleep last night?" Elly asked, with a note of concern.

"To be honest," Eric confessed, "I got very little, but I'll be fine." He yawned again.

9

"Oh, honey, you should have gone on home last night when you knew I would be okay, and slept in a real bed."

"And leave you here all alone? Not on your life!" Eric declared. "Besides, if I'd done that, I wouldn't have enjoyed one wink of sleep. I would have been too worried about you."

There was a tapping at the door. "I'm here to check on the patient," a nurse announced, one whom Eric hadn't seen last night. She must have just come on duty. "I'm Linda." She introduced herself, validating the name on her badge. "I'll be your nurse from now until four o'clock."

"Oh, I do hope I won't be here all day," Elly said in alarm. Realizing her statement might sound offensive to the pleasant nurse, she added hastily, "That's not because of you, Linda, of course. It's just that I'm hoping the doctor will let me go home this morning."

Linda smiled cheerfully. "I hope so, too. Hospitals aren't the happiest places to be, especially when you're the patient. Even though I truly love my job, sometimes it's not the happiest place for me, either. I'll check to see when the doctor will be doing his rounds and let you know, if you'd like."

"Oh, that's so kind of you," said Elly. "I really would appreciate knowing."

"No problem," Linda told her. "And now that you're awake, are you ready for some breakfast? As soon as I'm finished here, I can bring it straight away."

Elly, who hadn't been able to consume a morsel since arriving at the hospital, suddenly realized how ravenous she was. "That would be lovely, Linda. I'm really hungry."

Eric smiled at his wife's words, happy that her appetite had returned to normal. It was then he realized how little he had eaten the day before. His stomach reminded him with a particularly annoying growl. "Elly," he said, "while Linda is fetching you something to eat, do you mind if I run to the cafeteria? I'll hurry back so we can eat together."

"Oh, yes, please go," Elly insisted. "I'll be fine until you get back."

"Are you sure?"

"Eric, you have to eat, too," she said, giving his hand a squeeze.

"I love you," Eric mouthed the words to his wife, as Linda was still in the room.

"I love you more."

***

David and Sarah Murray were utterly exhausted by the time they arrived at Hartsfield-Jackson Airport in Atlanta. As they stood bleary-eyed and jet-lagged at the luggage carousel, where they hoped and prayed their suitcase with the bulk of their clothes would show up, Sarah had a thought.

"David," she said, "since both of us are extremely tired, why don't we take a taxi to the hotel? I know it costs extra, but it would cost a lot more in the long run if we had an accident in the rental car because we couldn't keep our eyes open."

Feeling the same way she did, David readily agreed. "That's a great idea, Sarah. Neither of us needs the stress of driving in Atlanta traffic right now. To heck with the expense! We're on vacation, aren't we?"

Sarah laughed. "Don't most folks on vacation call it Island Time? Our island time is every day. So what should we name our vacation?"

As punchy as he felt, David's quick response surprised them both. "I suppose since we're heading for the mountains, we're on Highland Time!"

CHAPTER 2

PADDLES AND PRAYERS

"Sharp-eyes! Reverend! Wake up!" Mrs. Sharp-eyes whispered urgently. "I hear noises upstairs. Someone is awake." The hawk and the owl roused themselves from what had been, for both of them, a delicious slumber. Mrs. Sharp-eyes, well aware of their eventful and tiring day, had decided to keep the entire night-watch for them. When they realized the sacrifice she had made on their behalf, Reverend and Sharp-eyes were beside themselves with thankfulness.

"My dear," said Sharp-eyes, "you shouldn't have taken all that on yourself, but I must admit, I feel good as new after sleeping through the night."

"As do I," Reverend chimed in. "You have gone above and beyond the call of duty, Mrs. Sharp-eyes. There is only one thing left for you to do."

"And what would that be?" she inquired, suddenly overcome with drowsiness.

"Return to The Glade at once and get some much-needed rest," Reverend ordered gleefully. "Sharp-eyes and I will take it from here."

Mrs. Sharp-eyes sighed with relief. "Oh, thank you, Reverend. That will be quite the tonic for me. Once I've rested, I'll return with more food for all of us."

"Splendid, my dear," said Sharp-eyes, nuzzling her beak with his. "We shall see you this evening, then?"

"You will, dearest," she said. "I'll be off just as soon as someone can let me out of this house."

"Hmm," Sharp-eyes mused, "how can we go about setting you free?"

Reverend said, "Perhaps we should check to see if any doors are unlocked. Since the handles of the doors leading outside are like a lever, it would be easy to push down on it with my talons to loosen the latch. I say we start the search immediately."

The owl and the hawks wasted no time in testing every door to the outside world. All were locked. They were beginning to give up hope when Reverend spied the door leading to the garage. "We haven't tried that one yet," he said excitedly. It could be unlocked because the garage doors are shut."

"But what good will that do?" Mrs. Sharp-eyes wondered. "I'll just be stuck in the garage, won't I?"

Reverend grinned mischievously. "If we can get into the garage, my dear hawk, I know how to get you out."

Sharp-eyes and Mrs. Sharp-eyes exchanged confused looks, but followed Reverend to the aforementioned door and held their breath. The owl flapped his wings a time or two to gain the necessary height to land on the handle. To their absolute delight, the moment his talons gripped it, the latch gave way and the door swung wide. They hastened into the garage. Reverend once again took flight and perched on the side of Ronnie's truck bed, which was near a central support pole.

"See this white switch with the blinking red light?" he asked. "It's the way we will get the garage door to open. I just caught a glimpse of Ronnie using it after our close encounter yesterday. If you're ready for take-off, Mrs. Sharp-eyes, I'll pull that switch."

"Oh, I'm way past ready," she declared, giving Sharp-eyes a quick hug. "Let's do this, Reverend!"

Ronnie was just toweling himself dry from his morning shower when he heard the unmistakable sound of the garage door being opened. *What in tarnation?* Hastily, he finished drying off, wrapped the towel around his waist, and dashed through the bedroom where Betty Rae was still sleeping, taking time only to grab his rifle in case he met with an armed intruder. Ronnie thundered down the stairs to the living room and made a beeline to the door leading to the garage. When he saw it was ajar, he stopped dead in his tracks. His heart pounding, he eased the safety off the rifle and crept stealthily toward the door. With his back against it, Ronnie surveyed what he could see of the garage without revealing his presence just yet. Yes, the garage door behind his pickup was wide open. He strained to listen for any sound that would betray an unwanted guest. All was silent, except for the chirping of birds in the trees.

Feeling a bit braver now, Ronnie swung the door open with his rifle at the ready. "All right, you danged varmint, show your face!" he yelled menacingly. Reverend and Sharp-eyes practically jumped out of their feathers. When they beheld their nemesis clothed only in a towel, the two wanted to laugh until their sides ached; the sight of the rifle sobered them up instantly.

"Quick!" Reverend exclaimed. "We have to get back into the house before Ronnie shuts the door and decides to lock it!" Sharp-eyes needed no prodding. In a flash, the two flew inside the house, keeping a healthy distance from the armed and potentially dangerous Ronnie. Not wishing to risk any contact, the owl and hawk perched on the broad mantelpiece of the stone fireplace.

"That was a close one," Sharp-eyes said, once he had recovered his breath.

"Yes, my friend," Reverend agreed, "and way too close for comfort. Oh, I hope today is the day when Ronnie will do something that truly incriminates him. This spying business is weighing heavily on my heart and trying my very soul."

***

The journey to the raft launch location was painfully slow. Davy knew the reason: Buses from the NOC and other rafting companies were creeping toward the same destination. Davy wondered if the river would be too crowded to even navigate. He decided to ask Bampa about it, since he had ridden the river before. "Bampa, look at all this traffic. Will it be this bad on the river, too?"

"It will feel that way at first, Davy, when everyone is boarding the rafts and shoving out into the rapids," Bampa told him, "but it doesn't take long for the packs to separate. Sure, we will more than likely have rafts in view ahead of us and behind, but it never feels crowded."

Reassured by this, Davy leaned back on the seat and sighed. "Everything okay, Davy?" Racer asked.

"Now it is," the boy answered. "I was worried that if the river was too crowded, Silky and Mrs. Silky would have a hard time staying with us."

"Don't you give that a second thought, child," Racer said with a chuckle. "Those two are pros when it comes to navigating the river. And as you haven't had the pleasure of spending a lot of time with them since the Naming, you'll especially enjoy watching their antics; regular water acrobats, those two."

Davy had a thought. "Racer, can you swim?" he asked.

"Me? Swim? But of course!" Racer declared. "Not with the grace of the otters, let me assure you, but I can dog paddle and I use my tail to steer in the right direction. I don't like to swim unless it's absolutely necessary, though."

"Why is that?" Davy asked. He loved swimming so much and couldn't fathom why everyone else, including the Old Ones, might not share the same sentiment.

"Two reasons," the squirrel said. "The first is that the waters in these mountains are frigid, as you learned on our creek hike, and I'm not suitably padded against the cold like the otters are." Racer leaned in closer to Davy as if he were about to share a deep, dark secret. "And secondly, when I *do* get into the water, I become visible."

Davy was shocked. "You mean, if you somehow fall in the river today, everyone would see you?" he asked in a heightened tone, which grabbed everyone's attention.

"What's that, Davy?" Anna piped up. "What about seeing Racer?"

"Racer says when he swims, he becomes visible to anyone who happens to be around."

"Well in that case," Jim observed, "I hope you'll take every precaution to stay in the raft, Racer. We don't need a Mad Squirrel Sunday *and* a Mad Squirrel Tuesday."

Racer laughed enthusiastically at this comment. When he finally got hold of himself, he said, "Davy, tell Jim I have every intention to stay high and dry. I've quite had my fill of personal appearances of late, and I don't desire to make any in the near future."

When Davy relayed the squirrel's message, Anna was dismayed. "Oh, Racer, does this mean I won't get to see you anytime soon?" In answer to her question, the True Squirrel of the Old Ones appeared, big as life, before Anna's startled and wondering eyes. He remained in that state for only a few seconds, but in that brief time, he leaped to the girl's shoulder and planted a whiskery kiss on her cheek.

***

After she finished her breakfast, Kate felt renewed and ready for her lesson in canning from Susie. The two worked all morning together, chatting and laughing as they did so, but neither brought up the probability of Kate's pregnancy until they took a break for lunch. Susie was the first to broach the topic. "You certainly paid meticulous attention to all I showed you today, Kate. I'm amazed by how you were able to concentrate, what with all that transpired this morning."

Kate took another bite of her chicken salad sandwich, chewed thoughtfully, and swallowed before she answered. "I think that's exactly why I *could* pay attention to you, Susie. You see, it's such unexpected, too-good-to-be-true, over-the-top news, I really haven't processed it. I mean, you could be spot-on, right about my condition, but don't you think I should take one of those pregnancy tests before I share any of this with Jim? I'd hate to tell him our suspicions and have them turn out to be only that—suspicions."

"By all means," Susie agreed. "A pregnancy test is absolutely in order, and the sooner the better."

"I'd run out this afternoon to buy one if I had any idea where to go," Kate lamented. "I haven't left the farm except to attend church the whole time we've been here. I'm afraid I'd get lost."

"Not to worry," Susie said, reaching across the table to pat Kate's hand. "I have some errands to run in Bryson City this afternoon, and I'll be more than happy to pick one up from the drugstore for you."

"Oh, Susie, would you? That would be a godsend!" Kate said gratefully.

"There's only one hitch," said Susie, with a gleam in her eyes.

"And what's that?"

"We're not quite through with the canning, but I think you've learned well enough, to the point where you're ready to go it alone. Can you do that so I can leave in a minute? That way I can get back before the others come home. It wouldn't do for me to hand you a pregnancy test in front of prying eyes, now, would it?"

Kate had to laugh. "No, it wouldn't. Even if you had it wrapped in a bag, the kids would want to know what Nana bought me. And yes, I feel confident enough to finish up the batch for you, Susie. You've been a marvelous teacher."

"And you the apt pupil, my dear," Susie assured Kate. She popped the last bite of sandwich into her mouth and rose to take her plate to the sink. She then gathered her purse and keys from where she had left them on the buffet, and walked back over to Kate to give her a motherly hug. "I'm so happy for you," she whispered. "I have no doubt the test will be positive."

"Oh, I pray so," Kate said in earnest. "I pray so."

***

Eric did what he could to make himself look presentable before leaving for the cafeteria, but the wrinkles in his uniform and still swollen eyes just could not be helped. Secretly he hoped he wouldn't run into anyone he knew, but that was not to be. "Eric! Is that you?"

The unmistakable voice of Mildred Mason caught him off guard. He stopped where he was and turned to greet her. "Good morning, Mildred. How is Edgar feeling today?"

"Oh, he's much improved," she told him. "The doctor is fairly certain we can go home this afternoon." She paused to study Eric's face, and knew instantly that something was far from right. "Why are you here at the hospital this morning? I thought you left yesterday." When Mildred saw the pain in Eric's eyes, she wished she had never asked the question.

Eric bowed his head and squeezed his eyes shut, willing the tears to stay put. He took a deep breath and addressed Mildred in the softest of tones. "I'm here because Elly lost our baby yesterday."

"Oh, dear, oh, no," Mildred said shaking her head in sincere sympathy. "I didn't even know Elly was pregnant. Oh, what a shame and sorrow!"

"No one knew, except us. We chose to wait a bit longer. And now, we have nothing to tell," Eric said, his voice hoarse with emotion.

"Does Pastor Russell know what happened?" Mildred asked.

Eric shook his head and sighed. "I don't have his number. Sure could have used some prayers last night."

"You still need prayers, "Mildred insisted. Hastily, she rummaged around in her oversized pocketbook and produced a tattered but still functional address book. Holding it up to Eric, she announced, "I have the pastor's home number in here and Janet Marshall's, too. She organizes the prayer chain at church. If you like, I'll give them both a call when I get back up to Edgar's room." Eric, now too choked up to trust his voice, simply nodded. "It's all settled then," Mildred said, reaching on tip-toe to give the sheriff a grandmotherly pat on his stubble-covered cheek. "Don't you worry about a thing, my dear. Prayers are on the way."

***

Pastor Mike had just grabbed his keys from their hook beside the back door when the phone on his desk jangled demandingly. For a split second, he thought about letting his answering machine get it, but something made him feel the call coming through was of utmost urgency. He ran to his office and picked it up. "Hello, Pastor Russell here."

"Hello, Pastor, it's Mildred again." She had called Mike yesterday about Edgar's spill and subsequent overnight stay at the hospital, but had insisted he need not visit, just keep them in his prayers.

"Mildred? How is Edgar faring this morning?"

"Much better," she said. "He'll be his ornery old self in no time. It's not him I'm calling you about. It's about Sheriff Eric and his wife, Elly."

***

When Jim saw Zach's truck signal a left-hand turn, he followed suit. Within moments, the two vehicles were parked side-by-side in a grassy area a fair distance away from the raft buses. Davy and Racer were the first ones to bound out of the car, with the others exiting at a more sedate pace. Zach and his two grandchildren had already hopped out of the truck, and were standing there waiting to greet their rafting companions. Zach's expression was befuddled when he saw Bob getting out of the car.

"Thought you said you were bringing the wife, Jim," Zach said. He reached a hand out to the unexpected guest and introduced himself. "I'm Zach Jones," he said cheerfully. "Nice to have you aboard today."

18

"Bob Fairchild," said Bob as the men shook hands. "I'm glad I had the opportunity to come along."

"Kate wasn't feeling well this morning," Jim explained, "so Bob here was gracious enough to come with us."

"Good deal," Zach said. "These are my twin grandchildren, Tyler and Taylor." The brother and sister waved at everyone shyly. Davy guessed they were probably twelve years old.

"And these here are my kids, Davy and Anna," Jim said proudly. The fact that he didn't introduce him and his sister as stepchildren was not lost on Davy. He flashed Jim a bright smile to show his approval.

"You're twins?" Anna asked in amazement. "Why don't you look alike?"

Everyone had a chuckle at this except Anna, who thought she'd asked a valid question. Taylor spoke up first. "We're what they call fraternal twins, Anna," she told her. "Only identical twins look like each other."

"Oh, I see."

"Okay," said Zach, "now that the introductions are out of the way, what say we unload the truck and get this raft in the river?"

***

At ten o'clock, Nurse Linda returned to Elly's room to check her vitals and bring some much awaited good news. "Just saw Dr. Harris in the hall making his morning rounds," she said brightly. "Shouldn't be long before he's in to see you."

"Oh, that's a relief," said Elly. "I do hope he'll tell us I'm good to go." There was a soft knock on the door of the room. "Maybe that's the doctor now!"

"Come in," Linda called out. Eric walked to the door, anxious to see if the visitor was the doctor. When he realized their caller was Pastor Mike, his tired face managed a welcoming smile. He knew Dr. Harris's care for Elly's physical health was all important, but her hurting spirit needed the pastor's brand of healing.

Eric shook Pastor Mike's hand warmly. "Thanks for coming," he said, finding to his dismay that he was on the verge of choking up all over again.

"I'm thankful I chose to answer the phone when Mildred called," Mike said softly. "I left right then."

"Pastor Mike?" Elly queried, as she couldn't see around the corner. "Is that you?"

"Yes it is, Elly," Mike said cheerily as he came into view, with Eric right behind him. "I'd have been here earlier had I known." He approached Elly's bedside and took her hand gently, his eyes behind his wire-rim glasses luminous with empathy. "My heart aches for both of you. I'm so, so sorry you've had to go through this."

Elly's eyes welled with tears she didn't know she had left. Sensing their need for privacy and prayer, Linda excused herself. "I'll just go see if I can track down Dr. Harris," she said as she exited the room. As soon as she left, the dam broke. Elly's sobs were so heart wrenching, neither Eric nor Mike could hold back the tears that streamed down their cheeks. Mike prayed silently as he held one of her hands, and Eric held the other. Patiently and lovingly, they allowed Elly to grieve all over again for the loss of her child.

***

Susie Fairchild stood in the drug store aisle, which hosted too vast a variety of pregnancy tests, she thought. With her readers on her nose and a studious look on her face, she examined the promised features of each and tried to determine which one she could trust to be the most reliable. *It won't do to have any false alarms. I wish I'd taken the time to research this online before plunging into the unknown.* As she replaced one test on the shelf and removed another, Susie observed two women about Kate's age staring curiously at her. She knew why right away, but decided to ignore them and continue browsing.

After about ten minutes, Susie finally chose what she hoped would be the test with the most dependable results. She took it from the shelf and when she turned to head for the cashier, realized that not only were those two women still gawking at her, but a small crowd had gathered at the end of the aisle, all bearing quizzical expressions. Uncharacteristically, Susie shamed them with a scowl as she strode past them with head held high and made a straight for the checkout counter. When she handed her purchase to the clerk, a pimple-faced teen with the nametag "Larry," she watched as he looked at the pregnancy test then back at her with the same disbelief as the nosy crowd she had just left behind. This, unfortunately, was the straw that broke the camel's back.

"Yes, I'm buying this; my name is Sarah and my husband's name is Abraham," Susie stated brusquely. "Get over it!" Hastily, and without so much as a "thank you for shopping with us," Larry rang up the purchase, stuffed it in a bag with the receipt, and gave Susie her change with shaky hands.

Sporting an indignant look on her usually genial face, Susie marched determinedly out of the store. As she got in her car and began backing out of her parking place, she noticed a throng of shoppers gathered at the pharmacy window, all with the same looks of disbelief on their faces. Susie gave them what she hoped was a withering stare and took off with a squeal of her tires. Once she was out of their sight, she broke into gales of laughter so intense she had to pull off the road to compose herself. Susie took the pregnancy test out of the bag and started laughing all over again.

"You better give us good news," she told the box. "And Kate, if it's a boy, you're going to have to name him Isaac!"

***

Ronnie slid his chair back from the table; he'd just finished breakfast.

"I'm going to be doing some work in my office," he announced to his family. They had only just begun consuming their morning meal, which for Betty Rae, consisted of only a cup of coffee.

"I thought you we're going to check on those properties in Pigeon Forge today," Betty Rae remarked.

"Changed my mind," Ronnie stated flatly. He got up, leaving his plate right where it was, and lumbered off to his destination.

"Follow him closely," Reverend advised Sharp-eyes. "We have to make sure we get into that office right behind Ronnie, as he's liable to shut and lock the door."

"Why would he lock it?" Sharp-eyes wondered. "It's only his family here, at least to his knowledge."

"I just have a hunch," said the owl. "If he altered his plans for the day, there must be a reason. And that reason just might provide us with another clue as to what Ronnie's really up to."

The two Old Ones, awkward on their talons, kept as close to Ronnie as they dared without betraying their presence. To their immense relief, the door to the office remained open long enough for them to slip in without a mishap. As Reverend predicted, Ronnie did lock the door. They waited until Ronnie was seated at his sprawling desk to fly to the top of a bookshelf, where they would have an advantageous view of whatever it was he was preparing to do. Their eyes grew wide when they saw Ronnie finger a small, delicate looking key on his chain and insert it into the lock on his desk drawer. They heard the fine click it made as Ronnie turned it. He pulled the drawer open noiselessly and retrieved an impressive-looking ledger, and what the owl and hawk concluded must be a checkbook. Ronnie opened the checkbook first and shoved it to his left before he took a pencil from the cup on his desk and opened the ledger. This gave Reverend and Sharp-eyes a chance to study the check itself. Simultaneously, they gasped.

The name printed on the check was not Ronnie's.

***

Before heading for the river, Zach handed each person a life vest. He insisted the children wear protective helmets, too.

"The river is running high, which makes it easier to avoid the rocks, but I don't like to take chances when it comes to the young'uns," he stated. "And then there's that last section of rapids before we reach the NOC, which is quite a doozy if we're not careful. If someone was to fall into the river, it would more than likely be the place it happens."

Davy saw Anna's eyes grow round with fear.

"Don't worry," he whispered. "At least you didn't bring Mary and Smokey. Even if one of us does fall in, we've got the vests and helmets to protect us."

"Make sure Anna knows the otters will be with us, too," said Racer. "In fact I see them now, waiting for us in the shallows."

When Anna heard this from Davy, she was mightily relieved. "I'm glad they're here," she said, loudly enough to be overheard.

"Glad who's here?" Zach asked as he removed the paddles from the truck bed.

Davy thought fast. "Tyler and Taylor," he blurted. "Anna was worried she'd be too little to handle a paddle, and she's happy some older kids can do it for her." As soon as the words tumbled out of his mouth, Davy regretted saying them. His instinct to protect the Old Ones was so fierce, it overwhelmed his new resolve to tell the truth. He had lied, and it didn't feel good or right or true. Racer, sensing the boy's inner turmoil, gave his hand a reassuring pat. For the first time ever, Davy found little comfort in his friend's touch.

Zach grinned. "And so she should be. These two are seasoned river rafters. Anna and Davy, you can sit in the front of the raft and just relax and enjoy the ride." Both Tyler and Taylor smiled at their grandfather's compliment as he handed them the paddles to carry. The men were going to transport the raft to the river's edge.

Taylor handed Anna one of the paddles. "You may be too small to use them," she told Anna with a smile, "but you can help carry one." Anna took the paddle delightedly and returned Taylor's smile. The older girl balanced her remaining paddles in one arm, took Anna's free hand in hers, and strolled with her toward the river. "You can sit on my side of the raft, Anna," Taylor said. "I'll be right behind you."

Right on cue, the men hoisted the raft over their heads, and the entire party, except for Davy and Racer, followed Tyler, Taylor and Anna. The boy wanted a few words with his friend. "Racer," he said in an almost inaudible voice, his head hanging in shame, "I feel awful about what I just said a minute ago. I shouldn't say anything at all unless it's the truth. I know that and I really, really *want* to be truthful. It's just, it's just…"

"Now child, we all want to tell the truth," said Racer, "but look what happened to young Will when he tried to be forthcoming. And I must admit, in having you keep me and the other Old Ones a secret from your family, I was setting an awfully poor example for you. Afraid it's my fault for planting such a notion in that trusting head of yours."

"Oh, Racer, please don't blame yourself," Davy insisted. "I just have to get my tongue under control. As Jim says, it's my responsibility."

Racer gave Davy one of his amusing, lop-sided grins. "Yes, you will, and yes, it is," he said. "Step by step, my child, step by step. You'll get there."

CHAPTER 3

LOVE AND LAUGHTER

Abby McGuire was always friendly and polite to each and every customer who came through the doors of the Nantahala Outdoor Center, but today she radiated an exuberance and warmth that left each person with whom she came in contact feeling brighter and happier about the day. When her mother told her that Pastor Mike was coming around dinner time and would be invited to eat with them, Abby had been less than enthusiastic. She had just finished a long day at work, and was not looking forward to entertaining a man who she assumed would be stiff, formal, and boring, just like all the other ministers she had known. To Abby's utter surprise, Pastor Mike turned out to be nothing like what she had imagined. Cordial, down-to-earth, quick-witted, and engaging were the adjectives that came most readily to her mind.

Not to mention cute! This thought made Abby blush. She had dated different guys off and on during her time in college, but she had never found one she felt met her high standards and expectations. When Abby saw other young women with their steady beaus, she had often felt a twinge of jealousy, wondering why it was so easy for others to find true love while it constantly eluded her. She knew that her reputation for being studious, a non-partier, and a church-goer were, for many college-aged men, a huge turn off. *But those aren't the kind of guys you want to date anyway,* Abby would always console herself. Then she'd recall what her mother always told her: "Honey, you won't find true love; it will find you."

True love? Abby, be real! There's no such thing as love at first sight, you know that! But why does my stomach do happy flip-flops when I think about Mike? I've never felt this way before. I like this feeling! Oh, I so hope Mike will drop in to visit me today!

***

"Can you read it?" Reverend whispered to Sharp-eyes. "Can you read the name on the check?"

"Yes, yes I can," the hawk answered. "Calvin C. Holbrook. Who in the world is that?"

"Is there an address on the check? A phone number? The name of the bank?"

"P.O. Box 111, Murphy, NC, 28906. No phone is listed. Bank of America."

"We must remember that information," Reverend said. "I so wish Cleverhands was with us so he could write it down. I truly think we're onto something critical in this case."

Ronnie reached for the checkbook and pulled it in front of him, blocking the view of the Old Ones. Sharp-eyes knew he had to move from the safety of their perch to be able to see whom Ronnie could be making out a check to, using someone else's account. He ran the risk of discovery if the man detected a breeze from the movement of his wings, but there was nothing else for it. The hawk propelled himself from the bookshelf and soared up to the ceiling where he could observe Ronnie's activities in relative safety. When he saw to whom Ronnie was making out the check, he gasped.

"Reverend! Ronnie's making the check out to Bill Cunningham, his foreman! He's signing it Calvin C. Holbrook! What can this mean?"

"I don't know," Reverend admitted. "It's another puzzler upon which to ruminate."

"Now he's scribbling something in his ledger," Sharp-eyes said excitedly. "It looks like the amount is five thousand, the same as he wrote on the check! He's recording that amount as being from CCH to BC."

"From Calvin C. Holbrook to Bill Cunningham," said the owl thoughtfully as Sharp-eyes, his job successfully completed, descended from the heights and resumed his place by Reverend's side. "I know from our dear Will that checks are written from one human to another when paying in cash is not feasible. But I never imagined a person could write a check *as* another person without that party finding out they had been swindled. Unless...."

"Unless what?" Sharp-eyes interjected.

"Unless," said Reverend slowly as he looked directly into his friend's eyes, "Calvin and Ronnie are, in some sense which I don't understand, one and the same."

***

Bampa had been right about the rafts separating as they all flowed downstream toward their destination. Davy was beside himself. As if the sun sparkling on the river and the twists and turns they took to avoid the rocks and navigate the swifter rapids weren't enough, he had the joy of watching Silky and Mrs. Silky glide effortlessly alongside the raft, chatting away to him and to Racer, though Davy didn't dare utter a response. Still, the broad smile fixed on Davy's face said it all.

"Cat got your tongue, Davy?" Silky teased him.

"Now Silky," Mrs. Silky scolded, "You know Davy can't talk to us while surrounded by strangers! Don't make him feel all the worse for it!"

"Yes, dear," said Silky. This made Davy laugh out loud; the playful otter sounded exactly like Jim when he spoke those words to Mom in a sing-song voice.

Tyler, sitting next to Davy and directly across from Taylor, had yet to say a word. Davy's unexpected outburst prompted a reaction from the older boy.

"Hey, kid, you've had a goofy smile on your face the whole time we've been floating down the river, and now you're laughing. What's up with that?"

Davy turned to Tyler and said, "I'm just having fun, that's all. Doesn't riding on the river make you happy?"

"'Course it does," Tyler confirmed. "Just not looney happy."

"Tyler!" Zach barked at him. "Where are your manners?"

"He doesn't have any," Taylor quipped.

"Shut up, you!" Tyler snarled at her.

"Enough!" Zach commanded, then added in a more genteel tone, "Y'all just pay attention to the paddles and what I'm telling you to do, deal?"

"Deal," the twins replied simultaneously, though not enthusiastically.

Racer folded his arms over his chest, cocked his head, and tapped his foot impatiently on the bottom of the raft. "Yes, that boy could use a dose of good manners," he remarked. "Oh, we Old Ones could show him a thing or two about those!"

Davy leaned down toward the squirrel's ear and whispered, "You sure taught me."

Racer gave Davy a quick peck on the cheek and said, "You, my child, were teachable."

Davy laughed out loud again. Tyler said nothing, but gave Davy a contemptuous look which he chose to ignore. Instead, he concentrated on the antics of the otters, who were now leisurely floating on their backs; they had reached a quieter stretch of the river. To his amazement the otters began a remarkable routine, which looked exactly like the synchronized swimming Davy had seen when he'd watched the Summer Olympics. Right paws were held up in the air at the same moment, then the left ones, tails switching in time to an imagined beat, rolling to their stomachs and returning to their backs. Davy was completely enthralled. Except for the wonder of Racer's singing and the hawks' flying dance at the Naming, this was one of most delightful things he had witnessed the Old Ones doing. Oh, how he wished everyone else could see this astounding show of precision and grace!

"Elegant, isn't it?" Racer observed. "Yes, child, you are seeing Silky and the missus in their most agreeable environment, and it is a wonder to witness!"

Davy nodded his head ever so slightly t, so as not to draw attention from Tyler, and continued to watch in awe. It wasn't long before the dance was over. The river soon met more prominent rocks, with which the otters and the raft had to contend.

"Left side! Push paddles out," Zach ordered. "Keep us to the center of the current." Bob and Taylor followed Zach's directions and the raft was back on course, moving faster now, the front end bowing and bobbing and sending sprays of freezing water into the faces of Anna and Davy.

Anna squealed and laughed when the droplets hit her skin, warmed by the sun. "This is so much fun!" she declared. Turning to Taylor, she asked, "Do you do this every day?"

The girl chuckled. "No, not every day," she said, "but not near enough as I'd like."

"How often would you raft if you could?"

"At least once a week," Taylor said, "except in the winter. That would *not* be fun."

"Right side! Paddles in, paddles in!" Zach called out. Jim and Tyler immediately complied, and on and on, down, down, down the rapids they flew. "It won't be long before we'll be at the biggest rapids on this stretch. Everyone ready for it?"

Davy and Anna glanced back at Bampa for reassurance. He knew what they were thinking and gave them a big thumbs-up. "I think I hear it already," he said. "Am I right, Zach?"

"Indeed you are!" Zach declared. "Soon we'll see the tourists standing on the bank, where they can watch the rafters and kayakers take the falls. Also, there's a professional photographer poised to take a photo of each raft as it tips over the edge. I'll make sure I get y'all some copies."

***

When she heard tires crunching on the gravel, Kate knew it must be Susie returning from her errands. She put down her camera and went to open the back door. Kate had been looking again at the photos Davy and Anna took on their recent hike, hoping beyond hope to see Racer as more than just a shadowy smudge on the images. *Davy told me to believe. Am I too distanced from my childhood to have the faith of a child? Lord, why can't I see? Please help me with my unbelief.* Kate, who had found herself becoming more and more frustrated by this endeavor, was genuinely relieved to be in Susie's company once again. She held the door wide for Susie and noted that her face, while always cheerful, seemed infused with a joyful glow. "Why, Susie," Kate said, "You are absolutely beaming! What on earth is going on?"

"Oh, just wait 'til I tell you, dear," Susie said, her eyes twinkling like merry stars as she handed Kate the bag containing the pregnancy test and a box of herbal tea. "But let's brew a steaming cup first, and I'll happily fill you in on all the details."

***

No sooner had Eric and Elly said their good-byes to Pastor Mike when Dr. Harris, accompanied by Nurse Linda, entered the room. Though they both looked exhausted, the doctor noted that there was a deep peace in their eyes. He knew right away what it was. The power of prayer never failed to comfort even the most grief-stricken. He shook both of their hands warmly and said, "I'm sure you'd like me to say you're ready to go home, young lady. If you wouldn't mind stepping outside the room for a moment, Sheriff, I'll get right to it." Eric bent down to give Elly a kiss on the forehead and slipped out of the room just as Nurse Linda was taking her temperature and blood pressure. He was pleased to find a chair in the hallway beside the door, and sat down gratefully.

Eric hadn't been there two minutes before he saw a nurse walking briskly toward him with what appeared to be a slip of paper in her hands. When she reached him, she asked, "Are you Sheriff Peabody?" He nodded in the affirmative. She handed him the note and departed as quickly as she had come. Eric opened it slowly, hoping it didn't contain more bad news.

Hi, Eric,
Just to let you know, I've managed to cover your shifts through Thursday. Thought you would need time with Elly. Please give her my love.
Connie.

Eric grinned from ear to ear.
"Hallelujah," he whispered. "That gal finally called me Eric."

***

When Sarah Murray woke the morning after they had arrived in Atlanta, she was momentarily disoriented. They had entered the hotel room in such a drowsy haze, she hadn't paid attention to any details except the bathroom and the bed. Her still sleepy eyes took in the details now as if she were seeing the room for the first time. It was modest, but it would do as a place to recuperate after the long journey from home. David, lying beside her, was still sleeping. As stealthily as she could so as not to wake him, Sarah got out of bed and glanced at the digital clock on her bedside table. *Eleven o'clock? Oh, my, how in the world did we sleep this late? The day is half gone!* Then it struck her. This was eleven o'clock Eastern Time. Five time zones back in Hawaii it was only seven in the morning, the usual time she rolled out of bed.

David turned over, yawning and stretching, as he, too, roused from slumber. "What time is it?" he muttered to Sarah.

"It's time for both of us to be up," she said. "We've got to adjust to this new schedule quickly, or we'll never be ready to make the trip to the mountains on Thursday."

David didn't need any more coaxing. Throwing back the covers, he tumbled out of bed and headed straight for the bathroom. "I'll make it quick," he told Sarah. "I'm in dire need of coffee and some breakfast."

Sarah laughed. "Coffee's no problem because we can brew it right here in the room, but breakfast? I think it's going to have to be lunch."

***

Pastor Mike glanced at his watch as he departed the hospital. It was close to eleven o'clock. His first appointment wasn't until one thirty, and the family didn't live far from the Nantahala Outdoor Center. After sharing in and praying for the sadness and grief of the Peabody's, he knew he had to see Abby. Even if she couldn't take a break from work, just gazing at her face and exchanging a few pleasantries would lift his spirits.

Mike arrived at his destination in thirty minutes. As luck would have it, a pickup was just backing out of an otherwise jammed parking area in front of the store, and he was able to slide his car in without a hitch. *It sure is busy here. I wonder if Abby can even manage to take a break.* Mike knew there was only one way to find out. He got out of his car, locked it, and headed straight for the entrance. Once inside, it took only a moment to spot Abby behind a cash register, flashing her endearing smile at every customer with a purchase to make. The line was somewhat long and getting longer. Mike realized the only way he could talk with Abby under these circumstances was to get in that line before anyone else beat him to it. His eyes darted around furtively as he searched for something he could buy without doing too much damage to his wallet. When he spied a display of energy bars, he didn't hesitate. Mike scooped one up and hurried to get in the line which would bring him face to face with Abby. He felt fairly confident she had not seen him yet; as he stood behind a man of impressive stature, Mike hoped he could remain hidden until he was at the counter.

As the line slowly continued to move forward, Mike found he was both nervous and excited about this impending encounter. It reminded him of how he felt when he had his first crush on a girl, back in seventh grade. Her name was Claire. It was Valentine's Day, and he had brought her a card declaring his undying love for her and one red rose with a lacy ribbon tied to its stem. Palms sweating and his insides quaking, he had placed the gifts on her desk before she arrived at school and had taken his seat on the other side of the room to wait anxiously for her reaction to them. It wasn't long in coming. Claire had flounced into the classroom, ponytail swinging, and went straight to her seat. Mike had watched in hopeful trepidation as she slowly opened the card and read his words written there. After staring at them for what he had thought was an eternity, Claire had raised her head, met his gaze and smiled. Oh, how that smile had melted his heart! That smile!

"Pastor Mike, how nice to see you again!" Abby's voice sliced through his reverie like a hot knife through butter. *That ponytail! That same smile, so bright, so attractive!* He almost laughed at the coincidence, but instead returned Abby's smile with one of his own.

"It's great to see you again, too, Abby," he said, as he placed the energy bar on the counter and dug out his wallet. "But please, just call me Mike." He thought he detected a crimson flush rising on Abby's cheeks, and hoped his invitation to familiarity had not been too bold a move.

"All right," she answered as she rang up his purchase. "Mike it is."

Abby was just about to hand back his change when Mike realized that with so many other customers behind him, he had to move fast. "I was

31

wondering, since it's close to lunch time, do you have a break soon?" he blurted out, moving to the side to allow the next customer to come to the counter.

"In five minutes," Abby said, flashing him that priceless smile. "Can you wait?"

"Can I wait? Yes, yes, of course I can wait. I'll be right outside the door," Mike assured her, and with every step he took, he felt as though his heart was soaring toward the heavens.

***

When Kate heard Susie's story about her misadventures in the drug store, it launched both of them into riotous gales of laughter. Kate laughed so hard, the tears rolled down her cheeks and her sides ached. It took some time before she could even catch her breath. When she finally did, Kate said, "Oh, Susie, when you volunteered to pick up the test for me, the thought never crossed my mind how it might look to others. The way you handled the whole thing was nothing short of inspired!"

"I simply couldn't resist pulling that stunt," Susie admitted with a chuckle. "The look on those folks' faces is something I'll never forget. Although truth be told, I don't think I'll be darkening the door way of that drug store in the future. And I can't imagine how many tongues will be wagging about this at the dinner table tonight."

"Or over the phone," Kate added. "As fast as news of Mad Squirrel Sunday spread around here, I wouldn't be surprised if you wake up tomorrow and find you are quite the celebrity."

"Celebrity?" Susie exclaimed in horror. "Oh, I hope not! I like my anonymity just fine, thank you. I'm so glad I paid cash instead of using a credit card; they may talk about the grandma in the pregnancy aisle, but at least they won't know my name!"

***

"You can come back in, Sheriff," Dr. Harris called to Eric. One glance at Elly's eyes told him what he would hear the doctor say. "I've decided to keep Elly one more night, just to be safe side. Her blood pressure is still

32

a bit elevated and she's running a low-grade fever. I'm afraid if I send her home today, you both would end right up here in a day or two."

"That's disappointing news, doctor," Eric said with a sigh, "but I want what's best for Elly. If you say she needs to stay, then she needs to, no question."

Dr. Harris turned to Elly. "I want what's best for you and best for your husband," he said. "I'll put you at the top of my patient priority list for release tomorrow as long as your symptoms improve, and I feel sure they will."

"Thank you, doctor," Elly said, managing to give him a weak but sincere smile.

Once the doctor and nurse departed, Elly reached out, inviting Eric to share a much-needed hug. He willingly obliged, holding her tenderly, knowing without even looking at her face that the tears were streaming again. Eric pulled back ever so slightly to reach for a tissue, which his wife accepted gratefully.

"Honey," she said as she wiped her face and nose, "I want you to go home tonight and get some real rest. I'll be fine here. I've got 'round the clock care."

Eric was taken aback. "You don't want me here?"

"Oh, no, Eric, that's not it! I love having you here," Elly assured him, "but you will feel so much better if you can shower, shave, and change your clothes. Speaking of which, I need you to bring me some clothes from home, so I have something to wear when I'm released tomorrow."

Eric gave his wife a loving look, stroked her hair affectionately, and bent down to kiss her on the forehead. "You know I'm going to miss you," he said softly. "I can't imagine I'll sleep much better in our bed than I did in the chair last night, because you won't be there."

***

Abby was as good as her word. In exactly five minutes, she popped out of the store carrying a paper sack and a faded quilt that had seen many years of wear. "Lunch," she announced to Mike as she held up the bag. "Would you like to share?"

"Do you have enough?" he asked, feeling hungry, but knowing the energy bar would tide him over for now.

Abby blushed as she recalled making the extra sandwich on purpose that morning in the hope that Mike would stop by.

"Yes, I have plenty," she told him. "How would you like to walk over to where we can have a good view of the last section of rapids as rafters go over it? It's the biggest one on this river. We could picnic there and have something fun to watch at the same time."

"I'd love to," Mike said with enthusiasm. "I've wanted to do this ever since I moved here, but just never made the time to actually do it. Lead on!"

The two struck out at a healthy clip. Mike had always fancied himself as a fast walker, and was surprised when he actually had to pick up his pace to stay alongside Abby. It wasn't long before they reached what she deemed a suitable place, away from the crowds along the river bank, but still close enough to have a decent view of the rafts as they careened over the rapids. "Is this spot good enough for you?" Abby asked, pointing to a large, flat slab of granite at the river's edge.

"Perfect," Mike replied. Once they spread out the quilt and sat down, Abby promptly revealed the contents of their lunch: Grapes, chips, cookies, and two sandwiches. *Why are there two sandwiches? Does Abby usually eat this much for lunch, or did she think I might actually join her?*

"It's egg salad," she said as she handed him his sandwich. "I hope you like it."

"One of my favorites," Mike said with a broad smile on his face. "I haven't had one in ages."

"Don't you cook?" Abby asked.

"Not really," he confessed. "And the generous ladies in the church are constantly providing me with meals, so there's not much impetus for me to learn."

"Oh, I see," Abby said. "That's so sweet of them, looking out for you like that. You're one lucky guy!"

Mike stopped in the middle of unwrapping his sandwich and looked Abby right in her warm, brown eyes. "Yes, I *am* one lucky guy," he said and watched that now-familiar blush rising on her cheeks. *Does she feel the way I do? Can it even be possible?*

"Before we eat, Mike," Abby said, "would you say the blessing?"

"Certainly," he said, and caught himself instinctively reaching for her hand, a habit he had formed in childhood when the family said grace over each mealtime. Flustered at what he thought Abby would take as an untoward move, Mike snatched his hand back. Now it was his turn to feel the red-hot flush of embarrassment spreading over his face. He opened his mouth to apologize. "Abby, I'm sorry, it's just that I...."

"Shh!" she said, melting him to the very core with her smile. Abby reached for the hand he had withdrawn and held it gently in hers. "Can you say the blessing now? I'm starved!"

CHAPTER 4

OVERBOARD!

A fter eating lunch with Elly, Eric followed her directive and set out for home. He had to admit, he was downright exhausted and emotionally drained. His mind, usually keen and alert, felt fuzzy and full of incoherent thoughts. This made it difficult to give his full attention to driving, but Eric fought through the fog with every ounce of concentration he could muster. It wasn't until he pulled up safely in his driveway that he realized he had driven the patrol car home. His was in the sheriff's office parking lot.

"Dang!" Eric said as he fumbled for his cell phone, dismayed to see how low the charge on it was. "Guess I'd best use the radio to let Connie know the situation."

"It's not the first time that's happened," Connie assured him when she heard Eric had forgotten to stop and pick up his car. "You just bring it back in one piece tomorrow, y'hear?"

"I hear," he said, "and I will. Elly should be coming home tomorrow. Am I still off through Thursday?"

"That's a fact, Sheriff," Connie said.

"After your note, I thought you'd be calling me Eric from here on out."

There was an uncharacteristic silence on the other end of the radio. Eric thought he heard Connie sigh. When she spoke, he could hardly hear her.

"I felt so bad about what happened to y'all. I did a lot of crying and praying," Connie confessed. "After that, well, calling you Sheriff at a sad time like this just didn't seem right."

Eric was so moved by Connie's sympathy that tears sprung to his eyes once more. In a voice he knew sounded choked and unsteady, he said, "Thank you, Connie. And if you'd keep us in your prayers, we would be most grateful."

"You can count on that! Now go get some rest, Eric!" The radio on Connie's end clicked off. It made him smile when she used his name, not his title.

***

When she arrived home after her visit with Kate, Susie hung her purse and keys on the wall-mounted coat hooks Bob had made several years ago as a Christmas present for her. She loved the convenience of always knowing where these items were, and treasured the rustic design Bob had rendered with this creation. It fit their log home perfectly. Susie had turned to go into the kitchen when she noticed the light on their answering machine was blinking. Since she had been gone most of the day, she hoped the call wasn't an urgent one that she should have returned right away. Susie pushed the play button.

"Hi, Susie, it's Janet Marshall here. I'm afraid I have some sad news to share. Elly Peabody lost her baby yesterday, and both she and Eric are in need of our prayers. Could you pass this along to your contact on the prayer chain as soon as you can? Also, mention that I'm coordinating meals to take to them for at least the next two weeks. If you can contribute, give me a call back. God bless!"

Susie felt as though the breath had been knocked out of her. She slumped into the armchair next to the telephone table, covered her face with her hands, and wept bitterly. Elly's tragic loss in light of the hopeful joy she and Kate felt today tore at Susie's tender heart. She prayed for Elly and Eric. She prayed for Kate and Jim. Susie prayed until she had no more words to say and no more tears to shed. As her tsunami of emotions ebbed, Susie dried her eyes and with unsteady hands reached for the phone and her address book to call Cheryl Mann on the prayer chain. She'd also return Janet's call, to confirm she would be more than happy to help with the meals. Cheryl's phone rang three times before she answered.

"Hello?"

"Hi, Cheryl, it's Susie Fairchild. I have some sad news..."

***

After Susie left, Kate put the box of tea away in the pantry and picked up the pregnancy test, which she had left on the table. She knew she had to wait until morning to get the most accurate results, but her mind wanted to know for sure what her heart, and Susie, were already telling her. Kate sighed. "I know I can't use you right now," she said to the box, "but where will I hide you in the meantime?" Kate knew it made sense to hide it in the bathroom where she could use in first thing in the morning, but felt hesitant since everyone in the family had to share the only one in the house. There were no cupboards in the bathroom, only open shelves to store towels and toiletries.

"I suppose I could slip this behind a stack of towels," she said aloud as she headed toward the bathroom. "I can't see any other options right now."

When she returned to the kitchen Kate saw Maggie sitting patiently by the door, with Frisky pouncing happily on her tail. "Somebody wants to go out, I see," she said as she scooped the rambunctious kitten up in her arms and swung the door open for Maggie. "I'll just come outside with you two. I need some fresh air and scenery to take my mind off all that's happened today." *And I hope, take my mind off all that might possibly happen tomorrow.*

***

Davy felt his pulse quicken with excitement the closer the raft swept toward the last, and decidedly most exhilarating, rapids on the Nantahala. Anna was already emitting squeals of delight, anticipating nothing different from her experience on the log ride at Six Flags. Racer, perched on the prow of the raft, was chatting away to Davy and not being as mindful as he should have been of his precarious position.

"Oh, we're almost there! We're almost there!" Racer shouted. "See? There goes Silky down the chute! Now Mrs. Silky! Did you see them, Davy? I do hope this raft goes over it as gracefully as they did, because here we go!"

Everyone on board whooped, screamed, or shouted as the nose of the raft dipped over the edge and plunged into the rapids at an unprecedented speed. But the thrill of the ride ceased the moment the raft hit the river below with a jolting slap. Not prepared for the impact, both Anna and Racer were tossed unceremoniously into the icy water.

"Anna!" Everyone shouted in panicked unison, but Zach hollered, "Float on your back, Anna! You'll be fine! We'll get you out."

"Hey! What's that thing floating next to Anna?" Tyler yelled, pointing frantically.

When Davy realized everyone could see Racer, his heart sank. As if Anna's tumble into the river didn't grab enough attention from the sightseers lining the bank, he knew that Racer's unusual appearance would definitely be noticed. The shouts and pointed fingers of the baffled crowd confirmed his fears. What would happen when Racer finally emerged from the water? Would his wet fur keep him visible? Already, he saw people scrambling back up to the road and racing down it to try and follow the path of his sister and beloved friend. How many of these folks, he wondered, knew of Mad Squirrel Sunday and were now dashing to get a better glimpse of the legendary creature?

"It looks like a squirrel," Zach remarked, "but that's the biggest danged one I've ever seen!"

As they paddled furiously to catch up with Anna and Racer, no one but Davy could have predicted the next astonishing event. Instead of floating with the current, Anna and Racer were going against it and moving swiftly toward the safety of the shore.

***

Though the shock of hitting the water had Racer reeling, he was fortunately close enough to Anna to latch onto her life jacket. Her eyes were wide with terror and her teeth were already chattering.

"Anna, my child, there's nothing to fear," he assured her.

"Racer?" she said, eyeing him with disbelief. "I can see you. I can hear you. Why?"

Thinking the shock of hitting the icy water had confused Anna, Racer simply answered, "It's a long story, but don't worry. The otters have seen our plight and are coming to our aid. Don't be alarmed when you feel them bump you."

Seconds after Racer announced the otters, Anna felt a powerful force beneath her back as both Silky and Mrs. Silky garnered all their strength to fight the current and escort Anna, with Racer clinging tenaciously to her life vest, to the shore and rescue.

***

Abby and Mike enjoyed watching the rafts as they plummeted into the final rapids and reveled in hearing the screams of excitement from the people on board.

"Does anyone ever fall out of a raft when they go through the rapids?" Mike asked, then popped the last morsel of his sandwich into his mouth. He had to admit that this egg salad was every bit as good as his mother's.

"Oh, yes," Abby confirmed. "It doesn't happen all that often, but when it does, it sure gets people's attention." She glanced at her watch and sighed. "It's about time for me to go back to work. I was so hoping we would see my boss, Mr. Jones, and his crew coming over the falls, but I guess it's not meant to be."

Mike stood up promptly and helped Abby to her feet. As they turned to go, she took one more longing look back at the river.

"Oh, see, Mike, see!" she exclaimed excitedly. "There they are! See the raft with green and tan markings? That's Mr. Jones'. Let's stay just a minute longer so we can watch them come over the falls."

"Who does Mr. Jones have with him?" Mike asked. "Do you know?"

"Oh, yes," Abby replied gaily, "his two grandchildren and Mr. Hunter's family."

"Jim Hunter, by any chance?"

"Why yes, how do you know him?"

"The family attends my church," Mike answered. He shaded his eyes for a better view of the raft, which was fast approaching the last rapids. "That must be Davy and Anna on board. And I can't really tell, but the older gentleman resembles Bob Fairchild."

"Oh, they're almost there, almost there!" Abby said, unwittingly mimicking Racer's utterance at that very moment. The way she said it with such childlike joy endeared her to Mike even more. He had to force himself to take his eyes off her and focus on the raft, which was just tipping over the edge. Down the falls it blissfully careened, but its landing was anything but a sweet one. Both Abby and Mike cried out when they saw Anna thrown from the raft and into the unforgivingly cold, rushing river.

"How awful!" Abby screamed, tears welling in her eyes. "That child must be frightened to death!"

"I believe it's Anna who fell out," Mike said agitatedly. "I do hope she won't be traumatized by this. She's such a sweet..." Mike stopped mid-sentence, and stared hard at Anna. *Is it? Could it possibly be?* "It's Racer! Racer's hanging onto Anna's life vest. Do you see him, Abby?"

Abby saw him, but couldn't believe for a moment that what she was seeing could even be real. But Mike saw him too, so she was convinced she really saw Racer.

"It's the squirrel!" she blurted out, as the revelation dawned. "The one who caused the ruckus at your church! It has to be!"

"One and the same," Mike confirmed. "I don't know why he can be seen at the moment, but I know his presence will have a calming effect on Anna, guaranteed."

What Abby and Mike saw next confounded the both of them. Here came Anna and Racer toward shore, pushed along by an invisible force powerful enough to defy the current. When they realized the two were heading to a spot only twenty feet away they scrambled down to the shore with the quilt as fast as they could go, so Mike could pull them out of the water. As soon as he could reach Anna's hand, Mike grabbed it tightly in his and deftly pulled her, shivering and soaked to the skin, to safety. A somewhat bedraggled Racer, still visible, hopped to the ground and bowed graciously to Mike.

"So nice to see you again, Pastor Mike," he said with that winning, lopsided grin on his whiskery face. "When I saw you and this lovely lady on the shore, I knew you would help us, so I had Silky and Mrs. Silky push us over to you."

"Silky and Mrs. Silky?" Abby asked weakly as she enfolded the quaking Anna in the warm quilt and vigorously rubbed the girl's arms in an attempt to revive her circulation. She was having trouble wrapping her head around the idea she was conversing with a squirrel, and such a gigantic one at that.

"Otters, of course, ma'am," Racer answered politely but froze when he spied an army of curiosity seekers, several with cameras in hand, careening full-tilt in their direction. "So rude of me, I know, to flee so abruptly upon arriving, but you aren't the only ones who can see me in my present state. I simply must be going!"

"Ready to do some water skiing, Racer?" Silky called out. He, too, was greatly alarmed by the size and the speed of the approaching crowd.

"Ready!" Racer responded. Hurriedly, he kissed the hands of Anna and Abby in turn and gave Mike a hug. Turning on a dime, the squirrel beat a hasty retreat to the river, looking to all watching as though he planned to plunge right back into it. Instead, to the speechless amazement of Mike, Abby, and the gathering mob, Racer sailed away on top of the water as if he were being towed on skis behind an invisible motorboat.

"Farewell!" His voice floated over the water. "Until we meet again!"

***

Showered, dressed, and braced by the coffee they brewed in their room, David and Sarah Murray took the elevator to the hotel lobby. The smartly dressed attendant at the front desk greeted them cheerfully as they approached.

"Good morning," he said brightly, "how may I be of service to you today?"

David cut right to the chase. "Are there any restaurants within walking distance of the hotel? We were too tired to rent a car last night, and took a taxi here instead."

"Oh, dear, oh dear, a taxi?" the attendant, whose nametag read Tim, asked in dismay. "Did you not know we have a free shuttle service to and from the airport?"

"Believe me," Sarah spoke up, "if we had known, we definitely would have opted for that. Free is always good."

"Yes, indeed, it is," Tim agreed. "So when you are ready to rent a car, know we will gladly carry you back out to the airport to do that."

"Sounds great," said David. "Now about those restaurants..."

"Yes, sir, of course," said Tim. "The closest one to us which I would recommend is Ruby Tuesday. Are you familiar with that chain?"

"Yes, we are," David confirmed. "We have a few where we live."

"And where might that be?"

"Hawaii."

Tim gave a low whistle. "That's one long flight from there to here!"

"You can say that again," said Sarah. "We're still quite jetlagged from the trip; it's the only reason we slept through breakfast this morning."

"Ah, but don't do that tomorrow," Tim advised with a bright smile. "We have complimentary breakfast here every morning. And as you said, ma'am, free is always good!"

"We'll be sure not to miss it, "David assured him. "And I'll get with you about the shuttle as soon as we get back from lunch."

***

Reverend and Sharp-eyes saw Ronnie close the ledger and return it, along with Calvin C. Holbrook's checkbook, to the desk drawer, locking both away. He then reached into a side drawer and pulled out an envelope, into which he slipped the check he had made out to Bill Cunningham. After addressing, sealing, and placing a stamp on the envelope, Ronnie pushed himself up from his chair and proceeded to the door.

"Time to go!" Reverend exclaimed. He and the hawk swooped after Ronnie as fast as they dared, and darted out of the open door as deftly as they could. It was another close call. The air stirred up by the movements of their wings made Ronnie jump and look around in confusion. It felt like a breeze generated by a ceiling fan, but there wasn't one above his head. Fortunately for Reverend and Sharp-eyes, Ronnie scratched his head, shrugged, and headed for the door to the garage.

"Betty Rae, I'm goin' to the post office," he shouted when he'd opened it, giving the owl and hawk ample time to enter the garage without another unwanted incident. "I'll be back in time for lunch."

"Please tell me that after this last brush with doom, we are not getting into the truck cab again," Sharp-eyes said glumly.

"No, no, no," Reverend assured him. "We'll just follow him by air today. Like you, I don't care for these chance encounters in the least. I'm afraid we might show our hand before the time is right."

"Before the time is right?" Sharp-eyes was understandably perplexed.

"That's what I said," the owl responded, giving his friend a wink. "Remember, I have the beginnings of a plan."

43

***

When Eric entered his house, he was immediately struck by how empty it felt without Elly there to greet him. He tossed his keys on the kitchen table and sank wearily into a chair. The grief and sorrow of these last twenty-four hours weighed heavily on his heart; Eric knew he would feel better if he cleaned up, but he didn't have the energy to budge. Instead, he sat where he was, listening to the mantel clock's rhythmic tick-tock, tick-tock, tick-tock, and as his eyelids drooped over his weary eyes, Eric felt again the hot sensation of tears burning them.

Dear Lord, I hurt. I've never hurt so much in my life. I need to feel your presence. I need your comfort. I need your strength to help Elly through this time. Help me, Lord, please help me.

The telephone in the kitchen pierced the silence like a siren. Startled, Eric leapt to his feet, and with remarkable energy considering his condition, ran to answer the call.

"Sheriff Peabody here," he said breathlessly.

"Hi, honey," spoke the sweetest and dearest voice Eric knew. "I tried your cell phone, but couldn't get you. I just wanted to make sure you made it home all right."

"I did," he confirmed," but this place sure seems lonely without you. I miss you already, Elly."

"I miss you, too," she said. "Oops! Here comes Linda again. Guess I need to hang up. Call me later?"

"You bet!"

"Bye. I love you!"

"Love you too," Eric told her, and as he hung the receiver back on its cradle, added, "More than you know, Elly, more than you know."

***

Jim was relieved beyond words when he saw Pastor Mike lifting Anna out of the icy waters and Abby, the young lady he'd met at the NOC yesterday, wrapping her up with the quilt. He knew, of course, the party responsible for delivering both Anna and Racer to safety. Jim tapped an awed Tyler on the shoulder, and said, "Can you get Davy's attention?" The boy nodded and poked Davy in turn, motioning him to look at Jim without ever taking his eyes off the amazing spectacle before them.

When Jim realized no one was looking at him, he mouthed to Davy, "Thank Silky and Mrs. Silky when you see them next!" Davy managed a half-hearted smile. He, too, was thankful for his sister's rescue by the otters, but was consumed with worry for Racer as his drenched fur betrayed his presence to the crowd, which threatened to reach him in a matter of moments. He was just about to shout a warning to his dear friend when presto! Off went Racer down the river, his feet not appearing to touch the water, waving merrily to the stunned audience he left behind.

Zach, Taylor and Tyler were rendered speechless by what appeared to be a larger than life squirrel jetting downstream. Zach was so amazed and confounded by the sight, he almost missed his landing point. If it hadn't been for some quick maneuvering by all the paddlers, they would have been in quite the pickle.

"Whew!" Zach remarked when everyone was safely out of the raft and it was hauled ashore. "That was a close one. That'll teach me not to let distractions, no matter how amazing, to keep me from paying attention to the river."

"Indeed, that was quite a miraculous feat we saw," Bob said with a twinkle in his eye as he sent a wink in Jim and Davy's direction. "Jim, Davy and you go on and see to Anna. I'll help Zach with the raft."

They required no further prodding. Davy had never seen Jim run so fast, and found it a challenge to even keep within ten paces of his step-father. When they drew near the spot where a still-shivering Anna was standing with Mike and Abby, Jim had to work his way through the sea of onlookers, who were still clustered about and murmuring to each other about the inexplicable event they had just witnessed.

"Let us through, please, let us through," Jim said impatiently as he pushed against the crowd with Davy, who had finally caught up, at his heels.

"Hey! You the girl's father?" A shout came from somewhere in the throng.

"Better check for squirrel bites!" This comment resulted in roars of laughter.

Jim was not amused in the least. "Show's over!" he yelled commandingly. "Every one of you go on back where you came from, and leave us in peace!"

At Jim's outburst, a hush fell over the gathering. One by one, people turned reluctantly away and meandered off; only a few stubborn souls remained at the scene, but even these spectators backed off to what they considered a respectful distance. At the sound of Jim's voice, the tears which Anna had so bravely fended off until now began to flow. When he reached her, Jim knelt down and gathered her tightly in his arms. Davy flung his arms around the both of them, and they stayed just like that until Anna's sobs subsided. Abby and Mike stood quietly by, silently sending up prayers of thanks for Anna's safe delivery from the river's clutches. When Davy finally looked up, he noticed a man in a blue plaid shirt still lingering in their vicinity. He seemed to be reviewing photos in his camera.

"I got 'em," the man whispered to himself, a satisfied smile on his face. "I got 'em."

CHAPTER 5

RENDEZVOUS AT RIVER'S END

When she finished speaking with Cheryl, Susie dialed Janet Marshall to volunteer to bring a meal to the Peabody's.

"Oh, Susie," said Janet, "I'm so glad you called! I hate to ask you this on such short notice, but I know you freeze meals from time to time. Is there any way you could deliver a meal to Elly and Eric this afternoon? I was going to, but my Henry is working late tonight and we only have the one truck."

Susie answered readily, "I certainly can, Janet. By the way, do you know for certain that Elly's come home from the hospital?"

"No, I don't," she admitted. "I guess the best way to find out is to call their house."

"Good idea," Susie said. "I should give them fair warning anyway, before I just show up at their door."

"Wonderful! Thanks again, Susie, you are a gem! Bye-bye!"

"Good-bye." Susie hung up and pulled the church directory from the small drawer of the phone table. She located the Peabody's number easily, as the membership at Nantahala United Methodist was a modest one. Before she lifted a finger to dial, Susie prayed. *Lord, give me the right words to say to Eric and Elly. Let them be words of healing and hope, and may You fill them with your love and peace. Amen.*

***

Kate returned to the house, refreshed and relaxed after her stroll in the yard with Maggie and Frisky. She loved having the animals around, especially when everyone was gone from the house. Kate glanced at the clock. It was almost two. *I wonder when Jim and the kids will get back. Sure hope they've had a marvelous time. I wish I'd felt well enough to go with them, but it doesn't really matter in light of the good news I'm hoping to find out tomorrow.* The strident ring of the ancient telephone interrupted Kate's thoughts. She trotted quickly across the kitchen to answer it.

"Hello?"

"Hi, Kate, it's Sarah. We're in Atlanta."

"Really? I'm so glad you arrived safe and sound! How was the flight?"

"Honestly, it was pretty grueling. David and I are still recovering, but think we'll probably be good to go by tomorrow. We just had our lunch, and David took the hotel shuttle back to the airport to rent a car. I know you didn't expect us until Thursday, but would it put Jim and you out too much if we arrived tomorrow instead? We'd be there late afternoon at the earliest."

"Tomorrow?" Kate felt a moment of panic. She was a conscientious housekeeper, but there were so many details left to do before her in-laws arrived. Would there be enough time? She fought the urge to keep to the Thursday schedule and said, "Of course you can come tomorrow. Davy and Anna will be absolutely thrilled when I tell them."

"Could I speak with them now?" Sarah asked eagerly. "I can't wait to see them!"

"Jim took them whitewater rafting today," Kate explained. "I know they will be disappointed they missed your call, but your arrival tomorrow will more than make up for all that."

"Whitewater rafting? How thrilling! Tell them I'm looking forward to hearing all about it."

"I will, Sarah, I will," Kate assured her. "And I can't wait to see you both. It's been such a long time."

"I agree, honey," Sarah said. "It's been too long. Way too long."

***

Eric's conversation with Elly perked him up considerably. He decided it was high time he jumped in the shower and into some clean clothes. Without hesitation, Eric strode toward the bathroom. He was just about to run the water when the phone on his bedside table rang. Thinking it might be Elly again, he grabbed for it as swiftly as he could.

"Sheriff Peabody here."

"Hello, Eric, it's Susie Fairchild."

"Hi, Susie," he said. He knew before she said anything else that she'd heard the news through the prayer chain. Eric drew a deep breath, not wanting any more words of sympathy right now, but bracing himself for what was about to hit.

"I know there are no words I can offer right now that would make everything all right, dear," Susie said gently, "but I want you both to know Bob and I are here for you. If it's okay with you, I'd like to bring supper to your house later this afternoon."

"That's so kind of you, Susie," Eric said sincerely, "but Elly's still laid up in the hospital. She'll be there at least until tomorrow. I can manage to whip up something to get me by."

Susie saw her opportunity. "Eric, I won't hear of that," she told him in her best motherly fashion. "Come have supper with us tonight. You don't need to be alone at a time like this, and Bob and I would love to have you. Please say yes."

Eric mulled the offer over in his head. Susie had the reputation at church as one of the best cooks in the county, and her shepherd's pie was legendary. *Besides, she's right. I don't need to be alone right now.*

"I'd be honored to eat with you," Eric told Susie. "Just tell me the time and I'll be there."

***

When Anna finally stopped crying, Jim gave her a smile and a loving tug on her sopping wet braid.

"You've had quite the adventure today, Miss Priss. We're all so proud of the way you stayed calm through it all."

"That was because of Racer," Anna said softly. "I could see him and hear him. He told me not to be afraid."

49

"Anna," Davy said with a most serious look on his face, "you're not the only one who saw and heard Racer. Everyone did."

"Everyone?" she asked in alarm. "I know Pastor Mike and Miss Abby saw him, but I thought that was because Racer chose to be seen."

Davy shook his head sadly. "Remember what Racer said about becoming visible when he gets wet, Anna? It looks like my worst fear came true today."

"Cheer up, Davy," Mike said encouragingly. "Good ol' Racer made a successful escape. And what an absolute pleasure it was to see him again."

"And to meet him for the first time," Abby chimed in. "What a thrill!"

"I'm glad you two could see him," Davy said sincerely. "It's the other people who were there who worry me. The ones I saw taking photos."

"But we took photos of Racer just the other day," Anna said, "and he didn't show up in any of them."

"That's because he was invisible to everybody but me," Davy told her. "What if he can be seen in these photos? What if someone puts their pictures of Racer on the internet?"

Jim took Davy gently by the shoulders. "Look at me," he said comfortingly. "If I saw a photo of a giant squirrel showing up on the internet, you know what my first reaction would be?"

"No, what?" Davy asked.

"It's been photo-shopped," Jim answered, "pure and simple. So let's not allow our what ifs to run away with us right now, okay, son?"

At that moment, Abby looked up and saw Zach fast approaching.

"Oh, no, Mike!" she lamented. "I'm late for work. I've got to go!" Abby bent down to give Anna a peck on the cheek. "You keep the quilt, honey," she told her. "You need it a lot more than I do."

***

Reverend and Sharp-eyes followed Ronnie to the post office, noting with relief that he wasn't talking on his cell phone. So far, they felt their choice to simply tail him by air was a fortunate one. When Ronnie brought his truck to a halt, the owl and the hawk descended to the roof of the cab just as he was getting out, and at that very moment his phone rang.

"Carson," Ronnie said gruffly. "You what? Where? Where are you now? Stay put! I'll be there in ten." Hurriedly, Ronnie shoved the envelope into an outdoor mailbox and clambered back into his truck.

"Wonder what that was all about?" Sharp-eyes said.

"I don't know," said Reverend, as the two soared into the sky, "but I think we're about to find out."

***

"Susie!" Kate exclaimed urgently the moment she heard Susie on the other end of the line. "I just heard from Sarah. They're in Atlanta, and they're going to be arriving tomorrow instead of Thursday! Will you be ready for them? Do you need my help?"

"Calm down, Kate," Susie said reassuringly, "I'm good to go. The guest bed has fresh sheets, I just finished cleaning the guest bathroom, and the rest of the house is in reasonable shape. The more important question, dear, is do you need my help with anything?"

"I have a few things left to do," Kate said, "but it's nothing I can't get done between now and tomorrow, before they arrive. Oh, Susie, I'm so thankful you volunteered to open your home to them during their visit. It means the world to me."

"I'm so happy we could help," said Susie. "I'm looking forward to meeting Davy and Anna's real grandparents."

"Adopted or not," Kate told her, "Bob and you are as real as grandparents can be. Remember that!"

***

As Abby and Zach approached each other, she offered him a genuine apology.

"Oh, Mr. Jones, I'm so, so sorry I'm late! It's just Anna fell in, and there was the squirrel, and..."

"Whoa, whoa!" Zach exclaimed as he caught her arm. "Slow down, Abby. I saw it all too. I just checked with Debbie, and she told me she was fine with filling in for you as long as need be."

"Oh, that's such a relief," Abby admitted. "I'll be sure to return the favor whenever Debbie needs a longer break."

"I know you will," Zach said. Nodding in Mike's direction, he added with a fatherly smile, "Why don't you walk back down with me? I don't believe you've said a proper good-bye to your beau."

At this comment Abby dropped her eyes, her face awash in crimson, but Zach saw the smile playing on her lips.

"He's not my beau, Mr. Jones, we're just friends," she informed him as she strolled with him toward Mike and the others.

"Debbie didn't see it that way," Zach said with a chuckle. "Said your face lit up like a lantern the moment you saw him in the store. Come to think of it, she said he was beaming, too."

"Oh, dear," Abby said with a shake of her head, a smile still on her face. "Debbie is an observant one, that's for sure. I can tell I'm in for a lot of teasing when I return to work."

"Good-natured teasing," Zach assured her. When they arrived at the spot where Jim, Mike, Davy, and Anna were still standing, Zach's first gesture was to surround Anna with a bear hug. "When you tumbled out of that raft today, my heart was in my throat. But you didn't panic. You followed my directions perfectly. I'm proud of you, Anna, and I want you to know that."

"Thanks, Mr. Jones," she said sincerely, "but I don't think I'll want to go rafting any time soon."

Everyone laughed at her remark, gratified to see that Anna was her old self again. Abby introduced Mike to Zach, and the two exchanged hearty handshakes.

"So you're a pastor?" Zach asked delightedly. "What church?"

"Nantahala United Methodist," Mike replied. "Hope to see you there some Sunday soon, if you don't already have a church home."

Zach threw back his head and laughed. "I've been going to Cold Springs Baptist Church for nigh on thirty years, son. Only the good Lord Almighty could tear me out of my pew, but the invitation is much appreciated."

Jim turned suddenly to Zach, a look of concern on his face. "Where are Taylor, Tyler, and Bob?" he inquired.

"Up at the store, waiting on us," Zach replied. "Bob's offered to take all the kids to River's End restaurant over yonder while you and I go get our vehicles. Davy, Anna, I'll bet you're hungry."

"Starving!" Davy readily admitted. "But what about you and Jim? What are you going to eat?"

"We'll grab us some sandwiches to go. Sound good to you, Jim?"

"Sounds great," he said, "as long as lunch is on me."

"Mr. Jones, who's carrying you back to the launch site?" Abby asked.

"Don't know at the moment," he replied, "but I'm sure one of the fine folks at the NOC will volunteer."

Knowing that his next appointment was in that very direction, Mike piped up. "Why don't I drive you both to the launch site? I'm scheduled to visit with a family down that way. It wouldn't be any trouble at all."

"You sure?" Jim asked.

"Absolutely!"

Zach gave Mike a friendly clap on the back. "Thanks, Pastor! I say we all retreat to River's End, get these kids settled in with Bob, and get ourselves those sandwiches!"

***

Showered, shaved, dressed, and with a fresh cup of coffee in his hand, Eric felt much better than he'd expected to, considering his overall lack of sleep. Dinner at the Fairchild's, he knew, was at six thirty. It was only three in the afternoon, and Eric wondered how he was going to pass the time. *Maybe I'll just give Elly another call to see how she's doing. She'll be glad to know I won't be trying to scrounge up dinner on my own tonight.* He retrieved his cell phone, which had been charging up on the kitchen counter. As he began to dial the hospital, his mind drifted back to the recent incident involving Ronnie's phone; those undeleted photos had cost the man dearly. Eric froze. He was supposed to have checked the county land records for Jim Hunter on Monday! Here it was, midafternoon on Tuesday, and he had yet to follow through. What with all that had transpired in the last twenty-four hours, he knew his lapse would be understood, even forgiven; still, Eric couldn't help but be remorseful for letting Jim down. He felt compelled to call Jim right then and there to apologize, and tell him he would definitely be at the courthouse first thing in the morning.

"Hello?" It was Kate Hunter.

"Hi, Kate, Eric Peabody, here," he said. "Is Jim around? I need to speak with him."

"I'm afraid not, Sheriff," she answered. "Can I take a message?"

Eric hesitated for a moment before he spoke. He didn't wish to lie to Kate, but he didn't feel up to another round of sympathy. "Just tell Jim I've had some complications come up the last two days, and haven't been able to check on the property information as I promised. Tell him I'll take care of that tomorrow."

"Will do," Kate said brightly. "And tell your lovely wife Elly that I really enjoyed meeting her last Sunday."

"She enjoyed meeting you, too," Eric assured her.

After they said their good-byes and hung up, Eric looked at his watch again. *It's only ten after three. The court house is open until five. I've got nothing else to do until dinner. Why wait until tomorrow? Let's get going, Eric!*

***

River's End restaurant was hopping when Bob arrived, with the four children in tow. The hostess immediately noticed Anna's wet braids and incongruous quilt in such hot summer weather, but greeted them cheerfully and escorted them to the last available table, outside on the deck which overlooked the river. Anna, still damp and cold beneath her now soggy wrap, was relieved to discover that at least one chair at their table was in full sun. "I call it!" she announced as she plunked herself down unceremoniously.

"You deserve it," said Taylor with friendly grin. She had taken a genuine liking to Anna while they were rafting down the river and now held her in high esteem for surviving her fall into the river with such grace. "I'll drape the quilt over this railing so it can dry out along with you."

"If you don't mind me asking," said the hostess, looking directly at Anna as she placed menus on the table, "are you the girl who fell into the river just a while back?"

Anna was about to open her mouth to answer when she caught a look from Bampa, which distinctly read *I'll handle this.*

"Why, yes," said Bob smoothly, "she is. She's been through quite the ordeal today and is very hungry, as are we all. I know it's out of season, but could you possibly whip her up a cup of hot chocolate? She needs all the warmth she can get."

It was obvious to all that the hostess was dying to ask more questions of Anna, but Bob's run of interference successfully deterred her.

"Yes, sir, I'll have your server bring it to her right away," she said politely, but Bob could tell her curiosity was not assuaged in the least.

"All right, kids," Bob told them, "let's look at the menu and get in our heads what we want to order. I'd like to place ours right when the waitress gets here."

Taylor, who was sitting next to Anna, raised her menu over her face and leaned in to whisper, "Why did you let Mr. Fairchild answer for you?"

Anna shrugged her shoulders. "I thought it was okay," she said. "I don't feel much like talking to strangers about it right now anyway. Bampa must have read my mind."

"Or he doesn't want anyone asking pesky questions about that amazing squirrel who looked like he was rescuing you," Taylor observed.

"Ladies," said Bob firmly, regarding them over the top of his reading glasses, "there will be plenty of time to talk once our food gets here, so let's get down to business."

"Yes, Bampa," Anna said, and the girls both dutifully obeyed his request.

"There are so many good things here," Davy commented. "What's your favorite, Tyler?"

"I like the pizza," he said, smiling at Davy for the first time that day. "That's what we usually get when Grandpa brings us here."

"I love pizza, too!" Davy exclaimed. "Bampa, why don't we just get a pizza to share?"

"Sounds good to me," Bob said. "How about it, ladies, will pizza do?" Anna and Taylor nodded enthusiastically. "Well, then, let's figure out what toppings we want on it, and we'll be ready to order when Anna's hot chocolate arrives."

***

Reverend and Sharp-eyes were taken aback when Ronnie turned his truck into the Nantahala Outdoor Center's spacious parking area, at the rear of the building.

"This is absolutely the last place I'd ever envision Ronnie wishing to visit," Reverend asserted. "I can't imagine why he has business here."

"Or with whom?" Sharp-eyes asked. "I can't fathom any crony of Ronnie's appreciating this beautiful place."

The owl and hawk followed Ronnie as he trekked the notable distance from the parking lot, past the NOC, and on toward River's End.

"Do you think he's meeting someone inside the restaurant?" Sharp-eyes wondered.

"It looks that way," Reverend answered. "My, my, though, it's quite crowded. I'm not sure how we're going to slip in unfelt by someone milling around down there."

"Look! There's an outdoor deck for dining," said the hawk. "Why don't we perch on the railing and get our bearings before we figure out how we can get inside?"

"Makes sense to me," said the owl. "If people are eating outside, there must be entry from there to the restaurant." The two swooped down, landing not three feet away from where, to their immense surprise, Davy was sitting with Anna, Bob, and two children with whom they were not acquainted. Davy's back was to them, and they dared not speak to him from this angle as his startled whirling around in his chair would certainly appear odd to the surrounding diners. "Let's hop along the rail until Davy has us in view. I'll keep my wing over my beak so he knows not to say a word."

Awkwardly, the two sidled along the railing toward Davy. He was just preparing to put a second slice of pepperoni pizza into his mouth when he caught the unexpected sight of Reverend out of the corner of his eye. Davy longed to jump up and hug his friends, but the signal from the owl to stay put and stay mute conveyed its meaning in full.

"Davy, my lad," said Reverend with a bow which made the boy want to giggle. "How fortunate it is to find you here! We've been tailing Ronnie, and we have every reason to believe he is meeting someone of interest in

56

the restaurant. Is there any way you can get us through that door and into the main dining area?"

Davy nodded imperceptibly and asked, "Bampa, may I be excused? I need to use the restroom."

"Of course, Davy, by all means," said Bob.

Davy got up quickly, and the owl and hawk fell in line directly behind him. When they reached the door, the boy held it open just long enough for his friends to safely enter. "Very good," said Reverend. "Now to find Ronnie."

"Over there!" Sharp-eyes exclaimed. "In the corner with—*Bill Cunningham?*"

"Davy, go ahead and run to the bathroom so Bob won't be suspicious and, worse, Ronnie doesn't catch a glimpse of you. When we find out what Ronnie's up to, we will fill you in as soon as possible. There's a good lad."

Reluctantly but obediently, Davy trudged off toward the restrooms, wishing with all his heart he could simply talk with Reverend and Sharp-eyes right here, right now. *I still have so much to learn about patience. Having to wait is so hard! I really hope Reverend and Sharp-eyes know what they're doing.*

CHAPTER 6

MY VERY BEST SHOT

It was a repeat of the poky ride Jim and Zach had made just that morning, but it gave them ample time to finish their sandwiches. Mike had graciously informed them he didn't mind people eating in his car.

"With as much running around as I do in these parts," he said, "I find myself frequently dining while driving. Why wouldn't I let my passengers do the same?"

"If you had kids in the car," Zach mumbled as he chewed, "you'd change that tune in a heartbeat!"

Jim had to laugh. "That's true, Zach. Before Kate and I got married, I had no idea it would behoove me *not* to let Davy and Anna eat while we drove around. I didn't so much mind the few crumbs, which were easy to vacuum up, but the day Anna dropped her milkshake and the lid popped off, well, let's just say the party ended right there."

Zach took another generous bite of his sandwich, but this time remembered to chew and swallow before he spoke. He turned to Jim, who was sitting next to him in the back seat of Mike's car.

"You know, Jim, you got one special little girl in that Anna. Seeing her come to shore and being pulled out safely gave me such a relief, I can't begin to tell you. I've never lost a rafter on my watch, and I'd sure as shootin' hated it if she'd gotten hurt." He paused to take another bite, chewing on it thoughtfully.

"It was a huge relief to me, too," Jim admitted, "but in retrospect, the greater relief was that her mother wasn't in the raft with us today. Knowing Kate, she would have plunged in right after Anna to try to save her."

"Sounds like something any mom would do," Mike commented, thinking of the close bond he shared with his own mother.

"What I don't understand about today, though," Zach observed, "is how and why, when Anna hit the water, that humongous squirrel popped up out of nowhere. I've seen squirrels swim across lakes from time to time, but never seen one try to navigate a river as hefty as the Nantahala. I could swear that critter was hanging onto Anna's vest and pushing her to shore. My mind tells me that's impossible, but my eyes tell me what I saw. And then, if that isn't confounding enough, seeing him glide downstream looking every bit like he's walking on water like the good Lord did? Well, that takes the cake!"

Mike glanced in his rearview mirror and met Jim's look of concern. He could tell instantly that Jim had no desire to elaborate on the incident with Racer today. Mike decided to intervene.

"You know what seeing that squirrel reminded me of, Zach? The one who appeared suddenly during Sunday's service two weeks ago when I was absent, flattened the guest preacher, and sent the entire congregation into a tail spin."

"Go on!" Zach exclaimed. "You're pullin' my leg now, son."

Jim was genuinely surprised.

"You mean you haven't heard about Mad Squirrel Sunday?" he asked, giving Mike a wink. "Why, I thought everybody in this neck of the woods had heard about what happened at our church!"

Zach regarded Jim with a look of amazement. "You mean to say you were there? You saw it, too?"

"Just as I'm seeing you at this very moment," Jim confirmed.

"Well, I'll be," Zach said, shaking his head in wonder. "I've heard strange things in my lifetime, but this beats them all. So you two think this critter we saw today is the same one who..."

"Came to church?" Mike said, completing Zach's question. "There's not a shred of doubt in my mind." He had reached the launch parking area at last. Mike slowly made his way in the direction of the two men's vehicles, which Jim had pointed out to him and pulled in right behind Jim's car. "Here we are," he announced unnecessarily.

Thanking Mike with a vigorous handshake and a thank you, Jim exited the car; but Zach seemed reluctant to leave. When finally he did, he tapped on Mike's window for him to roll it down.

"Pastor, I just got to ask you something," he said in all seriousness.

"Sure, anything," Mike assured him.

Zach lowered his voice, and Mike sensed the man's apprehension. "Think there's any chance of that ol' squirrel visiting Cold Springs Baptist?"

Mike thought a moment before he answered. Zach couldn't help but notice the twinkle in the young man's eyes. "Nope, not a chance, my friend," he said.

"And why's that?"

"Because," Mike said with confidence as he placed his car into drive, "he's a Methodist."

***

Eric changed as quickly as he could from street clothes to his sheriff's uniform before leaving for the courthouse. It would look incongruous for him to be driving his patrol car in anything but official attire. He grabbed his keys, locked the door, and threw his casual clothes in the backseat in case his visit to the courthouse took longer than he expected; he didn't want to dine with the Fairchild's looking like he'd come to arrest them instead. He decided he would leave the patrol car at the office and pick up his own, so he didn't have to do that in the morning—if time permitted.

Eric didn't have much experience in searching property titles. He had, of course, done so when he and Elly had chosen to purchase their present home from its owner without the help of a realtor. If memory served him right, he should simply look under the name of the current owner: in this case, the alleged owner, Ronnie Carson.

In twenty minutes, Eric reached the entrance to the courthouse and easily found his way to the large room where property records were stored. As he walked through the heavy doors, he met the gaze of the same pale clerk with the pinched face whom Cy Smith had an exchange with only the day before. Eric couldn't be sure, but he thought he detected fear in the man's eyes as he approached the desk.

"Good afternoon," Eric said with a friendly smile, which failed to make an impression on the clerk for better or for worse. "I'm here to look up some information on property I have an interest in purchasing. Would you point me in the right direction?" The clerk didn't say a word; he simply gestured in the direction of some double doors down a narrow hallway. The fact that his arm was trembling ever so slightly did not escape Eric's notice.

"Thank you, sir, I appreciate the help," he said, and promptly headed down the hall.

As he pushed open the doors, Eric had the uneasy sense that something was not quite right here. He couldn't put his finger on it, but the feeling made him edgy. Eric hoped it didn't mean that what he would uncover today would turn Davy's world upside down.

***

Reverend and Sharp-eyes were beside themselves with delight when they realized Ronnie and Bill were seated at a table for four. Two empty chairs, one on either side of the men, gave them the perfect perch from which they could see and hear all that transpired between them. They had only just settled silently in when the waitress approached to take their order.

"I wonder if they've said anything yet that we shouldn't have missed?" Reverend asked worriedly.

"Let's hope not," Sharp-eyes replied. "I wonder why Bill has a camera with him. Do you think there's a photo on there he wants to show Ronnie?"

"And if there is, I wonder what it could possibly be?"

The men completed their order, and the waitress promptly withdrew. Ronnie leaned across the table and said, "Okay, Bill, what is so urgent that you had to see me right away?"

Bill smiled smugly at Ronnie. "You know, Carson, when you told me about those critters the other day at church, I honestly thought one of the screws in your head got loose. Mind you, not to be disrespectful, but you got to admit that what you said sounded mighty far-fetched, like something out of a fairy tale, or a Disney movie."

"Yeah, yeah, so what," Ronnie said tersely. "Where's all this goin', Bill?"

Bill was obviously enjoying keeping Ronnie off balance. "Well, you see, I fancy myself a pretty good amateur photographer," he drawled. "When I get a day off, and I got a lot of 'em now, y'know, I like coming down here to the river and snapping pictures of folks riding down the last rapids. I like taking shots of other things, too."

"Quit yammerin' and get to the point!" Ronnie hissed menacingly.

"Okay, okay," Bill conceded. "I will. Wait! She's bringing our iced tea."

The two got quiet as the waitress delivered their tea, nodded their thanks, and waited until she was out of earshot to continue. "Enough stalling, Bill. Out with it," Ronnie snapped.

Bill sighed when he realized Ronnie was not playing along with his game of suspense. Defeated, he reached for his camera, turned it on, and pushed the button, which made his most recent photos pop up on the screen. He handed the camera to Ronnie. "Here," he said. "Look what I shot today at the river. I think it's one of my very best. What do you make of it?"

As Ronnie flipped through the photos, Reverend and Sharp-eyes saw his eyes widening and an expression of incredulity rising on his face. "Can you see the photos, Sharp-eyes?" Reverend asked anxiously.

Sharp-eyes twisted his head this way and that in an attempt to glimpse what had Ronnie spellbound. "I can't get a clear angle," he said morosely. "Ronnie's got the camera too close to his face. Let's just hope they start talking about the pictures."

Ronnie stared and stared at the images before him. After what seemed like an eternity to Bill, Ronnie slowly turned the camera off and handed it back. Bill found the smile on his face anything but heartening. It was ominous and cunning, with a touch of wickedness thrown in for good measure.

"I know who's in these photos," Ronnie whispered hoarsely. "His days are numbered."

***

Sarah was relieved to know Kate didn't mind their early arrival. She had been so tired the night before, the sound of jets taking off and landing in close proximity hadn't bothered her in the least. But now, she found the constant noise an irritant. Sarah was looking forward more than ever to the peace and quiet Kate had assured her the farm offered, day in and day out. She hoped, too, that she and David would enjoy staying with Bob and Susie Fairchild. Kate had described them in the most glowing of terms, and Sarah had always thought highly of her daughter-in-law's ability to correctly assess a person's character. *And even if the arrangement is less than perfect, we'll only be there two weeks. But I'm going to hope for the best.*

Sarah heard the key card click in the door to the room. In walked David, all smiles and holding up the keys to the rental car. "We're good to go, Sarah!" he declared. "What do you say we check out now?"

"Now?" Sarah asked in disbelief. "But I thought you'd already paid for tonight?"

"Just talked with the manager on duty," David informed her. "I was initially only going to cancel tomorrow night, like I told you, but thought I'd see if I could cancel both. The manager seemed a bit surprised, but he politely credited the charge to my account."

"But where will we stay tonight?" Sarah asked apprehensively.

"Honestly, I don't know," David replied. "All I know is, if I don't get away from this airplane racket, I'm going to lose my mind *and* my hearing."

"You, too?" she said with a smile. "Well then, let the adventure begin!"

***

Davy exited the restroom cautiously and glanced all around the dining room for Reverend and Sharp-eyes. He spotted them in a far corner; luckily Ronnie's back was to him, and he didn't recognize the man sitting across from him. But when the man reached for a camera, the light bulb flashed in Davy's head. *He was one of those people taking pictures! He was hanging near the back when everyone started to leave. I remember his shirt was the same blue as this man's!* Davy blanched. He felt his heart sinking like a stone into his stomach. *Photos of Racer; it has to be! Ronnie already knows about the Old Ones, but now he has proof. Proof! What will happen now?*

63

Just then, Reverend spied Davy and called out to him, "Davy! Go back outside before Ronnie turns around! And don't worry, lad, everything will be all right, you'll see." Davy took Reverend's uplifting words to heart; he wanted so desperately to believe everything would work out for good for the Old Ones. If Reverend thought it would, then he should think the same. Davy honored the owl's request and returned to the table. The large pepperoni pizza had dwindled down to two pieces, one of which he was hoping to have.

"Whoa, I'm stuffed," his Bampa announced. "Can anyone here finish what's left, or do I have to get a to-go box?"

"I'll take one!" Davy and Tyler exclaimed in unison.

"Taylor, Anna, do you want any more before I let these two at it?" Bampa asked.

"I'm good," said Taylor.

"Me, too," Anna said with a grin. "I'm so glad Taylor talked me into trying pepperoni on the pizza. It was really good!"

Davy reached for his slice, saying to Anna, "All this time I've been telling you how great it tastes, and you would never try it. But one suggestion from Taylor and you're ready to risk it."

Taylor laughed at this. "Davy, that's because girls rule and boys drool," she said good-naturedly. "Right, Anna?"

"Right!" Anna agreed with a giggle.

Tyler and Davy looked at each other and rolled their eyes. "It's tough having a sister, isn't it?" Tyler observed.

Davy looked at Anna and smiled. "Yes, sometimes it is," he admitted, "but I wouldn't trade Anna for the world."

***

When Jim and Zach arrived back at the Nantahala Outdoor Center, Jim helped load the paddles, helmets, and raft back onto Zach's truck. "Now all we need are Bob and the kids, and we're good to go," said Jim. "I wonder if they're still eating..."

Zach looked at his watch. "Knowing how fast my grandchildren eat, they could easily be finished by now. I told them to meet us at the store; if they're not there, we'll mosey over the River's End." The two men walked first to the store, where Zach popped his head inside and asked, "Abby, are the kids back yet? No? Okay, thanks." He turned to Jim and said, "Guess we'll hook up with them at the restaurant. I don't know about you, Jim, but I could sure use a long drink of iced tea just about now."

"I'm with you there," said Jim. "Let's go."

"Hi, Mr. Jones," the hostess greeted him the moment he stepped through the door, with Jim right behind him. "Table for two?"

"Not today, Mindy," Zach said. "We're just here to locate my grandchildren and their friends." He craned his neck, looking all around, until he spotted them through the picture windows. "I see them on the deck," he told Mindy as he pointed in their direction. "We'll join them and have two iced teas."

"Right away, sir," Mindy said.

As Jim's focus was on his destination, he never saw Ronnie sitting with his foreman at a corner table. But Ronnie saw him. His eyes narrowed to slits, and a scowl encompassed his face. Bill looked up from his hamburger and caught this unexpected shift in Ronnie's demeanor, which had noticeably improved once lunch had arrived. "What's wrong now?" Bill asked, sincerely concerned.

"That scum-bucket cousin of mine, that's what's wrong," Ronnie said through clenched teeth. "Seeing Jim is enough to make me lose my appetite."

"Don't let him get to you," Bill cautioned him. "I doubt he even saw you when he came through, but he's going to have to pass by us on the way out—that is, if we're still sitting here. We can keep an eye out for when he's headed this way, and just pretend we're too busy eating to even know he's there."

Ronnie heaved a sigh. "I suppose you're right, Bill. I shouldn't let Jim get to me like I do," he said, then added with a sly smile, "he may be on his high horse now, but he's in for the tumble of his life when I kick him out of the saddle."

***

When Jim came out onto the deck with Zach, Davy could tell by his jovial expression that he hadn't seen Ronnie seated in the dining room.

He hated to ruin his stepfather's day by informing him of his cousin's close proximity, but knew he had to warn Jim and let him know that Reverend and Sharp-eyes were still spying on the man's nefarious activities. The minute Jim grabbed a chair and pulled it up next to Davy, he knew something was amiss. "Is everything all right, son?" Jim asked softly, his eyes deep with concern.

"No, Jim," Davy whispered. "Can we go over to that corner of the deck where no one is sitting? We need to talk."

Jim got up as promptly as he had sat down. "Bob," he said, "could you bring my iced tea to me over there when it arrives? Davy and I need a few moments."

"Sure thing," said Bob. He knew instinctively that their conversation would most likely revolve around the Old Ones, Racer in particular. Thus the need for privacy was obvious.

When Davy and Jim reached the unoccupied corner, both leaned on the railing, pretending to be doing nothing more than gazing at the river below. Davy knew time was of the essence, if he was to communicate what he needed to without drawing the suspicions of the others. He plunged right in. "Ronnie's here," he said in a low voice.

Without looking at Davy, Jim asked, "Where?"

"In the dining room, with a man who I'm sure got some photos of Racer," he answered. "Reverend and Sharp-eyes are there, too, listening to the conversation. I hope they tell us what they know soon. Reverend promised me everything would be okay, and I really want to believe it will. But after today..." Davy's voice trailed off. Jim detected the catch in his throat that pointed directly to barely held-back tears.

Jim placed a reassuring arm around Davy's shoulder and drew him close. "You're letting the what ifs get to you again, son," he said calmly. "If Reverend says everything will be okay, I think we can trust him, don't you? And as for Ronnie, it's a free country and he can eat anywhere he wants to. Do I want to see him again? No, of course not, but I can't rule out an encounter today. I just appreciate the heads-up."

"Here's your tea, Jim," said Bob cheerfully as he held out the glass. Jim turned from the railing to take it. When he did, Bob noticed his serious expression and knew his hunch about the Old Ones had been correct. He leaned in to Jim and whispered, "You should know, the conversation at the table has turned completely to the miraculous squirrel antics today. I gave Anna 'the look' and I don't think she'll add anything to the mix that would show our hand, but I think it's best if you all come back and sit down with us."

"I agree," said Jim and looked directly at Davy. "Son, you let me know about anything Reverend and Sharp-eyes find out right away. In the mean-time, take the owl's good advice and put your fears to rest."

***

Dazed and disheartened by what he had read and reread so many times he could not count, Eric slowly closed the deed book before him on the table and buried his face in his hands. With so much sadness and tragedy in just two days' time, he could barely believe this last blow. He had studied every word on every page, searching for the one clue which could convince him these were counterfeit; his diligent perusal had uncovered no flaws. Eric knew he was no expert at deeds and titles, but the wording had been straightforward and understandable. Even the signatures, written several times, seemed to be authentic.

How am I going to tell Jim? At this thought, Eric's head began to pound. *Even worse, how will Davy react? I know I need to tell them, but Lord, please give me the strength to do it.* Eric rose stiffly from the chair and resignedly headed toward the shelf from which he had taken the book. It was then he noticed the sour face of the clerk peering through a window in the swinging door. It made the skin on his neck crawl. *Has he been watching me the whole time? Is he in cahoots with Ronnie?*

As Eric slipped the book into its proper slot, he felt a faint glimmer of hope. There was more to this story than met the eye, of that he was certain. But whether or not the missing link could be discovered in time remained to be seen. *I'm going to give it my best shot, Jim and Davy, my very best shot.*

CHAPTER 7

AN ENCOUNTER WITH RONNIE

Silky and Mrs. Silky carried the precariously balanced Racer on their backs through the water with amazing agility. They didn't stop until they'd reached a spot where no humans with their prying eyes were anywhere to be found. "Let's go ashore here," said Silky. "Hold on, Racer, this could be a bumpy exit."

"Like the ride wasn't bumpy enough?" Racer asked with mock indignity as he wobbled back and forth. "It's a miracle I managed to balance at all; I wouldn't have but for you two working in such perfect synchronicity." The squirrel leaped to much-welcomed solid ground as the otters heaved themselves up the bank. Racer turned to both of them and, with a gleam in his eyes and his signature, lopsided grin beaming, said, "In all sincerity, my dear Old Ones, I can't thank you enough. You sure got me out of jam in a hurry, and I owe my present safety to your swift actions."

"We wouldn't have had it any other way," Mrs. Silky assured him. "Are you starting to dry out?"

"All but my feet and the end of my tail," Racer said, "But I wonder if I'm still visible to the unchosen?"

"You could very well be," Silky observed. "Why else would I have selected this remote spot for us to land? I say it's time to get you back to The Glade for a bit of rest, don't you think?"

"And a bite to eat," Racer declared. "I'm ravenous!"

"So what else is new?" Mrs. Silky asked, causing all three of them to share in a vigorous laugh.

"Time's a-wasting!" Silky avowed, encircling Racer and Mrs. Silky in preparation for instant transport. "And come to think of it, I'm pretty hungry myself."

***

Jim glanced at his watch as he and Zach took their last swallows of iced tea. "Well, kids," he announced, "this has been fun, but I think it's high time we head home. Your mother is sure to be a bit worried by now."

"I'm ready," said Anna. She still hadn't dried out completely and was anxious not only to change into fresh clothes, but also to tell Mom all about her harrowing experience and her valiant rescue by Silky and Mrs. Silky.

Zach got up from the table, motioning to Taylor and Tyler to do the same. He reached out to shake both Bob's and Jim's hands. "Sure was grand having y'all along with us today," he said warmly. "Don't forget to stop in the store to fetch your photo of us all coming over the rapids."

"Thanks for the reminder. We will," Jim said.

Anna crinkled her nose and frowned. "I don't know if I want to see it," she admitted.

"Then don't look at it," Davy said matter-of-factly, "but you know Mom will want to see it, so we have to take it home."

"I suppose," she said with a pout.

"But Anna," Taylor protested, "what if that squirrel got in the picture? Wouldn't that be something?"

Immediately, Anna's face brightened. "I didn't think of that," she said. "All I thought about was seeing me thrown out of the raft all over again. Seeing Ra...I mean, that squirrel would be awesome!"

Davy cringed. Anna, who had been so vigilant in keeping her mouth closed while everyone else was discussing the miraculous events of the day, almost spilled the beans in the eleventh hour. Thankfully, Zach and his grandchildren didn't notice the slip. As everyone headed for the door, Davy spied the quilt left to dry on the railing. *Perfect!* "Jim! We have to return Abby's quilt," he said as he scooped it up and watched as his step-father held the door for everyone as they filed inside. Davy hurried over to him and whispered, "Ronnie's to your right. Just look straight ahead as you walk to the exit. Tell Bampa, too." Jim gave him a wink and gladly followed his directive.

After being in the bright sunshine, the restaurant seemed dim and gloomy. It was all Davy could do to keep his own focus on the exit door and not look to his right to see if Reverend and Sharp-eyes were still at their posts. There was no need to look. "Davy," Reverend addressed him, "tell Jim we will be coming by soon to share what we know about Ronnie's movements these last several days. We wish to rest in The Glade a while before we can make that happen. Otherwise, I'd give you a precise moment of arrival."

Davy nodded ever so slightly, but it was enough to catch Ronnie's eye. In a flash, a wicked and treacherous thought entered the man's mind. "Hey, Davy," he called out, "come over here, boy." Davy froze in mid-stride, watching Jim continue his progress with the others, apparently not having heard Ronnie's command. Tentatively, he turned to meet Ronnie's gaze; it was cold and steely, contradicting the smile playing upon his lips. "C'mon now, Davy, I won't bite. Don't you want to see a photo of your sister my friend, Bill, got today?"

"Don't do it!" Reverend warned him emphatically. "Don't come close to him, Davy! I may have removed part of the evil in him, but much remains."

"Follow Jim quickly, lad," Sharp-eyes implored. "We'll handle this!"

Davy tried to move, but his feet felt as hard and immobile as stone. He stood there like a statue, unable to wrench his eyes away from Ronnie's stare, so ghastly and sinister; the pupils, which should have been dark and round, were transforming hideously into fiery slits. Davy trembled all over as horrid memories that to this point had been held at bay came flying into his head, black and monstrous like the vision of thousands of bats swarming out of their cave at once.

"Stop looking at him!" Reverend screeched in a panic, knowing full well what the boy was seeing. "Run, Davy, run for your life!"

Jim's voice came to Davy's ears, echoing and faint as if heard in a dream. "Davy, there you are. I thought you were right behind me." Jim's voice trailed off. He saw instantly that Ronnie was staring straight at the boy. Bill Cunningham, his face beet red, seemed flustered and confused by the entire situation. Jim glared at his cousin. "All right, Ronnie," he said gruffly, "what's going on here?"

Ronnie diverted his gaze from Davy's to Jim's, and the spell Davy had fallen under was promptly and thankfully broken. "Why Jim, ain't nothin' going on except me trying to be friendly-like," he replied smoothly. "Seems Davy here doesn't know how to be friendly back."

"Davy's plenty friendly," Jim said tersely. "With decent people, that is."

"So let's see if I have this right," Ronnie drawled as he stood to his full height and took several menacing steps toward Jim. "First, you don't tell him nothin' about whose property you're really living on; second, you steal *my* property which was rightfully mine in the first place, and now you have the gall to say *I'm* not decent?"

Jim's temper burst the floodgates. Before Davy could grab for his stepfather, Jim had taken the two great strides required to place himself within a foot of his cousin. Ronnie tried hard to maintain his cool, but it was clear to all who were watching this scene unfold that the man was unnerved by Jim's aggressive move. Through gritted teeth, Jim growled, "If I *ever* catch you anywhere around my family or my property, Ronnie, you'll regret the day you were born!"

"Oh, another threat, Jim?" Ronnie said bravely, though there was an unmistakable quaver in his voice. "My, my! Maybe I'll just be making another call to the sheriff this afternoon. Couldn't hurt. Couldn't hurt. And look around, Jim, there are plenty of witnesses this time. You need to back off, and back off now."

"I'll back off," Jim said fiercely, "but I won't back down when it comes to protecting what's mine, y'hear? If you keep your distance and your hands off what's not yours, you got nothing to worry about."

"Actually," Ronnie snarled, summoning up his courage, "it's *you* who needs to be worried. If anyone's on the wrong side of the law, it's you, and I plan to prove it."

"Really?" Jim asked sarcastically. "Is that a threat I hear spewing out of *your* mouth?"

"No, not a threat, cousin," Ronnie sneered. "It's a promise!"

***

Bob, Zach, and the children were just entering the Nantahala Outdoor Center when Bob realized Jim and Davy were missing. He stepped out the door and looked back the way they had come for any glimpse of them. He spotted them just leaving the restaurant. One look at Jim's face, even from this distance, told Bob something untoward had taken place. *Did he have an encounter with Ronnie? I thought we all agreed to keep our distance. He sure looks riled up! I hope I can get him to calm down, or I'm going to be the one driving us home.* As the two drew nigh, Bob opened the door for them without a word. Jim's clenched jaw and furrowed brow confirmed Bob's suspicions that there had indeed been an unwelcome run-in with Ronnie. Bob knew Jim would tell him about it later, once he regained his composure, and wisely decided not to ask him anything at the moment. But the look of consternation on Davy's face moved Bob to speak to him, at least. He reached for the boy's arm and gently grabbed hold. "Davy," he said quietly, "is everything okay?"

Davy looked into his Bampa's eyes, so kind and filled with concern, so contrary to those hideous ones, which had held him fast only moments ago. They filled Davy with such relief, he hugged Bob right then and there, squeezing him tight as if he would never let go. "I had a memory back at the restaurant," Davy confessed against Bob's chest, "and it wasn't a good one."

"Can you tell me about it?" Bob asked.

Davy pulled away ever so slightly in order to look at Bob's face. He shook his head. "I can't really explain it," he said, "but I know what it means."

"So what *does* it mean, Davy?"

Davy motioned to his Bampa to bend down so he could whisper in his ear. "Ronnie's not just bad, Bampa," he said. "He's evil."

***

Betty Rae was finding it impossible to concentrate on any of her usual pastimes for long. She had been so overwhelmed with joy and relief when Ronnie had shared the good news about his health, she didn't even think to question whether or not her husband was telling her the truth. But now, the possibility that Ronnie could have glossed things over simply so she would not worry kept nagging at her like a pesky mosquito. The descriptions Buddy and Sammy had given her of Ronnie's serious condition up there on the mountain had been so vivid and congruent in detail, she hadn't doubted their veracity. Betty Rae wondered if, perhaps, Ronnie had only fainted in the heat, frightening the boys into believing the worst. *That must be it. I'm just letting my imagination run away with me. Ronnie seemed as right as right can be when he got home yesterday, and when he left this morning. Stop fretting, Betty Rae; it's just a waste of time!*

Determinedly, Betty Rae picked up her latest romance novel off the coffee table. She was just heading out to the porch when Buddy and Sammy burst through the front door, hot and perspiring from a long round of shooting hoops. "Hey, Mom!" they greeted her.

"Hey, yourself," she answered. "Looks like the two of you need to jump in the shower."

"Aw, Mom," Sammy whined. "It's just sweat. It'll dry."

"I need somethin' cold to drink first," Buddy said. "Man, it's hot out there today!"

Both boys headed for the kitchen. Betty Rae decided to follow them. There was a question she needed to ask. "Buddy, Sammy, you haven't said much about your father's clean bill of health except that you were glad everything is okay. Have you changed your minds about what really took place on the mountain? Do you think you misjudged what you actually saw?"

Buddy took a long swig of iced tea. "I know what I saw, Mom," he said. "I don't know how it could have been anything other than a heart attack, but if the doctor said it wasn't, then I guess it wasn't."

"Do you think he might have just fainted?" Betty Rae asked. "When people faint, they look an awful lot like the way you described Dad's face."

"Maybe that's it," said Sammy brightly. "Maybe that's why he came around so sudden-like."

Buddy frowned and took another sip of tea. "I don't know, Mom. I've never seen a person faint before. I guess I got so scared, I jumped to conclusions. I feel bad now, knowin' how much we worried you."

Betty Rae gave both her sons a sincere smile. "Yes, I was very worried," she admitted, "but better to be safe than sorry. I'm so glad I had the doctor run those tests. Now we can all rest a little easier, can't we?"

"Sure, Mom," Sammy said, "but can I wait 'til tonight to take my shower?"

***

Mrs. Sharp-eyes, refreshed from her visit to The Glade, was now perched on the Carsons' roof with Mrs. Reverend, who had insisted on accompanying her. "We need to give both our loves a rest," she'd said, "and you shouldn't be alone lest any misfortune befall you." The hawk had been delighted by the offer. She truly did not want to stand watch by herself, and she enjoyed the owl's company in all times and circumstances.

Now, as they watched Buddy and Sammy playing basketball in the driveway, Mrs. Sharp-eyes had an idea. "Those two probably won't last much longer in this heat, as hard as they're going at it. Why don't we try to get in the house right behind them, instead of waiting for Sharp-eyes and Reverend to return? There's an outside chance we could glean more information."

"That sounds like a good plan," Mrs. Reverend agreed. "If Reverend and Sharp-eyes return and don't see you here on the roof, they'll probably assume you have yet to arrive or you found an opportunity to slip into the house without them."

The owl and hawk watched and waited for the subtlest of signals to let them know the boys could be growing weary of the game and were ready to return to their comfortably air-conditioned house. The moment they saw Sammy rolling the ball into some bushes by the door, they swooped down and landed as close to the boys as they dared. Both were hoping and praying they could gain easy entry. Buddy had his hand on the door knob. "Go get the ball, Sammy," he said as he opened the door wide. "You know Mom don't like us leaving our stuff outside." Blissfully and thankfully Mrs. Reverend and Mrs. Sharp-eyes winged their way inside and soared up to the mantelpiece, just in time to see Betty Rae picking up her book and walking toward the porch. When they saw her and both boys heading for the kitchen, they traded their fireplace perch for the top of the refrigerator.

As they listened intently to the discussion of Ronnie's health, Mrs. Reverend and Mrs. Sharp-eyes were deeply troubled. "Ronnie hasn't told them the truth," said Mrs. Sharp-eyes dolefully.

"Does that surprise you?" Mrs. Reverend asked. "Ronnie certainly doesn't have a reputation for being honest. But in this case, where it is so serious, one would think he would divulge the matter in full."

"One would think," the hawk noted, "being miraculously revived from the massive heart attack Ronnie *knows* he suffered, and is living to tell about it. Wouldn't that be incredible news to share with one's family?"

"I think you pegged it, dear friend, when you said 'miraculously,'" said Mrs. Reverend.

"How's that?" Mrs. Sharp-eyes inquired.

The owl regarded the hawk solemnly. "Ronnie doesn't believe in miracles."

***

All the way home, Anna couldn't stop looking at the photo of their raft as it plunged over the last rapids. There she was in the water with Racer, big as life, right beside her. Zach had generously given Jim and Bob several copies, as souvenirs to keep or send to family or friends. "After all," he'd said with a grin, "that's not something you see every day!" Davy had simply placed his photo on the seat beside him and stared unseeing out the window. His day had been nothing less than a rough and tumble roller coaster ride of emotions and experiences. He had gone from the exhilarating thrill of rafting down the river with Racer, Silky, and Mrs. Silky, to the murky depths of an encounter with Ronnie, running the gamut of fear, worry, and what ifs in between those high and low points. Davy's thoughts were whirling dizzily in his head. He desperately wanted to shut them off, or at least slow them down. He closed his eyes wearily and leaned back against his seat, hoping this would help calm them. Before Davy knew it he'd drifted off into a much-needed, peaceful sleep.

Jim, still agitated, had wisely given the car keys to Bob, who glanced in the rear view mirror and observed that the boy was sleeping. "Looks like Davy's day has done him in," he commented softly to Jim, sitting beside him.

Jim turned around to see for himself. "The boy's had quite a long day," he sighed. "We all have." The men were silent for the next several minutes. Bob could tell by the look on Jim's face that he was deep in thought, and knew it was best to leave him be just as he had earlier, at the Nantahala Outdoor Center. To Bob's relief, Jim opened up earlier than he would have expected. "You know, Bob, something happened back there that I don't understand, but it really has me concerned," Jim said. He spoke barely above a whisper so as not to disturb Davy.

"Does it by any chance have something to do with Ronnie?" Bob asked.

"Yes. Well, no...I'm not sure," Jim said hesitantly. "When I went back into the restaurant to fetch Davy, the boy was standing stock still, almost as if he was in a deep trance. It appeared to me he was staring in Ronnie's direction, but I got the feeling he was seeing something else, something..."

"Compelling?" Bob suggested.

"Yes, exactly," said Jim. "It wasn't until I touched Davy's shoulders that he seemed to snap out of it. Any ideas, Bob?"

"Actually, yes," Bob answered readily, to Jim's surprise. "You see, Davy was looking right at Ronnie, but that's not who he was seeing."

"Then who *was* he seeing?" Jim asked, intrigued.

Bob took a deep breath and spoke in a somber tone. "Davy saw the demon within."

***

Susie glanced up at the clock hanging in the kitchen. Here it was, almost three o'clock, and still no sign of Bob. She sighed and turned her attention back to the pie crust she was rolling out on the counter. Susie wanted this meal shared with Eric to be memorably cheerful and satisfying, especially with all he was going through at the moment. She purposely decided to make an apple pie for dessert so she could send whatever remained of it home with the sheriff, along with the leftover beef stew, which was already simmering on the stove.

At that moment, Susie heard the front door open. "My, oh, my, does this house ever smell wonderful!" Bob exclaimed. "Let me guess—beef stew!" He entered the kitchen and greeted Susie with a generous hug, which she gladly returned.

"You're right as always, Bob," she told him, and added teasingly, "at least when it comes to food."

He had to laugh at this remark. Spying the pie crust on the counter, he said, "Wow, Susie, you haven't made a pie since my birthday. What's the special occasion?"

Susie explained to Bob about Eric and Elly's sad situation, and why only he could make it to dinner. "The church is planning meals for the rest of the week, maybe longer, once Elly comes home. But since she's still in the hospital, Eric agreed to come to our house. I do hope we can lift his spirits."

Bob smiled warmly at Susie and stroked her cheek. "If you can wait until this evening to hear about our amazing adventures on the Nantahala," he said, "I'm certain I have plenty of stories guaranteed to amuse you both and take Eric's mind off his current troubles."

Susie smiled. "Yes, I can wait," she assured him. "Now let me get my apples cut up so I can bake this pie."

***

"You're home! You're home!" Kate called gleefully. The moment she had heard the car tires grinding on the gravel, she had sped out of the house as fast as her feet would fly to greet her family. "I'm so glad to see you!" Davy and Anna leaped out of the car and rushed to hug their mother. Anna was still damp from her fall into the river, and Kate noticed right away. "Oh, dear, Anna, how did your clothes get wet?" she asked in alarm.

"We'll tell you inside," said Jim, as he and Bob got out of the car. That's when Kate noticed that Bob had been doing the driving. She was puzzled, but sure that Jim would explain all momentarily.

"Here you go, Jim," said Bob as he tossed Jim the car keys. "It's time I checked in with Susie, so I'll be off."

"Want me to give you a lift?" Jim offered.

"Thanks, but no thanks," Bob answered. "I could use the exercise. Bye, everyone! It was great fun!"

"Bye, Bampa!" Davy and Anna said in unison. Anna added, "Come back soon!"

"Don't worry, Anna," he said with a grin, "wild horses couldn't keep me away from my grandchildren!" With that, Bob headed down the road toward home, and the Hunters and Murrays gladly entered theirs.

"Boy, Kate, I could sure use a cup of coffee," Jim declared. "Do you have any made?"

Kate flushed ever so slightly. She had been tempted to brew some that afternoon, but had heeded Susie's advice and drank a cup of herbal tea instead. "It's not made, honey, but I'll get right on it. I can't wait to hear about today."

"And by the looks of things," Jim said as he gave Kate a big hug, "you're feeling much better. Are you?"

"Feeling right as rain," she said with a laugh. Davy and Anna were both very relieved by this news, although the way Mom had greeted them had already assured them she was her old chipper self again.

"Mom, hurry and make Jim's coffee," Anna pleaded; she was holding the photo backwards against her chest so the image wasn't revealed. "I can't wait to show you this picture!"

"While your mother is brewing the coffee," Jim suggested, "why don't you two run along and see what Maggie and Frisky are up to. I bet they've really missed you today."

Davy and Anna didn't need further prompting. "I'll bet they're on Maggie's bed, snoozing away," Davy told Anna as they headed in that direction. Just the thought of his beloved dog was enough to make all his lingering worries melt away. Sure enough, there the pets were, curled up together on the porch. When Maggie heard the footsteps approaching, she let out a bark of welcome which, of course, startled poor Frisky once again. But the kitten was soon comforted in Anna's loving arms, while Maggie showered Davy's face with exuberant kisses.

"You want to hear all about our day, Frisky?" Anna asked as she cuddled him close. Frisky replied with a resounding purr which would have sounded more suitable coming from a cat twice his size.

"C'mon, Maggie," Davy said, "you need to hear all about the day, too."

"And what about yours truly? Don't I get in on all the fun?"

"Racer!" Davy shouted with delight as he ran to open the screen door for his friend.

"Racer's here?" Anna asked, looking all around. "He must be dry, because I can't see or hear him. At least I have the photo."

"Photo? Photo of what?" Racer inquired eagerly.

Davy sighed and answered him. "The one of us coming over the rapids, with Anna and you plain as day in the water."

"Aha!" Racer exclaimed. "I'm willing to bet it's not the only one out there. Did you see that crowd of people running toward us, holding cameras and cell phones?"

"Yes, I did," Davy said. "Doesn't that worry you a little? I mean, first you show up at church, and everyone is talking about it. Now you appear to another bunch of people, who take photos to back up the fact that you do really exist. Isn't this going to cause problems for the Old Ones?"

"Why should it, my child?" Racer asked, patting Davy's hand comfortingly. "The only problem we have right now is keeping Ronnie away from The Glade for good. I truly don't think the occasional Old One sightings will hurt at all. In fact," said the squirrel, leaning closer to Davy as if they could be overheard, "my hunch is it will actually help."

CHAPTER 8

IN THE NEWS

When Reverend and Sharp-eyes returned with Ronnie to his house, they were astonished to find Mrs. Reverend and Mrs. Sharp-eyes perched on the mantelpiece, waiting expectantly for their arrival. "What a sight for sore eyes!" Reverend declared jovially as he soared upward and landed next to Mrs. Reverend. Sharp-eyes, just as relieved as the owl to see his missus, joined her and affectionately nuzzled her head with his beak.

"We were fortunate to slip into the house when Buddy left the door open," Mrs. Reverend informed them. "Although we're not sure it's a piece of the puzzle that will make a difference in our reconnaissance, we have learned that Ronnie hasn't told his family the truth about what happened on the mountain."

Reverend's amber eyes grew wide. "Well, well, well," he said, shaking his head. "I cannot predict at the moment if this information will be helpful, but it does give us a fact we might not have known otherwise."

"Except for the initial phone call Ronnie made from the hospital yesterday," Sharp-eyes observed.

"Are you two still planning to rest up at The Glade and visit Jim and Davy this evening?" Mrs. Sharp-eyes asked. "We are more than happy to stay here in your stead."

"That's what we were hoping, my dear," Sharp-eyes said. "I, for one, am feeling terribly drained—especially after our excursion today." The hawk and the owl proceeded to fill the ladies in on all that had transpired since they'd followed Ronnie into his office that morning.

"And you were never able to see the image on the camera?" Mrs. Rev-erend asked worriedly. "The one who Ronnie said 'he knew' and that 'his days are numbered'?"

"We're hoping Davy can answer that for us," said Reverend.

"I know who it is!" Mrs. Sharp-eyes exclaimed suddenly to the bewil-derment of the others. "I was talking to Mrs. Racer at The Glade this morning. She told me Racer was planning to raft the river with Davy and that Silky and Mrs. Silky would be swimming along with them. Do you think Racer could have fallen into the river?"

Everyone fell silent. They all knew what happened to the True Squirrels of the Old Ones when they became wet. Reverend was the first to speak. "If that is true, my dear Mrs. Sharp-eyes," he said, "then it is the second time in a fortnight an Old One, namely Racer, has become visible to the unchosen. And my feeling is, as fast as the news of Mad Squirrel Sunday travelled, this will travel faster and farther than we could ever imagine."

***

Eric, dressed in street clothes and once again in his own car, drove in the direction of the Fairchilds'. He knew he would first have the unpleas-ant obligation to stop at the Hunters' home and fill Jim in on the details of the deed he had seen at the courthouse. As much as he dreaded telling Jim, Eric feared Davy's reaction even more. Certainly, the boy would be devastated. Still, Eric couldn't shake the feeling that there was a clue some-where out there that could render Ronnie's claim null and void. *If only I could put my finger on it.*

As Eric pulled into the Hunter's drive, Jim jumped up when he heard the noise of the tires to see who the unexpected visitor could be. The family had been happily seated at the kitchen table, relaying to Kate the adven-tures of the day. As she listened to them all share the tale and looked at the remarkable photo innumerable times, she couldn't help but wish she had been able to go with them. "We'll take you another time, Mom," Davy assured her right before Jim left the table to exit the back door and greet whoever might be outside. "We really missed having you there."

Mom sighed. "I missed so much today," she said, "but you've all done such a marvelous job of relating all the news, I feel like I was there with you, at least in spirit. And Davy, please tell Racer I'm so thankful he kept my little girl calm through the entire ordeal."

"Why don't you tell him yourself?" Davy asked, grinning mischievously. "He's been sitting here the whole time!"

"Has he now?" It was Mom's turn to smile. "Well, then, dear Racer, thank you from the bottom of my heart. And please, thank the otters, too."

Racer bowed graciously in Mom's direction and said, "Thank you most kindly, m'lady. It was my honor, duty and pleasure. I will be sure to let Silky and Mrs. Silky know of your gratitude."

When Davy repeated the squirrel's words verbatim, even adding the bow, both Mom and Anna erupted in a storm of giggles. They were still chuckling when Jim entered the door with Sheriff Eric in tow. The looks on the men's faces immediately squelched the merriment. Mom stood up quickly. "Oh, Sheriff, do forgive me," she said earnestly. "I forgot to tell Jim about your phone call when he got home. There's nothing wrong, is there?"

Jim walked over to her and placed an arm around her shoulder. His green eyes were moist, and his voice sad and subdued when he spoke. "Davy, Anna, could you two possibly hang out on the porch for a little while? Or go play outside with your pets? The sheriff here needs to discuss something with your mother and me."

"Go on, Davy," Racer urged. "I'll stay here and listen in. Oh, and let's pray Reverend and his entourage show up before the sheriff leaves!"

"I forgot to tell Jim," Davy said out loud, before he realized it.

"Forgot to tell me what, son?"

"The Old Ones," Davy said. "Reverend and Sharp-eyes told me to tell you they will visit tonight."

Jim raised an eyebrow, but didn't say anything. Eric appeared a bit nervous at this prospect, and secretly hoped they wouldn't show up until he was safely ensconced in the Fairchilds' residence. It was Mom who posed the question. "Davy, you mean they're coming to see you, right?"

"Not just me," Davy stated. "According to Racer, we will all be able to see them."

***

David and Sarah Murray reached Blue Ridge, Georgia, about mid-afternoon, and decided to look for lodgings there for the night. It was the height of tourist season, but they were hoping beyond hope they could secure an available motel room. Good fortune found them when they inquired about availability at the Comfort Inn. They had spotted the sign from the highway. While David took care of the arrangements, Sarah stood at a distance from the reservation desk perusing a rack of pamphlets advertising all the interesting attractions the area offered.

The hotel clerk, whose name badge read "Roger," greeted David warmly at the reservations desk. "How long will you be staying with us?" Roger inquired.

"Just one night," said David. "We're heading up to North Carolina and the Nantahala Mountains tomorrow."

Roger grinned broadly. "That's some mighty gorgeous country up there," he noted. "God's country, I call it. I've been up that way countless times. Is this your first visit to that area?"

"No," David admitted, "but that was so long ago, it will seem new all over again."

Roger took David's credit card and was prepared to swipe it when he noticed the "check I.D." in the place reserved for a signature. "Sir, may I see your driver's license?" he asked courteously.

"Why, certainly," David said as he retrieved it from his wallet. "I'm glad you caught that, son. Most folks don't, and that's a shame. You can't be too careful nowadays."

"Yes, sir, I agree," said Roger as he scrutinized the license. When he saw David's last name and realized his place of residence was Hawaii, he had a sudden flash of memory. It was a long shot, but curiosity got the better of him. Roger studied David's face and noticed a familiar green in those eyes, such a rare color he had only seen in one other person his entire life. "Begging your pardon, Mr. Murray," he said, "but is your wife's name 'Sarah' by any chance?"

David was understandably taken aback. "Why yes, it is," he admitted. "How did you know?"

"I really didn't know, but I took a guess based on your last name and the fact you live in Hawaii," Roger told him. "Plus, sir, I've only seen eyes like yours on a friend I served with in the military. His name's John Murray. Is he, by any chance, your son?"

At this most unexpected question, David once again experienced the grief he thought was buried all those years ago come churning to the surface like a tidal wave. Before he could stop them, he felt tears stinging his eyes and a lump rising in his throat. David lowered his eyes trying to gain his composure. He was barely able to croak out an answer. "Yes, he was," he said haltingly. "John was killed in the line of duty."

Roger's face fell and his hands began to shake. "I'm so sorry," he stammered awkwardly. "John was a good man, a loyal soldier, and an even better friend. If I'd known, sir, I'd never have brought it up."

David forced a smile. "It's not your fault, Roger," he said with as much grace as he could muster. "Thank you for your kind words about John. Any father wants to hear good things about his son."

"You have every reason to be proud, sir," Roger said, a bit more confidently now. "We were only in the unit together for two months, but he looked after me like I was his kid brother. I was only eighteen, and scared out of my wits. His encouragement was the glue I needed to hold myself together and make it through."

"I'm glad to know that," David said sincerely, letting a tear fall as he reached over the counter to shake Roger's hand.

"And there's one more thing you need to know, sir," Roger said, as he raised the charge slip with his free hand. "Your stay tonight is on me."

***

All afternoon, throughout his many calls on prospective church members, Pastor Mike struggled to stay focused. He was fine when actually sitting down and chatting with folks. It was during the driving from one destination to the next that he found his mind wandering back to thoughts of Abby, their wonderful picnic by the river, and the incomparable ruckus caused by Racer's unanticipated appearance on the shore, with a soaked-through and shaken up Anna in tow. Mike said a prayer of thanks that Anna had not been hurt in the mishap, and asked God's protection over Racer. He did not know if the incident would in some way put this amazing creature in jeopardy, but he sincerely hoped not. Mike couldn't dismiss the fact that so many people had captured photos of Racer, and wondered if it would be front page news in the Nantahala community.

Mike turned into his own driveway a little before six o'clock that evening. He planned to fix himself a bite to eat and retreat to his office to begin working on this week's sermon. He had just popped a slice of meat-loaf and generous helping of mashed potatoes into the microwave when he heard his phone ring. He sprinted to his office to get it, and noticed with alarm that his answering machine was ablaze with messages: fifteen, to be exact. His spirits sagging, Mike answered the phone. "Hello, Pastor Russell here."

"Pastor, it's Valerie Green," the caller said in a breathlessly excited voice. "Did you catch the five o'clock news?"

"No Valerie, I just now got home. What did I miss?"

"You! That's what you missed! Standing with that pretty lady at the Nantahala and that little girl, what's her name? She adopted one of my kittens. Oh, Anna, that's right, Anna! And right smack dab in the middle of y'all is that danged Mad Sunday Squirrel! It has to be! Leastways, that's what the reporter referred to when she broke the story. She said the station got flooded by photos of this happening right in our backyards today, so it can't be photo-shopped. No way! And they say Anna got tossed from a raft? Poor thing! Guess she's okay, though, or they would have said something, wouldn't they? Anyway, Tommy thinks because of this latest incident, we're in for another boom in attendance this coming Sunday. Wouldn't that be something? Better put some humor in that sermon now, ha, ha, ha! Oh, and that pretty gal, are y'all dating or something? I hope so. You need to find you a good woman, Pastor, it's about time! Well, gotta go heat up Tommy's supper. Maybe you should put your television on and see if they repeat the story in the six o' clock news. Bye-bye!"

Click! Valerie hung up. Mike stood there a moment, shell-shocked by her non-stop barrage of verbiage. He knew without having to check them that his string of messages was more than likely about the same topic. Slowly, he placed the receiver back on the handle and, still in a daze, reached for the television remote. The screen flickered to life. The news was just starting.

***

Bob Fairchild rarely watched the evening news, but he was feeling fatigued after the long day and didn't want to be underfoot in the kitchen while Susie was bustling about preparing tonight's meal. He plopped down on the living room couch, put his feet up, and turned the television on, prepared to be bored. But after a day like today, Bob welcomed a little boredom. He closed his eyes and simply listened.

"And in local news today, tourists at the Nantahala Outdoor Center got the shock of their lives, when what appears to be a gigantic squirrel was seen swimming alongside an unidentified girl who had been thrown from her raft."

Bob's eyes flew open. "Susie!" he yelled. "Susie, come quick!"

Hearing the panic in her husband's voice, Susie dashed out of the kitchen and into the living room, where Bob was pointing animatedly at the television. Her hand flew to her mouth as she gasped in dismay. "Racer! Anna! Oh, no!" They watched the remainder of the news report in stunned silence, both wondering what impact this revelation would have on the safety and obscurity the Old Ones had enjoyed up to this point. "Oh, Bob," Susie said sadly, "shouldn't we call Jim and Kate about this? Shouldn't they know what's going on?"

"We do need to let them know," he agreed. "I tell you what, Susie, I'm going to set up the VCR to record the news at six o'clock, in case they air this segment again. My gut tells me they will. Then instead of just telling Jim and Kate about it, we can show them."

"Okay," Susie acquiesced, "but I'm still going to give them a heads-up."

***

When Davy and Anna retreated to the porch, both wore worried looks on their faces. They sat side by side on Davy's cot, Anna cuddling Frisky, and Maggie's head placed gently and comfortingly in the boy's lap. Anna turned to her brother and asked, "Why do you think the grown-ups don't want us to hear what they're saying?"

Davy sighed, then said, "I think it has something to do with this property. Reverend and Sharp-eyes have been following Ronnie around for the past several days, and they're convinced he's up to no good. That's why they want to talk to Jim."

Anna brightened at this. "Oh, I'll be so happy to see them, really see them, again. And I hope they bring us good news."

"Me too," Davy agreed, giving Anna's braid a tug. "We could sure use some of that."

"And what exactly could you use more of?" asked a voice on the other side of the screened door.

"Reverend! Sharp-eyes! Scout! Prancer and Cleverhands, too?" Davy was beside himself as he dashed to the door to let them in.

"I don't see them," Anna whined. "I thought you said we would be able to!"

Reverend chuckled. "Tell your sister, lad, that first we must prepare the sheriff for our appearance. From what I understand, the poor man was completely overwhelmed by his initial encounter with Racer and Cleverhands."

"That he was!" Cleverhands attested. "Thought he'd bumped his head falling off that bench, but he came through like a trooper." This pun elicited groans from his fellow Old Ones, but it was clear to Cleverhands that Davy hadn't grasped the play on words. "Davy," he explained, "I said 'trooper' as in 'state trooper.' Get it?"

Davy smiled. "Yes, I get it. Good one, Cleverhands!"

Prancer entered the porch with great care, not wishing to repeat cracking his head on the door post as he had done on a previous visit. He said, "Davy, if you would be so kind as to announce our arrival, we can get down to the business at hand."

"C'mon, Anna," said Davy taking her hand. "You'll see everyone in a minute. We have to let Sheriff Peabody know we have company."

***

Abby was scheduled to get off work at five that evening, and she was more than ready. All afternoon she had fielded questions from tourists who witnessed the dramatic rescue of Anna, and the oversized squirrel, earlier in the day. Some even begged to have their photo taken with her, which Abby found awkward. She didn't want her picture out there for everyone and anyone to see, but she also didn't want to offend her custom-ers, many of whom had waited in line with purchases they neither needed nor wanted just for the opportunity to speak to her. Abby strived to be agreeable and as truthful as possible, but jealously guarded Anna's identity. She had witnessed Jim's reaction to the sea of people gathered like hungry vultures around a fresh carcass, and knew he wished for anonymity. And when it came to the persistent inquiries into the nature of Racer, who and what he was, her pat answer was "I'm not sure." *After all, that's not lying. I really don't know anything about him, except that I saw him and heard him speak.*

Promptly at five o'clock, a cheerful Debbie appeared to relieve the grateful Abby. "Thanks so much for being on time," Abby told her. "I'm absolutely worn out."

"I'll bet you are," Debbie said. "I sure don't envy all the attention you got today, but it did boost sales. Mr. Jones will be happy about that."

"I suppose he will," Abby agreed. "But if I've learned one thing today, I know I never want to be a celebrity. How do those stars even handle all the attention they get?"

"I guess it's because they like to be center stage," Debbie said, and added with a grin, "so if someone decides to make a movie about giant squirrels that rescue little girls and walk on water, I guess you won't be looking for a cameo?"

Abby had to laugh at this. "Exactly!" she concurred. "No limelight for me! If you're all set here, I'll head to the office to fetch my purse. I can't get out of here soon enough."

With that said, Abby made a beeline for the office in back of the store. Brad, a fellow employee who was on break, was watching the news and sipping on a glass of tea. "Hey, Abby," he said as she entered. "You had quite the day, I heard."

"You can say that again," she said as she walked over to her locker and began fiddling with the combination. "I don't know when I've ever been so tired after a day's work. It will be so nice to go home." Abby's jaw dropped when the reporter's words sank in. She whirled around just in time to see a photo of Mike, Anna, Racer, and herself, plastered as big as life on the television screen.

Brad leaped to his feet. "It's you! It's you!" he cried out excitedly. "Look, Abby, you've made headline news!"

Abby, feeling more anxious and dismayed with every passing second, watched and listened as the story unfolded. This was sure to garner her the very attention she so dreaded. *And Mike? What about Mike? Anyone at his church will know immediately who he is. What if one of them calls the station? What if the same happens to Anna? And dear God in heaven, what will happen to Racer?*

The instant the report concluded, Abby snatched her purse out of her locker and dashed for the door without so much as a good-bye wave to Brad. "Hey! Where are you going in such a hurry?" Brad called after her. "Didn't you like the story?"

"No!" Abby shouted over her shoulder. She dodged and weaved her way through the aisles and the shoppers, in a frenzy to reach the front entrance, her gateway to freedom from all the craziness of the day.

"Abby! Wait! Don't go that way!" Debbie was calling to her frantically, but Abby was too keen on exiting the store to heed her. The moment she popped out into the bright sunshine of a summer's evening, Abby wished with all her heart and soul she had listened to Debbie.

***

When Davy and Anna reached the entryway to the kitchen, Davy cleared his throat loudly so as to get the adults' attention. When he had it, he said, "Excuse me. I'm sorry for interrupting, but they're here."

Jim saw a hint of apprehension in Eric's eyes. He knew the man was most likely not keen on seeing any more Old Ones after the shock of meeting Racer and Cleverhands for the first time. "Okay, Davy, can you tell us exactly which of the Old Ones will shortly make themselves visible? I thing we owe Sheriff Peabody a fair warning."

"Yes, I know," Davy said. "That's what the Old Ones said, too. That's why you can't see them yet. It's quite the, what was that word you used, Racer? Oh, entourage! It's quite the entourage."

"Entourage?" Eric asked nervously.

"Yes, sir," Davy answered. "We have Racer and Cleverhands—you've met them. Then there's Reverend the owl, Prancer the buck, and Sharp-eyes and Scout, the hawks. Are you ready to meet them, Sheriff?"

Eric took a deep breath and managed a faint smile in Davy's direction. "Ready as I'll ever be, I suppose," he declared. "Let's do this!"

CHAPTER 9

WHERE'S THE PROOF?

When the Old Ones materialized in the Hunters' kitchen, Eric was unable to contain his awe and wonder. He sat there, stock still, mouth agape, as he watched the loving reunion taking place between Jim's family and these creatures, indescribable in their size and elegance. Even when Racer and Cleverhands approached him, wearing the merriest of smiles, he found himself momentarily at a loss for words.

"So glad to see you again, Sheriff!" Cleverhands exclaimed, extending his paw for a friendly handshake. In somewhat of a daze, Eric slowly stretched out his hand toward the raccoon. Cleverhands grasped it so quickly and firmly, it took Eric by surprise.

"Likewise, I'm sure," said Racer as he, too, reached out his paw which Eric took in turn. "See? That was easier than you thought!" Still tongue-tied, Eric just nodded his head in agreement. "Now please allow yours truly to introduce you to the rest of our company."

Once the introductions were genially concluded, everyone except Prancer, who was simply too large to fit, took a seat around the kitchen table. Reverend was the first to address the gathering. "We are so gratified to be with you all again and grateful that the sheriff just happens to be here this evening, for we believe what we have to share tonight will be of as much interest to him as it will to you, Jim. But that brings me to another point." Here the owl stopped and fixed his amber eyes directly upon Eric. "Sheriff Peabody, my intuition tells me you are here on the same business we are, am I correct?"

Eric hesitated before speaking, coughing and clearing his throat, never imagining in all his born days that he would be conversing with an owl, albeit an exceptional one. "If that business involves this property and its rightful ownership," he said, "then yes, we are here for the identical reason."

"Excellent!" Reverend declared. "Then if I may be so bold to suggest you take notes with regard to our undercover espionage of late, dear Sheriff, we can begin. Scout, since you and Mrs. Scout were the first to spot suspicious activity on the part of Ronnie and a certain Cy Smith, would you do the honors of being the first to speak?"

Scout fired away without hesitation and as the facts spilled out, Sharpeyes and Reverend chimed in whenever one or the other thought something needed clarification, or if they had their own tidbit of information to divulge. Eric, attentive to it all, was particularly interested in the license tag number and the mysterious check book printed in someone else's name. "Can you give me those numbers from the tag again? Okay, got it. And do you have any idea what kind of car this man was driving?"

"Sadly, no," said Scout. "I mean, we Old Ones are keen on a lot of things, but cars humans drive are not high on our priority list."

"Okay, then," Eric continued, "what was the name on the checks again?" At this question, Cleverhands stepped forward and handed the sheriff a slip of paper.

It's all there," he said proudly, "name, address, bank, everything!"

Eric studied the paper and copied down the information before passing it on to Jim to see. "There are a few odd things here," Eric remarked. "There's no phone number, and the only address is a post office box. Additionally, the bank is in Murphy. That's a long hike from here."

"Maybe," Jim suggested, "distance is exactly what Ronnie wanted with this account. Think it could be a way he's hiding funds he doesn't want others to find out about?"

"Jim, you just might have hit the nail on the head," Eric said, smiling for the first time since the entire interview started. "Reverend, were you able to read to whom the check was made out?"

"Bill Cunningham," Sharp-eyes blurted. "He's Ronnie's foreman. The one he told to recruit workers and make them carry pistols at the work site."

"Pistols?" Kate asked fearfully. "Whatever for?"

Reverend turned his soulful eyes toward her. "My dear Kate, mother of the Chosen One, Ronnie has figured out we can be killed and he has every intention of doing so if we try again to thwart his project."

Kate gasped in shock. "How can this possibly be? How does he know you even exist?"

"Stories," said Reverend. "Ronnie grew up hearing the same stories from Will as Jim did. We figure when he couldn't logically explain what took place at the work site, he had to fall back upon what, to his mind, was the illogical. And now that he's actually seen us in the flesh as of today," the owl continued, focusing his gaze directly on Racer, "not a smidgen of doubt remains in his mind."

"What do you mean by that?" Racer asked apprehensively. "Was Ronnie in that crowd when I came to shore?"

"No," Reverend said evenly, "but Bill Cunningham was. He snapped your photo and showed it to Ronnie. That's when we overheard Ronnie say he knew who you were, and that your days were numbered."

"Sounds like a threat to me," Davy observed. "You want to write that fact down, too, Sheriff?"

Eric looked sympathetically at Davy as he slowly laid his pen on the table. He then turned to Jim and asked softly, "You think it's time to let them know what I know?"

Jim sighed heavily. "I suppose we shouldn't postpone the inevitable, especially since we have such a gathering of Old Ones here," he said. "They deserve to hear the truth."

"The truth?" Prancer interjected. "What do you mean, Jim?"

"The truth about the predicament your mountain is in right now," Jim replied resignedly. "Go ahead, Sheriff."

Eric, noting that all eyes were expectantly glued on him, wished with all his heart he didn't have to relay the discouraging news to them, but he knew he had no other choice. "I went down to the courthouse this afternoon," Eric told them, "and found what I never hoped to see. There is a deed, signed by both Ronnie Carson and Will Hunter, giving the land in question to Ronnie. In checking the date with Jim, the deed was signed two weeks before Mr. Hunter passed away and a month and a half after he had updated his will. That means for all intents and purposes, the deed is valid."

The silence which ensued hung like an impenetrable fog in the air. Davy felt as helpless and hopeless as he had in The Glade when he was knocked flat by an invisible force, one he now knew was evil. He couldn't breathe. He couldn't move. Sheriff Peabody's words spun around in his head like a manic dog chasing its tail. *The deed is valid. The deed is valid. The deed is valid.*

Suddenly, the air was rent by a deafening cacophony of shouts and protests and questions from all the Old Ones all at once. "Impossible!" "Will would never!" "How can this be?" "There must be a way around this!" "It has to be a mistake!" Frustrated by the din, Reverend rose up into the air and signaled with his wings for quiet. The Old Ones, still clearly upset and beside themselves, reluctantly complied.

Once peace had been restored, Reverend said, "Now then, we all have questions, and we are all confused by this most unexpected and upsetting news, but we need to speak in turn. If no one objects, I would like to pose the first question to the good Sheriff." The Old Ones nodded their assent, and the owl, turning toward Eric, said brusquely, "Sir, I would like to know why you allowed us to ramble on about our reconnaissance efforts when you already knew about the contents of the deed?"

Eric looked so crestfallen upon hearing these words that Reverend immediately regretted asking the question. Eric willed himself to meet the owl's gaze and said, "I hoped that something you discovered would give me the one piece of evidence I need to call the deed into question. Certainly Ronnie's movements have been suspicious, and I appreciate all the information you have shared with me, but the most important element missing in all of this is proof."

"Proof?" The Old Ones chorused. At that very moment, the phone emitted its raucous alarm. Kate ran to answer it.

"Hi, Susie! What? No, really? Oh, they won't believe it! We have quite the crowd here now; Sheriff Peabody and some of the Old Ones, believe it or not. He is? You don't mind the gang of us coming? Okay, okay, we'll be right down!" She hung up and turned toward the expectant faces gathered around the table. "Well Racer, Anna," she said with grin, "seems you two were on the evening news tonight. Bampa recorded it and Susie has invited all of us to come over to view it. And aren't they expecting you for dinner, Sheriff?"

"Yes, they are, at six thirty," Eric answered.

"Dinner!" Racer exclaimed, the thought of food temporarily lifting his dampened spirits. "Are we invited too?"

"Everyone is invited," Kate assured him. "Although I doubt if Susie will have prepared enough to feed us all."

"That's not a problem," Reverend assured her. "Scout, Sharp-eyes, will the two of you be so kind as to speed to The Glade and gather up some tasty victuals to add to Susie's dinner tonight?"

"Certainly," said Scout.

"We'll meet you there," Sharp-eyes said. "Will you please open the door for us, Davy?" Still reeling from the shocking news, Davy forced himself out of his seat and wordlessly led the two hawks to the kitchen door. Just as they were exiting, Sharp-eyes turned to the boy and whispered, "Don't you worry, lad. We'll straighten this situation out one way or the other. I promise."

They vanished in a twinkling, and Davy found himself wondering bleakly if this would be the only promise the Old Ones couldn't keep.

***

As everyone prepared to depart for the Fairchilds', Reverend approached Eric, who was still seated, and laid a gentle wing on his shoulder. "I'm sorry I was so blunt with you just now," he said apologetically. "I know you are doing everything you possibly can to be of help to Jim, and to us. If I may accompany you as we walk to the Fairchilds' home, I just may have the proof you need to resolve this case." Eric smiled weakly and Reverend noted a deep sorrow in his eyes, which he sensed had little to do with the current tribulations. "If I may," the owl whispered in his ear, "could I place my wing over your heart?" The request bewildered Eric, but he knew this most ancient and honorable of creatures had only the best interests of others in mind. Eric nodded his approval.

It only took seconds for Reverend to detect from his heart, so pure and good and strong, the source of Eric's grief. And he knew, beyond a shadow of a doubt, that he could offer words of comfort and peace. Reverend bowed his head, praying silently. When he finished, he regarded Eric kindly and compassionately. "This is your time of mourning, my friend," Reverend said, "and in your loss, I grieve with you. But take heart! Have hope! One day soon, Elly will give you a son."

***

When the curious crowd arrived at the Fairchilds', Jim held the door open for all to enter, and noticed for the first time that Eric and Reverend were lagging behind at a significant distance. It was clear to him that the two were deep in conversation, most likely about the unfortunate matters at hand, and he wondered if the words they were exchanging would shed new light on a way to prove Ronnie's dealings were underhanded. *I've got to get down to the courthouse first thing in the morning, and get copies of the documents. Maybe if Bob and I have a close look at them together, we can figure a way out of this mess we're in. There must be a way!*

Out of the blue, Scout and Sharp-eyes appeared on the porch. Each carried a sack containing something delicious; Jim could tell from the appealing aroma arising from them. He couldn't help but chuckle. "Now you Old Ones aren't going to spoil Susie's always excellent food by sharing your incomparable fare, are you?"

"Perish the thought!" Scout exclaimed. "Indeed, after we all partake of a bite or two from the food we brought, it will actually make Susie's taste better than ever."

"That's good to know," Jim said, relieved. "Go on in and join the throng. I'll wait here for Reverend and the sheriff."

The hawks gladly obliged, and the house, already fragrant with the dinner Susie was keeping warm, at once became an olfactory wonder. "Oh, what a sweet surprise!" Susie said enthusiastically as the hawks placed their sacks on her kitchen counter. "Now there will be plenty to go around and, I must admit, I've missed the food of The Glade terribly ever since we feasted with you. Thank you both so much!"

"The pleasure is all ours," said Sharp-eyes, bowing graciously in Susie's direction.

"It's all queued up and ready to roll!" Bob announced. "Let's go!" Everyone scrambled for a spot on the living room floor to see the news report just as Eric and Reverend entered. Jim was pleased to see a smile on Eric's face and a twinkle in the owl's eyes.

"Good news?" Jim asked expectantly.

"It's hopeful, Jim," Eric answered.

"And where there is hope," said Reverend, "all things are possible. Let's watch the news, shall we?"

***

"Welcome to Channel Ten's *News at Six*. I'm Bonita Varney."

"And I'm Robert Spann."

"As we reported to you in the five o'clock hour, the Nantahala Outdoor Center was the scene of a highly unusual, and what some viewers are calling miraculous, rescue of an unidentified girl by a larger-than-life squirrel when she tumbled out of the raft she was riding in. Channel Ten was flooded by a host of photos similar to the one you see on your screen. Oddly enough, less than two weeks ago, rumors about a huge squirrel barreling down the aisle at Nantahala United Methodist Church and knocking down the pastor spread throughout our area. Now the sighting of this animal again today is raising both questions and eyebrows. Is this the same creature who terrorized a church? Are there others like it, living in the mountains? Is it really a squirrel, or some other previously unidentified beast?" asked Bonita.

Robert added, "To find some answers to that question, we join reporter Chad Newton, live at the Nantahala Outdoor Center. Chad?"

"Robert, Bonita, I'm here at the entrance to the Nantahala Outdoor Center where Abby McGuire, the woman whom several sources identified in the photo, is employed. We are told she is due to leave work any moment now, and we're hoping she can shed some light on today's most mysterious event. As soon as she emerges...wait! Here she is now! Miss McGuire, Miss McGuire! Chad Newton, Channel Ten news reporter. Our viewers have many questions about what happened today when the little girl fell into the river, and we're hoping you have the answers. First of all, do you know the girl's name? Does she live in this area?" Chad asked.

Abby, obviously flustered, replied, "No! I don't know her name, and I don't know where she lives."

Chad asked, "What about the squirrel? Or, as many are asking, is it a squirrel at all?"

"I believe it's a squirrel," she answered.

"Do you think it's the same one reported to have wreaked havoc at Nantahala United Methodist Church, two Sundays ago?"

"I can't say for sure because I wasn't there." Abby was growing more anxious by the second.

"So this is the first time you saw anything like this?" Chad pressed Abby for information, ignoring her obvious discomfort.

"Yes, sir."

"Did it appear to you as though this squirrel was actually trying to help the girl to shore and safety?" Chad continued his barrage of questions.

Slightly defensive, Abby replied, "That was how it looked."

"The man standing with you, we're told, is Pastor Mike Russell, the minister of the church where the squirrel made its appearance. Can you verify that for us? Was he the one the squirrel toppled?"

"Yes and no," she said.

"And just how did the both of you happen to be at the exact location where the squirrel seemingly decided to direct the girl?" Chad shoved his microphone even closer to Abby's face.

"Stop! No more questions!" Abby cried, pushing the microphone away. She darted around the reporter and ran as fast as she could to her car..

Chad called after her. "Miss McGuire! Can you come back? Just for a moment?" Abby didn't even acknowledge his request. "Well, folks, it looks like our star witness suddenly got camera shy. Let's hope someone can get in touch with Pastor Russell, or tip us off as to who the lucky little girl who experienced such a fantastic rescue is. Back to you, Bonita, Robert."

"Or better yet, someone get a hold of that squirrel. Maybe it could make a television appearance right here in our studios," Bonita laughed.

Robert agreed. "That would make for some awesome headline news! Now on to other stories we're following..."

***

When the news segment ended, no one in the Fairchilds' living room uttered a word. All were pondering in their minds what effect Racer's sudden and unexpected notoriety might have on the future of The Glade. It was Reverend who broke the silence, and the words he spoke shocked everyone. Everyone, that is, except Eric. "My dear Racer," he declared, "I never realized you were so photogenic. It makes me wonder if each and every one of us will look that handsome on camera when the time comes."

"What???" Davy and the Old Ones cried simultaneously.

"You mean to tell me, Reverend," said an incredulous Racer, "that I should accept Miss Bonita's invitation to appear on television? Surely you jest!"

"It sounds to me," Prancer stated, "like Reverend was not just referring to you, Racer, but to all of us. Am I correct?"

"As usual," Reverend said with a deep throated chuckle. "There is still a chance, outside perhaps, but still a chance, we will not have to pull off that stunt to pull the rug out from under Ronnie."

"I'm hoping not," said Scout flatly. "If I had to be in front of a camera, I'd be as anxious as that poor girl, Abby, was."

"She was so nervous," Kate agreed. "I felt truly sorry for her. Poor thing! All those questions thrown at her when she was not expecting them! I wouldn't like that either."

"Mom?" Anna wanted to know. "Abby knows my name. Pastor Mike told her. Why didn't she say who I was?"

Kate gave her daughter an affectionate smile. "Abby was trying to protect you, Anna. For one thing, you're underage, and she would have to have Jim's or my permission before mentioning your name publically."

"On top of that," said Jim, "Abby knew that you, we, all of us, don't need one more inch of publicity right now. How would you like to wake up tomorrow morning and have a pack of television trucks surrounding our house, Anna?"

Anna wrinkled her nose in distaste. "I wouldn't like that at all; neither would Mary and Smokey."

"But Jim," Davy interjected, "what if someone not as responsible as Abby calls that television station and gives away Anna's name? What then?"

"We'll deal with that if and when it happens, son," Jim answered. "Right now, I say it's high time we enjoy our meal and leave our troubles until tomorrow."

"Here! Here!" shouted the Old Ones.

Reverend added with gusto, "Let the feast begin!" And so, it did.

Chapter 10

A Promising Morning

Mike awoke with a start. Only the faintest gleam of light seeped through the curtained windows of his bedroom. He rolled wearily out of bed, not at all feeling up to facing the day ahead. The previous evening had been a nightmare. After the news segment in which he was featured aired, Mike's telephone began ringing off the hook. He valiantly tried to field each call and give the person on the other end of the line the time of day, but no sooner would he replace the receiver when another ring would sound. Being a pastor inevitably made him available to his congregation no matter what the hour of day or night, something Mike had not minded until now. But these endless inquiries about the reappearance of the mad squirrel had pushed his patience to the limit.

The most frustrating factor during Mike's frenzied evening had been that he couldn't get in touch with Abby. Every time there was a brief lull between calls, Mike had dialed her number, but all he succeeded in getting was a busy signal. He had wondered if she'd taken the family phone off the hook. *I know that's what I wish I could have done with mine. I don't blame Abby one bit. I just wish that reporter hadn't ambushed her like he did. It made her so upset. Maybe I can try to reach her this morning.*

Mike checked his watch. It was six-thirty, much too early to call anyone. He decided instead to clean up, grab some coffee, and head out to the McGuires in person. His morning run could wait.

***

Jim slipped out of bed as noiselessly as he could so as not to wake Kate. Between his worries about the property and the alarming presence of the news truck, cameras, and reporters that had met them when they had returned from the Fairchilds' last evening, Jim had tossed and turned all night. This morning as he fixed his coffee, he recalled how fortuitous it had been having Sheriff Peabody with them. Eric had directed the family to not say a word to the reporters as they headed for the safety and privacy of their home. Jim wished he could have overheard exactly what Eric had said to the news crew, but it must have been mighty convincing. Within five minutes, the entire team had vacated the property, much to the relief of the Hunters and Murrays. But the incident had caused Jim and Kate understandable concern. Someone had to have tipped off the television station as to Anna's identity. Why else would they have been there?

Now as Jim shaved and brushed his teeth, preparing to leave momentarily for the courthouse, he couldn't help but wonder who could possibly be so thoughtless, heartless even, to reveal a child's name to the media. Only one person came to mind. *Ronnie. It has to be. I don't know anyone lower or meaner than he is. If I find out that he's the one who did this...* Jim scowled at the mirror, hastily hung up his towel, grabbed his keys, and hurried out the door to his truck.

The sound of the engine woke Kate from a deep sleep. It took her a moment or two to realize that this was the morning when all their lives could be changed forever. Hastily, she threw back the covers, slid off the high bed, and padded on bare feet to the bathroom. Once there, she closed the door as quietly as she could and dug behind the stack of fresh towels for the pregnancy test. Kate's hands trembled as she tried to open it, and a wave of unwelcome nausea came over her just as it had the morning before. Fighting against that feeling as best she could, Kate finally opened the package and raced for the toilet. *Dear Lord, let it be positive, let it be positive, let it be positive...*

***

As he brewed his coffee that morning, Eric thought it ironic that he had fallen asleep in his easy chair last night. *Here Elly sends me home so I can get a good night's sleep in bed, and what do I do? Crash in a chair, just like I did*

100

the night before. The first thing Eric had done when he'd arrived home from the Fairchilds' was call Elly. She was eager to hear how his dinner went, and wanted to know if he had caught the news about the gargantuan squirrel at the Nantahala. Eric had told her the dinner was exceptional and that, yes, he had seen the remarkable story on television. He had so longed to tell Elly about Reverend's promise of a child and all the details of what he knew about Racer and the Old Ones he had met, but he'd known he must keep the information to himself just a little while longer. *Maybe we'll have a breakthrough in this case sooner rather than later. I'd sure like to have proof without having to involve the Old Ones, but Reverend may be right. It might have to come to that.*

***

Davy's eyes fluttered open. He lay unmoving on his cot, listening to the chirping birds in the oak trees and across the meadow, and to Maggie's whiffling snore as she snoozed on her bed with Frisky curled up beside her. It was so peaceful and calm, Davy wondered for a moment if he shouldn't try to go back to sleep. It was then he remembered this was the day his grandparents were arriving, to stay for two glorious weeks. He felt the same excitement as he had the morning of the day he and Anna had planned to go exploring. Up Davy jumped, and with a big smile lighting up his face, trotted merrily to the bathroom. To his dismay, it was closed and locked—just as it had been the previous morning, when his mom was so ill. He wondered if she had gotten sick all over again. Timidly, he knocked on the door and said softly, "Mom? Are you in there?" Are you okay?"

"I'm fine, honey," she said, though the unmistakable sounds of retching indicated otherwise. "I'll be out in a minute. Can you hang on, Davy?"

"Yes, Mom, but are you sure you're all right? You don't sound all right." Davy heard his mother vomit again, followed by the swooshing noise of the toilet flushing. When she appeared in the doorway, she was as pale and drawn as she had looked yesterday, but her eyes were glowing.

"It's all yours, sweetie," she said, patting him fondly on the head as she stepped into the hall. Davy gave her a strange look and, shrugging his shoulders, took his turn in the bathroom. "Oh, Jim," Kate whispered as she headed for the kitchen, "how I wish you were here right now! I so desperately want to tell you! How will I make it through the day?"

***

When Susie entered her kitchen that morning, she couldn't wipe the smile off her face. Having entertained the Old Ones last evening so soon after they had dined with them at The Glade had been the highlight of her day. Not only was the food amazing, but the Old Ones had also insisted upon cleaning Susie's kitchen after the feast. It was absolutely spotless and the sun, streaming through the large windows, danced so brightly on the countertops and stainless steel sink that Susie had to squint when she looked at them. To top it all off, there was a lingering fragrance of honeysuckle in the room that Susie found both cheerful and soothing. With the other rooms in the house already freshened for their impending company, Susie was overwhelmed with gratitude for the help offered to her last night. Now she could spend the day as leisurely as she wished. "Maybe I'll even do some painting," Susie said aloud as she turned the coffee maker on. "I haven't done that in ages."

"Who are you talking to?" Bob asked as he strode into the room. "Are there any Old Ones still hanging around?"

Susie giggled. "I wish they were," she said. "No, just talking to myself."

"So you're thinking of heading to the art studio, eh?" Bob said, pulling up a chair at the table.

"I'd like to," Susie confirmed. "After all, everything's clean and set for the Murrays' arrival, and we've been so busy with Jim, Kate, and the kids, I just thought a bit of painting would do me some good."

Bob sniffed the air, a curious look on his face. "Susie, do you smell honeysuckle?"

"I do," she confirmed. "Isn't it lovely? I'm sure it was left as a parting gift from the Old Ones."

"No doubt," said Bob with a grin. "I can't get over the crowd we managed to cram in here last night. And I'm even more amazed by how the Old Ones, even in the face of what could be serious trouble, were able to show such positive attitudes."

"A good lesson for us all," Susie said as she poured their coffee. She brought Bob's cup to him. "I do hope Jim can discover something in those documents that will reveal evidence against Ronnie."

"I promised to help him with it," Bob said. "Who knows? Something might jump out at me that Jim doesn't catch, especially when it comes to dates."

"Dates?" Susie asked, giving her husband a quizzical look. "What would be so important about those?"

Bob gave Susie a sly grin. "You know how I've always teased you about writing everything down on your calendar? Well, I shouldn't have, because that might just prove to be the chink in the otherwise seamless armor."

***

David and Sarah enjoyed a leisurely, complimentary breakfast at the Comfort Inn. They were both feeling refreshed after a good night's sleep, and David was eager to hit the road. "But honey, we can't leave too early," Sarah protested. "I told Kate we wouldn't be there until afternoon. Why don't we explore Blue Ridge this morning, have a good lunch, and then head up to the Nantahalas? What do you say?"

David smiled at her. "What do I say? Don't argue with the smartest woman you know."

Sarah laughed merrily. "I'm glad you realized that," she said. "I know how anxious you are to get there, David, but we never picked up a house-warming gift for Kate and Jim, let alone something for Davy and Anna. Maybe we can find something unique at a shop in town."

"Something expensive, more than likely," David said good-naturedly, "but we'll take a stab at it. Let's go back to the room to get our things, and we'll be out of here in no time."

"Good!" Sarah exclaimed, rising from her chair. "And David, one more thing: If we don't find any gifts we like, there is a Walmart right up the street."

"Really? How do you know that?"

"I asked the desk clerk this morning," she answered. "Did you forget you're not the only one in this marriage who loves to save money?"

It was David's turn to laugh. "No," he confessed, "I hadn't forgotten. And if it won't disappoint you too much, I say we just do our gift shopping there. That gives me more leeway to splurge on that lunch you mentioned."

"It's a deal," Sarah said.

***

When Reverend and Sharp-eyes arrived that morning at the Carson home to relieve Mrs. Reverend and Mrs. Sharp-eyes from their duties, they were dismayed to find that every door on the ground level was locked. What was even more disconcerting, as they peered through the glass panes of each door, was not finding the ladies anywhere. "Sharp-eyes, why don't you stand guard at the front entrance where the garage doors are, in case somebody in the family comes out that way?" Reverend suggested. "I'll try the upper deck. It seems to me there would be little need of bolting those doors." The owl and the hawk spread their massive wings and were at their respective destinations in a twinkling. As Reverend hobbled toward the first set of French doors, he was immensely gratified to see Mrs. Reverend and Mrs. Sharp-eyes perched on top of an ornate, oversized wardrobe. *If they're in this room, Ronnie must be here, too.* Reverend reached for the door handle with his beak and pushed down hard. To his delight it opened easily, and he slipped soundlessly into what he surmised must be Ronnie's and Betty-Rae's bedroom.

"Reverend!" Mrs. Reverend shouted when she spied him. "I'm so glad you're here!" The owl and hawk swooped gracefully to his side.

"Where is Sharp-eyes?" Mrs. Sharp-eyes inquired worriedly. "Is he back at The Glade?"

"No," Reverend answered. "He's guarding the front door in case Ronnie comes out that way, as I had to come up to the second level and hope I could gain entry. It is fortunate that I did, but where is Ronnie now?"

"In the bathroom," said Mrs. Reverend, nodding her head in the direction of a closed door. Reverend caught the faint sound of running water, and guessed Ronnie was in the shower. "And oh, my dear," Mrs. Reverend continued in a voice both sad and subdued, "last evening that man stooped to a level of low we could never have imagined possible."

104

"What?" Reverend was aghast. "What heinous act has Ronnie committed now?"

"There was a news report on television last night," Mrs. Reverend began.

"You mean the one revealing Racer?"

"You saw it? How in the world?"

"We were at the Fairchilds'," said Reverend, "but that's a long story for another time. So tell me, please, what did he do?"

Mrs. Reverend and Mrs. Sharp-eyes exchanged mournful glances. The segment had been disturbing enough when they realized Racer had made another public appearance, but when they had realized it was Anna in the photo, they were beside themselves with fear Ronnie would recognize her, too. Mrs. Reverend heaved a sigh and said sadly, "Ronnie called the television station last night. He identified Anna, first and last name; not only that, he also gave them the address of the Hunter farm."

"Did anyone from the station show up?" Mrs. Sharp-eyes asked Reverend. "You were there. Did you see anything?"

Reverend shook his head. "When the family departed the Fairchilds' with Sheriff Peabody, we Old Ones said our farewells and set out for The Glade. We were beginning to feel the strain of being visible to everyone, not just Davy. So unfortunately, my dear ladies, I have nothing to contribute to the story which is, indeed, a dreadful one."

The three Old Ones heard the flow of water stop. "Hurry!" Reverend urged. "Out the door, you two! Tell Sharp-eyes where to meet me and retreat to The Glade for some rest. If Racer is there, tell him to go see Davy and find out what transpired last night." The owl and hawk gratefully heeded Reverend's advice. Sharp-eyes joined him before Ronnie even came out of the bathroom.

"I'd like to say I'm glad we've found a way in," Sharp-eyes observed, "and I'm happy the ladies are on their way to The Glade, but I wish we were headed in that direction, too. I must admit this sleuthing business is becoming tiresome."

"Yes, it is," Reverend agreed. "I grow weary, too, my friend, but we must press on toward the goal. The more information we can gather, the better chance it will, I believe, make all the difference."

***

When Eric strode through the doors to the sheriff's office, he caught Connie totally off guard. "What are you doing here, Sheriff? I thought sure I wouldn't see you until Friday."

"I'm not staying but a minute," Eric assured her as he went to a file drawer to retrieve a copy of the Hunter property's survey map. "I just need you to do a couple of things for me, if you don't mind."

"That's my job," Connie quipped cheerfully. "What do you need?"

Eric handed her the slip of paper with the license number written on it. "Will you run a check on that plate, please? I need to find out to whom it's registered. See if the person has a criminal record. Handing her the information on Calvin C. Holbrook's checking account, he said, "I know this won't be a piece of cake by any means, and my gut tells me you'll probably hit a dead end, but see if you can find anything to verify that this is a real person. Start by looking up birth and or death records in North Carolina. Let me know what you uncover as soon as you can."

"Will do," said Connie. "And Sheriff? If I do manage to find anything out about this Calvin guy, do you want me to run a background check, too?"

"By all means," Eric told her. "Gotta run. They're discharging Elly at eleven this morning."

"That's great news! Give her my love, will you?"

"Sure thing."

***

Just as Eric had done the day before, Jim now stared at the ominous deed in disbelief. What upset him the most was seeing his grandfather's signature on the document. Though his memories told him it was familiar handwriting, Jim felt in his heart that this must be a forgery. *It has to be. Grandpa would never, ever do something like this. He loved the Old Ones too much. He would never betray them like this. I hope I can find something at home with his signature, so I can compare them.* The moment Jim stood up to return to the clerk and request copies of the deed, he felt an unexpected twinge of pain in his back. Whether it was caused by the way he had been sitting at the table or was a symptom of the stress he was experiencing right then, Jim couldn't tell. Stiffly, he approached the clerk's desk, paid the copying fee, and handed the documents over to the same unpleasant-looking individual whom Eric had encountered. Something about the way the clerk regarded him made the hair on Jim's neck stand at attention. He breathed a huge sigh of relief when the copies were handed to him and he was free to go.

Once he was outside the courthouse, Jim checked his cell phone to see if it had a decent signal. He would call home before he left, to give Kate time to do some snooping around for anything sporting Grandpa Will's signature. Thankfully, he got through.

"Hello?"

"Hi, Kate, I'm done here and I'll be heading home as soon as we hang up," he said. "Can you do me a favor? Look in all the drawers of the house for anything that Grandpa Will signed. Have Davy and Anna help you."

"Okay, honey, I will," Kate answered, "but the way Susie and Bob cleaned up here after Grandpa passed, I doubt we'll find anything."

"Try," Jim said firmly and hung up. Kate knew from the abrupt end to their conversation, Jim was deeply worried. She said a prayer and got straight to work.

***

Mike arrived at the McGuires' and walked briskly up the driveway. Just as he reached the top step of the porch, the front door opened, and there stood Bessie McGuire, her blue apron coated in flour, inviting him in. "We've been expecting you, Pastor Mike," she told him. "I'm in the middle of making biscuits to go with our eggs and bacon. Will you join us for breakfast?"

"I'd be delighted," Mike answered as he stepped across the threshold, "but Mrs. McGuire, I don't understand why you expected me to be here."

"It's Bessie," she corrected him. "Did you, by any chance, try to call our house last evening?"

"Why, yes. Yes, I did," Mike admitted, "but I could never get through. For my part, I was barraged by phone calls well into the night, and really wished I could have unplugged the thing."

"That's what we had to do," she said. "It was literally ringing off the hook. That's why you couldn't reach Abby, and she couldn't reach you. She was so upset by the first news report, which aired while she was getting ready to leave work, and then to be ambushed by a reporter outside the Nantahala Outdoor Center? It completely overwhelmed her." Mrs. McGuire motioned for Mike to take a seat at the table, returned to her biscuit dough, and continued talking. "Mind you, Abby is not a shy girl, but she's never liked notoriety, and that mess last night really put her out of her comfort zone. She was convinced people in your congregation would be calling you endlessly, after seeing your photo with that oversized squirrel on the news, and she knew you would see how distraught she was during her interview. She thought you'd be as worried about her as she was about you, am I right?"

"Yes, ma'am," Mike answered readily. "I was worried about Abby. I had to see her in person so I'd know if she was doing better today."

"I am," Abby said, smiling warmly at Mike as she strolled into the kitchen. Mike automatically stood up when she entered, having been taught proper etiquette from a young age. This made Abby smile even more, but Mike could tell by her puffy eyes that she had done her fair share of crying last night. Even with swollen eyes and no make-up, however, Mike thought Abby was the most striking woman he had ever laid eyes on. "Do you want some coffee, Mike?" Abby asked as she opened the cupboard where the mugs were stored.

"Good gracious me!" Bessie exclaimed. "Where are my manners? Forgive me, Pastor, for not offering you some. I should have done it first thing."

"Don't worry about that, Mrs. Mc...I mean, Bessie," Mike said kindly. "I had some before I came, and wasn't even thinking about having another cup until Abby mentioned it. Yes, I'll take some coffee, nothing in it, just black."

"That's how I drink mine," Abby said as she poured them each a cup. She placed Mike's in front of him and took her seat at the table. Just then, they heard the slam of a screen door and in walked Abby's father, Hank, arms to the elbows covered in dirt.

"Well, this is a howdy-do," Hank said enthusiastically, "looks like you were right about our visitor this morning, Abby. I'd shake your hand,

Pastor Mike, but I need to clean up first. Been out back in the garden since the crack of dawn. Gotta get to weedin' before the sun gets too hot. I know there's some folk who feel closest to God when they sit in church, or look at a sunset over the mountains, or view the stars on a clear night; but for me, it's workin' the soil, plantin' the seeds, and watchin' 'em grow. Ain't nothin' to compare with that!"

As Hank continued his monologue about gardening, Abby leaned toward Mike and whispered, "Daddy loves to talk."

Mike just grinned at her and took another sip of his coffee. Hank's proclivity for long-windedness reminded Mike of Valerie Green's same penchant. Why he found hers so irritating and Hank's actually entertaining, he couldn't figure out. *Maybe it's because Hank talks for the pleasure of it, but Valerie always asks a bunch of nosy questions, just as she did last night about Abby. She sees one photo and she's already got us married off. Of course I'm sure the whole congregation is already speculating about my relationship with her. Why let them speculate? Why don't I give them something concrete?*

"Excuse me for interrupting, Hank," Mike said boldly, "but might I have a word with you out on the porch?"

"Why certainly, Mike," Hank replied affably, holding out his hand in that direction, "after you."

"I'll be right back," Mike said to Abby, whose face told him she was confused by his actions.

When the two men were settled in wooden rockers and safely out of earshot of the women, Hank said, "So Pastor, what's on your mind that we couldn't discuss in the kitchen?"

Mike opened his mouth to speak, but no words were forthcoming. His palms began to sweat and he could feel his cheeks growing hot. He coughed, cleared his throat, and struggled to pull himself together. *What if I ask and Hank says no? What then? Ask, you fool, this is Abby we're talking about!* Mike took a deep breath and a leap of faith. "It's about Abby," he stammered. "I'd, I'd like to ask her out on a date, sir, but thought I should ask your permission first." *There! I said it!*

Hank was uncharacteristically silent for several moments, which didn't serve to calm Mike's already frayed nerves, and he seemed more interested in studying his own calloused hands than answering Mike's question. After what seemed like an eternity, Hank turned toward the pastor. His face, leathery from decades of labor in the outdoors, showed little expression. But there was, Mike noted, a most genial twinkle in his eyes. "How old are you, Mike?" Hank asked quietly.

Being a question he had expected, Mike answered promptly. "I'm 28, sir," he stated, "and I realize Abby just turned 21. I know that's quite an age gap, and it's one of the reasons why I thought it only right to ask your permission to ask her out."

"And what's the other reason?" Hank asked.

"She's living under your roof, not out on her own yet," Mike answered. "I just felt it was the right thing to do, considering the circumstances."

Hank looked thoughtful for a moment as if he was searching, atypically, for the right words to say. Suddenly, a smile spread across his face like a ray of sunshine. "Mike," he declared, "I like a man who does the right thing by others, and you've certainly done the right thing by me today. After seeing you and Abby interacting the other evening, I figured something like this was coming. But knowing young folks today, I just figured you'd flat out ask her without getting me involved. As for your ages, it makes no difference to me. Why, I'm ten years older than my Bessie; started dating when she was only eighteen and got married when she turned twenty. Why, I'll never forget how she looked walking down that aisle, all smiles and graceful-like, while I'm waiting with the preacher and shaking like a leaf. It was all I could do to..."

"Breakfast!" Bessie shouted. "Come and get it!"

Mike took full advantage of the interruption. "If I ask her," he said quickly, "do you think Abby will say yes?"

Hank smiled reassuringly at Mike. "I don't *think* she'll say yes," he said. "I *know* she will. Now that my hands are clean, Pastor, let's have that handshake."

CHAPTER 11

GRANDPA WILL'S SIGNATURE

"**M**om, what are you doing?" Davy asked. When he'd walked into the kitchen with Maggie, he saw his mother rummaging through the drawer which had originally contained the map of the property.

She whirled around to face him. "Davy, when you straightened this drawer up a while back, did you find anything with Grandpa Will's signature on it?"

Davy thought for a moment. "No," he answered, "but I didn't pull any of the letters out of their envelopes. Maybe you could check those."

"Maybe," Mom said hesitantly, "although I don't know why Grandpa would have written any letters to himself, do you?"

Davy shook his head. "Why do you need to find Grandpa's signature, anyway?" he asked.

"Jim's bringing a copy of the deed home from the courthouse," Mom answered. "Grandpa Will's signature is on it. We have to be able to compare it to the real thing, if we want to prove the document is forged."

Davy felt his heart once again plummeting to his stomach. All morning he had been struggling to not worry about the problems with the property, focusing instead on the excitement of seeing his grandparents that afternoon. Now the dark clouds of the what ifs descended upon him once more, raining fear and foreboding in his soul. *How I wish Racer was here. He'd know how to make me feel better. I know he has to stay at The Glade all day to regain his strength, but I miss him so much.* As if she read his thoughts,

111

Maggie nuzzled Davy's hand and whined. Davy immediately dropped to his knees and put his arms around the dog's silky neck.

"What are we going to do, Maggie?" he whispered. "I'm scared for the Old Ones, aren't you?" In response, the old dog wiggled away so she could bathe Davy's face with generous and slobbery kisses. Despite how he was feeling, the boy couldn't help but laugh. "Cut it out, Maggie, that's enough," he gently chided her. "You want to go outside?" Maggie barked, but instead of heading for the kitchen door, she latched onto Davy's belt and led him into the adjacent room. When she reached the bureau where Grandpa Will's books were tucked away safely in their box, she stopped and whined at Davy again as she stared at the drawer. The boy's eyes grew wide as he looked from the dog to the drawer, and a smile replaced the confused look on his face. "Mom! You can stop looking for that signature," Davy shouted. "We've got it right here!"

***

The ride home was a quiet one for Eric and Elly, as both were lost in their own thoughts. Eric had brought Elly a dazzling bouquet of flowers, which she now cradled in her arms, breathing in the soothing scent they emanated. When she was in the hospital, all Elly could think about was going home; now that she was actually doing so, knowing that days of grieving stretched endlessly before her, she felt nothing but melancholy. She longed to tell Eric how she was feeling, but didn't trust her voice or her control over her tears. Elly knew if she started crying, it would create a distraction for Eric, one he didn't need when driving. She turned from the flowers to look at his face. His expression was serious, stoic even, and it made Elly wonder if his thoughts were running on the same track as hers, or on something else entirely.

When they finally rolled to a stop in their driveway, Eric hopped nimbly out of the car, ran around to open Elly's door for her, and offered his hand to her free one. This time, Elly didn't protest. If she needed any-thing right now, it was to feel the warm, firm grasp of her husband's hand holding hers. Eric helped her out of the car and shut the door. Together, they strolled slowly up the walkway which led to their front porch. Because of the tall hedges surrounding the porch, neither had glimpsed the charming surprises awaiting them there. Now as they turned to climb up the steps, they gasped in disbelief. There, spread before their amazed eyes, was a sea of flowers and potted plants, which had transformed their weathered entryway into veritable meadow of loveliness.

Tears sprang to Elly's eyes. "Oh, Eric!" she exclaimed. "I can't believe it! Who has been so thoughtful and generous?"

"Lots of folks, by the look of it," he said, giving her hand a gentle squeeze. "Let's check to see if there are tags or cards on these gifts telling us who sent them."

"Oh, yes, let's!" Elly said as she bounded up the stairs eagerly, smiling for the first time since Eric presented her with his bouquet that morning. She stopped at the first pot, which was filled with marigolds, one of her favorites. "It's from the Andersons," she told Eric excitedly. "Emma knows how much I love these. I'll look forward to finding a place for them in my flower bed."

Eric watched with delight as Elly moved from one gift to another, here reading a tag, there opening a card to read comforting words from neighbors and friends. It was then he spied a small ice chest to the left of the front door. Curious, he walked over to it and removed the card taped to the top. He opened it and read: "This should tide you over for your next two suppers. More is on the way! Thinking of you both with love, Gary and Janet Marshall." Eric opened the lid and called to Elly, "Beautiful, I don't think you're going to worry about doing any cooking for a while. Come look at this!"

Elly stopped where she was and joined Eric at the ice chest. "Oh, my, how wonderful, she said. "Who sent this?" Eric handed her the card to read. "I should have known," Elly said with a grin. "That Janet probably has the whole church in line to feed us. What a blessing she is!"

"Have you looked at all our gifts yet?" Eric asked.

"Not quite," Elly answered, "and I'm going to have my work cut out for me writing thank you notes to all these dear, sweet people, but it will be a labor of love, that's for sure."

Just then, Eric spotted a modest spray of wildflowers draped over an odd looking tin in the far corner of the porch. He wondered why this inconspicuous gift had not been lumped in with all the others. He pointed it out to Elly. "See that strange container over there? Why don't we check that out next?"

Elly agreed, and they headed straight for this peculiar offering. Although the wildflowers were cut and not placed in water, Eric and Elly were amazed to find they were still fresh and vibrant. Eric handed the bunch to Elly and picked up the tin. The decorations adorning it were like nothing either one of them had seen before. There were swirling vines and leafy branches filled with birds which appeared so real, the two expected to hear them sing at any moment. And the longer Eric and Elly stared at the container, it seemed to them that the colors changed and shifted, now iridescent, now primary-color bright. It reminded Eric of the kaleidoscope his grandmother had given him when he was a child. "Eric," Elly said softly, "it's so, so...oh, there aren't words to describe it. Should we, dare we, open it?"

Eric didn't say a word. Gently, he pried back the wondrous lid. The moment he did, the air was filled with a fragrance like nothing he had ever smelled before. Both Elly and he were transfixed by the enchanting aroma, so much so that it took Eric a few moments before he realized there was a small note folded neatly on top of what appeared to be some sort of delectable tea mixture. Carefully, he removed the slip of paper, opened it, and these were the words that greeted him:

A tea to comfort, cleanse and heal;
Brew one cup at morning's meal.
Love and blessings,
The Old Ones

Eric, beside himself, stared at the note for so long that Elly's impatience got the better of her. She sidled next to him and craned her neck to read what her husband couldn't stop looking at. "The Old Ones?" she inquired, completely baffled. "Who are they, Eric?"

In that instant, Eric realized he no longer had to keep his knowledge of the Old Ones clandestine. They had revealed themselves to Elly through this gift. He was free, he knew, to tell her all about them, investigation or no investigation. The thought of being able to share his experiences with these marvelous creatures with the one person in life he loved the most worked like a tonic on Eric's heart. He felt his spirits lifting, as one does when a sliver of sunshine breaks through stormy clouds. "The Old Ones?" Eric told Elly with a chuckle. "They are my newest friends. Let's go inside, and I'll tell you all about them."

***

Jim burst through the kitchen door. "Did you find it, Kate?" he bellowed breathlessly. Kate emerged promptly from the bathroom, where she had been doing some last minute cleaning before company arrived.

"No, honey, I didn't," she announced as she ran over to Jim and threw her arms around his neck, "but Davy did!"

Jim hugged her back and brushed his lips against her forehead. "Where did he find it?"

"Here, Jim, it's here," Davy said happily, as he rushed into the room carrying one of Grandpa Will's books in his arms. "Grandpa signed his name after every story!"

"He did, did he?" Jim's face brightened considerably at this news. "Can you show me, Davy? I have to meet with your Bampa in a few minutes so we can look at this deed together. Oh, and Kate, Susie's fixing lunch for us, so no worries there. I'm not sure how long this will take."

"Just remember that David and Sarah will be arriving this afternoon, honey," Kate said. "I can't wait for you to meet them."

"And I want to meet them too, but first things first," Jim said with a smile. He couldn't help but notice a fresh radiance in Kate's face. It made her look prettier than ever.

"Here's the signature, Jim," said Davy as he held the book open for his stepfather to see.

Jim's face turned as white as the blank pages confronting him. Agitatedly, he snatched the book from Davy's hands and thumbed wildly through it. "Jim, whatever is the matter?" Kate asked in alarm.

"It's empty! Empty!" Jim shouted. "I don't see one blessed word, let alone a signature!"

"But it's there, I promise!" Davy protested, tears of frustration filling his eyes. "Mom, you look at it. See if you see anything."

She removed the book gently from Jim's hands and opened it cautiously. *Believe, Kate, believe!* Words danced in front of her eyes, faint and fragile, as if printed from a cartridge in desperate need of ink; but they were there. Kate beamed. "I see them, Davy," she said triumphantly, "but not clearly, not like you can. Jim, there *are* words here."

A light went on in Jim's head. "It's because you have Davy's gift, Kate," he said, "that's why you can see something. But what about Bob? He read a story from this very book just the other day. He must have seen words. How could that be?"

"I know!" Davy exclaimed excitedly. "It's because Racer and Mrs. Racer were here. That has to be the answer."

"It makes sense, son," Jim said thoughtfully. "There seems to be no end to the powers the Old Ones possess. I wish one of them was here right now to help us."

"They can't be," Davy told him. "They're resting at The Glade after last night and I'm not sure how long that will take, but since I can see Grandpa's handwriting, why don't I go with you to Bampa's? Maybe I can tell if the signatures look alike."

"That's a good idea, Davy," Jim said, "although if you had other plans, I could let you look at the deed right now."

"No, I want to come with you," Davy insisted. "I need to do something to take my mind off Grandpa and Grandma coming here today, or I'll get too excited."

"Then it's settled," said Jim as he took the book from Kate and handed it to the boy. "I'll let you be in charge of this. After all, it does belong to you."

***

"Anna!" Kate called to her daughter, who was curled up with a book in the living room. "I'm taking out clothes to hang on the line. Why don't you come with me and bring Frisky and Maggie? Some fresh air will do us all some good."

"Coming, Mom," Anna answered, lifting Frisky from her lap where he was dozing peacefully and tucking him under her arm. "Let's go, Maggie." The old dog lifted her head when she heard her name and struggled to her feet. She followed Anna and Frisky to the kitchen and out into the sunshine. Maggie couldn't believe how attached she had become to the little kitten, and she thoroughly enjoyed watching him play outdoors where he leaped at butterflies and pounced on grasshoppers. It reminded her of her own puppy days, when she was literally bursting with energy and could chase balls or sticks for hours without flagging. *Those were the days. Poor Will! I'd wear him out with all my antics, but he never stopped playing with me. I love you, Will, and I miss you so much. I'll see you one day, though. One day.* Maggie flopped wearily on a particularly springy patch of grass near the clothesline and rested her head on her paws, observing Frisky and Anna frolicking with amusement.

"Pssst! Maggie!" The dog whipped her head around to see Racer and Mrs. Racer standing next to her. "Where's Davy, girl?" Racer asked. "Is he inside? We need to see him."

"He went with Jim to the Fairchilds' house," Maggie answered. "Davy's helping them read Will's signature from his book."

"Aha," said Mrs. Racer, "because we're not there to facilitate Bob's or Jim's ability to see the words."

"Then we've timed it just right, sweets," Racer declared. Giving the dog a comforting scratch behind her ears, he added, "Maggie, we'll stop by and visit with you when we're finished with the business at hand, okay?"

"Why can't I just come with you?" Maggie asked.

"Wouldn't you worry Kate if you just wandered off?" Mrs. Racer inquired.

"Oh, I hadn't thought of that," she whined. "Just tell Davy to hurry and get back here as soon as he can. I miss him."

"We know you do," Racer said giving her neck a hug. "He'll be back before you know it."

"What's Maggie whining about, I wonder?" Kate mused.

"Old Ones!" Racer and Mrs. Racer shouted gaily as they bounded off in the direction of the Fairchilds' home.

Old Ones? Did I just hear those words, or is it my imagination? Kate looked down at Maggie. "I sure wish you could talk to me like you can to Davy," she said with a sigh. "As smart as you are, I'm sure you have lots to tell." Maggie gazed up lovingly at Kate's face, her plume of a tail waving in the grass. Kate couldn't resist bending down to stroke the dog's head and give

117

her a gentle hug around her neck. "I'm so glad you're with us, girl," she whispered. "Can I tell you something I've been longing to tell Jim? I feel if I don't say it to someone, I'm going to burst! And I know you'll keep it secret." Kate put her mouth to Maggie's silky ear to make absolutely sure Anna wouldn't overhear her. "Maggie," she said, "I'm going to have a baby."

To Kate's utter amazement, Maggie sat bolt upright, emitted an enthusiastic woof, and began cavorting energetically, first around Kate and then loping over to where Frisky and Anna were playing to run rings around them. "Mom!" Anna exclaimed in disbelief. "What's happened to Maggie? The only time I've seen her like this was the day we saw the rainbow cloud."

Just as astonished as Anna, Kate declared, "She's acting as if she were a puppy again! Oh, how I wish Davy was here to see this!" *Did Maggie understand what I told her? How could she possibly? It can't be. Or can it? Believe, Kate, believe!*

***

After breakfast, Hank returned to his work in the garden. Though both Mike and Abby offered to help her clean up, Bessie shooed them away. "You two go on out to the porch and chat before you have to leave for work, Abby," she said with a wink and a smile. "I've got this covered."

Mike and Abby obligingly did as they were told. Once seated in the comfortable rockers, Mike was the first to speak. "So you have to work today?" he asked worriedly. "Won't that be stressful, after yesterday's incident?"

Abby gazed at her hands, folded in her lap, reminding Mike of Hank's identical pose just thirty minutes ago. Without looking up, she said softly, "I don't want to go to work, Mike, but I have to. I'm lucky to have a summer job, and I can't risk losing it. I thought about asking Mr. Jones for the day off, but I decided to face the music instead. Who knows? Maybe this whole thing has already blown over, and I won't be the center of attention."

"Something your mother said you don't like," Mike observed.

"And she's right about that," Abby said, lifting her eyes up to meet Mike's. "There are times I wish I wasn't that way. It would have made yesterday a lot easier to handle."

"Well, let's look on the bright side," Mike said. "You *did* make it through yesterday. You *did* survive. And you're facing today with courage that the Lord will help you handle anything thrown your way. I'd call that progress."

Abby chuckled. "Mike, you're giving me more credit than I deserve," she said, "but I would appreciate some prayers today."

"You got it," he told her. "I've been holding you in prayer since the evening we first met."

Abby dropped her eyes again and the familiar blush rose to her cheeks. "You want to know something?" she said shyly. "I've been praying for you, too."

Genuinely touched by this, Mike reached bravely for Abby's hand, hoping she would let him hold it just as she did yesterday. He was not disappointed. The touch of her skin warmed Mike from head to toe. *This is the moment to ask her, Mike. Quit stalling and just do it!* "Abby," he said, "there's something I'd like to ask you."

"Ask away," Abby said invitingly.

"Would you consider going out with me? On a real date, I mean?"

Abby looked thoughtful, as if she were trying to process the words Mike had spoken. Then she raised her head, looked Mike squarely in the eyes, and with a mischievous grin on her face, inquired, "Is that what you and Daddy were talking about this morning?"

"Yes, it was," Mike admitted, returning her smile and giving her hand a squeeze.

"And I know he gave his permission," Abby confirmed, "or else you wouldn't be sitting here right now, waiting for my answer."

"What *is* your answer, Abby?" Mike persisted. "Yes or no?"

"Abby!" Bessie called to her. "Have you lost track of the time? You're going to be late for work!"

"Oh, no!" Abby exclaimed in dismay as she looked at her watch, leapt up, and dashed inside the house for her purse and keys, leaving Mike hanging out to dry. He stood up, determined to intercept her as she left the house. He had to have her answer. He simply *had* to.

As Abby careened out the door, ponytail flying, Mike grabbed her by the arm. "I know you're late, but I need an answer, Abby. Yes or no?"

She paused just long enough for Mike to drink in the sparkle in her eyes and the glow on her face. Impulsively, Abby stood on tip-toe and did the last thing Mike ever imagined she would do, something so wonderful he would remember its sweetness for years to come.

Abby kissed him on the cheek.

***

Bob and Jim watched anxiously as Davy studied Grandpa Will's signature on the deed, comparing it meticulously with the one penned in the book. Davy traced each flow of cursive letters, one at a time, first in the book, next on the deed, hoping to find a variant that would jump out at him. To add to this challenge, the signature on the deed, though it appeared the same as the original, was smaller due to the size permitted on the document. Davy knew he needed some help. "Bampa, do you have a magnifying glass?" he asked.

"Why, yes, Davy," Bob answered as he got up to hunt it down.

"Why do you need a magnifying glass, son?" Jim wondered.

"Grandpa Will's writing in the book is larger than the one on the deed," Davy explained. "It makes it hard to check for differences if I can't make the letters the same size."

Jim sighed. "Sure wish I could help you with this," he said glumly.

"Here you go, Davy," Bob said. He handed the boy the magnifying glass and reclaimed his seat at the kitchen table.

Davy grabbed it eagerly and held it hovering over the script on the deed. "Wow! This really helps," he declared. "Now let me try again." Painstakingly, he traced the 'W' in 'William' in the book and then switched to the deed, noting no obvious difference. Davy kept at it, sometimes checking a particular letter repeatedly to make sure he hadn't overlooked the slightest jot or tittle. The close scrutiny was placing a strain on Davy's eyes, and he could feel a subtle hint of an oncoming headache, something from which he rarely suffered. He was just beginning to wonder if he should ask Jim if he could take a break for a few minutes.

"Bob, look!" Jim exclaimed so unexpectedly, it made Davy jump. "The words! The words in Grandpa's book. They're coming into view!"

"The Old Ones!" Davy shouted, running to the front door and fling-
ing it open eagerly. As if on cue, Racer and Mrs. Racer bounded into the
living room. They each gave Davy a warm hug.

"How did you know we were here?" Racer asked, sporting his familiar
grin.

"The letters in Grandpa's book," Davy told him. "Jim and Bampa saw
them reappearing, so I knew one of the Old Ones was close by."

"Have you found any deviance yet from Will's signature and the one
on the deed?" Mrs. Racer asked as they followed Davy to the kitchen.

"Not yet," he said, "but now that you're here, maybe you or Racer can
see what I can't. Jim, Bampa, Racer and Mrs. Racer are here to help us."

"Fantastic!" Jim declared. "I'm all for some assistance right about now."

The True Squirrels of the Old Ones wasted no time. They sprang to
the table and eyed each signature methodically. "Do you need the magnifying glass?" Davy asked.

"No, child," said Racer, "but thank you." Using the tip of an ebony
claw, Racer traced Grandpa Will's signature in the book. As he did so, he
was suddenly filled with an overwhelming presence as if his dear friend
were standing right next to him. Racer felt his heart swelling with love
for Will, yet aching with sorrow at his loss. He fought back tears and said,
"Mrs. Racer, it's your turn. Trace slowly. Tell me what you feel."

Mrs. Racer willingly complied while Racer turned his attention to the
signature on the deed. *Nothing! I feel nothing! Oh, I hope and pray Mrs. Racer
experiences the same!* When Mrs. Racer finished tracing Will's signature,
there were tears in her eyes. "You felt it, too, didn't you?" Racer asked excitedly. "Will's presence!"

"Oh, yes," she sniffled, "so real, so strong, so incredibly haunting."

"Try the other one, sweets," Racer encouraged her.

Mrs. Racer traced the signature on the deed once, twice, three times.
She turned to Racer and announced emphatically, "Nothing! It's not
Will's! It can't be!"

Upon hearing this, Davy gave a whoop and a cheer. "Jim, Bampa, the
Racers say the deed is forged!"

"What? How do they know that and so quickly?" Jim asked.

When Davy explained to the men how the squirrels had deduced the
difference, Bob shook his head. "I don't mean to rain on anyone's parade,"

he said, "but what if Racer and Mrs. Racer can't feel Mr. Will's presence in the deed because this isn't the original? It's a copy."

The squirrels were crestfallen at Bob's sensible, yet disappointing, observation, and Davy's spirits fell just as quickly as they had crested just a moment before. "Jim," he implored bitterly, "what do we do now?"

Jim thought for a moment before he answered. When he did, there was a smile on his face. "This may be a copy," he told them, "but the original, or what should be the original, is filed at the courthouse. Perhaps after lunch, Racer and Mrs. Racer could accompany us on a drive over there to see what happens when they trace *that* signature."

"Oh, yes, dear Jim!" Racer exclaimed as he jumped up and down for joy, "We'll gladly go with you, won't we, sweets?"

"But of course!" Mrs. Racer agreed. "It's high time we solve this mystery."

"Bob," Susie called as she entered the kitchen. She had come from the living room, where she had been doing some knitting, and was carrying her calendar in her hands. "Weren't you going to use this today?"

Bob slapped his forehead. "How could I forget?" he chided himself. "Look here, Jim, we might not have to make that trip to the courthouse after all."

"What do you mean?" Jim asked.

"Give me the date that deed was supposedly signed by Mr. Will."

Jim glanced at the document, and answered, "March thirtieth, this year."

Hastily, Bob flipped to the month of March and his eyes zeroed in on the date. He emitted a low whistle as a smile spread across his face. "Well, I'll be," he said. "This is most fortuitous, most fortuitous indeed."

CHAPTER 12

PHONE CALLS AND FORGERIES

David and Sarah stood in the Walmart check-out line, reassessing the contents of their cart. Kate had given them several suggestions about what Davy and Anny would enjoy having during their summer at the farm, so selecting gifts for them had been a breeze. The cart held child-sized hoes, shovels, and rakes to use in the garden, art supplies for Anna, a container of BBs for Davy, and a watch to be wrapped and set aside for Davy's birthday. When it came to Kate and Jim, however, the choice was more problematic. Sarah had no idea what they needed or wanted, and David, totally dependent upon his wife when it came to shopping, was usually no help, but this time, he remarkably came to the rescue.

"Sarah, I saw those photos of the garden they have, with Jim seeming to be enjoying himself there. Why don't we get them some flowers to plant along the border of it?"

"David, I do believe you're a genius," Sarah complimented him. "That's the very thing! Why, I remember like it was yesterday, our John always bringing flowers to Kate just because she loved them so much. Jim will enjoy planting them, and she'll enjoy the blooms."

"And with their new tools," David remarked, "Davy and Anna can help him."

They had chosen the most colorful array of flowering plants, which they now beheld admiringly as they inched their way up toward the cashier, and loaded their plunder onto the belt. "Someone's going to be doing some planting, I see," the friendly clerk remarked as he began to ring up their purchases.

"Don't look at me," David said with a chuckle. "I don't play in the dirt. These are gifts for those who do."

"Children, by the looks of it," said the clerk. "It's great to know kids get outdoors these days. Too many just plop themselves in front of the television or the computer. Such a shame!"

"I agree," said Sarah. "Believe it or not, our grandchildren are spending an entire summer at a place where they have neither, and from what we hear, they're having the time of their lives."

"So these are for them, I guess," noted the clerk. "Lucky kids, I say."

"Lucky grandparents, too," said David as he swiped his card to pay for the merchandise. "Getting the opportunity to spend time with family means everything."

"Yes, sir," said the clerk as he handed David the receipt. "Y'all have fun now, y'hear? And thanks for shopping at Walmart."

***

As Eric relayed his encounters with the Old Ones to Elly, she was overwhelmed with awe and delight. She had to admit that all this would be harder to swallow had she not seen the squirrel she now knew to be Racer on television the evening before, but the idea that these creatures, invisible to most, actually lived and breathed practically in their backyard...it just enchanted her. Elly laughed heartily when Eric told her of his first meeting with Racer and Cleverhands, and his confrontation with Ronnie. "So that explains why Ronnie was so nervous around us at the grocery store," she remarked. "And you had the nerve to say 'take a photo' after you rescued his phone from the water? Oh, Eric! Then you invited him to join us in the check-out line. He must have wished a hole had opened in the floor and swallowed him then and there!"

Eric laughed heartily. "Yep, I bet he did. I just couldn't help giving that underhanded crook a hard time. I couldn't understand how that following Monday, when we literally bumped into one another in the corridor at the hospital, how he had suddenly become so rude and abrasive, so sure of himself, until Reverend shared the reason with me last evening."

"What did he tell you, honey?" Elly asked. Eric filled her in on all the details of Ronnie's heart attack, the owl healing him, and the consequent and inexplicable results at the doctor's office. "No wonder Ronnie had such attitude," Elly observed. "He must have thought after that diagnosis that he was unassailable, even by a sheriff."

"I think he still does," Eric said, "and I know he's up to no good, but all the evidence provided by the Old Ones can't be backed up unless they show their hand."

"You mean go public, just like Racer did?" Elly guessed smartly.

"Just between you, me, and the good Reverend," Eric answered, "that's the plan, should everything else fall through."

"And Reverend shared his plan with you?" Elly was incredulous. "Does Davy know about it?"

"I think he suspects," said Eric thoughtfully, "but the owl knows the whole idea worries the boy. He is sparing his feelings until there is no alternative left."

"Poor Davy," Elly said sympathetically. "How that boy must love his friends. How blessed he is to be the Chosen One. What I wouldn't give to meet the Old Ones in person!"

"If they met with me," Eric said, "and cared enough to send us this unique gift, I think they will certainly make themselves known to you sooner or later."

"I hope it's sooner," Elly said wistfully.

Eric reached across the table to take her hand. "There's something more I need to tell you, Elly," he said, "something wonderful Reverend promised us."

"Us?" Elly asked, confused. "But he doesn't even know me!"

"In a strange way even I don't understand, I think he knows us better than we can know ourselves at times," Eric said, tears brimming unsolicited in his eyes. "Reverend promised me you would bear us a son. A son, Elly! And as Davy says, 'Old Ones always keep their promises.'"

＊＊＊

"What is it, Bampa?" Davy asked eagerly. "What's on the calendar that day?"

Bob smiled broadly and said, "That's the day Susie and I took Mr. Will up to Highlands for an early birthday lunch. We also did some sightseeing at Bridal Veil Falls and Dry Falls, since they are in the area. As I recall, we picked Mr. Will up around nine thirty that morning and didn't arrive back home until dinner time."

"Then that means Grandpa Will couldn't have been anywhere near that courthouse on the date recorded on the deed!" Jim said excitedly. "Guess Ronnie didn't figure on that wrench being thrown into the works."

"Bampa, Racer wants to know if the calendar is proof enough," said Davy. "He's afraid others will think Nana wrote that down once we actually had a copy of the deed."

"It could be misconstrued that way, I imagine," Bob conceded, "but take a look at just this one page in Susie's calendar. See how full it is? It's her habit to write everything important happening on each day of the year, from birthdays to doctor appointments, you name it."

"Plus," Susie interjected, "I keep my old calendars in a drawer; I must have them going back fifteen years at least. That's proof that this has been a long-standing practice on my part. They serve my memories like a short-hand journal."

"Well, this certainly proves to all of us here that Ronnie had the deed forged," Jim said, "but if I know Ronnie, he'll find a way to wiggle out of this, too. I think we're going to need something more, but I'll give Eric a call and make him aware of this new information. Maybe he can help."

"Don't forget to tell him what Racer and Mrs. Racer said about the signature, too," said Davy.

Jim rubbed Davy's head affectionately. "I'll be sure to, son," he said, pulling Sheriff Peabody's card from his wallet and excusing himself to use the phone in the living room. Bob got up too, in order to help Susie with lunch.

"You try it, Davy," Mrs. Racer suggested.

"Try what?"

"Running your finger over the signatures."

"I already did that. I didn't feel anything special."

"But did you trace it in its entirety, child, or just one letter at a time?" Racer asked.

"One letter at a time."

"Then try again," Mrs. Racer urged. "Let your finger flow along each letter gradually and gracefully. Take your time."

Hesitantly, Davy placed his index finger on the tip of the W in Grandpa's book and began the twisting, turning journey along the cursive trail. Racer and Mrs. Racer watched the boy expectantly, uttering not one word that might distract him. By the time Davy reached the second L in William, he felt a warm, tingling sensation beginning in his finger tip. As he continued tracing the signature, the warmth spread up his hand and into his arm, moving faster with each stroke, until Davy felt his whole body encased in what he would later describe as the best hug he had ever experienced. The squirrels knew by the look on the boy's face that this exercise had been a resounding success.

"Well done!" Racer exclaimed, when Davy rounded the last curve in the last letter.

"Now Davy," said Mrs. Racer, patting him on the shoulder, "try the one on the deed."

The moment Davy's finger touched the first letter on Grandpa's supposed signature, the glow in which he was basking instantly vaporized. "It's gone," he lamented. "Oh, how I wish I'd never touched this paper!"

"That's how we felt, too, child," Racer assured him, "but wasn't it marvelous while it lasted?"

Davy managed a smile. "Yes, it was," he said. "I'll never forget it."

"Never forget what, Davy?" Bob asked over his shoulder.

Before Davy could answer, Jim strolled back into the kitchen. "The sheriff is off duty today," he announced. "I called his home phone, but no one picked up, so I left a message; I hope he'll return my call soon."

"I'm sure he will," said Susie confidently. "After his visit with the Old Ones last night, I think Eric is as invested in their future as we are."

***

Jim and Davy, with Racer and Mrs. Racer in tow, had no sooner returned to the farmhouse when the phone sounded its raucous ring. "I'll get it!" Jim hollered as he sprinted to pick it up. He thought for sure the call would be from Eric, but it was instead a call he wasn't expecting to receive so soon. "Yes, this is Jim Hunter. Be there at two? Certainly, I can make it. Yes. Yes. Looking forward to meeting you as well. Good-bye."

"Who were you talking to, honey?" Kate asked from where she was standing washing dishes in the sink.

Jim ran to her and gave her a quick hug. "No time to explain, Kate," he said. "I have to change clothes and run off to meet with someone. I'll tell you all about it when I get back, I promise."

"But Jim," Kate protested, "what about being here when David and Sarah arrive?"

"You'll have to do the honors," he said, as he dashed for the bedroom.

And when are we going to have a moment alone, Jim? I have such good news to tell you! The best news ever!

"Mom," Davy's voice interrupted her reverie, "can we have a cookie?"

"Who's we?" she asked playfully, knowing full well it was probably Racer.

"Racer and Mrs. Racer are here," Davy explained. "Racer has promised to only eat one."

"That's good," Mom said with a laugh, "because I've made them especially for your grandparents." She glanced at the clock, and added, "I expect them to be here around two, so don't go skipping off to The Glade or anything."

"I won't," Davy said, as he reached for the cookie jar. "I'm too excited about seeing Grandpa and Grandma to go anywhere. But Racer and Mrs. Racer will be going back there after we eat these."

Kate turned just in time to see two chocolate chip cookies dangling in mid-air and disappearing one dainty bite at a time. She fancied for one moment that she had glimpsed a paw holding one of them, but the image faded as quickly as it had come. Kate couldn't help but feel a stab of disappointment. She so wanted to believe like Davy, and see as he did.

"On my way!" Jim hailed them as he bolted out the door.

"Bye, honey," said Kate, but Davy noticed the slight frown on her face.

"Why is Jim all dressed up like he was going to work or church? Where is he going? He didn't say anything about having to be anywhere but here today."

"Jim got a call, but said he was in too big of a hurry to explain it this minute or to even tell me who it was," Mom said with a sigh. "I guess we'll just have to be patient."

"Being patient isn't easy, is it?" Davy remarked.

"No, it's not," Mom agreed, "but it is one of the seven virtues and is well worth the practice, honey." She winked in the direction of the vanishing cookies and added, "Maybe the Old Ones will help you improve in that area."

"No worries there, Mom," Davy assured her as he turned to head for the porch followed by two tiny morsels of cookie. "Oh, and Racer and Mrs. Racer say 'thank you.'"

"They are most welcome," she said, wishing with all her heart she could have heard them speak those words aloud. *Believe, Kate, believe.*

***

It was a quiet, uneventful day of spying at the Carson home for Reverend and Sharp-eyes. Betty Rae had departed mid-morning to have her hair done, and Buddy and Sammy had retired to the den to play their customary video games. Ronnie had lazed on the couch most of the morning, watching television and reading some magazines. He hadn't made any phone calls or received any. At lunch time, Ronnie wandered into the kitchen to fix a sandwich and a glass of tea. Then it was right back to the sofa, where he plopped himself down and began surfing channels with his remote.

Sharp-eyes stifled a yawn. "How can humans be so easily entertained?" he asked sleepily.

"I have no idea," Reverend answered. "Ronnie is certainly not doing anything to pique our interest today. I can tell, my friend, that you are still in need of rest after last night. Why don't you nap for a bit and let me stand guard."

"Are you sure?" Sharp-eyes asked doubtfully. "You didn't get any more rest than I did."

"I'm fine for now," the owl assured him. "If I start to feel drowsy, I'll wake you up to take your turn."

"If you insist," said the hawk, yawning yet again. "I think I'll go to the dining room to rest, though. It's too noisy in here."

As he watched Sharp-eyes glide away and around the corner, Reverend flew from the mantelpiece to the floor, thinking a bit of pacing would get his blood flowing and keep him more alert. He, too, was still feeling drained from their last adventure, but was highly gratified by the support Eric had shown for his plan. *But when to implement it? That's the immediate question. I'll just go through every detail in my head right now. It will help keep me awake and attentive.*

The sudden clamor of Ronnie's cell phone gave Reverend a start. He crept as close to the man as he dared, hoping to catch some of the words from the caller on the other end of the line, but Ronnie's words were all he heard. "Carson, here. You what? Bill, that's the best news I've had all day! How did you manage to round guys up so quickly? The photo? Really? Well, well, imagine that, imagine that. Who knows, maybe they will see that varmint lurking about. Tell 'em to be at the worksite this Friday, ten o'clock sharp. I've lost enough time as it is. And Bill, remind them to be packing." Ronnie snapped his phone shut and leaned back on the couch, hands behind his head and a sinister smile on his face. "It's all over now, Jim," he said aloud. "It's all over now."

***

When Eric heard his home phone ring, he leaped up to grab it as quickly as he could. Elly, still feeling tired from her recent ordeal, had retired to the bedroom for a nap, and he was anxious that nothing disturb her. "Sheriff Peabody," Eric said as softly as he could into the receiver, noting for the first time that afternoon that his answering machine was blinking.

"Hi, Sheriff, it's Connie. I have some interesting news for you."

"I'm all ears," said Eric as he pulled his notebook and pen from his shirt pocket. "Let's have it."

"The car with that license number is registered to a Gary Allen Burdette," Connie began. "He was convicted of forgery, about ten years ago. Since he didn't have a previous record, the judge let him off on probation and community service. His record's been clean ever since."

"Or he's just never been caught," Eric astutely observed.

"I thought of that," said Connie. "Now this other fellow, this Calvin C. Holbrook, so far, no leads, but I'll keep working on that if you want me to."

"I'd like that, Connie," Eric said, "but don't stress too much over it. The more I mull over this one, the more I think it's a wild goose chase. I'm not even sure if it matters in this case I'm investigating at the moment, although I'm planning to call someone's bluff with it."

"Oh, now that sounds intriguing," Connie said. "I'd love to be there for that one."

"I'll be sure to tell you all about it," Eric assured her. "Now if you'll please give me Burdette's address, I'll pay him a visit as soon as I can round up some friends."

"Friends?" Connie was genuinely perplexed.

"I'll tell you all about that later, too," said Eric with a laugh. "Right now, I have to check a message on my answering machine. Thanks for everything, Connie."

"You bet!"

Connie hung up and Eric pushed the button on his answering device. As he listened to Jim's voice, he couldn't help but smile with satisfaction. He didn't waste another moment, but dialed the Hunter's home phone.

"Hello?" Kate's pleasant voice sounded on the line.

"Hi, Kate. It's Eric, is Jim around?"

"I'm afraid not," she said. "Do you need his cell phone number?"

"No," he said. "How about putting Davy on the line?"

"Davy?" Kate asked. "Then this must have something to do with the Old Ones."

"Yes, ma'am, it has everything to do with them."

"Hang on just a moment, and I'll get him," she said. Kate quickly put the receiver down and ran out to the porch to summon Davy. When she arrived, he was talking animatedly with what she knew must be the Racers. "Davy, come quickly. Sheriff Peabody wants to talk to you."

"To me?" Davy asked in surprise.

"Yes, honey. He says it has to do with the Old Ones."

"Then there isn't a moment to lose, child!" Racer exclaimed. "Come on, Mrs. Racer, let's go see what the sheriff has to share with Davy, and let's hope it is good news!"

CHAPTER 13

GRANDPA AND GRANDMA ARRIVE

After a pleasant lunch in Blue Ridge, David and Sarah grabbed some coffee to go and started on what would be the last leg of their long journey. Sarah, thrilled at the prospect of seeing Kate and their grandchildren, chattered happily away. David drove the entire route, hardly speaking a word until they reached the city of Andrews. Spotting an inviting rest area up ahead, he pulled into it. "What are you doing, honey?" Sarah asked.

"Don't you need a pit stop after all that coffee?" David ventured.

"Come to think of it, I do," Sarah confirmed. "My, this is an attractive place with the mountains all around. Hope the restrooms are as neat and clean as the grounds here are."

"Only one way to find out," said David as he pulled into a parking spot. He'd started to get out of the car when Sarah caught his arm.

"David," she said gently, "you've been so quiet ever since we left Blue Ridge. Is everything okay?"

David slumped back into his seat and sighed. "Yes, and no," he said resignedly. "On the one hand, like you, I can't wait to see Kate and the kids. On the other hand, well, what if Jim doesn't believe me? Or worse, what if I've jumped to the entirely wrong conclusion? Sarah, honestly, I can't even decide on a way to break the news, even though I've had lots of time to think about it."

Sarah patted her husband's hand comfortingly. "Not lots of time for something this potentially momentous, David," she said. "Don't be so hard on yourself. Pray that when the time comes, God will give you the right words to say."

David gave her a wan smile. "That's all I have been praying about," he admitted.

"And I'll join you in that prayer," Sarah assured him. "Now let's use the restroom so we can be on our way. And David," she added with a confident smile, "I have no doubt today will be a superbly joyful one!"

***

Davy watched anxiously out the living room windows, not for his grandparents this time, but for Sheriff Peabody's arrival. When it was clear the boy couldn't accompany Eric that afternoon due to the imminent arrival of the Murrays, Racer concocted a brilliant solution. "Tell the sheriff that Mrs. Racer and I will return to The Glade and send Mrs. Scout and Mrs. Reverend back here to the house. They are the only ones who saw this Gary fellow clearly. If they recognize him, they can poke him once with their beaks, twice if he's not the right man."

Eric had readily agreed to this plan, and was speeding toward the Hunter's place to pick up the deed and his two invisible partners. Davy was relieved to see Mrs. Reverend and Mrs. Scout swooping into sight and perching on the roof of his mother's car just as Sheriff Peabody's car came into view. Davy ran to the back door, grabbing the deed Jim had left on the table on the way.. "Mom," he shouted, "the Sheriff's here, and so are Mrs. Reverend and Mrs. Scout. I'm going outside to meet them!"

When the owl and the hawk spied Davy, they flew to him and engulfed him in their strong, warm wings. "Oh, Davy, you are a sight for sore eyes, my dear," said Mrs. Reverend. "I've missed you so!"

"As have I," Mrs. Scout told him. "We are so glad we can be of service to the sheriff. It's nice to see our sleuthing is finally paying off."

"Yes, it is," Davy agreed, stroking each of their feathered heads in turn. When Eric pulled up, he couldn't help but smile, knowing from Davy's gestures that his two witnesses were by the boy's side. Davy hurried over to the car and opened the back door, held it for several moments, then closed it once he was sure Mrs. Reverend and Mrs. Scout were safely inside. "They are ready to go, Sheriff, and understand what they need to do."

"Excellent," said Eric, "but there's one more thing: Do they have any idea where our suspect might work? I have the home address, but he might not be there this time of day."

"Tell him to drive to Smith & Sons," Mrs. Scout suggested. "My instinct tells me that is his place of employment."

Davy passed on the information to Eric and added, "Just be sure you give them plenty of time to get out before you shut the car door; any door, for that matter."

"I promise I'll be extra careful, Davy," Eric said as he took the deed from the boy's hand. "Maybe to be on the safe side, either Mrs. Scout or Mrs. Reverend could tug on my pants leg to let me know they're good to go."

"Splendid idea, Sheriff," said Mrs. Reverend, clapping her wings together. "We shall do just that."

"They like that idea," Davy said with a grin.

"Good," said Eric, returning the smile and reaching out his hand to shake Davy's. "Then it's off we go!"

***

"Sharp-eyes! Sharp-eyes! Wake up!" Reverend commanded as he nudged the hawk on the shoulder.

Sharp-eyes blinked sleepily, "What is it?" he mumbled as he made an effort to rouse himself. When he caught the glint of excitement in Reverend's eyes, the hawk rallied remarkably. "Good news, Reverend? Is it good news?"

"That depends on one's perspective," the owl said mischievously. "For us, I think it's the best news yet. We must fly to tell Davy, then it is back to The Glade for us."

"You mean we don't have to watch Ronnie anymore?" Sharp-eyes asked incredulously.

"No more," Reverend assured him. "I know his plans. Now it's time for ours."

***

"I can't take this waiting anymore," Anna declared to her mom as she entered the kitchen carrying Mary and Smokey, with Frisky pouncing along behind her. "When are Grandma and Grandpa going to get here?"

Mom glanced at the clock and smiled. "Honey, it's almost two. That's when they said they hoped to arrive, when they last called me. Why don't you fetch Davy and go wait in the front yard for them? Maybe you could play some ball to pass the time."

"Okay," Anna agreed and headed for the porch, where she knew Davy was more than likely hanging out with Maggie. She peeked her head around the corner and saw Davy was jotting down something in a notebook. "What are you writing, Davy?" Anna asked as Frisky bounded toward Maggie and her plume of a tail in hopes of a romp.

"Reverend and Sharp-eyes are here," he told her. "They're giving me some important information to pass on to Jim when he gets home. I have to make sure I get all the details straight. They can't stay long."

"Why not?" Anna wondered. "Why can they only stay a short while?"

"They have to get back to The Glade," Davy responded tersely. "Let me finish my notes, then we'll talk, Anna. I promise."

Anna sighed disappointedly, but didn't interrupt again. Instead she walked over to Maggie and Frisky and sat on the floor where she could stroke them as she kept watch. She hoped she would soon see her grandparents coming down the gravel road. "I wish I knew when they'll be here," Anna whispered to Maggie. At the sound of her voice, the dog waved her tail and Frisky went into a series of frantic leaps trying to catch it. This made Anna giggle, but she quickly covered her mouth with her hand, knowing any noise right now could be distracting. She had never seen such a serious expression on her brother's face. The facts the Old Ones were giving Davy must indeed be critical. He seemed compelled to get it all straight, down to the last tiny detail. It made Anna wonder if Davy would tell her about it first, or wait to tell Jim only. *Where is Jim, anyway? Davy said he left the house in a hurry earlier. He was all dressed up. What could that be about? If he's not home soon, he'll miss greeting Grandma and Grandpa.*

"I think I have it all down right," Anna heard Davy say. "But what do I do if anything changes? Will one of you come back tomorrow, after I've had a chance to go over all of this with Jim?"

Anna heard nothing, but Reverend spoke to Davy. "I will send the most rested among us to check the final plans and movements tomorrow evening. Be looking for your visitors just around dinner time."

"I will," Davy said. "But does this mean I can't even see Racer until Friday?"

"I'm afraid so, lad," said the owl as he laid a sympathetic wing on Davy's shoulder, "but with your grandparents coming today, you should have plenty of companionship. I'm afraid we, too, must now take our leave. We are weary to the bone."

"I understand," said Davy sadly, giving Reverend and Sharp-eyes each a hug. "I'll miss you until Friday. Please be safe."

"As safe as possible, always," Reverend reassured him. "Now if you will be so kind as to unlatch the door, we will be on our way."

Davy rose reluctantly from his cot, but did as the owl asked. Anna noted the dejected look on his face as he opened the screen door. Though she couldn't see Reverend and Sharp-eyes, her heart told her this was a somber and solemn farewell.

***

As Mike made his numerous pastoral rounds that day, he couldn't stop smiling. Abby's unforeseen kiss had launched him onto cloud nine, and he had yet to descend from it. Time and again, Mike placed his hand to his cheek where Abby's lips had touched it, as if by doing so, he could capture the sensation anew. Not even the prospect of meeting with Tommy Green at the church, where a crew was scheduled to install the new air conditioning unit that afternoon, could dampen his spirits. Mike knew in his head it was too early to call this feeling love, but his heart, soaring on the wings of eagles, told him a different story. He pulled into the church driveway waving heartily to Tommy, who had just stepped out of his car. Right behind him, as if on cue, a van sporting the logo "Bryson City Heating & Air" arrived on the scene. It gratified Mike no end that everyone involved in this afternoon's project was right on time.

"Hello, Tommy," Mike called cheerfully. "Beautiful day, isn't it?"

Tommy regarded his pastor askance. Although he knew Mike to be an upbeat person, he had never seen him quite this animated. "I guess you could say it's beautiful if you're standing in the shade," he remarked. "And just wait 'til you get inside the church. It's so hot, Preacher, you could give a sermon about hell and folks would think they were already there."

Mike threw back his head and laughed enthusiastically. "Not my style, Tommy, you know that," he said, "but I appreciate your observation."

Two technicians emerged from the van and sauntered over to where Mike and Tommy were standing. "You must be Pastor Russell," a burly, balding man said as he extended his hand toward Mike. "I'm Don, and this here is Rupert. We'll be installing your new unit for you. Mr. Green here got you a sweet deal if I say so myself. I'd have the exact same a/c if it were for my own church."

"Well, that's good to hear," said Mike, genuinely pleased, "but you can call me Pastor Mike."

"Wait a minute!" Rupert exclaimed suddenly. "Ain't you the fella on the news last night? The one standin' by the river with that giant critter what looked like a squirrel?"

"Looked like a squirrel?" Tommy asked somewhat indignantly. "That's the very creature that caused a mad panic in this church just about two weeks ago. Isn't that right, Preacher?"

"I do recall hearin' about that from my neighbor, Mrs. Mason," Don remarked. "Didn't take it serious, though. Sweet lady is getting up in years."

"She may be aging," Mike said, "but Mildred is as truthful as she is sweet. Yes, the squirrel is one and the same."

"Did it try to bite you?" Rupert asked apprehensively. "Was the little gal okay?"

The image of Racer singing so sweetly at the Hunters' kitchen table flooded Mike's mind. He smiled and stated simply, "He's not the biting kind. And yes, she's okay; the little one was cold and scared by her fall into the river, but she wasn't hurt."

"That's a relief," said Tommy sincerely. "Why that's all my Valerie could talk about last night because she recognized her as being..."

"No names, no names!" Mike stopped Tommy in his tracks, much to the man's bewilderment. "I apologize, Tommy, for being so abrupt, but I know for a fact this family would wish for anonymity."

"I understand, Preacher," Tommy said, rather coolly. "No offense taken."

"Well, on that note," Don said, "I think it's high time Rupert and I got to work. This could take a couple of hours."

The two men returned to the van, but Rupert couldn't resist posing one more question. "Think you could arrange a way for me to meet this squirrel myself, Pastor Mike? You do that, and my labor here today is free."

***

Bob was checking his e-mail when he heard their phone ring. As Susie answered it in the kitchen, he couldn't make out who she was talking to. He didn't have to wonder for long. Susie addressed him as she entered the living room. "That was Kate, Bob. She said their phone rang shortly after Jim returned from our house. He took the call, then dashed to get changed into church clothes and rushed out the door like a whirlwind, saying he'd explain it all later. Do you have any idea what this could possibly be about?" Bob winced ever so slightly, but the gesture was not lost on Susie. "You *do* know something, don't you?" she asked, with a hint of accusation in her voice.

Bob sighed and gave his wife a sheepish grin. "I've never been good at keeping secrets from you," he said, "nor do I even like making that a practice. I've wanted to tell you ever since Jim told me, but he wished to keep it under wraps until he knew something for sure."

"Knew what for sure?" Susie inquired.

"He's probably interviewing for a teaching job," Bob answered. "Ken Anderson told him there was an opening for a JROTC position at the high school, and Jim decided to apply for it."

"So that's why he had to use our computer the other day!" Susie exclaimed. "Jim was working on his resume and application. And you think this call might have something to do with an interview?"

"Honestly, I think it's a rather quick turn-around to be called for an interview so soon," Bob offered, "but it's the only scenario I can think of right now. Why else would Jim get all gussied up?"

"But why didn't he tell Kate?" Susie wondered. "Why tell you and not her?"

"Two reasons," Bob answered. "First of all, he didn't want Kate to get her hopes up if he ended up not landing the job. They both so desperately want to be able to stay here. Secondly, Jim told me because he needed someone to pray for him and the situation. He knew I would gladly do this and keep his secret, too."

"Well, now that this cat's out of the bag," Susie said, "I'll join you in prayer for Jim. But there's something you need to know, honey." Here Susie paused and took a deep breath. "I must confess, I've been keeping a secret from you too, one I've been dying to share ever since I've suspected it."

"Another one we need to pray about?" Bob asked.

"Definitely," said Susie. "I think Kate is pregnant."

***

After Reverend and Sharp-eyes departed, Davy took a seat on the floor with Anna, Maggie, and the energetic Frisky. "I think it's so cool how Maggie has taken to your kitten, Anna," he said. "It's almost like she thinks she's his mom." At this statement, Maggie licked Davy's face in affirmation. "You *do* think you're Frisky's mom, don't you girl," said Davy with a laugh.

"You understand what she's saying?" Anna queried. "I thought you could only do that when the Old Ones were around."

"I can't hear her talk," Davy confessed, "but the more time I spend with her, it seems, the more I understand her and she understands me. We don't need words."

"Oh, I see," said Anna, "kind of like how Mary and Smokey always know what I'm thinking."

Davy resisted the temptation to chuckle. "I guess you could say that," he said, giving her braid a pull. Just then, Maggie tensed. She lifted her head and perked up her ears, nose twitching as she sniffed the air eagerly. "What is it, Maggie?" Davy asked, concerned. "What do you hear?"

The old dog struggled to her feet and stiffly walked the few paces from her bed to the side of the screened porch that looked out on the gravel road leading to the farmhouse. "Woof!" Maggie barked excitedly. "Woof! Woof!"

"I know what Maggie hears!" Davy shouted gleefully. "It's a car in the distance! It must be Grandpa and Grandma!"

Both Anna and he leapt to their feet and made a mad dash for their mom, who was in the kitchen. "They're here! They're here!" Davy and Anna announced simultaneously, running for the back door.

"They're here?" Mom asked, jumping up to follow them. "That's funny. I didn't hear a car coming down the drive."

"Maggie heard it!" Davy declared. "The car will be in sight really soon. I just know it!"

All three tumbled out the door, Anna carrying Frisky and Maggie trotting behind them, and hurried around the side of the house so they could glimpse the car the moment it rounded the bend. Davy's stomach teemed with butterflies as he kept his keen eyes focused on the spot where he knew the car would first appear. It had been over two years since he had seen his grandparents, and he couldn't wait to spend these next two wonderful weeks with them. For Davy, the timing of their visit could not have been better. Reverend was right; Grandpa and Grandma would help him keep his mind off the temporarily absent Old Ones, from whom he had not been separated for one day since meeting Racer.

"I think I hear the car!" Davy shouted merrily.

Anna strained to listen. Within seconds she, too, heard the faint but unmistakable crunch of tires on gravel. "I hear it too!" Anna confirmed. "And look! They're turning the corner!" Kate, Davy, and Anna began waving wildly in greeting. Maggie proceeded to welcome the newcomers with loud, continuous barks, which made Frisky cringe in Anna's arms.

"Do oo havta do dat, Maggie?" Frisky asked. "Oo hurt ear!"

"So sorry, little one," Maggie apologized, nuzzling the kitten. "It's just that I'm so excited for everyone, but I'll stop now, okay?"

"Tank oo," said Frisky, much relieved until Anna, bubbling over with enthusiasm, began jumping up and down.

"Anna!" Mom cautioned when she heard Frisky's frenzied meows. "I know you're excited, but you're scaring your kitten half to death with all that hopping around."

Anna stopped immediately. "Oh, Frisky, I'm sorry," she said, stroking his fuzzy head to calm him down. "I didn't mean to upset you. You know I love you." Frisky purred his forgiveness.

***

"Oh, look, David!" Sarah exclaimed as they rounded the bend and the farmhouse came into full view. "We have a welcoming committee! They must have heard the car from quite a distance to know we were almost here." She rolled down the car window to wave back at them.

David saw the grandchildren and Kate, but his focus was on the house; towering oaks still majestically shaded its roof. Memories washed over him like a crashing wave. *This is the place. I wasn't mistaken. At least about that part.* David felt his hands begin to tremble. He gripped the steering wheel tighter to steady them. In brief moments, he would be hugging three of the most important people in the world, to him. *But where's Jim? I thought surely he would be here to greet us. Maybe it's all for the better. At least it gives me a little more time.* As they crept closer, David saw a beaming Kate signaling where he should park the car. He smiled, gave her a thumbs-up, and followed her direction.

"Oh, we're here!" Sarah said gleefully. "Here at last!" She flung open the passenger door the second David stopped the car. By the time David disengaged himself from the vehicle, Sarah was already hugging Kate and the kids and planting kisses all around. He hung back briefly to let her have her moment in the sun. There would be plenty of grandpa time in the days to come. *Grandpa time and more. I hope. I pray.*

CHAPTER 14

PINNED TO THE POST

Eric pulled slowly into the parking lot behind Smith & Sons Surveyors, examining the license plates of every vehicle there, hoping one would match the numbers on the slip of paper he held in his hand. His reward came quickly. "Ladies," Eric announced to the invisible Mrs. Reverend and Mrs. Scout, "we've hit pay dirt!"

"Pay dirt?" Mrs. Scout queried. "Whatever in the world is that?"

"I haven't a clue," Mrs. Reverend admitted, "but Eric sounds happy. Maybe the car is here."

Eric swung into an empty parking space. "This is the place where we'll find our man. Great detective work, ladies, if I may say so myself. Are you ready to roll?" Mrs. Reverend gave Eric one light peck on the shoulder, their signal for yes. "Good enough," Eric said. He grabbed the manila envelope containing both the map and the deed, exited the car, and held a back door open for the Old Ones, who hopped out and let him know they were in the clear. "The main entrance is around front," he explained. "I suppose you'd be more comfortable flying there than walking. I'll meet you there, okay?" He set off briskly, but the owl and hawk, swift of wing, beat him by a country mile.

As they waited patiently, Mrs. Scout remarked, "How I do like this young man, Eric. He's so kind and courteous."

"And complimentary," added Mrs. Reverend. "He had such nice things to say about our sleuthing skills."

"Yes, he did," said the hawk. "I do hope we will recognize the man in question. He entered and exited the building so fast."

"Have faith, my friend," the owl assured her. "We've come this far, haven't we?"

"We have," Mrs. Scout agreed, "but it's been a bumpy, exhausting ride. I'll be so glad when all this is behind us."

Eric took the stairs two at a time, and the three of them entered the building without incident. Eric approached the receptionist's desk. The middle-aged woman sitting behind it was on the phone, and merely nodded in his direction. There were many times Eric regretted not wearing his uniform and this was one of them; it never failed to garner immediate attention. Thankfully he had remembered to slip his badge into his pocket. Since he had no official appointment with the man in question, Eric felt this would get his foot in the door no matter what.

When the receptionist finally replaced the receiver on its hook, she regarded Eric dismissively over her reading glasses, her face stern and her eyes steely. "Do you have an appointment, sir?" she asked flatly.

"No, ma'am," Eric admitted, "but I'd like to speak with a Mr. Gary Burdette, please."

Her eyes narrowed and she glanced quickly at a large calendar spread across her imposing desk. "He's with a client," she said curtly.

Unruffled, Eric pulled his badge from his pocket and flipped it open in front of the rude woman's nose. "I'll wait," he said. With great satisfaction, Eric watched the receptionist's face drain of color as her eyes grew wide with fear. He noticed her hands were shaking as she reached for the inner-office intercom to contact Gary.

"What is it, Ruth?" a voice crackled in the speaker.

"Mr. Burdette, there is someone here to see you," Ruth told him with a quaver in her voice.

"Didn't I make it clear this morning that I was not to be interrupted today? I'm swamped with work! Have him or her make an appointment for tomorrow."

Ruth looked at Eric pleadingly. He simply mouthed the word, "Now!"

"I'm sorry, Mr. Burdette, but I think you need to see this person right away."

"Why?"

"It's the sheriff."

***

Elly roused from her nap, feeling ever so rested and more like her old self. As soon as she sat up, she spied the note beside her pillow. It read:

Hey, Beautiful!
Sorry I had to run out, but this has to do with helping the Old Ones. Hope you understand. Be back just as soon as I can.
Love, E.

Elly smiled as she read Eric's words over again. She thought about the Old Ones she had only learned about today, their mystical gift, and Reverend's promise. Elly touched her abdomen tenderly, tears welling in her eyes. "I miss you," she whispered longingly. "I miss you so much. I know you are safe with God, but I can't help wishing you were still safe here with me." Elly stood up slowly, reached for a tissue from a box on the bedside table, and wiped her eyes. "You may be right, Reverend," she said aloud between sniffles, "but it won't be soon. My heart is too broken to even think about it. Still, thank you for giving us hope."

***

Abby had never been so grateful for short hours that day at work. From the moment she'd taken her post at the cash register at nine, the stream of customers and curiosity seekers had been non-stop. All she could think about was being able to clock out at two and go home, far away from the circus she felt the NOC had become. When Zach arrived at work around ten, he noticed immediately that all this unwanted attention was taking a toll on her. He could tell Abby's smile was uncharacteristically forced, and her eyes were moist as if she was constantly on the verge of tears. "Brad!" Zach called to another employee, who was busy restocking some T-shirts, motioning for him to approach.

"Yes, sir, Mr. Jones," said Brad. "What can I do for you?"

"I need you to spell Abby for a few," Zach said. "She's having a rough time of it, after yesterday's news report. I'm going to take her back to the office and try to talk to her, give her some time to sort through her feelings before putting her back on the floor."

"Sure thing, Mr. Jones," Brad said. "Abby was sure in a bad state when she left here yesterday. I hope you can help."

"Me too," said Zach, giving Brad a friendly pat on the back. "Thanks, son."

Thirty minutes after having been relieved from her duty, Abby emerged from the office looking much calmer and steadier than she had all morning. Brad was genuinely impressed. "What did Mr. Jones say to you, Abby? You look like a whole different person," he said softly when she arrived at the cashiers' station.

Abby smiled at him, a real smile this time. "He said a lot of comforting things," she told him, "but the one thing that helped the most was reminding me that we work as a team here, and we're all here for each other, no matter what."

"That's the truth," Brad agreed. "If things get rough again today, Abby, don't hesitate to let me take over, y'hear?"

"Thank you, Brad," she said sincerely. "I won't hesitate in the least. You can count on it."

***

When they left Davy, Reverend and Sharp-eyes hastened to The Glade as fast as their weary wings would take them. They were much too fatigued to even consider instant transport, but knew that time spent in the Sanctuary would make them both good as new. Upon their arrival, Sharp-eyes, per Reverend's instructions, flew to the Bell of Meeting and rang it vigorously while Reverend took his place at the high table to await the influx of Old Ones into the Banquet Hall. He watched as they trickled in from their chambers or the kitchen and took their seats at the many long tables provided. Reverend was pleased to see that Wily, True Fox of the Old Ones, was already taking attendance, but wondered worriedly why Mrs. Reverend had not yet shown up to take her customary place by his side. Scout saw the look of confusion on the owl's face, and flew directly to his side.

"Your missus and mine are on a mission," Scout said, with a twinkle in his eye.

Reverend arched an eyebrow. "Are they, now? And what sort of mission might that be?"

"Helping Sheriff Eric finger the forger," he answered. "Racer and Mrs. Racer came to fetch them a while back. Hopefully they can identify the man in question as the one they saw both entering and exiting the building, on that most unfortunate day when I was laid low by a door."

"I'll agree," said Reverend, "that that was a tough day for us all. When I saw you crumpled in a helpless heap on the pavement, I prayed the Creator would give me the power to heal you."

"And He did," Scout said brightly.

Reverend smiled and gave the hawk a kindly pat on the shoulder. "So tell me," he continued, "was it the license plate info the ladies got that helped lead the sheriff to this particular individual?"

"Indeed," said Scout. "According to what Racer told me, this fellow has a previous conviction for forgery. Of course I doubt the chap would admit to any wrongdoing, but do you think this knowledge could help your plan succeed, Reverend?"

"It couldn't hurt," he said, "and as soon as everyone is gathered together, the plan is precisely what we will discuss."

***

Kate gave David and Sarah the grand tour of the farmhouse. They were appropriately awed by the gigantic stone fireplace and hearth, the antique bed in Jim and Kate's room, the huge, hand-hewn table in the kitchen, and the Civil War memorabilia in Anna's cozy loft space. "But Davy," Sarah said curiously, "you haven't shown us your bedroom. Where is it?"

"Come and see," Davy said with a grin. He proudly led the way out to the screened-in porch. He had been extra careful that morning to make his bed up neatly and tidy up his shelves. When David and Sarah saw Davy's military set up and the photo of his father, John, prominently displayed, they were deeply moved. Davy saw the tears welling in his grandmother's eyes and he reached for her hand. Giving it a gentle squeeze, he said softly, "Don't cry, Grandma. I miss Daddy, too, but I know he is in heaven. We'll all see him again one day."

Sarah had no words. She simply wrapped her arms tightly around Davy and held him close. Not one to be left out, Anna joined them, saying, "C'mon, Grandpa, c'mon, Mom, group hug! Group hug!"

David and Kate didn't hesitate a moment to answer Anna's invitation. As soon as the five were entangled in a giant cluster, Anna began to giggle. It was contagious. Before they knew it, they were all laughing together; deep, cleansing belly laughs to chase away the tears and renew their spirits. David was the first to depart the group. "I just thought of something, Sarah," he said. "We didn't get the surprises out of the trunk for Kate, Jim, and the kids. Davy, you want to help me with those?"

"Sure thing," he said enthusiastically.

"Can I come, too?" Anna asked. "I love surprises!"

"Of course you can, sweetie," David said, giving her braid a tug.

"That's what Jim does all the time," Anna observed, smiling up into her Grandpa's face as she took his hand in hers. David's heart melted at his granddaughter's spontaneous show of affection, and his green eyes, always bright, twinkled more merrily than usual. Anna cocked her head as she studied them, wondering if she had ever really noticed them before. After all, she hadn't seen Grandpa or Grandma since she was six, and that, for her, was a long, long time. "That's funny, Grandpa," she said. "Your eyes look just like Jim's, too."

***

While Don and Rupert were busy installing the air conditioning unit, Mike decided to brave the stuffy interior of the church to see if Rhonda Banks, the church custodian, had been by yet to clean after last Sunday's service. He doubted that she had, considering the uncomfortable temperature of the interior; he was right. The minute he opened the door, a suffocating wall of heat rudely greeted him, as did the narthex floor, littered with everything from dropped tissues to a pacifier and Valerie's abandoned kitten box. If this weren't enough, the wastebaskets were full to the brim, and the extra chairs set out for last week's service were still in the nave. Mike sighed at the chaos and felt beads of perspiration forming on his brow. He knew he had to air out the church the best he could in order to bring the temperature down. Mike propped open both front doors and made his sweaty way to the back of the church to open the side exit, through which Racer had purportedly escaped after his run-in with Pastor Williams. The very thought of the squirrel made Mike smile. While he hoped yesterday's mishap at the river hadn't put Racer in danger, Mike couldn't help feeling he was one fortunate man to have been in the presence of this Old One not just once, but twice.

"Good idea, Preacher," Tommy's voice boomed in the acoustically favorable church. "I'll get the windows open in the office and in the restrooms, and prop open those doors, too."

"Thanks, Tommy," said Mike as he headed back up the side aisle. "While you're doing that, I'm going to try to clean this place up a bit to make Rhonda's job a bit easier."

"You might think about cleaning it up a lot," Tommy remarked. "My Valerie told me just this morning that Rhonda's down with a stomach bug. She usually comes on Thursdays to do some cleaning for us. Guess we won't be seeing her tomorrow."

Mike groaned. This was not the way he wished to spend his afternoon, but since he was already here, he decided to endure the heat and get it over with. He headed first for one of the trash cans, grateful to feel a soothing breeze blowing from the open doors.

"Oh, and one more thing before I forget, Preacher," said Tommy as he kicked a wooden wedge underneath the door to the men's restroom. "Valerie told me to ask you who that sweet young gal is, the one who was with you in that photo they aired last night. Mind telling?"

"Not at all," a voice sounded in the doorway, a voice as sweet as heavenly music to Mike's ears. "My name is Abby."

***

"Hello?" Bob answered the phone.

"Hi, Bob, it's Kate. David and Sarah are here, and I wondered if you and Susie would like to come over sometime this afternoon to meet your new houseguests."

"We'd love to," Bob confirmed. "Susie's outside doing some painting, right now. I don't know if she's at a stopping point yet, but I'll go check with her."

"Tell her not to rush," Kate said. "Anytime you want to drop in is just fine."

Bob and Kate exchanged good-byes, and he strode out of the house and over to where Susie was sitting in the shade with her easel, canvas, and paints. She was so focused on her work that she didn't see him approaching until he was within two steps of her. "Lord, Bob!" Susie gasped, almost dropping her brush. "Don't sneak up on me like that!"

"I'm sorry, dear," he said sincerely. "I knew you were concentrating, but I didn't realize how much."

"It's okay, honey," Susie assured him. "I know you didn't mean to scare me. What brings you out here?"

"Kate called, and said David and Sarah have arrived," Bob said. "She invited us to come over anytime this afternoon to meet them. Since you're busy with painting at the moment, I'll leave the time we go up to you."

"I'd really like to keep at this for a while," Susie told him. "Since you're here, why don't you take a peek?"

This last remark took Bob by surprise. Susie almost never showed him a painting or drawing until she was completely finished with it, down to the last detail. He was delighted to be privy to her work in progress. Walking around to Susie's side of the canvas, Bob expected to see a fledgling replica of the meadow and mountain vista, which spread before them, but the painting that greeted him filled him with greater delight than any scenery ever could have. "It's Davy and Anna!" Bob exclaimed. Susie was creating the portraits of their adopted grandchildren from a photograph she had tacked to the corner of her canvas. "You're capturing them perfectly, Susie! Is it a gift for Jim and Kate?"

"A Christmas gift," Susie confirmed. "I'm so glad you like it, Bob. I'm doing my level best to capture their personalities here, not just their looks."

"And you're doing very well at both," Bob affirmed, "but may I make a small suggestion?"

Susie was taken aback as Bob, who had no artistic talent whatsoever outside of woodworking, never trusted himself to offer any critique at all. "Yes, go ahead," she said tentatively, wondering what Bob would say.

Bob grinned broadly and said, "Include Racer."

***

When David opened the trunk of the rental car, Davy and Anna immediately saw the child-sized garden tools; there hadn't been a bag large enough to contain them. They were beside themselves with excitement. "Davy, this is just what we wanted!" Anna squealed as she grabbed a hoe.

Davy retrieved a rake, a shovel, and a second hoe. "Grandpa, these are great! Mom must have told you we need these to help Jim and Bampa in the garden."

"Bampa?" David asked with a puzzled look on his face. "Who is Bampa?"

Davy's cheeks flushed crimson. He had assumed, mistakenly he now realized, that his mom had told his real grandparents about their recently adopted ones. Would Grandpa and Grandma be jealous of the Fairchilds? Would their feelings be hurt? Davy cringed inside at the mere thought of causing his grandparents any grief or disappointment. He was just opening his mouth to try and explain when Anna delivered the blow for him. "Bampa and Nana are Mr. and Mrs. Fairchild, Grandpa, the people right down the road that you're staying with while you're here. When Davy didn't know when we would ever get to see you and Grandma again, we asked if we could adopt them as grandparents. Is that okay?"

David looked first at Anna and then at Davy. The boy, so worried about his grandfather's reaction to this news, saw only his solemn expression, not the gleam in his eyes. "Well, children," David said thoughtfully, "this certainly is news to me. But you know what?" Here David bent down and gathered his grandchildren in his arms. "It's great news! As far as I'm concerned, a child can't have enough grandparents."

"Really?" Davy asked as a wave of relief washed over him. "Then you're not upset about it?"

"Upset?" David countered. "Why should I be? If Anna and you think so highly of Mr. and Mrs. Fairchild that you wanted to adopt them as grandparents, they must be fine people indeed. How lucky your grandma and I are to be staying with them and getting to know them better."

"Oh, you'll love them, Grandpa, I just know it," Anna said confidently.

"I'm sure I will, honey," said David. "I'm sure I will."

***

The moment Gary Burdette appeared in the waiting area of Smith & Sons, Mrs. Reverend was certain it was the man they had seen days ago, but Mrs. Scout wasn't convinced. "I don't know if this is the same fellow we saw," she told the owl. "Somehow he looks different to me, but I can't figure out why."

"Wasn't he wearing glasses that day?" Mrs. Reverend said. "He doesn't have them on now. Maybe that's confusing you."

But Eric was, perhaps, the most confused. As he shook hands with Gary and introduced himself, he was puzzled when no poke from a beak was forthcoming to indicate Gary was the one. *Do we have the wrong guy? If so, this will be a colossal waste of our time.* Eric and his invisible companions followed Gary down the hall to his office, which Eric noted was lavishly decorated with Victorian-style furnishings and drapes. Gary motioned to a chair facing his sprawling desk. "Have a seat, Sheriff," he said. "Make yourself comfortable." Eric did so as Gary walked around his desk and sat in his own chair. "Now," he said, folding his hands on top of the desk, which Eric observed was impeccably neat for a man who claimed just moments ago to be swamped with work, "how can I be of service to you today?"

Still uncertain as to the verdict of identity, Eric plunged in anyway. He reached into the manila envelope and removed the altered survey map that had been created in this very establishment. Unfolding it, he handed it to Gary and said, "This is a map of property owned by a friend of mine," he said. "As you can see, someone at Smith & Sons is responsible for drawing it. Does it look familiar to you?"

Gary took the map and fumbled for something in his desk drawer. Mrs. Reverend and Mrs. Scout hopped up onto the edge of the desk's broad surface to secure a better vantage point. They saw Gary pull a small case from the drawer and open it. "Glasses!" they cried in unison. The instant he put them on, all doubt vanished. Mrs. Scout hastened to drop to the floor and give Eric the confirmation he had been hoping for. Eric nodded imperceptibly in the hawk's general direction, and then turned his full attention to Gary, watching closely as the man perused the map meticulously. If looking at it made him nervous in the least, Eric couldn't tell. Gary was a cool as a cucumber.

"This was, of course, drawn up in this office," Gary admitted as he pushed the map across the desk toward Eric, "but it's not one I worked on personally. Why is this of any importance?"

151

Eric produced the original map from the folder. "This is the map my friend's family has had for years. It, too, as you can see, originated in this office. Would you mind comparing the two for me?"

Gary studied them both for several minutes before he spoke. "Yes, I see the difference," he stated, holding up what Eric knew to be the bogus map. "This one reflects the decision of an owner to sell off some of his property. He must have wanted the survey altered to reflect that move."

"And that's what I'm having a hard time understanding," said Eric. "This is land that belonged to my friend's grandfather, and was passed down to his family after the elder gentleman passed away. Knowing his grandfather's character as he did, my friend swears he would never have sold a square inch of the property to anyone, no matter how high the offer was. So how do we reconcile the two, Mr. Burdette?"

"We don't," Gary replied. "The altered map could have been drawn up with the intention of sale, which was never consummated. It has to be backed up by a deed. Is there a deed involved, Sheriff?"

"So glad you asked," Eric replied as he reached back into the envelope to produce the one piece of evidence he hoped would pin Gary to the post. "If you would be so kind as to look this over for me, I'd appreciate it."

Gary accepted the paper from Eric and there were actually the beginnings of a friendly smile on his face. He unfolded it carefully, adjusting his glasses as he did so. The smile vanished. His complexion paled and his hands trembled. Eric knew it was time to go for the jugular. "Mr. Burdette," he began in a steady but serious tone, "there are several things you should know at this point. I have evidence that on the date Mr. Hunter purportedly signed this document and had it notarized, he was nowhere near Bryson City. Additionally, I am aware of your previous conviction for forgery. If my suspicions prove true, which I have no doubt they will, you are headed for a world of hurt." Eric stood up abruptly, collecting the deed and the maps before leaning his towering frame intimidatingly over the desk to look Gary straight in the eye. "Thank you for your time, Mr. Burdette. You've been most helpful. Have a great day, now, y'hear?"

CHAPTER 15

A JOYOUS OCCASION

Bob and Susie strolled down to the Hunter's farmhouse around three thirty that bright and sunny afternoon. Noting that Jim's truck was missing in action, Bob commented, "I'm taking that as a good sign, Susie. If I'm right about where Jim is, the longer he stays gone, the better."

"I agree," she said. "Now remember, Bob, loose lips sink ships. Let's not share any news not ready for the telling."

"My lips are sealed," Bob assured her as they approached the kitchen door and knocked.

Kate looked up from the table where she was sitting with Anna and Sarah. Anna was showing her grandmother all her latest drawings, and was basking in the generous praise Grandma offered. "Come in, it's open," Kate said as she stood to greet the Fairchilds. Sarah stood as well, anxious to meet the people gracious enough to open their home to her and David for two weeks.

"You must be Sarah," Susie said delightedly as she gave Sarah's hand a hearty shake. "Welcome to the lower forty-eight!"

Sarah laughed at this and said, "It's wonderful to be here, and to finally meet you in person. I've heard nothing but glowing reports from Kate about her neighbors. I'm glad you are here for Kate and Jim and the kids."

"The pleasure is all ours," Susie said warmly.

It was Bob's turn to shake hands with Sarah. "How was your trip?" he asked.

"Long, but uneventful," she answered. "Getting over the jet lag was the most difficult aspect of it, but we've finally recovered. Thank you so much for offering to put us up, Susie and Bob. Are you sure it isn't too much trouble?"

"No trouble at all!" Bob insisted. Looking around, he asked, "Where are David and Davy?"

Kate grinned ear to ear. "Out in the garden," she said. "Come see what David and Sarah brought for us." Kate led the way through the side room and out to the porch with everyone traipsing merrily behind her. "David!" she called as she opened the screen door. "Bob and Susie are here!"

When Bob caught a glimpse of the colorful flowers and saw Davy using his new garden tools to help with the planting, his pleasure knew no bounds. "Looks like you're going to turn into a real gardener after all, Davy," he declared as he trotted toward David and met him halfway. "Bob Fairchild," he unnecessarily introduced himself as the men shook hands. "I'm guessing you not only brought the flowers, but the children's garden tools, too. Boy, is that something they needed! Davy has really taken a liking to playing in the dirt."

"And you've taught him well," David said sincerely. "He's already shown me a thing or two; I'm not the green-thumb type. I have to say, you've planted a magnificent garden here, Bob. I feel good knowing my family is eating healthy this summer."

Bob chuckled. "I think they eat healthy all year 'round, David," he said. "Kate sees to that!"

"What is it I see to?" Kate asked as the group approached.

"A healthy, nutritious diet for the family," Bob answered. In an aside to David, he added, "Though we do manage to give the kids an occasional soda."

David smiled broadly. "Isn't that what grandparents are supposed to do? Spoil the kids and then send them back to mom and dad?"

"Aha! I see you know we aren't just Bob and Susie, but Bampa and Nana, too," Bob remarked.

"That I do," David confirmed. "I told Davy and Anna today that children can't have too many grandparents. Don't you agree, Bob?"

"Amen to that!"

As the adults continued chatting, Anna ran over to where Davy was industriously digging another hole in the soft, yielding soil in which to place the next flowering plant. "Can I help, too?" she inquired.

"Of course you can, Anna," said Davy as he wiped perspiration from his forehead. "These tools are not just for me, they're for both of us." He handed his sister the shovel he had been using. "See if you can dig another hole while I put the plant in this one."

Anna happily took the shovel and began digging in the spot Davy pointed out to her. It was harder than she thought, but she was determined to keep at it. She certainly didn't want Grandpa and Grandma to think she didn't appreciate the new tools. As she plugged away, Anna thought she heard a car honking faintly in the distance. It struck her as odd. When they lived in the city, a tooting horn was nothing out of the ordinary. But out in the country where most days the only sounds were birdsong and the whispering wind, the noise, incessant and repeated, seemed highly unusual. "Do you hear that, Davy?" Anna asked.

"Hear what?" Davy asked, as he tamped the soil firmly around the base of the plant.

"A car horn," she said. "I think it's getting louder."

Davy stood up and cupped a hand around one ear. Immediately he heard a faint but raucous chorus of honks, drawing nearer and nearer. Now it seemed the adults, too, had heard the unusual racket and were conferring amongst themselves as to who could be creating such a ruckus. Davy and Anna left their planting to join them.

"It certainly is getting louder," Bob observed. "I think this someone is coming down our road, actually."

"By the sound of it, I think you're right, Bob," Kate said, her brow puckered with worry. Who in the world could it be, I wonder?"

"Maybe the horn has a short in it," Sarah suggested.

"Or maybe someone just likes to toot his own horn," David said, grinning. All the adults laughed at this remark, but it left Davy and Anna scratching their heads.

"Whatever the reason," said Susie, "it's certainly grabbed our attention, hasn't it? I can't wait to see who's behind this."

Davy had a thought he knew was probably off base, but he decided to give it a shot. "Mom, do you think it could be Jim making all that noise?"

Mom regarded him as if he had suddenly grown an eye in the middle of his forehead. "Davy," she said sternly, "have you ever known your step-father to act so rashly? Really! I'm surprised at you."

Davy had seen Jim act rashly when he confronted Ronnie at the work site and in the restaurant, but he decided this was not the time to bring those incidents up. Instead, he simply said, "Sorry, Mom," and continued to listen to the horn blasts, which were most definitely getting closer by the moment.

"I have an idea," said Bob. "Let's go around to the other side of the house, where there is a better view of the road. At least we'll know who it is the moment they come around the bend." Everyone assented to this idea and followed Bob quickly, the horn blasting vociferously and more frequently with every step they took. They had just taken up the same positions where Kate, Davy, and Anna had stood earlier that afternoon in anticipation of the Murrays' arrival when Davy caught the merest glimpse of the approaching vehicle through the trees. He saw a flash of chrome, far above the last curve in the road where all would at last be revealed. His breath caught in his throat. The color he barely saw was the same as that of Jim's truck. *Was I right all along? Could it possibly be?*

Davy felt a tug on his shirt. It was Anna. She had heard him catch his breath and knew something was up. "It *is* Jim, isn't it?" she whispered in his ear. Davy nodded, but didn't utter a word. Jim's truck would be barreling around the corner soon enough, and the truth of the matter would divulge itself.

***

"So that, my dear Old Ones, is the plan we must follow to the letter on Friday," Reverend stated. "Are there any questions?" Racer's paw shot up. "Yes, Racer," the owl acknowledged him.

"Are you absolutely, positively sure about our needing to rest up all day Thursday to be able to pull off this stunt?" Racer asked. "I'm sure going to miss seeing Davy, if that's the case."

"I know you will miss him," Reverend answered sympathetically, "but I've already informed the boy and he is taking it in stride. He, too, realizes sacrifices must be made at a time like this."

Smokey's paw was next. "Reverend, I just want to say that I commend your plan. Although there is risk involved, a big risk at that, I do think it's our only hope if we wish to save our hallowed ground."

"Hear! Hear!" The shouts arose from every Old One in the cavernous room.

"Then there's just one more detail to be settled," said Reverend. "Should the plan change in any way that Jim and the sheriff would need to be notified of, I must know who amongst you has spent the most time in our Sanctuary since the Great Healing occurred. Wily, if you will kindly take a poll while we are all gathered here, I'm sure Mrs. Hopper, Mrs. Racer, and Mrs. Silky will be happy to round up some refreshments for us all."

A great cheer went up at the prospect of wondrous food and drink being served. It had been a long, though productive, afternoon and everyone was ready for a respite from talking about the serious endeavor that lay ahead. Reverend left the high table to join the throng below. He, too, needed this time to place cares and concerns aside and simply make merry with his friends. "A glass of mead, my dear," he said jovially to Mrs. Racer as she hurried past him. "That should work like a tonic."

***

"Abby! What are you doing here?" Mike asked, simultaneously surprised and delighted. "I thought you had to work."

"I got off at two," she explained. "I was driving home and noticed your car was parked at the church, so I thought I'd drop in to see what was going on. My goodness! It's an oven in here!"

"That's why the heating and air guys are here," said Tommy, striding boldly over to Abby to introduce himself. "Name's Tommy Green. My wife and I saw you on television last night with the Mad Squirrel. I'll be the first to admit my Valerie is a nosy one, so forgive me inquiring about you to the preacher here. She'll be so happy to find out I actually got to meet you."

"No doubt," Mike remarked, hoping his tone didn't sound sarcastic as he walked over to join Abby. He fixed Tommy with a steady gaze. "Tell Valerie that Abby and I are friends, very new friends. She is, along with her parents, looking to join our church."

"Well, I'll be doggone!" Tommy exclaimed. "Ain't that exciting! The more the merrier, that's what I say. Will you be here this Sunday?"

"I wouldn't miss it for the world," Abby declared, glancing at Mike and shining her winning smile his way.

"Good then," said Tommy. "Valerie will be pleased as punch to meet you, that's a fact."

"I look forward to meeting her, too," said Abby graciously.

"Well then, Preacher," Tommy said, "we best get back to work if we want to have this place looking worthy on Sunday."

Abby was puzzled by Tommy's comment. "Don't you have someone who cleans the church for you, Mike?" she asked.

"Yes, we do," he told her, "but Tommy informed me she's fallen ill this week, so we're taking it upon ourselves to get it done. Might as well do it now, as we have to wait on the technicians to complete their job."

"Oh, do let me stay and help!" Abby exclaimed. "The job will go a lot quicker with a third pair of hands."

Mike was genuinely touched. "Are you sure you want to help out in this miserable heat, Abby? Neither of us would blame you one bit if you'd rather head for home."

"Yes, I'm sure," she said. "I want to stay."

"Speaking of staying," Tommy remarked, "all those extra chairs? I think they need to stay, too. Why, after all the added notoriety this week, I think we could be in for another record breaking crowd. That would be good news for the bishop, wouldn't it, Preacher?"

Mike couldn't help but smile. *Thank you, Racer. Thank you.*

***

Eric exited Smith & Sons as swiftly as possible, with Mrs. Reverend and Mrs. Scout right behind him. He maintained a stoic demeanor until he reached his car. He then squatted down beside the driver's side door and addressed the owl and the hawk with a broad smile spread across his face. "Are you right in front of me, ladies?" Eric asked. In answer, he felt a gentle breeze generated by their wings upon his face. "Good! You have done a marvelous job, one that I think will go far in stopping these underhanded crooks and saving your home. Tell Reverend that Elly and I will be

158

praying for you all, and assure him I will help in any way I can. Just contact Davy or Jim if you need me. Oh, and before I forget, thank you for the tea. I'm looking forward to trying it tomorrow with Elly. Do you need me to drive you back to the Hunters' in order to get home?" Two gentle pecks told him no. "Okay, then I guess this is farewell, for now. Thanks again for everything." Before he could stand up, Eric felt the oddest yet most comforting sensation he had ever experienced. It didn't take him a second to realize he was caught in a warm, feathery embrace. *The wings of angels. You've been my angels today.*

***

Ronnie was snoozing on the sofa when his cell phone jolted him awake. "Hello?" he answered groggily. Ronnie recognized the agitated caller as Cyrus Smith; he was talking so fast that Ronnie, barely coherent, couldn't understand a word he was saying. "Slow down, man, slow down!" Ronnie bellowed into the receiver. "I just woke up, and I can't follow anything you're jabbering about. Start over again, will you, Cy?"

Ronnie heard a hefty sigh on the other end of the line as Cy got hold of himself before speaking, this time in a measured tone which likely took great effort to maintain. "Sheriff Peabody was here today," he said, his voice tremulous. "He had both maps and the deed to the Hunter place with him. He strongly suspects that Mr. Hunter's signature is not authentic."

"What do you mean, not authentic?" Ronnie spluttered in frustration. "How could he have any evidence that it isn't? You got some kinda mole working for you?"

"I assure you, Mr. Carson, there are no moles here," Cy replied icily. "They know all too well what side their bread is buttered on. Somehow Peabody knew to corner Gary Burdette, my son-in-law, and was fully aware he had a past conviction for forgery. Needless to say, Gary is a basket case. He's convinced Peabody won't stop investigating until he digs out the truth, and we both know what that is."

"Sheriff Busybody can pry and poke and bluff all he wants," Ronnie declared arrogantly. "Our case is solid as a rock, and you know it. I don't know how he guessed when it came to Gary's past, but unless Gary acts the fool and confesses, how can the accusation possibly hold any water?"

"I don't know," Cy confessed morosely. "But I feel certain someone tipped Peabody off. How else could this unfortunate turn of events be explained?"

"Unfortunate or not," said Ronnie, "it would take months, maybe even years, to dig up enough evidence to prove anything against any of us. By that time, my cabins will be up and running. In fact, we resume work Friday morning."

"That soon?" Cy was incredulous. "Shouldn't you let the dust settle just a bit before leaping headlong into this project?"

"I've waited long enough!" Ronnie fumed. "I ain't waiting any longer. No one and nothing is going to thwart me this time, y'hear? And tell Gary to untwist his shorts and quit worrying about something that ain't gonna happen."

***

As he rounded the last bend, Jim was elated to see that his horn alarm had definitely had the desired effect. The family, gathered outside, was waiting anxiously to see who the maniacal driver with a penchant for laying on the horn could possibly be. *And if I know them like I do, the last person they suspect is me!* Jim bowled down the long drive toward home as fast as he dared, beeping all the way, grinning ear to ear when he saw the startled looks on everyone's face. He had them exactly where he wanted them. Jim swung the truck wildly into his parking spot and slammed on the brakes, which squealed in protest. As he leaped out of the cab and sprinted toward the bewildered group, Davy noticed Jim was carrying papers in his hand and waving them jubilantly above his head as if they were first prize ribbons.

When he reached them, Jim scooped Kate up in his arms and whirled her around and around, laughing the entire time. "Jim, have you lost your mind?" Kate asked, embarrassed by his brazen show of affection in front of in-laws, to whom he had yet to be introduced. "Put me down before you hurt your back again!"

"Not before I do this," he said, planting an ardent kiss on her lips. Then seeing the stunned looks of David and Sarah, who were standing with the Fairchilds, Jim recovered his manners. "It's wonderful to finally

160

meet you!" he said enthusiastically, as he shook David's hand and gave Sarah a hug. "You've made it just in time to hear the fantastic news!"

"What news could possibly be so fantastic that you honked the horn all the way down our road?" Kate wondered.

"This," said Jim, handing her the papers he had been holding. "You need to be the first to know."

Kate took the papers tentatively from him. As she began to read, Davy noted his mother's expression transforming little by little from one of concern to one of sheer joy. "Oh, Jim, I can hardly believe it," she said as she looked lovingly into his eyes. "You did this for us; for all of us."

"Did what? Did what?" Davy and Anna chanted impatiently as they crowded close to their mother and Jim. The adults wanted to do the same, but refrained. Bob took Susie's hand in his and gave it a knowing squeeze.

"You tell them, honey," Kate said, barely able to contain her own impulse to break the momentous news.

"If you insist," Jim said, squatting down in front of the children and taking their hands in his. "Davy, Anna, I have to ask you something, and I expect an honest answer."

"Okay," they responded, momentarily confused by Jim's request.

Jim cleared his throat, and looking from one to the other, asked, "Are you looking forward to our move back to Atlanta at the end of the summer?"

Both shook their heads and frowned. . Davy said, "How could you think we would ever want to go back? I don't want to leave the Old Ones, ever!"

"What if I told you didn't have to?" Jim asked, smiling warmly. "What if I told you we can stay here for as long as we want?"

"Are you serious?" Davy was astonished. "How is that possible? What about your job? What about Mom's?"

Jim showed the children the piece of paper with the heading *Nantahala High School*. "I have a job," he said brightly. "Say hello to the new JROTC instructor!" Anna squealed, Davy cheered, and they both rushed Jim to hug him, knocking him off balance so that all three landed in a celebratory heap on the grass.

"Oh, this is a joyous occasion, indeed!" Susie exclaimed as she embraced Kate.

"It's an answer to prayer!" Bob declared as he helped Jim and the children to their feet.

Suddenly, Davy had an unsettling thought. "But Jim," he said, "what about Mom? Will she have to find a job here, too?"

Jim grinned and rubbed Davy's close-cropped hair. "Only if she wants to," he said. "Since we're not paying rent here, there really isn't any need for the extra income. Maybe your mother would prefer to just stay home with you and be, well, a mom for a change."

At this remark, Anna threw her arms around her mother's waist and hugged her tightly. "Stay at home, please, Mom?" she begged. "I love having you around all the time."

Mom stroked the top of Anna's head affectionately. "And I love being around you two all the time," she said. *And this little one coming along will need me around all the time, too.* "Susie, could I borrow your computer tomorrow to write my resignation letter to Winston High?"

"Of course, Kate," Susie said.

"And Kate," said Jim with a wink in her direction, "while you're at it, will you write mine, too?"

Kate reached for Jim's hand and pulled him close. "Anything for you, honey," she whispered in his ear. "I love you."

CHAPTER 16

A LOT TO CELEBRATE

Mrs. Reverend and Mrs. Scout arrived at The Glade just as the first round of refreshments was being served. Spying Reverend and Scout together at the table with Sharp-eyes and Mrs. Sharp-eyes, the owl and hawk lost no time in swooping toward them for a grateful reunion. "We have news!" Mrs. Reverend exclaimed as she threw her wings around Reverend. "Glorious news!"

"By all means, my dear, do share with us," said Reverend eagerly. "If it changes our plans in the least, we must notify Davy and Jim at once."

Mrs. Reverend and Mrs. Sharp-eyes recounted in tandem the events of the day and the success of their mission with Sheriff Peabody. "Oh, you should have seen the look on Gary's face when he saw our Will's signature that he'd forged!" Mrs. Sharp-eyes said gleefully. "There was not a shred of doubt in my mind that he was guilty of this misdeed."

"Nor in mine," Mrs. Reverend said. "I wish you all could have been there to witness how masterfully our dear Eric cinched the figurative noose around Gary's unsuspecting neck. I'm sure this unforeseen turn of events elicited some alarm among the ranks of those at Smith & Sons."

"One can only hope," said Scout. "They deserve a bit of a scare after the stunts they've pulled."

Reverend took a sip of his mead and said, "I do believe this is another feather in our cap as we confront Ronnie on Friday. Wily," he called to the fox who was winding up his tally of recent rest hours for the Old Ones. "Have you completed the task at hand?"

Wily promptly trotted over to the owl. "Just now completed, my friend," he said.

"And who, then, among us is able to serve as an envoy to Davy this evening?" Reverend asked.

Wily grinned and gave the owl a salute. "You're looking at him," he said, unable to keep a note of pride from creeping into his voice. "Oh, and the missus qualifies, too," he added. "We would be most honored to serve on this mission."

"Splendid!" Reverend declared. "Mrs. Reverend and Mrs. Scout, would you follow Wily over to where he was seated with Mrs. Wily and fill them both in on the new developments?"

"Certainly," they answered, and followed Wily promptly.

***

The moment he heard Jim's marvelous news, Davy's first impulse was to tell Racer. It made him sad to think he would have to wait until Friday to see his dear friend, and he hoped with all his heart that there had been a change in Reverend's plan that would grace him with a visit from the Old Ones strong and rested enough to be able to leave The Glade. Davy found consolation in hugging Maggie and whispering to her, "Did you understand what Jim said, girl?" She whined and pawed the ground, a sign Davy took to mean she needed an explanation from him. "We don't have to go back to Atlanta when summer's over. Jim found a job right here. That means you and I can be together forever and ever!" Overjoyed, Maggie let out a tremendous woof and bathed Davy's face with grateful kisses.

Seeing this, Mom laughed and said, "Maggie is sure happy about something, Davy. What do you suppose it is?"

"I told her Jim's news," he answered, continuing to submit to the dog's unbridled affections.

"Davy," Sarah said apprehensively, "you mean to tell us Maggie understands what you say to her?"

"She does, Grandma," Davy affirmed. "She's one smart dog."

David had a question, too. "Davy, a few minutes ago you said something about not wanting to leave the Old Ones. Were you referring to Maggie?"

164

Before Davy could answer, Jim intervened. "Man, it sure is getting hot standing out here! Why don't we all go into the house for some refreshments and cool air?"

"I second that," said Bob. "And don't you think this amazing news calls for a celebration, Jim?

"You know it does!" Jim declared as he put his arm around Kate and began walking toward the house. Everyone followed suit, with Davy and Anna walking hand-in-hand with Grandpa and Grandma. Davy wondered why Jim had interrupted his impending answer to Grandpa's question about the Old Ones. *Does Jim think I shouldn't tell them about my friends? Why would he act like that? Is it because he's just met them and isn't sure how they'll react? I want to tell Grandpa and Grandma all about Racer and everyone else in The Glade. I'll ask Jim first chance I get. I have to talk to him about the plan anyway. Right now, that's the most important thing.*

***

When Eric pulled up into his driveway, he saw Elly, pen and paper in hand, walking around on the porch. "What are you doing, Elly?" Eric called to her as he got out of the car.

"I'm making a list for thank you notes," she informed him. "I want to be sure I don't leave anyone out."

Eric joined Elly on the porch and greeted her with a hug. "With all these gifts," he said, holding her close to his chest, "you'll be busy for days to come."

"And that's exactly what I need right now," Elly said as she pulled away from him just enough so she could look him in the face. "But more than staying busy, Eric, I need you."

"You've got me, you know that," he assured her as he planted a kiss on her forehead. "Did it upset you that I took off this afternoon?"

"A little," Elly confessed, "but when you explained in your note that the Old Ones needed your help, I completely understood. It's just that when I woke from my nap, this house, which always seemed comforting and cozy even on the days when you were working and I was here by myself, felt cold and empty as if it knows how I feel inside."

At this, Elly dissolved into tears. Eric held her in his arms, feeling her body shake with each heart-wrenching sob, struggling to give her comfort as he, too, was hit by a fresh wave of grief. He squeezed his eyelids tightly shut, as though he could will the floodgates to remain closed, but to no avail. *Oh, Lord, I hurt for Elly. I hurt for us. I hurt for the little one. Help us, Father, help us.*

***

By the time Mike, Abby, and Tommy finished cleaning and straightening the church, the first welcome breath of chilled air from the new unit arose from the vents. "Time to close the doors and windows, Pastor," Don announced as he entered the narthex with Rupert, bill in hand. Both stopped dead in their tracks when they saw the now disheveled, perspiring threesome. "Don't tell me y'all been workin' in this heat!" Don exclaimed. "You coulda passed out!"

"Well, we didn't," said Mike a bit gruffly, mopping his brow with a paper towel. He removed his glasses to clean them on a dry end of his shirttail, which was harder to find than one might think. Abby and Tommy were just as drenched in sweat, and Abby's ponytail sported plentiful wisps of rebellious hair. "I'll get the back door," Mike said. After putting his glasses back on, he continued, "Tommy, if you get the windows and Abby shuts these front doors, we'll be good to go." Everyone hastened to close up the church as fast as possible, not wishing to waste one more moment in allowing the air conditioner to restore the interior to normalcy. When they regrouped in the narthex, Tommy went into the modest office and produced the church's checkbook from the safe. Don handed him the bill. Settling his reading glasses on his nose, Tommy perused it carefully. "Seems to be right there in the ballpark you quoted," he said with satisfaction as he handed the bill to Mike.

"Y'know, Pastor, that bill could go lots lower if you take me up on that offer," said Rupert, an expectant look on his face.

Mike grinned and said, "Sorry, Rupert. I think we're going to have to bite the bullet for the full amount." He passed the bill back to Tommy so he could cut the check. "You see, I have no control over this particular squirrel, so I can't make you a promise like that. But who knows? If you

166

keep your eyes and your heart open, one day, you just might see him for yourself."

"Wouldn't that be sumthin'!" Rupert said in genuine awe. "Tell you what, Pastor, if you see this here squirrel again, would you put in a good word for me?"

"Will do," said Mike congenially. "Now that's a promise I can keep!"

***

While Bob retreated to his house to retrieve a bottle of wine to toast Jim's new job, everyone else took a seat at the sprawling kitchen table with glasses of water or lemonade to quench their thirst. Jim intentionally sat right across from the Murrays; he was feeling a bit self-conscious about his initial introduction. He knew that though they would try their level best to conceal it, David and Sarah would be comparing him to John in everything he said and did over the two weeks of their stay. Jim didn't blame them for this, but it didn't set well with him. They loved Kate and the kids dearly, and the last thing Jim wanted was for them to think he was unworthy of any of them. He cleared his throat nervously and said, "David, Sarah, I think I may have caused things to get off on the wrong foot back there. By the looks on your faces, I could tell you were not expecting such craziness from me, and I apologize. It's just that I…"

Sarah reached out to touch Jim's hand. There was an unmistakably amiable smile on her face. "Don't apologize, Jim," she said. "There's no need to. Kate has told us from the moment she arrived here how much she hoped you all could stay and never have to go back to Atlanta. Just seeing how excited everyone is warms my heart."

"Mine, too," David admitted. He was smiling and regarding Jim in a way which made him feel suddenly comfortable, almost like he was in the presence of a long lost friend. "Although I do have to say," David added with a chuckle, "your behavior came as quite the surprise. I haven't been that entertained in I don't know when."

At his words, Jim visibly relaxed. He sensed they truly wanted to get to know him for who he was. He felt the same toward them, though he couldn't quite put his finger on the why of it all. Still, it was a comforting feeling, and Jim was cheered by it. "I don't know if you'll see another such display of abandon from me during your visit," he said as Kate took her seat next to him, "and I'm willing to bet you're relieved by that. Kate here will tell you I'm usually a pretty practical, level-headed guy."

"She already has, Jim," Sarah assured him. "And we know, too, you're a man who loves her with all his heart. We love Kate like a daughter. All we want is for her to be happy."

"And taken good care of," David said. "Seems to me, Jim, you're doing both exceedingly well."

Jim blushed and fumbled for Kate's hand. "I try," he said, "and I'll keep trying as long as I live."

"That's the spirit!" David exclaimed. "Well, well, look who's returned with the wine. Uncork that bottle, Bob. We have a lot to celebrate today!"

***

While the adults sat around the livliest of tables that afternoon, Davy and Anna quietly asked to be excused and retreated to the porch with Maggie and Frisky. "Let's take Maggie and Frisky outside," Davy suggested.

Maggie yawned. "I'm too tired, Davy," she said. "I think a little nap is in order after all this excitement."

"Old Ones!" Davy shouted joyfully.

"At your service," said Wily as he appeared at the screen door, accompanied by Mrs. Wily. "May we join you, Davy? We bring news."

"Of course! Come in! Come in!" Davy flung the door wide and the two elegant foxes with their ruddy red fur, brilliantly white chests, and ebony leggings trotted inside and lovingly began licking the boy's hands in greeting.

"Who's here?" Anna asked impatiently. "Which Old Ones are here?"

"Wily and Mrs. Wily," Davy responded as he squatted down on the floor to give each fox a hug.

"Hi, Wily and Mrs. Wily!" Anna greeted them. "Oh, how I wish I could see and hear you!"

"How I wish you could, too, my sweet child," said Mrs. Wily. "What a joy it was to spend time with you at the feast!"

"My dear," Wily reminded her, "we can't risk the energy it takes to become visible right now. We have used up enough simply coming here. Davy, have you spoken with Jim yet?"

"Not yet," Davy answered. "It's been a busy day and I haven't had time to pull him aside."

Wily looked serious. "Promise me you will, the moment we leave. It is urgent that he be prepared for Friday."

"Yes, I promise," Davy said, sobered by the tone in the fox's voice.

"There's a good lad," Wily said. "Now if you'll fetch the notes you took from Reverend, Mrs. Wily and I will give you some fresh details to share with Jim."

Davy promptly obeyed and began scribbling down every detail relayed to him by the foxes. Curious, Anna got up from where she was playing on the floor with Frisky and plopped herself down right beside Davy on his cot. Instantly, Davy turned his back to his sister, hiding the notes he was taking from her. "Please, Davy," Anna pleaded, "I want to know what you're writing down."

"It's for Jim, Anna," he told her. "I don't think it's a good idea for you to see these right now."

"Because you think I'm too little to keep a secret, don't you?" Anna pouted.

"Davy, tell Anna the Old Ones said Jim must see them first," Wily said urgently. "He alone can choose to share them."

"Anna," Davy addressed her, "Wily says only Jim must see these, okay? And the foxes are in a hurry to return to The Glade, so I need to concentrate."

"Oh, all right," Anna conceded despondently, turning her back on her brother to give him the privacy he requested. Mrs. Wily, who had taken a particular liking to Anna when they first met, felt sorry for the little girl. She wished to cheer her up in the worst way. *I have it! Anna may not be able to see us, but whoever said she couldn't touch us?*

"Davy," Mrs. Wily said, "tell Anna to expect a nudge from me. When she does, she is welcome to stroke my fur. Maybe that will help her to not feel so left out."

Davy cheerfully relayed the message to his sister. The moment she felt Mrs. Wily leaning against her legs, Anna buried her hands in the thick, silky-smooth coat of the fox. The sensation thrilled Anna beyond her wildest dreams. "Your fur is so soft," she whispered, "softer than Frisky's, softer than anything I've ever felt before. Thank you, Mrs. Wily. I love you."

"She loves you, too," Davy told Anna while jotting down the last of Wily's instructions.

"Any questions, Davy?" Wily asked.

"No, I think I have it," he replied.

"Good! Then the missus and I will be off, won't we dear?"

"Of course," Mrs. Wily said reluctantly as she gave Anna's cheek a good-bye lick. "I hope I see you soon, Anna. You too, Davy."

"Wait!" Davy shouted excitedly, suddenly remembering what he had longed to tell Racer. "I have news that you need to take back to the Old Ones!"

"Out with it quickly, my lad," Wily said. He was already standing at the door.

"We're not going back to Atlanta!" Davy exclaimed. "Jim found a teaching job here!"

Wily and Mrs. Wily, despite their pressing need to depart, danced gleefully all around Davy, singing a song of rejoicing as he laughed at their amusing antics. "There will be a celebration in The Glade tonight!" Wily assured the boy when the two foxes finally calmed down and caught their breath. "I can't wait to see Racer's face when we break the news!"

"I wish I could be there," Davy said regretfully.

"You will be soon, Davy," said Mrs. Wily jauntily. "Good things come to those who wait."

In a twinkling, the foxes were out the door and gone in a flash. As sad as he felt at not being able to accompany them, Davy managed to smile. "I think all the Old Ones are determined to teach me patience," he said to himself, "but, oh, how I wish Friday was already here!"

***

Ronnie heard the garage door opening and knew it was Betty Rae returning from the hair salon. Hurriedly, he cleared his plate and glass from the coffee table and carried them into the kitchen. Ronnie knew Betty Rae was always in a good mood when she returned from having her hair cut and highlighted, and he knew better than to spoil that for her. *No tellin' what we'd get for dinner if I left any mess around. Think I'll say something nice about her hair, too, even if I don't like it.*

"Hey," Betty Rae called loudly to Ronnie as she came through the door, "where are you, Ronnie?"

"In the kitchen putting some dishes in the washer," he answered.

"Really?" Betty Rae was delighted. "That makes two times in one week! Thank you, sugar."

"No problem," Ronnie said. "Boy, you're sure looking good with that new hair-do."

"You like it?" Betty Rae fluffed her curls and smiled coyly at him.

"No, I don't like it," Ronnie told her as he put his arms around her. "I love it."

"Oh, how you do go on," she teased him. "You've been so sweet to me lately, I'm beginning to wonder what happened to the old Ronnie."

"I've turned over a new leaf," Ronnie declared, "at least when it comes to you and the boys. Now that being said," he continued, "why don't you come with me Friday to the work site? You haven't seen it yet, and it's impressive, if I say so myself."

"Work site?" Betty Rae said indignantly as she pulled away from Ronnie's embrace. "Have you lost your mind? Why would I even want to be near all those sweaty, stinky workers and those hideous machines roaring and kicking up all kinds of debris?"

"We won't stay long, I promise," Ronnie said soothingly, "just long enough for me to get the men in the right frame of mind. Bill can do the rest, at least for that day."

Betty Rae softened a little. "Okay, so we won't stay long," she said, "but why do I need to tag along in the first place?"

"Because," said Ronnie, reeling her in toward him again, "I'm going to take my sweet gal up to Highlands for the day. How does that sound?" Betty Rae's immediate and passionate response assured Ronnie he wouldn't be in the doghouse any time soon.

CHAPTER 17

DAVID'S PRAYER IS ANSWERED

Following Wily's orders, Davy reentered the kitchen. Sidling up next to Jim, he waited for an opportune moment to interrupt as politely as possible. He hated taking his stepfather away from this high-spirited celebration, but he had no choice. There were an awful lot of details for Jim to see to, and Davy wished to give him ample time to prepare. "Excuse me, Jim," Davy said, the moment there was a lull in the conversation. "I need to talk to you."

One look at the boy's face told Jim that the matter at hand was of utmost importance. He knew better than to postpone this conversation. Jim promptly stood up. "I hate to leave this party," he said, "but there's something Davy and I need to discuss that can't wait. If you'll excuse me..."

"Don't be too long, honey," said Kate.

"Mom, I'll have Jim back in no time," said Davy reassuringly, although he wasn't at all certain that he would. As Anna was still playing with Frisky on the side porch, Davy led Jim out to the front porch where the worn, but comfortable, rockers begged to be sat upon. Jim helped Davy push them close together so he could better see the piece of paper the boy had produced from his pocket. "It's Reverend's plan," Davy explained as Jim donned his reading glasses. The Old Ones need your help, and Sheriff Peabody's."

Jim unfolded the paper and read it carefully, paying close attention to every detail. Davy waited for Jim's appraisal anxiously. He thought the plan was sound and had every chance of success if implemented just as Rever-

172

end instructed. But Jim, with all his worldly experience, would be a better judge. When Jim finished reading, he meticulously folded the paper and slipped it into his shirt pocket, along with his readers. He turned toward Davy and, taking the boy's hand in his, smiled and said, "I think this is our best shot, son, and it looks like I'm going to have a few phone calls to make. Could you possibly entertain your grandparents in the living room, once Bob and Susie leave, so they won't overhear my conversations in the kitchen?"

"Sure, I can do that," said Davy, "but why don't you want them to hear what you have to say?"

Jim sighed. "It's just such a complicated situation," he said. "They don't even know about the Old Ones yet, much less the property dispute."

"Jim, I was wondering," Davy said. "Why did you interrupt today when Grandpa asked about the Old Ones? Shouldn't they know about them?"

"I apologize for that, Davy," Jim said sincerely. "It just didn't seem like the right time or place. But I think now *is* the right time. You could certainly hold their attention with your tales of Racer, Reverend, and the whole gang while I'm on the phone, couldn't you?"

Davy had to laugh. "I can't wait to see their reaction," he said. "Do you think I should ask Mom to come in the living room with us, too, just in case they don't believe me?"

"Ask her if you want to, son," Jim said, giving Davy a pat on the shoulder. "But somehow, I think your Grandpa and Grandma will believe you just fine."

***

When Don and Rupert departed, Tommy said, "Why don't you two go on home and get cleaned up? I've got a few things to do in the office, and I need to check the thermostat before I lock up. No sense in walking into an ice box come Sunday."

"Are you sure, Tommy?" Mike asked. "You've already helped out so much today."

"I was glad to do it," Tommy said, "and doubly glad I got to meet you, Abby. You're one hard worker, I tell you what. The preacher and I would still be at it if we hadn't had you to pitch in."

"Yes, Abby, thanks a million," Mike told her.

"You're welcome," she said. "And yes, Tommy, I for one would love to go home and jump in the shower. I must look a sight!"

"A sight for sore eyes," Mike said honestly. This time, as Abby's cheeks were still flushed from all her exertion in the heat, he couldn't tell if his remark had flustered her. Mike so hoped she'd taken it as a compliment.

Mike's comment wasn't lost on Tommy. He could see exactly what was happening between these two. *Chemistry, that's what they got, chemistry. New friend or not, Preacher, you're fallin' and you're fallin' hard. Won't my Valerie love hearing about this!* "Okay, y'all," he said, waving them toward the doors "time to get a move on now, and Preacher?"

"Yes, Tommy?"

"Don't drag your feet."

***

Wily and Mrs. Wily, upon returning to the Sanctuary, rushed over to Reverend and whispered in his ear. The owl's face transformed from somber to ebullient in a matter of seconds. "By all means, my dear friends," he said jovially. "Take the platform! Announce the glad tidings! I'll quiet this crowd." Reverend ascended swiftly into the air and within moments, a hush fell in the Banquet Hall. "All eyes and ears on Wily and Mrs. Wily," he boomed. "All eyes, all ears!"

When the noise subsided, Wily began, "We went to tell Davy the good news, and we returned with news that is ever so much greater."

"So wonderful we scarcely dared believe our ears when he told us," Mrs. Wily chimed in.

"Racer," Wily called jubilantly, "would you kindly step up to the platform? Mrs. Racer, you come, too. We want to see your faces up close when you hear our announcement."

Puzzled, but keenly curious about the news the foxes had brought the Old Ones, Racer grabbed Mrs. Racer's paw, and the two hurried to join Wily and his missus as requested. When they arrived on the platform, they were greeted energetically by the foxes. "We can't wait to tell you!" Mrs. Wily said. She danced about as much as she had on the porch with Davy.

"We can't wait to hear!" Racer exclaimed. "Pray tell! Tell us all!"

Wily, a broad smile encompassing his face, announced elatedly, "Davy, our dear Chosen One, will not be leaving us at summer's end. He is here to stay!"

***

Eric hung up the phone and looked over his notes again. Jim had explained Reverend's plan pretty much the way the owl had presented it to him the night before. He felt confident that even if the plan did not produce immediate results on Friday morning, it was sure to buy them the time necessary to put everything to rights once and for all. At that moment, Elly entered the kitchen and headed for the sink to wash her hands. She had been busy planting her new flowers, in the holes Eric had dug for her in the soft dirt in front of the porch hedges that afternoon; she was wearing the dirt to prove it. Knowing how much Elly loved gardening, he thought the activity would at best cheer her up, or at least take her mind off their troubles for a time. "How's the planting coming along?" Eric asked, folding up his notes and slipping them into his pocket.

"Wonderfully!" Elly affirmed. "I'm almost finished, but I needed to take a break and get something to drink. It's thirsty work, planting."

"That it is," Eric agreed as he took down two glasses from the cupboard. "So was digging all those holes. Do you want ice water or tea?"

"Water's fine," she said, drying her clean hands on a dishtowel. "Thank you honey, for all your hard work out there this afternoon so I could simply enjoy the fun part."

"Anything for you, Elly," Eric said as he handed her water to her and poured himself a glass of tea. "I'm glad you're having a good time. Let's carry our drinks out to the porch. I want to see your progress." Seeing how Elly had so artistically laid out the plants, with their colorful blooms complimenting and enhancing each other, Eric was duly impressed. "This looks as beautiful as anything I've seen in those gardening magazines, Elly," he said proudly. "You've outdone yourself, that's for sure."

"Eric, you're exaggerating," she insisted, but the smile on her face revealed how pleased she was by his thoughtful words. The two sat down together on the top step of their porch. Elly took several sips of water and leaned her head against Eric's chest. He placed his arm around her and held her close, content to listen to her breathing and inhale the sweet fragrance of her hair. They remained in companionable silence for several minutes, savoring the view from the porch and the light breeze that caressed their faces. When Elly finally spoke, her voice was barely audible. "Eric, I've been thinking," she said. "We should do something special tomorrow on your day off. Do you have anything in mind?"

"Hmm," said Eric, "I honestly hadn't thought about it, but you're right. We should do something special. How about you, beautiful? What would you like to do?"

Elly sat up so she could look into Eric's face. She wore an impish smile he didn't expect to see; he was glad of it. "Do you remember where you took me on our first date?" Elly asked.

"How could I forget?" Eric said, feeling a bit sheepish at the remembrance of it. After all, it had only been a long, leisurely walk through the Joyce Kilmer Memorial Forest and a picnic on a bench. What Eric had really wanted to do was take Elly to the fanciest restaurant in Highlands. "Are you saying you actually want to go back to Joyce Kilmer?"

"Yes! I do," Elly affirmed, "but this time around, *I'll* pack the picnic."

"What?" Eric pretended to be shocked. "You didn't like my bologna sandwiches and Cheetos?"

"And Hostess cupcakes for dessert?" Elly added, giggling as she did so. "Eric, I hate to think what you'd look like now if you'd stayed a bachelor."

"But I didn't," he said, cupping her face fondly in his hands, "because the loveliest woman in the world said 'yes' when I asked."

***

When Jim wrapped up his business on the phone, he felt a great sense of relief wash over him. *I've done as you've asked, Reverend. Everything's set in motion. Now to see if the story has a happy ending.* Suddenly, he heard gales of laughter coming from the living room. Jim imagined Davy had probably just finished telling his grandparents about Mad Squirrel Sunday; that had been quite the day for shock and awe. *Then again, the Old Ones are ever a reason to be both shocked and awed. Reverend, I hope the public thinks as we do.* Smiling broadly, Jim entered the living room and took a seat on the hearth.

176

"Well, by the sound of it, Davy here has been quite engaging in telling you about his one-of-a-kind adventures," he said.

"It has been delightful!" Sarah declared. "Oh, I can't get over the miracles that have gone on here. Davy, do you think your Grandpa and I will get to meet these fantastic creatures while we're here?"

"I'm sure they'll want to meet you," Davy assured her, "but it won't be today or tomorrow."

"Why is that?" David asked.

"They have to rest up," Davy explained. "They have a big day on Friday."

"Big day?" David was understandably bewildered.

"Oh, my!" Kate exclaimed in alarm when she glanced at her watch. "Look at the time! I haven't even started our dinner. What was I thinking?"

"Let me help you with that, Kate," Sarah insisted, hopping up to follow her daughter-in-law to the kitchen. "Save those other stories, Davy, so I don't miss out, okay?"

"Okay, Grandma," he said. "They can wait."

"Well, just darn," said David with a grin, "and here I am all geared up to hear more. So, I guess that means I'll have to wait to hear about the 'Big Day?'"

Davy sighed and said, "I don't want to leave Grandma out."

"I know you don't, son," David told him. "I don't want her left out either. So as it seems that's the end of story telling for now, I'd like to spend a little time with Jim to get to know him better. Is that okay, Davy and Anna?"

"It's okay by me," Davy answered.

"Me, too," said Anna. Both children hugged Jim and their grandpa in turn, then scooted out to the screened porch to visit with Maggie and Frisky.

David cleared his throat a bit nervously in Jim's estimation. "Jim," he began, "would you mind if we sat in the rockers on the front porch? I'd like to take in the view while we talk."

"By all means," said Jim genially, leading the way.

When the men were settled into the rocking chairs, Jim thought that for someone who had just now expressed interest in conversation, David was unusually reticent. He seemed to be drinking in the scenery, yet his eyes looked like they were far, far away. Jim recognized this at once as being the look of someone lost in distant memories. He decided to break the silence. "David? You wanted to chat, right?"

David quickly recovered. "Yes, yes, of course I do, Jim," he said, as convincingly as he could. "It's just this scenery all around. So different from where we live now, but so familiar to me. I grew up in North Carolina."

"You did?" Jim said in amazement. "Kate never told me that. I grew up in North Carolina, too, right in this very house."

"Such an idyllic place to be a child," David observed. "I'm so glad Davy and Anna will have the chance to grow up here, too. That's a blessing."

"Yes, sir, it certainly is," Jim agreed. "Landing that job answered lots of prayers."

David took a deep breath and exhaled slowly. When he spoke again, his voice was low and soft. "I'm hoping to have some prayers answered, too," he confessed as he turned to look directly into Jim's eyes, just as green as his own. "You see, Jim, I have memories of this place, special memories that I need to share with you."

Jim was thrown for a loop. "Memories? Of this farm?" he asked incredulously.

David nodded his head. "From many years ago," he confirmed, "Memories long buried until I saw Kate's photos of this place." Jim thought he detected a catch in David's throat. "This is where I met Mary."

"Mary? My mother?" Now Jim was genuinely confused and confounded.

"Mary Hunter. Yes, Jim, your mother," David affirmed. "You see, Jim, my father was a much sought-after preacher for summer revivals. When he'd ride the circuit, he always took the family with him. As a kid, I thought this was a great vacation, but as I got older, I started to resent being dragged around from this place to that when I could have been working a summer job. Anyway, the year I turned eighteen, I was the typical preacher's kid: rebellious, surly, and full of wild oats in need of sowing. That's the summer your grandfather had a revival camp set up in that huge meadow of yours. People came from miles around, stayed the whole week, sang hymns, got baptized down at the lake, and heard enough fire and brimstone to last a lifetime."

"With all those people here," Jim interrupted brusquely, "how did you happen to meet my mother?"

178

"It was expected of the host of the revival, in this case your grandfather, to feed the preacher's family a nightly meal. The first time I walked through that back door and laid eyes on your mother, I was smitten. She was the most beautiful girl I'd seen in all my eighteen years, and I made up my mind right then and there to spend every moment I could with her. And having those throngs of people on the grounds made it easy, far too easy, for us to slip away unnoticed." Here David paused as if searching for the way to phrase his next words. He didn't need to do so as Jim filled in the gap for him.

"Your trysts were intimate, then," Jim concluded. There was bitterness in his voice that he didn't even attempt to hide.

"Yes," David admitted, knowing how difficult all of this must be for Jim to hear. "I don't know if this makes it any easier, Jim, but I truly loved your mother. On the last day we were at this farm, I pleaded with her to come with me. I promised to marry her. That's when she told me she was only sixteen and knew her parents would never give their consent. Oh, how that broke my heart! I told her I would write to her every chance I got, begged her to wait for me and not let another beau come between us in the meantime." David stopped again. He could feel the composure he had tried so hard to maintain ebbing away with every word he spoke. David knew he was standing on the brink of a slippery slope, where facts would soon give way to conjecture, and Jim would either find his speculations credible or preposterous.

"And did you?" Jim asked, his voice hesitant and unsteady. "Did you write to my mother?"

"I did," David confirmed, "many times. But I never heard back from her, not once. It crushed me at the time, but like most teenage boys, I found myself unable to dwell on it for long. As I told you, I was pretty wild at that stage in my life. If it wasn't for going into the army and then meeting Sarah down the road, I don't know that I'd ever have straightened up and flown right."

Abruptly, Jim stood up and strode to the edge of the porch, his back to David. He was not only upset about hearing about his mother's youthful indiscretions, but also bewildered as to why David felt he had had to share these with him. Jim's heart began to pound, and he could feel the searing heat of anger rising. The last thing he wished to do was lash out at David,

179

yet it took every inch of will-power to refrain from doing so. *There must be a reason David wished to share this with me. Surely, he didn't mean to be hurtful. So why am I so furious right now? Am I embarrassed for my mother or embarrassed for me? I have to get a grip. I can't hurt Kate and the kids. There must be a reason. Just ask him. Ask David.*

Jim whirled around to face David who wore an unmistakable look of concern. The clench of Jim's jaw and the fire in his eyes were the only visible signs of the rage seething within. He kept his voice calm and measured as he spoke. "David, I need to know why," Jim said. "Why are you telling me all this, about you and my mother? What difference does it make, all these many years later?"

David pushed himself up carefully from the rocker and walked in Jim's direction until they stood face to face. Jim was surprised to see tears standing in David's eyes. The shimmer made them look greener than ever. "When I saw Kate's photos, it brought back more than memories," he said. "I made the connection between your last name and your mother's." David reached into his back pocket and produced a folded document, which he handed to Jim.

"What's this?" Jim asked as he took the paper from David's hand.

"It's a copy of your birth certificate," David explained. "Go on. Open it." Jim did so hesitantly. David moved to stand next to him so he could peruse the document with him. "Kate told us that you never knew your father," David said gently, "and this confirms that fact, as you took your mother's name as your last one. But it's your date of birth that is most significant."

"March twenty-first?" Jim asked, baffled. "What's so significant about that?"

"Jim," David said quietly, "it is exactly nine months from the week I spent with Mary."

Jim was dumbfounded. He looked from the birth certificate to David's face as if seeing it for the first time. Jim's knees went weak and wobbly and his hands began to shake. It was all he could do to keep his balance. In a voice choked with emotion, he whispered, "Are you saying what I think you're saying?"

David nodded, the tears in his eyes at last overflowing. "Yes, Jim," he said. "I'm your father."

***

Jim and David tactfully waited until the family had almost finished eating dinner before they broke what they knew would be earth-shaking news. Sarah, privy to their intentions, knew Kate had best be sitting down when the life-changing announcement was made. "Kate, honey," Sarah called to her where she was standing at the sink, "don't fuss with the dishes now. I'll help you later. Come on back to the table. There's something Jim and David want to tell you. Something they want to tell all of us."

Obediently, Kate resumed her place next to Jim and regarded her husband and father-in-law apprehensively. "Is it good news, I hope?" she ventured.

"Yes, it is," Jim said, taking her hand in his, "but it's going to come as a bit of a shock. I know it was for me. I practically keeled over when I heard it."

"What does 'keeled' mean?" Anna asked just before stuffing her last bite of mashed potato into her mouth.

"It means to fall over in a faint," Mom said and shot Sarah a meaningful glance. "You know what this is all about, don't you, Sarah? Is that why you made me sit down?"

"Yes, that's exactly why," Sarah said. "Jim, you keep tight hold of that girl's hand, now."

At Sarah's admonition, Kate felt her stomach flip-flop; she clutched Jim's hand for dear life. She hoped she wouldn't be ill again, like she'd been that morning.

"Kate, Davy, Anna," Jim began, "you remember I told you I never knew my father?"

"Yes," Davy spoke up. "You told me he abandoned you and your mom."

"Well, I found out today," said Jim, "that my father didn't abandon me. How can you abandon someone you don't even know exists?"

"But Jim," Kate protested, "your mother said..."

"I know what she said, Kate," Jim stopped her. "And I don't really understand why she didn't want me to know the truth. But I talked it over with David, and my suspicion is she, along with my grandparents, chose to keep it secret in order to protect my father's family from scandal."

181

"And quite the scandal it would have caused," David asserted. "Would have toppled the Murray ministry like a house of cards."

"Murray ministry?" Davy asked, perplexed at hearing the family name. "What's that, Grandpa?"

"My father, your great-grandfather, was a prominent preacher in the South, Davy," Grandpa explained. "Not quite up there with Billy Graham, mind you, but he was sure popular."

In a shock of sudden realization, Kate's free hand flew to her mouth and she uttered a shriek. "Oh, dear God! Oh, dear God! David? You? *You?* How can this possibly be?"

"It's a long story, Kate," David said, sympathizing with her reaction to such unbelievable tidings. "A story I'll let Jim tell you later. But for now, Davy and Anna, just know that I'm not only your grandpa, I'm Jim's father, too."

Davy and Anna were speechless as they looked from Jim to David and back to Jim again. As he compared the sets of green eyes, Davy instantly recalled the day he had been studying the family photos on Grandpa Will's table and came across one of a young, smiling Jim: dapper in his uniform, his eyes just the same color and shape as his own father's. Anna was the first to find her voice. "Remember, Grandpa, when I said your eyes looked like Jim's? Now I know why, but it still makes no sense."

"It doesn't?" David asked, perplexed by Anna's comment. "In what way, sweetie?"

"Don't people have to be married to have children?" she asked innocently.

The adults shifted uncomfortably in their seats, and exchanged nervous glances until Sarah came to the rescue. "Most times, that's the way it happens, Anna. But sometimes, God sees fit to grace someone with a child whether they're married or not."

"Oh," she said. "Is that what people mean when they say 'God works in mysterious ways?'"

Jim, David and Sarah laughed heartily at her comment. Even Kate, as stunned as she was by the turn of events, managed a weak smile.

Davy had an instantaneous revelation. "Wait a minute!" he exclaimed. "If you're Jim's dad, Grandpa, and you were my dad's dad—that means Jim is Daddy's brother!"

182

"Half-brother, Davy," David corrected him, "and your uncle, too."

"Sounds like I just got promoted," Jim said with a smile.

Kate simply shook her head in disbelief. "It's unfathomable," she said. "What are the odds of something like this happening? I mean, I realized when I first met Jim that there were aspects of his features, especially his eyes, which reminded me of John, but to actually find out Jim is John's half-brother? I'm afraid it's going to take me a long while to adjust to all this."

Jim squeezed her hand and said, "Take all the time you need, Kate," he reassured her, "because I'm right there with you on this one. Yes, it will certainly take some time."

CHAPTER 18

DAVY'S DREAM

While Jim escorted David and Sarah to the Fairchilds' home to spend the night, Kate busied herself getting Davy and Anna ready for bed. "And no dawdling tonight," she told them, "you're both already up way past your bedtimes." Neither argued with their mother as both were worn out, physically and emotionally, from the day's staggering events. As Davy lay on his cot waiting for his mother to come pray with him and say good-night, scenes of the day flickered through his mind like a news reel. As weary as he was, Davy feared these thoughts, and one in particular, would surely keep him awake far longer than he wished. *Maybe I'll feel better after I talk to Mom and we say prayers. Maybe sleep will come easier after that.*

Davy heard his mother saying good-night to Anna. "'Night, night, sleep tight, and don't let the bed bugs bite!" He wondered why she had started using that silly phrase to wish his sister a good night's sleep. He didn't even know what it meant. Davy heard his mother's soft footfalls as she entered the porch.

"Mom?" he asked. "Why are you suddenly telling Anna good night the way you did just now? It makes no sense to me."

Mom laughed, but her voice sounded tired and drained when she spoke. "It's something my grandmother would always say when I was a little girl and spent the night at her house. I don't know why I suddenly remembered it, but I thought Anna might get a kick out of it, and she did."

"But what does it mean?" Davy persisted.

Mom sighed, but dutifully answered. "In the old days, honey, before people had mattresses like we enjoy today, they would lay on bedding stuffed with straw, which was supported on the bed frames by ropes underneath. If those ropes weren't good and tight, the bedding would sag and you would be uncomfortable. As for the bed bugs, just imagine lying down on what you think are clean sheets and waking up in the morning with itchy spots all over you."

"Gross, Mom!" Davy declared disgustedly. "I hope I never meet up with one of those."

"Chances are good you won't," she reassured him. "Are you ready to say your prayers? It's been an awfully long day for all of us."

"Before I do, Mom," he said, "can I ask you a question?"

"Sure, honey," she said, stifling a yawn.

Davy knew his mother was worn out and he felt badly for keeping her up any longer than necessary, but he knew he definitely couldn't sleep until this burning thought was extinguished. "Mom," he said quietly, "now that we know Jim is Daddy's brother, is that going to change anything? I mean you can stay married to him, can't you?"

Mom patted his cheek tenderly. "Yes, Davy, we can stay married," she assured him.

"But won't other people think it's kind of weird?"

"Possibly," she answered, "but right now, honey, I'm not worried about what other people think. I'm too overwhelmed with the news at the moment; it's barely had time to sink in. It's an adjustment for the whole family."

Davy sighed. "Y'know, Mom," he said, "I think it's great that my Grandpa is Jim's dad, but it's sad, too."

"Sad? Whatever do you mean, Davy?"

"All those years Jim hoped and waited for his dad to return to him," he said, "sitting right here on this porch and looking up the road thinking one day he'd drive down it. Now that he finally has, Jim wasn't even here to greet him when he arrived."

"Yes, sweetie, that does seem ironic," Kate said. With a smile on her face, she added, "but don't you think Jim more than made up for it, with his grand entrance today?"

185

Davy chortled. "That was pretty wild," he admitted. "But something that good deserved it, don't you think?"

"Yes, I do," Mom agreed. "But I think that's enough talk for one night, Davy. Let's say those prayers."

***

When Jim quietly opened the back door, he didn't expect to find Kate still up and waiting for him. She was sitting at the kitchen table, sipping tea and reading a book. She immediately put it down, the moment he arrived. "I'm sorry I'm so late," said Jim, as he leaned down to kiss Kate's head, taking a seat next to her. "I wanted to call, but I knew you were trying to get the kids to sleep, and I didn't want to disturb them."

Kate patted his hand gently. "I figured you might be a little late," she said, "and it's not like I didn't know where you were. I *am* tired, Jim, but with everything that's happened today, my mind doesn't want to shut down."

"Same here," Jim said. "I don't know that anyone will get much sleep tonight. Kate, you should have seen Bob and Susie's reaction to the news about David being my father. You could have knocked them over with a feather! But it didn't take long for them to recover and offer congratulations all around. Of course David gave them the background of how it all happened."

"Something I've yet to hear about," Kate remarked, "but I can wait."

Jim smiled and, taking her hand in his, said, "As I was walking back here tonight, I had a funny thought. All my life, I never had anyone I could call 'dad' and I've never been called 'dad' myself. David hasn't asked me to call him that and frankly, even though he's my father, I don't know if I'll ever feel comfortable using the word."

Kate saw in a flash the window of opportunity she had waited for since early that morning. "Why don't you try calling David 'dad' and see how it feels, Jim," she suggested. "I'm sure he would be delighted, and it would give you some practice in hearing it, too."

Jim regarded her quizzically. "Practice? What do you mean, Kate?"

"Can you stand one more bit of good news today?" Kate asked as she took both of his hands in hers.

"Who doesn't want to hear good news?" Jim replied cheerfully. "Let's have it; out with it."

Kate gently guided Jim's hands to her abdomen and laid them there, palms down. "You need to get used to hearing 'dad,'" she whispered as she leaned in close to him, "because you're going to be one."

***

As Mike lay in bed waiting for sleep to come, he replayed the conversation he'd had earlier that day with Abby. They had walked out of church together at Tommy's urging and headed for their cars, Mike following Abby to hers and chivalrously opening the door for her. A blast of heat met them. "I knew I shouldn't have parked in the sun," Abby lamented.

Mike ran around to the passenger side and opened that door, too. "A little cross breeze will help cool it down before you get in," he remarked. "Anyway, that gives us a minute or two, and there's something I'd like to ask you."

"Two questions in one day?" Abby asked playfully, as Mike hastened back around the car to stand in front of her.

"Yes," he said, fixing her with an affectionate gaze. "When is your next day off from work?"

"This Friday," she answered.

"Abby, if you don't already have plans for the day…"

"I don't," she interjected, flashing that smile Mike couldn't resist.

"Then how about planning to do something together?" Mike suggested.

"I'd like that," Abby affirmed. "Do you have anything in mind?"

Mike was stumped. He had gotten to the point of actually asking Abby out and now had no earthly idea where to take her on a first date. He wanted it to be special and memorable for her, something she would fondly reminisce about for years to come. He had to think fast. "Tell you what, Abby," he said, "let me give it some thought tomorrow while I'm home working on my sermon. I'll come up with something and give you a call. Is that okay?"

"That's fine," she assured him. "I should be home by four tomorrow, so you can ring me any time after that."

"Okay, you can count on it," Mike said. Abby eased herself onto the driver's seat and leaned across to close the passenger door.

"And Mike?" Abby added, as she placed her keys in the ignition and turned to look at him. "Don't fret over where we go or what we do. Just spending time with you is enough for me."

Just spending time with you. Just spending time with you. Mike closed his eyes as Abby's words played in his mind like the sweet refrain of an age-old hymn, comforting and full of promise. "And that's all I want to do, Abby," Mike whispered into the dark. "I want to spend time with you; as much time as I possibly can."

***

Davy dreamed he was frolicking in The Glade with Racer, Mrs. Racer, and all the Old Ones. Everyone was dancing to merry tunes as the sun shone down upon them from a cloudless blue sky. As he cavorted and skipped through the lush, green grass and wildflowers, Davy felt more light-hearted with every step he took, and his energy and joy knew no bounds. Racer suddenly grabbed one of his hands and Mrs. Racer took the other; they gleefully led him to join a circle the Old Ones were forming around the Blessed Portal, shimmering so brightly Davy could scarcely behold it. Once the ring was formed, Silky and his orchestra began a tune so lively and enchanting that no one could resist it. Faster and faster the Old Ones romped, round and round and round, until the speed was so frenetic, all Davy could see of their feet was a whirling blur. To his great alarm, he felt he was losing his grip on the squirrels' paws. He clung tighter and tighter, but his efforts were all in vain. It was in horror, then, that Davy realized he wasn't losing his hold; Racer's and Mrs. Racer's paws were slowly vanishing underneath his palms. "Stop! Stop!" Davy cried out. "Don't leave me! Don't leave me!"

Gone! Darkness! Not even a speck of light gleamed from the Blessed Portal. Davy couldn't see a hand in front of his face. His heart pounded in his chest. His breath came in short, panicked gasps, as if the very air about him had become hot and close and still. "Old Ones!" Davy called out in a terrified voice as despairing tears rolled down his cheeks. "Where are you? Why have you left me here? I'm scared! I'm scared!"

"And so you should be," hissed a menacing voice. Davy froze. He knew that hideous cadence all too well. "Turn around, Davy," it commanded. "You must look at me." Davy struggled to resist, but the force emanating from the malevolent demon overpowered him. He turned and unspeakable dread seized him. All Davy could see in the blackness were two glowing, red slits, glaring ominously at him. And as he stared back, he could see that the owner of those hideous eyes was creeping toward him.

"You had me last time, didn't you?" The creature spat the words hatefully. "Now it's my turn. I shall not lose again."

"Don't listen to him, Davy!" It was Reverend! The fragrance of honeysuckle permeated the air and the light, pale and weak at first, became brighter and brighter by the moment, revealing the presence of not only Reverend, but each and every Old One gathered behind and beside Davy. When the boy looked again in the direction of the red, foreboding eyes, there was Ronnie—glowering not at him, but at Reverend. In a flash, a pistol appeared in Ronnie's hand. A shot rang out.

"No!" Davy screeched at the top of his lungs. "No! No! No!"

"Davy! Davy!" Kate's voice called desperately from a distance. "Wake up, honey! Wake up!"

The Glade vanished. Davy opened his eyes, blinking at the intrusive morning light. His mom was sitting next to him on the cot, her gentle, comforting hands on his shoulders. Jim, coffee in hand and a worried look on his face, stood beside her. Davy sat bolt upright. "Mom, Jim, the Old Ones are in for trouble!"

"Davy," Mom said soothingly, "you just had a nightmare. I'm sure everything will be fine."

"No, Mom," Davy insisted. "This was more than a nightmare. I think it was a warning."

"A warning?" Jim asked skeptically. "What makes you think that, son?"

"It was so real," Davy said miserably. "Terribly real! It makes me so afraid about tomorrow, when the Old Ones face Ronnie." Davy covered his face with his hands and wept pitifully. Kate held him close and gave Jim a pleading look.

"I'll talk to him, Kate," Jim whispered. She gave him a grateful smile, knowing he could calm Davy's fears better than she could. When his mother left the room, Jim sat down in the spot she had vacated. "Davy," he said quietly, "would it help to tell me about the dream you had?"

Davy wiped his face with the bottom edge of his T-shirt and attempted to reign in his emotions. Jim waited in patient silence while Davy, still sniffling, composed himself. When Davy spoke at last, his voice was hoarse and low. "Jim," he said, looking at his stepfather with mournful eyes, "in my dream, Ronnie had a gun. He shot someone, but I don't know who it was. Everything went dark."

Jim placed a soothing hand on Davy's shoulder and said, "Davy, how is Ronnie going to have a gun tomorrow? Sheriff Peabody will be there. All the men, including Ronnie, will have dropped their weapons long before the Old Ones show up."

Davy sighed and hung his head. "I know that," he admitted, "but I can't shake the feeling that something will go awfully, horribly wrong."

"Instead of dwelling on those negative feelings, son," Jim advised, "why don't you focus on what could go down awesomely right? You know the plan. It's as solid as anything we have right now to stop Ronnie. Can you trust me on that?"

"I trust you, Jim," Davy said, "but could you do me a favor?"

"Of course, son," Jim answered.

"Will you call Sheriff Peabody and tell him about my dream?" Davy asked. "I want him to be prepared if Ronnie tries to pull something."

"I'll be happy to," Jim affirmed, "as long as you make a phone call, too."

"Who do you want me to call?" Davy asked quizzically.

"Pastor Mike," said Jim. "We could all use an extra dose of prayers."

***

"No, no, no," Racer mumbled agitatedly as he tossed and turned on his bed, tearing the covers off Mrs. Racer as he did so. She awakened immediately, aware he was having a bad dream, such a rarity for any Old One, and knew she should wake him at once.

"Racer!" Mrs. Racer called, shaking him by the shoulders. "Wake up! Wake up!"

"What? What?" Racer asked, bemused and disoriented, as his eyes flew open. He saw Mrs. Racer staring anxiously at his face.

"You were having a bad dream, my love," she explained. "I had to rouse you from it before it got any worse."

Racer sat up and rubbed his eyes, straining to recall what the dream had even been about. He could not remember the first detail of it, but the feeling of dread it engendered within him lingered; it made Racer shiver as if he were standing outdoors in an icy wind. Mrs. Racer, seeing as he was trembling all over, wrapped the blanket around both of them and snuggled close to try to warm him. He closed his eyes, trying to will the quivering to cease, but it aggravatingly persisted. The dream had left Racer with the unsettling feeling that something was sorely awry. Deciding that thinking good thoughts might ease the disquieting sensation, Racer let his mind drift back to his most recent visit with Davy. It was then the squirrel noticed something odd. No matter how hard he tried, Racer could not conjure up an image of the boy smiling. All he saw was sorrow and sadness on Davy's face. In a twinkling, he knew.

"It's Davy," he whispered to Mrs. Racer.

"Davy?" she inquired, mystified.

"He needs me now," said Racer dejectedly, "and here it is, the one day I cannot go to him."

"That was what your dream was about?" Mrs. Racer asked.

"Not the dream itself," he replied, "but the feeling it left me with. I sense Davy is frightened and worried about something. It grieves me to think of him that way."

"Me too," Mrs. Racer said empathetically. "But if we can't go to Davy, there is still something we can do for him right this very moment."

"And what's that?" Racer asked.

"We can pray," she said.

* * *

Eric and Elly were just about to head out the door on their day's outing when the phone rang. Swiftly, Eric answered it. "Sheriff Peabody here."

"Eric, it's Jim Hunter. Sorry to bother you at home again, but Davy has a concern he asked me to share with you."

"Share away," Eric said kindly. Jim told Eric all about Davy's dream and his worry about the Old Ones. When he concluded, Eric observed, "It sounds like Davy's imagination is running in high gear, but tell him I will be sure to take extra precautions tomorrow. You bet. Nine fifteen it is. See you then, Jim."

"What was that all about?" Elly asked, when Eric hung up the phone.

Eric smiled and put his arms around Elly. "Nothing to worry about, beautiful," he said. "How would you like to meet the Old Ones tomorrow?"

***

"Pastor Russell here."

"Pastor Mike, it's Davy Murray."

"Well hello there, young man," said Mike, "such a pleasure to hear from you. What can I do for you today?"

"I need...I mean, the Old Ones need some prayers," Davy told him.

"I'll be glad to pray for them, and for you, Davy," Mike assured him. "What exactly am I to pray for?"

At this question, Davy was unable to contain himself. He knew he could trust Pastor Mike to keep the plan for tomorrow to himself, and he was so aching inside from the hideous dream, he had to get it all off his chest. Mike listened with great interest and not a little amazement. Though he had seen Racer in person twice, the thought of that multitude of Old Ones appearing startlingly out of the blue to an unsuspecting crowd overwhelmed him. Mike found himself wanting with all his heart to see this sight in person. When Davy finished his story, Mike said, "Davy, rest assured, I will pray for all the needs of the Old Ones tomorrow and for your needs, too, as you stand with them. There is something I'd like to ask of you, if you don't mind."

"What's that?" Davy wondered.

"If I wouldn't be in the way, could I possibly join you and your family tomorrow?" Mike inquired. "It would be an honor and a thrill to meet all the Old Ones."

Davy, immediately thinking of how Racer held Pastor Mike in such high esteem, didn't hesitate for a second. "I'd love to have you there," he said, "and I know Racer will be glad, too."

"Wonderful!" Mike declared. "Just tell me where and what time, and I'll gladly show up. Oh, and Davy, one more thing. Might I bring Abby with me?"

***

Sarah and David showed up at the farm house around ten that morning. Jim had planned to take the whole family down the trail to the lake, but the overcast skies dissuaded him from risking that venture. Instead, he thought David would be intrigued by his grandson's prowess with a BB gun, and that activity would be likely to take Davy's mind off his worries. Jim was right on both counts.

"Wow, Davy!" David exclaimed, when the boy toppled each of the five cans Jim had arranged on the fence with one shot to each. "Nothing wrong with your eyesight, that's for sure! I'm impressed!"

"I am, too," said Jim as he trotted over to collect the cans and reset them. "Davy's a natural."

Davy smiled and blushed at the praise, and then he looked at David. "Grandpa, would you like to take a turn?"

"I don't know, Davy," he said with a chuckle. "It's been a good long while since I've had any target practice."

"C'mon, David," Jim cajoled. "Be a sport! Shooting a gun is like riding a bicycle; once you learn to do it, you never forget."

"Oh, all right," David conceded. "Hand me your gun, Davy. Let's see if your grandpa still has it in him." Jim and Davy looked on in utter amazement as David methodically took aim and fired at each can. It was the exact repeat of Davy's performance. Jim found himself recalling how Grandpa Will had taught him how to shoot. Grandpa Will had been good at it, but had nowhere near the accuracy Jim had shown early on. Now as he watched his biological father, Jim was instantly aware from whom he'd inherited that talent.

"That was great, Grandpa!" Davy exclaimed excitedly. "You're as good as I am!"

David laughed heartily. "What do you say we give Jim a turn now? "Jim!" David called to him; Jim was again resetting the cans. "Let's see how good you are at this, son!"

Jim froze momentarily, but his mind was racing. *I haven't been called* *"son" since my mother died. What if Kate's right? What if I should practice saying* *"dad?"* At this sweet thought, Jim felt a warm glow rising within him. The miracle of it all was so overwhelming; he felt that at any second his heart would burst with joy. He made his decision. "I'll be right there, Dad!"

***

The rain started just as the family sat down to lunch. Davy thought with relief that he was glad he'd taken Maggie out only moments before. Maybe she would be fine until the rain let up. The old dog was sleeping at his feet underneath the table. It seemed to Davy that in the short time they had been at the farm, Maggie was sleeping just a little bit more every day. Mom had assured him that as animals become aged, it is their natural ten-dency to rest more, and not a cause for unnecessary worry. Davy decided to be content with this, and was simply happy to know he wouldn't have to leave his beloved dog when summer drew to a close. He took a big bite of his grilled cheese sandwich and reached his hand down under the table to pat Maggie. Sarah noticed his gesture.

"Maggie must be sleeping at your feet," she said with a smile. "Your mother told us how thrilled you were when you found out you could finally have a dog."

"I was, Grandma," Davy said. "I still am. Maggie is the best."

"Hey, what about Frisky?" Anna protested. "Isn't he the best, too?"

"Best dog and best cat," said Jim, hoping to settle things.

"Oh, yes," said Sarah. "Anna, your little kitten is as sweet as can be. Guess where he is right now."

"Where?" Anna asked, her eyes darting all around.

"Sleeping in my lap," she answered brightly.

Anna smiled broadly at her grandmother. "He must love you a whole lot," she said, "just like I do."

"Just like I do, too," David said as he reached over to pat Sarah's hand. He was rewarded by his wife's beautiful smile.

"Just like we all do," Davy declared.

"Hear, hear!" Jim announced, holding his water glass high in the air. "I propose a toast!" Everyone held up his or her glass with anticipation.

"Here's to my amazing family," he said. "My lovely wife, my wonderful step-children and," here Jim paused to look directly at David and Sarah, "the best father and stepmother I could have ever dreamed of having. Cheers!"

"Cheers!" Everyone chimed in together. Glasses clinked merrily and happy conversation continued at the table. In that moment, Davy couldn't recollect when he'd ever felt so grateful for family.

CHAPTER 19

KATE'S GOOD NEWS

For most of the rainy afternoon, David and Sarah entertained Davy and Anna with endless rounds of Crazy 8s and Go Fish. Jim and Kate took this opportunity to retire to the porch swing, to watch and listen to the rain as it pitter-pattered through the leaves on the oaks and to enjoy a few peaceful moments together. Jim rocked the swing gently with his feet; Kate curled her legs up under her and nestled her head on his shoulder.

"It's so beautiful here," she said softly, "even in the rain, with mist hiding the mountains. I'm so thankful we never, ever have to leave."

"Oh, but we do at some point," Jim said as reached for her hand. "We have an entire apartment to pack up, remember?"

Kate sighed. "That's a chore I'm not looking forward to," she admitted. "When do you think we should return to Atlanta to do that?"

"After David and Sarah leave to go back to Hawaii," said Jim. "The sooner the better, so we can terminate our lease and not be paying for a place we don't need. And that's just the first step."

"What do you mean, honey?"

"It's this house," Jim stated flatly. "If we're going to be able to live in it year-round, I'm going to have to do some creative planning. Davy's fine in summer sleeping on the porch, but obviously that won't do in the winter."

"Why can't we turn the room between the kitchen and the porch into a bedroom of sorts for him?" Kate suggested. "I know that means putting much of the furniture already there in storage, but I suppose we're going to have to store most of our former furnishings anyway."

"That's a good solution for the moment," Jim said, "but with the baby coming and only one bathroom, I think we might have to seriously consider adding on in the near future."

"Oh, Jim, wouldn't that ruin the charm of this house?" Kate asked worriedly. "I love it so much just as it is. I don't mind in the least if we're a tad cramped."

"And you're not going to mind not having any closets for your clothes, Kate?" Jim said with a grin.

"Oh, dear, I hadn't thought about that," she said. "The wardrobe has been perfect for the few summer things we brought with us, but you're right. Where will we put everything?"

"Uh-huh, I thought so," he said as the reality of their situation was sinking in for Kate. "Not to mention a crib and playpen, our computer—I'll absolutely have to have that for work—and maybe even a second one for the kids to use for homework, and for you to enjoy, too."

Kate giggled at this. "When the little one arrives, I doubt I'll have much time for even reading, let alone messing around on the computer," she remarked.

"And speaking of the little one," Jim said as he tenderly patted Kate's stomach, "when do we tell everyone you're expecting?"

Kate leaned in to kiss Jim on the cheek. "If I keep having these bouts of morning sickness," she said, "I think everyone will know soon enough. After all, Susie guessed, and she was right."

"And I, for one, am so glad she was," Jim said. He wrapped his arms around Kate and held her tightly. "Do you know how happy you've made me?"

"If you're half as happy as I am, honey," she replied, "you're over the moon."

***

As Eric and Elly drove toward their destination, ominous looking clouds began gathering in the sky. "I don't know about our hike today, Elly," said Eric, "it's looking more like rain every second."

"I brought our ponchos," Elly said cheerfully. "I don't mind a walk in the rain, do you?"

Eric smiled. "Now that you mention it," he said, "I don't mind it at all, as long as I'm with you."

Elly returned his smile and said, "And if we do get rain, that will mean fewer folks on the trail. We might even have it all to ourselves."

"That's a possibility," Eric remarked, turning into the parking area for Joyce Kilmer Memorial Forest. "There are a few cars here at the moment, though."

"It doesn't matter," Elly said. "We're here, and I'm feeling ever so much better than I have in days. I wonder, Eric, could the Old Ones' tea we drank this morning possibly work this quickly?"

"Seeing as I'm feeling pretty chipper myself," he said, "I'd say most definitely."

"Oh, I can't wait to see them tomorrow!" Elly exclaimed. "It will be all too thrilling to be able to thank them in person."

"It will be quite the experience," Eric confirmed. "One you will always remember, beautiful. Are you ready to head out on the trail?"

"I've never been more ready," Elly assured him. "Let's grab those ponchos and go!"

***

Mike put the finishing touches to his sermon for Sunday and hit the print button. He knew he would look it over multiple times between now and then, tweaking it if necessary, and practice speaking the words aloud so that his delivery of the message would appear more relaxed and natural. As he pulled the pages out of the tray, Mike glanced at his watch. *Almost four? Where has the time gone? Just a few minutes more, and I can call Abby.* Mike felt sure she would jump at the chance to see all the Old Ones gathered spectacularly in one place, and he said yet another prayer for them and for Davy. Tomorrow, Mike knew, was a critical and pivotal day in the lives of all of them, and he felt humbled and gratified to be included in it. *Dear Lord, wrap your arms of protection around Davy and the Old Ones. Grant them the strength and courage to face the challenge of tomorrow. Fill them with your light, your peace, and your grace. In Jesus' name, I pray, amen.*

***

Bob entered the kitchen just in time to see Susie slipping something into the oven. "What are you baking now?" he inquired as he moved toward the coffee maker to brew an afternoon pot.

"A coffee cake to go with breakfast tomorrow," Susie replied. "Sarah mentioned that David really loves it as a treat now and then, so I thought I'd surprise them."

"It might be a surprise," Bob chuckled, "but I'm afraid it can't hold a candle to the bombshell they dropped last night."

"I know!" Susie exclaimed. "I've been thinking about it all day, and pinching myself to make sure I'm not dreaming. What a miracle it is—after all these years, Jim finally meets his father!"

"And finds out that Kate's first husband is his half-brother," Bob added, shaking his head. "Talk about truth being stranger than fiction; this situation sure fits the bill!"

"Speaking of Kate," said Susie as she retrieved two coffee mugs from the cupboard, "I wonder if she took that pregnancy test? Do you think I should call her? I'm dying to know if my suspicions are correct."

"I'm not sure about that, Susie," Bob ventured. "What if she is, but hasn't had a chance to tell Jim yet? She may feel put on the spot; not wanting to lie to you, but not wishing to tell you before she tells him."

"I hadn't thought of that," Susie admitted. "I certainly never want to put Kate between a rock and a hard place. I've grown to love her like a daughter these past two weeks, and I only want what's best for her."

"Then I think it's best you wait for the time being," Bob advised. "I'm sure Kate will let you know as soon as she can, especially considering all that trouble you went to in getting her that pregnancy test. I can't help laughing every time I think about it."

"Me either," said Susie with a grin. "I'm sure tongues are still wagging."

"No doubt," Bob said, as he poured their coffee. "No doubt they are."

***

At five o'clock, the rain finally ceased. Jim decided to take David and the kids outdoors with Maggie and Frisky, for a stroll through the apple orchard, leaving Kate and Sarah in the kitchen, where they were busily preparing dinner. Sarah chopped onion and celery for the potato salad, while Kate retrieved the package of ground beef from the refrigerator to make hamburger patties. "Thanks so much for your help, Sarah," she said sincerely as she laid a piece of parchment paper on the counter. "Fixing meals goes so much faster with an extra pair of hands."

"I thought you told me Jim helps you in the kitchen," Sarah remarked.

"Oh, he does, most of the time," Kate answered, "but things have been a bit crazy since the moment we arrived and we really haven't gotten back into our routine."

"'Crazy?'" Sarah asked. "I don't know if crazy is a strong enough adjective, what with Davy and his Old Ones. My, how I'd love to have a close encounter with those miraculous creatures!"

"I think you'll see them while you're visiting," Kate assured her, "but I can't predict when or where." She unwrapped the ground beef and was just reaching for the first portion when the nauseating odor of raw meat struck her nostrils. Instantly, Kate knew she was going to be sick. She flew to the bathroom without even so much as an "excuse me" to Sarah. There simply wasn't time.

Alarmed and not a little bewildered by Kate's abrupt departure, Sarah called after her. "Kate, honey, are you all right?" When Kate didn't answer, Sarah followed in her wake to be met by a closed bathroom door. Behind it, the unmistakable sound of violent retching almost made Sarah gag herself. When the noise ceased, Sarah tapped timidly on the door.

"Come in," Kate said weakly. When Sarah entered, she saw, much to her chagrin, her daughter-in-law draped over the toilet seat, pale as a ghost and trembling. Swiftly, Sarah grabbed a washcloth from the shelf, soaked it in cool water, and gently swabbed Kate's face with it. "Thank you," Kate whispered as she reached up to flush the toilet's unsightly contents. She sat down on the cool surface of the bathroom floor tiles and managed to smile at her mother-in-law. "Sarah," she said, "I have bad news and good news."

"What is it, honey?" Sarah asked anxiously. "Tell me."

"The bad news is, I'm afraid I can't help you with those burgers tonight," said Kate, knowing the moment of truth had come. "And the good news? I'm pregnant!"

***

When Jim and his entourage reached the kitchen door, a fully recovered Kate was there to greet them. "Did you all have a nice walk?" she asked. As she reached up to hug Jim's neck she whispered in his ear, "Sarah knows." Jim looked startled, but was soon reassured by the smile on Kate's face.

"It was a great walk, Mom," said Anna. "We even showed Grandpa inside the chicken coop! He thought it was cool, didn't you, Grandpa?"

"I sure did," he said, tugging on her braid.

"And we brought you and Grandma these," said Davy, producing two bouquets of wildflowers from behind his back.

"Oh, how lovely!" Sarah exclaimed.

"And how thoughtful," Kate added, giving each of her children a kiss on the cheek. "I'll get a vase right away." Jim followed her to the pantry.

"How did Sarah find out?" he whispered.

"I was at the counter, getting ready to fix hamburgers," Kate told him, "and the smell of the raw meat made me queasy. There was no way to explain my sudden episode in the bathroom by telling anything less than the truth."

"Yes, that was exactly the right thing to do," Jim said comfortingly. "Maybe it's time to let everyone else in on it, too."

"Even Davy and Anna?"

"Especially Davy and Anna," said Jim. "After all, they need to know why their mother has been unusually ill as of late. Telling them will at least remove that unsettling mystery from their minds."

"I suppose you're right," Kate conceded. "And after that, I need to do one more very important thing."

"And that would be?"

"Call Susie."

***

Sarah, with Jim's welcome assistance, served up dinner that evening. Kate's appetite had returned for the most part, but she was leery about tasting the hamburger. Davy noticed right away that his mother was missing what he considered the most desirable part of the meal. He dressed his with mustard and ketchup and passed the condiments on to Anna. "You know I don't like mustard," she said, wrinkling her nose at him.

"Then just pass it on to Grandma," he told her as he spooned a hearty portion of potato salad onto his plate. "You want me to give you some potato salad, Anna?" Davy asked.

"I think I'm old enough to do that myself," she quipped as she took the bowl from him.

"I know you are," Davy said. "I was just trying to be nice."

Anna sighed. "I'm sorry, Davy," she said. "I'm just feeling kind of grumpy tonight."

"That's because you didn't get enough sleep last night," Mom told her. "No staying up late for you tonight!"

"I'll go to bed whenever you say, Mom," Anna said as she stifled a yawn.

Davy took a hefty bite of his hamburger and chewed it slowly, savoring the warm, smoky flavor. *How can Mom not want a burger tonight? Grandma's are great!* "Grandma," he said, "these burgers you made are really good! Thanks!"

"Thank you, Davy," she said. "Only the best for my family!"

"I've been one lucky man all these years," David declared. "Sarah is an amazing cook."

"Oh, how you do go on," Sarah said, but he knew the compliment pleased her.

"Mom," said Davy. "Why aren't you eating a hamburger tonight? I thought you liked them."

"I do, Davy," she replied as she forked several string beans. "I'm just not up for one tonight, that's all."

"Well, Kate," said Jim, with a mischievous grin on his face, "I think this is as good a time as any to tell Davy why the hamburger doesn't interest you."

Mom laid her fork back on her plate. All eyes were looking at her eagerly, and Sarah's were twinkling brightly. "Okay, Davy," Mom said with a smile, "Anna, and David, we've had so much good news in the last two days. Do you think you can handle some more?"

"Good news?" Davy exclaimed. "How can not wanting to eat a hamburger be good news?"

Everyone chuckled at his comment, and Kate flashed him a warm smile. "Because," she said slowly, "sometimes when a woman is expecting, certain foods don't appeal to her."

A hush fell over the table. Davy stared at his mother in disbelief. Anna, not having understood what Mom had said, looked around at all the grown-ups' smiling faces. They were focused on Davy's reaction, and she wondered why he wasn't smiling, too. Then she watched, fascinated, as Davy's expression transformed gradually from one of incredulity to one of sheer delight. "Davy, what is it?" Anna asked, tugging on his sleeve. "Why are you acting this way?"

"Didn't you hear Mom, Anna?" Davy shouted joyfully. He sprang from his seat and raced around to table to hug both his mother and Jim. "She's having a baby!"

***

"Bob, the news is out!" Susie hollered to him as she hung up the phone.

Bob came running from his computer and into the kitchen to find an elated Susie. "The test was positive?" he asked excitedly.

"Yes! Isn't it fabulous?" Susie exclaimed. She threw her arms around her husband. "Kate's not only told Jim, but David and Sarah, and the children, too. They are beside themselves with excitement. Anna told Kate she wants a sister, and of course, Davy wants a brother."

"Did Kate explain that she couldn't take a special order on this?" Bob asked with a chuckle.

"Yes, she did," Susie said. "She told the kids that it was up to God to make that decision, and all they should pray for is that the baby be born healthy."

"Amen to that," Bob pronounced. "I imagine David and Sarah will be in high spirits when they arrive here to spend the night."

"I'll bet they're on cloud nine," Susie declared. "It's another grandchild for them!"

"It's not just another grandchild for them," Bob stated happily, "it's one for us, too!"

***

Davy emerged from the bathroom, clean and ready for bed. Grandma and Grandpa had already departed for the Fairchilds', and only Mom and Jim were sitting at the kitchen table. "Where's Anna?" Davy asked.

"In her bed," said Kate. "Poor thing fell asleep before we could even finish our prayers."

"I hope I can fall asleep that quickly tonight," Davy said wistfully, as he sat down across from his mother and Jim.

Jim's brow furrowed. "Are you still worried about tomorrow, son?"

"Yes, sir," Davy admitted. "We stayed so busy today, I really didn't think about the awful dream I had last night. But now that it's close to bedtime, I'm afraid I'll dream it all over again."

Mom reached across the table to lay her hand on his. "Davy," she said gently, "how many times in your life have you had the same dream twice?"

Davy thought for a moment before he answered. "I don't think I've ever had the same dream twice," he confessed, "but that doesn't mean it won't happen."

"Honey, we've talked about those what ifs before, haven't we?" Mom asked. "Take it from a still-recovering worrywart: They will only stress you out over something that will more than likely never happen. What good does that do?"

"I know you're right, Mom," Davy said with a sigh, "but can I ask you both a favor?"

"Sure. Anything for you, son," Jim said.

"When we finish the prayers, could you stay out on the porch with me until you're sure I'm asleep?"

"We'd be happy to, honey," Mom reassured him. "Speaking of bedtime and prayers, I think it's past time you headed in that very direction."

CHAPTER 20

CONFRONTING RONNIE

When Ronnie arrived with Betty Rae at the work site, he was pleased to see Bill Cunningham and a crew of ten hired men waiting for him. He pulled his truck alongside the trailer and exited the cab quickly. Betty Rae, who was all dolled up and wearing heels, slid off the seat and onto the gravel with great care. The last thing she wanted to do was turn her ankle; that would ruin the plans they had made to spend the day in Highlands.

"My, my, Miss Betty Rae," Bill Cunningham remarked when he caught sight of her. "Don't you look fancy! And are you in a sports coat, Ronnie? Are y'all headed somewhere special today?"

"That we are, Bill, that we are," said Ronnie jovially. "I'm only here to get the ball rolling and give these men a bit of a morale boost. Then I'm leaving today's work in your capable hands."

Bill smiled broadly. "Glad to have your trust, Carson," he said, and proceeded to introduce the crew.

"I'm gratified to have you all here," Ronnie said, "and I'm happy to see y'all are packing like we requested. Just for your safety, mind you, just for your safety."

"Excuse me, Mr. Carson," said a young man named Ben, "but rumor has it we're carryin' 'cause of critters like the one we seen on the news a couple of nights ago. Are they really that dangerous?"

"Once they see you packin' heat, they won't be," Ronnie assured him. "Now let's get down to business, so I can take this pretty lady out on the town."

***

Eric and Elly arrived at the Hunters' at nine fifteen that morning. Introductions were cordially, and swiftly made as Jim presented David and Sarah to them. "David will be coming with us today," Jim informed Eric. "After I told him Reverend's plan, he wouldn't take no for an answer."

"That's fine, Jim," Eric said. "David, an extra pair of hands and eyes might be just what we need. Bob, are you ready to handle that television crew when they arrive?"

"I sure am," said Bob. "I'll make sure they have a perfect view of the goings-on. Can't wait for the news reports tonight!"

"Are any of you ladies coming along?" Elly asked politely.

"No," Kate answered. "Even though Sarah here is dying to see the Old Ones, we thought it best to hang back today and let the men handle it. I'm sure the Old Ones will make themselves known to her very soon."

"I know they will," Davy said, giving his grandma a heartening hug.

"Well then, I guess it's time to get this caravan rolling," Eric said and added convivially, "Davy, would you like to ride in the patrol car with Elly and me?"

"Would I ever!" Davy exclaimed. "Thank you, Sheriff!"

"Don't mention it," said Eric, smiling and patting him on the shoulder.

"Okay, so we're off!" Jim declared, kissing Kate on the cheek and giving Anna's braid a quick tug. "Take good care of your mother, Anna. We'll be back before you know it."

"I will, Jim," Anna promised.

"And be careful," Kate cautioned, "all of you."

***

Reverend gathered all the Old Ones in the Banquet Hall that morning to review the plan one last time. "And I cannot stress this strongly enough, my friends. We are to wait for Davy's signal before we reveal ourselves.

You all know your positions on the road and the hill, and I know you will assemble yourselves accordingly. Lastly, but perhaps most importantly, this is *not* a time for heroics. If something untoward happens, you must vanish immediately and flee for The Glade. Let us be on our way!" he concluded.

"On our way!" they cheered in unison and readily followed Reverend and Mrs. Reverend up the Blessed Portal and into The Glade.

Mrs. Racer noticed with no little concern that Racer's brow was furrowed and his visage solemn as the two travelled with their counterparts to their destination. "What is it, my love?" Mrs. Racer asked. "Is the dream from the other night still bothering you?"

Racer took her paw in his. "I'm afraid it is, sweets," he said. "I can't shake the sense of foreboding I have about this whole thing. Ronnie is crafty, that's for sure, and I don't know that even our actual presence and testimonies will persuade him to cease and desist."

"But it's the only chance we have," Mrs. Racer declared. "You heard Reverend, the same as I did."

"I know it's our only chance," he said gloomily, "but I don't have to like it."

"Racer, look on the bright side," she said. "At least you get to see Davy today."

Racer brightened ever so slightly. "Yes," he said, "I can be with Davy. I'll try my best to focus on nothing but that. Maybe it will actually cheer me up."

"That's the ticket," Mrs. Racer said as she leaned over to give him a whiskery kiss on his cheek. "Focus on the Chosen One."

***

Mike arrived at Abby's home promptly at nine thirty, as he had promised. She greeted him at the door with that radiant smile of hers he so adored. "Come in, Mike," she said. "Daddy wants to know a little more about what we're going to see today. I don't know why he's worried, but he is. Do you mind talking to him?"

"Of course not," Mike assured her, but his heart sank just a bit at the prospect of a potentially long and one-sided conversation with the garrulous Hank. He didn't want them to arrive late at the construction site and run the risk of witnessing nothing at all. *But if I want to take Abby, I have to put Hank's mind at ease.*

"Howdy there, Pastor," Hank greeted Mike warmly when Abby and he entered the kitchen. "Have a seat. You want some coffee? Made it fresh just now. Bessie, you want a cup? Okay, it's coming. Now about this little jaunt you're taking my Abby on."

"Yes, sir," Mike told him, "It's perfectly safe, I assure you."

Hank frowned and took a sip of his coffee. "Ain't we talkin' about wild animals here? How close were you planning to get to these usually invisible critters? How do you know they won't attack?"

"Hank, the Old Ones are neither wild, nor are they dumb." Mike explained patiently. "They are cultured and civilized, far more so than many human beings I've met. They are making this once-in-a-lifetime appearance in a last ditch effort to save their home from destruction. We will not get too close, I promise you; we'll just watch from a distance as Davy suggested. And I can guarantee you, sir, the Old Ones will not attack."

"Davy? Who's Davy?" Hank inquired.

"Daddy, I told you," Abby said a bit petulantly. "He's the little boy who can see and hear the Old Ones any time they are around. He will be there, too. Don't you think if his parents think it's safe for him to socialize regularly with these creatures that it's safe for Mike and me?"

Hank looked at Mike, then at Abby, and back to Mike again. "You take good care of my little girl, y'hear, son?"

"I will," said Mike. "You can count on it!"

"And Abby?"

"Yes, Daddy?"

"Take the camera," Hank ordered. "I want me some pictures."

***

Eric turned his patrol car onto Willow Road with Jim right behind him. "How far is it, Davy?" he asked.

"It's a bit of a ways, as I remember, sir," Davy said. "We have to get past all these cabins to the right. Maybe about half a mile?"

"It sure is bumpy going," Elly observed as the car bounced and jostled its way through ruts and dips in the road.

"That's why I'm taking it slow," said Eric as he glanced at his watch. "We have plenty of time. Davy, when we're coming up on the site, you let me know, okay?"

"Yes, sir," he answered.

"Davy, I'm so thrilled for this chance to see the Old Ones," Elly said. She turned around so she could see him; he was seated in the back. "What is it like being able to see and hear them all the time?"

Davy grinned at her. "What's it like? It's like eating your favorite ice cream every day, as much as you want, but never getting sick or fat."

Both Elly and Eric laughed vigorously at this. "That's quite the original description, Davy," Elly declared. "I like it!"

"Thank you, Mrs. Peabody," he replied.

"You're most welcome," she said, "but you can call me Miss Elly, sweetie."

"Just like Pastor Russell says to call him Pastor Mike?" Davy asked.

"Exactly," she answered. "No need for friends to be so formal, is there?"

"In that case, Davy," Eric said, smiling at him through the rearview mirror, "why not address me as Sheriff Eric from here on out. Deal?"

"Deal!" Davy confirmed.

The car continued to crawl slowly along the uneven road, with Eric and his two passengers enjoying a companionable silence. Davy sat up straight in his seat, keeping his eyes peeled for what Jim described as the last turn before the work site would be in full view. Davy had felt confident he would recognize the spot, but now he wasn't so sure. He felt the same way as he had that day when Racer had pointed out the path to the lake, something the boy would have walked right past otherwise. *Help me know which curve it is, Lord. I'm not sure. I need help. Please help!*

"Are we close Davy?" Eric asked, thinking they should arrive any minute.

"I think so," he said uncertainly. The car veered right, then left, as the road curved before them. He was just about to declare that the upcoming bend was the last, when confirmation arrived in the welcome sight of Racer. He was holding up one paw in a signal to stop. Davy breathed a deep sigh of relief. "Stop right here, Sheriff Eric," he declared. "Racer is standing just this side of the turn and telling us to stop!"

"Racer?" Elly looked around eagerly. "But I don't see him!"

209

"You can't yet, Miss Elly," Davy told her as Eric stopped the car. Davy leaped out to run to his friend. Elly and Eric watched in amazement as Davy hugged the squirrel they could not see. Just then, Jim pulled up behind them, and spying Davy, knew one of the Old Ones had arrived to make sure they halted at the right spot.

"Okay, Bob," said Jim, "this is where I let you out. Whatever you do, don't let the television truck past this point. Only the cameraman and the reporter."

"Got it, Jim," Bob affirmed as he hopped out. "I sure hope they get here in time."

"I think they will," said David. "This is a huge scoop. Don't think they'd miss it for the world."

***

As the Channel Ten television truck maneuvered awkwardly along Willow Road, Craig Hewitt, the driver and cameraman, let out a low whistle and a string of oaths. "This better not be a wild goose chase," he growled at Chad Newton, the reporter sitting beside him. "This road is the pits, and no mistake."

"I'm not enjoying the ride any more than you are," Chad admitted grumpily, "but I'm telling you, this is no hoax. I feel it in my journalistic bones, my friend. This is destined to be the top story of the year for Channel Ten."

"Yeah, yeah, yeah," Craig grumbled sarcastically. "That's what they all say."

"Cut me some slack, will you?" Chad said with irritation. "That news report about the squirrel we posted on our website has gotten more hits than anything we've ever put up there. If this is what it's cracked up to be, we'll go national, guaranteed. Who knows? We could even see a Pulitzer Prize out of this baby!"

The truck hit another vicious dip. "Ouch!" Craig exclaimed. "If we ever make it there, that is."

***

Mike navigated the unexpectedly irregular road as judiciously as he could. "I apologize, Abby," he said after a particularly jolting pot hole. "I had no idea the road would be so rough. You'd think with all these pretty little cabins dotting this mountain, someone would take better care of it."

"You'd think," Abby said. "I know if I were vacationing in one of those cabins, I probably wouldn't come back for a return visit just because of this."

They rounded another curve and spotted the two cars parked there, one being the sheriff's, just as Bob Fairchild emerged from Jim's car. Seeing their approach and not readily recognizing who it was, Bob ran toward them, waving his arms. Mike rolled down his window and called to him. "Hi, Bob, it's Mike. Mike and Abby."

Bob reached the car breathless. "What are you two doing here?" he asked, sincerely bewildered.

"Davy invited us," Mike said. "Did he not tell anyone?"

"He didn't say a word to me," Bob admitted, "but that doesn't mean he didn't mention it to Jim. Pull on down behind Jim's car and see what he has to say. I've got to stay here anyway."

"Whatever for?" Mike asked.

"Television crew," Bob answered. "Got to intercept the truck before it rounds that last curve."

"Television truck?" Abby gasped in horror. "Mike! You didn't tell me they'd be news reporters here! What if they try to corner me again?"

"I didn't tell you, Abby, because Davy left that part out," Mike explained as he patted her hand comfortingly. "And don't worry about being cornered. I think they have bigger fish to fry today."

"That they do, young lady," Bob said. "Now why don't you all drive down to join the others so you can make your entrance in unison if Jim gives the okay, which I'm sure he will. And Pastor?"

"Yes, Bob."

"Say some prayers. Lots of them."

***

Ronnie heard the cars approaching before he saw them. "Bill, are we expecting any more workers today?" he asked nervously.

"Not by my count," said Bill, "but it does look like we have visitors."

When Eric's patrol car came into view, Ronnie had a momentary bout of panic. He thought about what Cy had told him concerning Gary and the forgery. *Get a hold of yourself, man! The sheriff has no proof, no proof at all. Stay calm and play the game. You're invincible, remember?* The patrol car pulled up a few feet from Ronnie's truck, and two other cars Ronnie couldn't identify stopped right behind him. He heard the sharp intake of Bill's breath. "Don't worry, Bill," Ronnie said with bravado. "This will be a short visit, I promise. I'll have that ol' Sheriff Busybody retreating like a dog with his tail between his legs in no time."

Eric surveyed the group carefully before getting out of the car. He saw right away that the men had gun holsters hitched to their belts, just as the Old Ones had feared. "Elly," he said haltingly, "you remember how to use the car radio, don't you?"

"Of course I do," she assured him. "Why are you asking, Eric? Do you think there could be trouble?"

"Whenever firearms are involved," he said, "there's always that possibility. Elly, I want you to stay with the car while we confront Ronnie and his crew. You'll still be able to see the Old Ones when they show themselves, but you'll be close to the radio should we need to summon help."

"Now you're scaring me, Eric," said Elly, her voice trembling.

"Don't be afraid, Miss Elly," Davy piped up. "The Old Ones won't let anything bad happen, and I won't either."

"Davy, stay with Miss Elly until I make sure these fellows lay down their guns, okay?" Eric asked, but Davy knew it was really an order.

"Yes, sir," he answered, "I'll wait for your signal."

Though he had checked his gun before he departed this morning, Eric did so again just to reassure himself it was good to go. He took the safety off, placed it back in its holster, and exited the patrol car. He saw that Jim and David were already standing outside their car. Pastor Mike and a young woman were standing together by another. With his back to Ronnie's group, he motioned to Jim to stay put, and leaned back into the open window of the car. "Davy," he whispered, "did you know Pastor Russell would be here today?"

"Yes, sir," Davy answered. "Is that a problem?"

212

"I hope not," Eric answered. "Having him here will at least remind us all to keep the faith." He turned and strode briskly toward Ronnie and his men, noticing with some surprise that Betty Rae was also in attendance. Both she and Ronnie were dressed fashionably, and it made him wonder what they were up to.

"Well, good morning, Sheriff," Ronnie hailed Eric as he approached. "And to what do we owe this visit by your esteemed self today?" Ronnie's tone dripped with sarcasm. He was acting the same way he had as when they met last, at the hospital: cocky, arrogant, and full of himself. "An even more important question is," Ronnie continued, his eyes narrowing into slits, "how did you know I was here, at this time and on this day? Been following me, Sheriff?"

"No, Mr. Carson, I haven't," Eric said coolly. "But I'm here at the invitation of someone who has been following you, so to speak."

"Betty Rae," Ronnie turned to her, a droll smile on his face, "you're following me around all the time, aren't you? Did you, by chance, invite the good sheriff to our groundbreaking?"

This comment evoked raucous laughter from the men. Betty Rae glared at her husband unforgivingly. "Why would I do something like that?"

"I didn't think so," said Ronnie, "but it looks to me, Sheriff, that you have some folks following you here today. Isn't that Jim I see? The one who is under the delusion that he owns every nook and cranny in the Nantahalas?"

"There are many reasons why Jim and the others are here," said Eric, "reasons that will become clear to all in a matter of moments. But first there's something I need to ask you and your men to do, Mr. Carson."

"And what might that be?" Ronnie asked with a scowl.

"Put your guns down," Eric said sternly. Some of the men, intimidated by Eric's very presence, immediately reached for their holsters and laid their weapons on the gravel.

"Wait a minute!" Ronnie yelled. "What right do you have to tell us to ditch our guns? Are you thinking we're that crazy, that we would shoot you or anyone else?"

"With what you're about to see," Eric said, this time looking at Bill and the men, not at Ronnie, "I'm concerned you will be shocked, alarmed and, quite frankly, fearful. I wouldn't want any one of you to land behind bars because you shot first and asked questions later." Bill carefully placed his gun on the ground and motioned to the rest of those still armed to do the same. Ronnie, glaring menacingly at Eric, was the last to comply. "There now," Eric told them, giving the others a thumbs-up behind his back, "that's more like it."

"What about you, Sheriff?" Ronnie snarled. "Aren't you going to put your gun down like the rest of us?"

"No can do," Eric stated flatly. "I'm here officially, on duty, and I'm here to protect—not provoke."

"Well, you just being here is provoking enough," Ronnie declared. "Not to mention the other uninvited guests making their way over here."

Jim and David, with Davy walking between them, approached the group. When they reached Eric, David and Davy stopped; Jim continued on until he was standing right in front of Ronnie. The intensity with which Jim was staring at him made Ronnie flinch ever so subtly. When Jim spoke, his voice was controlled and even, but Davy could tell by the set of Jim's jaw that a cauldron of anger bubbled just below the surface. "Ronnie, I have to hand it to you," Jim said. "When you want something, you don't take no for an answer. I know about the deed to this property. And though I know it's not worth the paper it's printed on, I can't prove it."

A villainous smile crept across Ronnie's face. "So in front of God, the sheriff, and everyone, you finally admit defeat? It's about time, since you've been all wrong about this from the get-go."

"I didn't say I was wrong," Jim corrected him. "I merely said I don't have the proof. But I know who does."

Ronnie's eyes narrowed as he took a step toward Jim. "You're bluffing," he hissed threateningly. "You're just trying to stall the inevitable. Well, guess what? It ain't working. This time, I win and you lose, and that's the way it's going to be."

"Not according to the Old Ones," Jim said calmly as he kept his eyes fixed on Ronnie's own. "You remember them, don't you? The characters in Grandpa Will's stories? The stories you wouldn't believe were true?"

Ronnie blanched. He could feel his heart beating loudly in his chest. The palms of his hands felt cold and clammy, and his stomach lurched like a sailboat caught in a violent gust of wind. "I remember," Ronnie croaked as he felt his former swagger ebbing away. *So that's what Sheriff Busybody meant by my being followed. This can't be happening! This can't be happening!*

Throughout this exchange, Davy had been watching the Old Ones scramble into their respective positions. At Reverend's signal, Davy walked over to join him; with Reverend on one side of him and Racer on the other, Davy felt confident and ready for the ensuing revelation. "It's time, Jim," he announced.

Jim took a few steps back from Ronnie, Betty Rae, and the men in order for them to experience an unobstructed view. "The Old Ones are here, Ronnie," he affirmed, "and they think it's high time you met them."

CHAPTER 21

REVELATION

In the split second the Old Ones appeared, the air was rent by shrieks and shouts and gasps. Betty Rae screamed uncontrollably. The man named Ben dropped to his knees and frantically prayed. Poor Bill Cunningham keeled over in a dead faint.

"Peace be with you!" Reverend called over the chaotic din, emitting the familiar fragrance of honeysuckle as he did so. "Peace be with you!"

Reverend's greeting combined with the sweet aroma had its desired effect. The crowd quieted. Even Bill came to, and was amazed to find he experienced none of the sickness in his stomach that was so common after one has passed out. Reverend swiveled his head from this person to that, his amber eyes seeming to cast a soothing spell upon each one as his gaze passed over them. When his focus turned to Ronnie, however, the owl shuddered. He knew the eyes of evil all too intimately, but discerned that the goodness all the Old Ones had carried with them to this place would sustain him.

Reverend cleared his throat, as was his habit, and addressed the gathering in a sonorous tone easily audible to everyone. "We are the Old Ones from the Ancient of Days," he began formally. "We have come here, risking our anonymity and safety, in order to save our home. To what we have to say to Ronnie, all of you here today are my cloud of witnesses. Listen well, and I pray, take all this to heart."

"Hear! Hear!" the Old Ones chorused, their voices resounding thunderously against the mountainside.

216

"Ronnie," Reverend continued somberly, "we are the ones who have been shadowing your every move since Saturday. We know where you have been, we know with whom you've met, and we are well aware of the lengths you are willing to go and the limits you are willing to push to get your way."

Ronnie's face turned beet red. "Following me?" he spluttered angrily. "How is that even possible?"

"Invisibility comes in handy at times," Reverend answered. "I could go into the full details of all we have learned, but I choose to keep it brief. Suffice it to say, the good sheriff has informed me that the evidence we have gathered is enough at the moment to issue a restraining order against you, until said time the matter comes to court. Our hope is that it won't, but that depends upon your cooperation."

"You ain't gettin' my cooperation, varmint," Ronnie spat viciously. "You got nothing on me. Nothing! This is my land, my property, and I want you off it *now*!"

"I'm afraid that's quite impossible, Ronnie," Reverend countered calmly. "Do you see this mountain behind me? The one upon which you are so intent to build? It leads to our home, our Sanctuary, The Glade. If you destroy the land by building your cabins here, you will destroy us, too. That is something we will not let happen."

"Do you think I give one hoot whether you critters live or die?" Ronnie exploded as any lingering sense of trepidation or fear of how the Old Ones could interfere with his plans dissipated.

Reverend took one step toward Ronnie; Davy followed suit. "There is something you must understand, Ronnie," the owl said evenly, raising his voice ever so slightly so that none could possibly miss his words. "If I hadn't cared whether or not you lived or died, you'd have perished on our mountain the day you brought your boys here to go on a shooting spree." Here, Reverend shifted his focus to Betty Rae who stared at him fearfully. "I hate to be the one to break the news to you, Betty Rae," he continued, "but your husband *did* suffer a heart attack that day. I could have left him to die, and I wouldn't be here right now trying to talk him out of exterminating us, had I done so." He turned back to Ronnie. "I chose to heal you, Ronnie, and I suffered terribly for my effort. I gave you back your life. Could you, in light of the mercy shown to you, show mercy to us?"

The ensuing silence was deafening. The eyes of everyone were trained on Ronnie, waiting in uneasy suspense for his reaction to Reverend's disclosure. For a brief and hopeful moment, Davy thought he caught a glimpse of remorse in Ronnie's eyes. *Could he show mercy? Is he able to?* As swiftly as his hopes had risen, they were dashed just as quickly. Davy saw Ronnie's eyes dreadfully transforming into the flaming crimson slits that had held him spellbound at River's End. This time, however, those venomous eyes were not looking at him; their fix was on Reverend. "Liar!" Ronnie roared in a terrifying, unearthly voice that set hearts to violent trembling. "All liars!"

In the split second Ronnie slipped his hand into his jacket pocket, Davy knew his horrific nightmare was coming true. He leaped in front of Reverend. There was a flash and a searing pain; Davy's world went black.

***

Kate, Sarah, Susie, and Anna were playing a lively game of Monopoly when Kate suddenly stiffened, all the color draining from her face. Sarah was the first to notice. "What's wrong, honey? Are you feeling nauseous again?"

"No," she said, with fear in her eyes and a quaver in her voice. "Something terrible has happened to Davy. I just know it."

Everyone looked at Kate in alarm. "How can you know that, dear?" Susie asked gently.

"I just do," Kate answered. Tears began to well in her eyes. She rose from the table and began to pace the floor. Sarah and Susie exchanged apprehensive looks. Anna, seeing her mother so distressed, left her place at the table to give Kate a comforting hug. Kate gratefully stopped mid-stride to return it.

"Don't worry, Mom," Anna said. "The Old Ones are with Davy. He's going to be fine."

"I wish I could believe that, honey," Kate said, squeezing her daughter tightly. "Oh, how I hope and pray my feelings are wrong."

***

The instant he saw Ronnie's movement, Eric drew his gun with lightning speed. Ronnie's bullet had only just left its chamber when Eric's hit his hand, still concealed in his jacket pocket, effectively dropping Ronnie to the ground. At the first sound of gunfire the Old Ones, as they promised Reverend, vanished from view, but did not vacate the scene. Their Chosen One, stricken, unconscious, and bleeding, could not be abandoned in his time of need. Neither could Reverend, who had been knocked out cold when Davy's body crashed into his upon taking the bullet meant for him. Racer and Mrs. Reverend were frantically trying to revive Reverend. Racer, tears streaming down his cheeks, was hysterical. "Wake up, Reverend, wake up!" Racer pleaded at the top of his lungs. "Davy needs you! You must breathe healing into him! Please, please, please!"

Sharp-eyes and Scout offered their assistance, propping Reverend into a sitting position and supporting him with their strong wings. Mrs. Reverend sped back to The Glade to fetch reviving herbs, praying and weeping the whole time that her beloved one would awaken in time to aid the one who had saved him. All the Old Ones cried and prayed fervently as they watched Jim and David, leaning over Davy's limp and lifeless form and shouting frantically for help. Elly had radioed 911 the instant she saw Davy fall. Once ambulance dispatch was confirmed she sprinted over to Eric, who was still standing with the shocked and mortified workers and the stricken, inconsolable Betty Rae. "The ambulances are on the way," she announced breathlessly, tears standing in her eyes. "Oh, I pray they get here in time."

"I pray they do too," said Eric stoically. "I don't know how much time we have."

Just at that moment, Mike and Abby ran up to the scene; Mike was carrying a first aid kit. "Eric! Will this help?" Mike asked, as he waved it in the air.

"Yes! Give that to Jim and David. Elly, get my first aid kit out of the car and we'll see if we can at least stop Ronnie's bleeding! And radio Connie for back up."

David, who had been a trained as a medic in the army, had already stripped off his shirt to try to staunch the flow of blood from Davy's shoulder. He thankfully took the kit from Mike and wasted no time using the contents. "Davy's bleeding heavily, Jim," he said chokingly as tears coursed down both men's faces. "I pray that bullet didn't hit a main artery. Please God, let the ambulance get here fast!"

***

While the cameraman stayed focused on the Old Ones, Bob was being questioned by Chad and had his back to the scene. "So let me get this straight, Mr. Fairchild," said Chad. "The young boy standing in the midst of these amazing creatures is the only one who can see and hear them all the time?"

"Yes," Bob answered. "It's Davy's gift. They call him the Chosen One."

"Wow, that's truly amazing," Chad remarked. "Do you think when all this is over, Davy would consent to an interview?"

"It would be up to his parents to give permission," Bob told him, "but I imagine..." *Crack! Crack!* The gunshots rang out. Bob whirled around in a panic. "Oh, my God, oh, my God!" he yelled as he sprinted down the long hill toward the group. He couldn't see Davy, but knew by the hunched figures of Jim and David that it was he who had been struck down. Bob prayed with every breath, with every step, with every tear: prayed from his heart that Davy would make it.

Bob had just reached Jim and David when Mrs. Reverend returned to the Old Ones in the very nick of time. "Hurry, Mrs. Reverend!" Racer shouted frantically. "David said Davy's bleeding too much! He can't die! He can't!"

Without a second's hesitation, Mrs. Reverend held the medicinal herbs under Reverend's beak and prayed. It only took a few seconds for the owl to revive, yet to those watching, it seemed an eternity. "Davy? What happened?" Reverend asked dazedly as he blinked his amber eyes at the faces surrounding him.

"He's been shot!" Racer screamed. "Now, Reverend, now! Heal him!"

At the squirrel's words, the haze vanished instantly from the owl's mind. "Help me over to him!" Reverend commanded Scout and Sharp-eyes, who immediately braced him and dragged him close to Davy. The owl inhaled deeply, prayed deeper still, and slowly let his breath flow out, invisibly surrounding Davy with a cloud of comfort and healing.

"How bad is it?" Bob managed to ask, staring in alarm at the now abandoned blood-soaked shirt of David's.

Jim looked up at his friend's stricken face. "If David can't get the bleeding to stop..." He couldn't bring himself to finish the thought aloud. Instead, Jim cradled Davy's head in his lap and prayed, the tears coursing unabashedly down his cheeks.

David removed the thick, soiled gauze he had been pressing hard on Davy's wound to replace it with a fresh one. He was just about to apply it when he gasped in amazement. "Look, Jim! Look at the wound!" David ordered urgently. "The bleeding! It's slowing down!"

Both Jim and Bob stared in awe at what only moments ago had been a life-draining floodgate. The bleeding not only slowed , it stopped completely before their wondering eyes, forming a sturdy scab in mere moments. "Reverend," Jim whispered. "This must be his doing."

"It was, dearest Jim," said Reverend as he appeared suddenly at Jim's elbow, his eyes shining with joy. "Davy will be fine now until he reaches the hospital."

Impulsively, Jim threw his arm around the owl's shoulder, pulled him close, and kissed the top of his feathery head. "Where would Davy be without you, Reverend?" he asked, a broad and blissful smile contrasting beautifully with his stray tears.

"The better question is," said the owl solemnly, "where would I have been today if not for Davy and his sacrifice?"

"You would no longer be with us," Mrs. Reverend spoke as she came into view. "And I would die of a broken heart. Jim, we owe everything to Davy."

"And now, I have one more person I must tend to," said Reverend with a heavy sigh.

Mrs. Reverend frowned at him. "Don't you go near that monster," she admonished him fiercely. "Do you not recall what happened the last time you tried to do Ronnie a good deed? I'll not hear of it!"

"My dear," Reverend said soothingly, "I have not forgotten what happened and I have no intentions of repeating such a foolish and prideful act. I'm only going to stop the bleeding in Ronnie's hand. Whether he heals or not will be up to the Creator."

"All right then," Mrs. Reverend grudgingly conceded. "But you're not walking over there alone. I'm coming with you."

"If you insist," he said with a chuckle. "But I think we should approach them invisibly; Betty Rae is shaken up enough as it is."

With that, the owls vanished from Jim's sight.

***

Kate was just beginning to wonder what was taking the men so long to get back, when she heard a car approaching down the road. "Anna," she said, "would you run to the living room window, and see if that's Jim and the others? If it is, I need to start fixing some lunch."

"Okay, Mom," said Anna. She jumping up from her seat at the table, where she had been helping her grandmothers pick up the Monopoly game. Everyone heard the car coming closer and closer, and expected it to stop at the house any minute; instead, it kept on going in the direction of the Fairchilds'. Anna ambled into the kitchen, a puzzled look on her face. "It was our car," she said, "but Jim wasn't driving; Bampa was. Why would that be?"

Mom's brow furrowed. "I have no idea," she said, and the anxious feeling she had had about Davy earlier in the day reared its ugly head. "Could you see who else was in the car, sweetie?"

"No, just Bampa," Anna confirmed.

"Maybe Eric is bringing the others home in his patrol car," Susie suggested, "though I have no clue why."

"Nor do I," Kate said as she slumped onto the table bench. "Now I truly am worried."

Sarah reached over to pat her hand. "Honey," she said, "worrying isn't good for either you or the baby. Let's think positive thoughts, shall we?"

Kate smiled wearily. "I'll try," she said.

At that moment, the phone sounded its unnerving jangling. "I'll get it!" Anna offered as she ran to pick it up. "Hello? Hi, Bampa! Yes, she's here. Just a minute. Nana, it's for you," she said, handing the receiver to Susie.

"Bob? Is everything all right?"

"No, it isn't," he answered shakily. "Just listen to the facts without reacting, if at all possible; Kate needs to hear this news in as calm a way as she can. Jim is at the hospital with Davy. Ronnie had a small pistol in his jacket pocket." A sharp gasp escaped Susie's lips. Bob continued, "I need you to be strong, Susie, for Kate and Sarah's sake. Davy will need surgery to remove the bullet. As soon as David finishes changing his clothes, I'm going to drive them all to the hospital. Can you stay here and keep Anna?"

"Of course I can," she whispered weakly, "but why did David have to change?"

"Long story," he said. "I know you'll make sure both Kate and Sarah are sitting down when you tell them. We should be there in a matter of minutes."

Click! Susie lowered the receiver slowly onto its cradle, trying to control the tears threatening to spill. When she turned to face the women, they knew instantly from her troubled expression that something was terribly wrong. "Susie, what is it?" Kate asked in trepidation.

"Why don't we all sit down," Susie suggested. As she was suddenly feeling weak in the knees, she took her own advice, too. She reached out her hands to take Sarah's in one and Kate's in the other, and took a deep breath. "This isn't easy," she admitted. "Kate, I'm afraid the fear you felt earlier today wasn't simply a feeling."

***

Eric's back-up arrived not five minutes after the ambulances; one of his deputies, Hoyt Darnell, had been patrolling in the general vicinity. The shock on Hoyt's face at the sight of the violent confrontation, Eric knew, was the result of seeing a child as one of the wounded. "What in the name of God happened here?" Hoyt asked, his eyes wide with disbelief.

Nodding toward the pile of handguns still on the ground, Eric answered soberly, "Nothing I could have imagined, with all the precautions I took. Don't let any of the men standing here move for their guns until we've gotten names, addresses and phone numbers. They are witnesses to the shooting. Wait until I rejoin you to begin. I need to see if I can find Elly a ride home."

"Yes, sir," Hoyt said.

Eric walked briskly over to Elly; she was standing with Mike and Abby. All three of their faces were tear-streaked, and Abby was unreservedly sobbing against Mike's chest. Eric put his arms around his wife and said, "I have to stay here for a while to finish up business. Pastor Mike, would it be too much trouble for you to take Elly home for me?"

"I'd be happy to," Mike said agreeably.

"But Eric," Elly protested, "I don't want to go home. I want to go to the hospital and wait with the family."

"That's what I want to do, too," Abby asserted, lifting her head up to look Mike in the face. "Will you take us there?"

"Of course," Mike assured her. "That's not just where I need to be right now, but where I *want* to be."

"Wonderful," said Eric as he reached out to shake Mike's hand. "I'll join you all there just as soon as I wrap things up."

"We'll wait until the ambulances have left before we leave," Mike said. "That way, they can have clear sailing up that treacherous road."

"Another good idea," Eric confirmed with a grin. He leaned down to kiss Elly on the cheek, "I'll see you soon, beautiful," he said and then turned and strode back to the scene to join Hoyt.

***

"I'm riding to the hospital with Davy," Racer announced to Mrs. Racer as he leapt effortlessly up and into the wide-open doors of the ambulance. He scrambled onto the foot of the gurney upon which the boy's limp body lay so helplessly. "If he wakes up, he'll need me. I just know it!"

"Be safe, Racer," she said anxiously. "It's liable to be a perilous ride. I will join you soon, my love!"

"As many of us who can do so will join you too, my friend," Reverend declared, and turning to the throng of Old Ones still gathered there, added, "Seeing as we all can't fit into an already cramped waiting room, it will have to be one small delegation at a time. I suggest we return to The Glade for a spot of rest, and then pull straws to see who of us, and how many, will go first. To The Glade!"

"To The Glade!" the Old Ones boomed.

Mrs. Racer blew Racer a kiss. "I love you," she said.

Racer flashed his lopsided grin at her. "I love you, too, sweets!"

***

Davy leaned comfortably against the shoulder of the Good Shepherd, gazing out across the endless pasture with its countless sheep. He breathed a cleansing sigh of contentment. "I love it here with you," he whispered. "Will I be staying this time?"

The Good Shepherd held Davy close and kissed the top of his head. "You will stay, my child, for a while; you need to abide in me, but it is not your time. Not yet."

Davy sighed again, but this time with a hint of sadness. "Life is painful," he confessed. "It's hard, and it's confusing. But you already know that. There's a part of me that wants all that to be over."

"Ah, but your life has only just begun," said the Good Shepherd comfortingly. "I have plans for you; plans to prosper and not harm you. You will be my hands and feet in the world for many who otherwise may never know me. Yes, Davy, I have great plans in store for you."

Davy was silent for several minutes, simply drinking in the ethereal scenery and breathing in the boundless peace. Like a still, small echo in the recesses of his mind, he could hear shouts and screams, cries and sirens; but the chaos seemed so removed and distant, it did not disturb him—he was rapt in this moment. Davy closed his eyes and snuggled closer to the Good Shepherd. "Sleep, my child," he whispered tenderly. "Rest. Rest in me."

CHAPTER 22

IN THE WAITING ROOM

To all appearances, Jim and Betty Rae were the only occupants of the emergency room waiting area. Davy, had he been there instead of lying unconscious on the operating table, would have seen a bevy of Old Ones gathered by Jim's feet or perched on vacant chairs near him. Reverend's decision to limit the amount of Old Ones who could keep vigil in the waiting room had been a wise one. Though it was accommodatingly empty now, he suspected it could fill up at any time with Davy's family and friends. Reverend glanced over at Betty Rae, noting that she was sitting as far away from Jim as was physically possible, and wondered if anyone would arrive to be with her and offer her words of solace and a shoulder to cry on.

As if she read his mind, Mrs. Reverend remarked, "I feel sorry for poor Betty Rae. She looks so pathetic and forlorn. If I thought it would do her any good, I'd speak with her myself."

"I know you would, my dear," said Reverend, placing a wing around her shoulder, "but I think only another human can comfort her." The owl looked at Jim, who was sitting next to him. He was hunched over with his elbows on his knees head bowed. Reverend knew Jim was carrying the weight of the world on his shoulders as he awaited the outcome of Davy's surgery. His heart ached to relieve Jim of the hurt and guilt he suffered at this moment, but Reverend knew his power to heal had already been stretched to the limit. The brief time he had spent in The Glade before coming here had not been enough to restore it. *But there is something else I can do. Something we can all do.* "My dear Old Ones," Reverend said quietly

226

as he knew most were deep in prayer for Davy. "As we pray for our beloved Chosen One, let us also lift up Jim and Betty Rae for healing in mind and spirit."

"Amen," the group answered; they took Reverend's request to heart.

The Old Ones hadn't been engaged in these prayers more than a few minutes when Mike, Abby, and Elly entered the waiting area. Racer, though his eyes were closed, heard their footsteps. "Visitors, everybody," he whispered hoarsely. "Look lively! You don't want to get stepped on or sat upon." The eyes of all the Old Ones flew open and their bodies tensed, ready to spring into action if need be. Jim, his head down, didn't even know anyone was approaching until Mike was standing right in front of him.

"Jim," Mike said quietly, "we've come to wait with you."

Jim immediately stood up and threw his arms around Mike as tears flowed afresh. "Thank you," Jim said as he hugged all three in turn. "I really would appreciate some company right now." Looking directly at Mike, he added, "And some prayers."

"You've got it," said Mike as the four joined hands and bowed their heads. "But before I begin," he whispered, "isn't that woman in the corner the one who was with Ronnie?"

Jim looked confused. "Yes, she's his wife," he said.

"What's her name?" Mike asked.

"Betty Rae," Jim answered. "Why do you want to know, Pastor?"

"Because," said Mike, "she looks like she could use some prayers too, don't you think? I mean, after all, she's not the one who pulled the trigger."

Jim turned his head to look at Betty Rae. She was staring, unseeing, at the far wall and the tell-tale streaks of mascara on her cheeks looked like cracks in the face of a fragile, porcelain doll. With her hair disheveled and her clothes spattered with blood, Betty Rae was the epitome of pitiful. Jim couldn't help but feel sorry for her. *And on top of all that, the poor woman is married to a man with the morals of a worm. Wait. You shouldn't insult a worm. You should...* In a flash, Jim remembered his conversation with Davy from days ago. *Is Ronnie your enemy? Is he yours?* He knew immediately what he had to do. Meeting Mike's gaze, Jim said resolutely, "Yes, Pastor, let's pray for Betty Rae. And while we're at it, say a prayer for Ronnie, too."

***

After the ambulances departed, Chad and Craig hurried to the crime scene. "We'll film a short piece here, to go before the segment we've already got," Chad informed Craig. He went to place himself not ten feet away from where Davy had fallen. Eric had already put up the plastic police barriers, which made for a dramatic backdrop. "Ready, Craig? In three, two one..." Chad counted down. "I'm standing just a few feet away from where two tragic shootings took place today, at an event which was touted to be the most mystical, magical sight ever witnessed in these parts—or any other place, for that matter. Cut! At this point, we'll edit in the footage you got of the Old Ones today," Chad said.

"Got it," said Craig.

"So, next segment," said Chad. "Start the shoot! Now the place where the Old Ones appeared to the marvel and wonder of all who witnessed it stands silent, barren and cold in light of today's unfortunate events. Neither of the wounded victims has yet to be officially identified, nor is either victim's condition known; at the time of this filming, the ambulances have only just departed. All we know is that Davy is the first name of the boy who was shot, and he is called the Chosen One by the Old Ones; for only he can hear and see them at all times. What an amazing gift that is! Let us all hope Davy's wound is not serious, and that he will enjoy many long and happy days surrounded by these remarkable creatures. When we learn of the victims' status, we will update you as soon as possible. Cut! Now let's see if we can wrestle some information out of the sheriff over there, and hustle back to the station. This needs to get on the News at Noon!"

***

When Mike concluded the prayer, he glanced again at Betty Rae. Her head was down and her hands, lying in her lap, were fidgeting anxiously with a tissue. "I think I'll go over and introduce myself," he said softly, nodding his head in her direction.

"That's a good idea," said Jim. "Maybe you can give her some hope."

228

"Jim," Elly said kindly, "can I get you anything? A cup of coffee? A snack?"

"Coffee would be great," Jim told her. "I'm feeling pretty spent."

"Why not coffee for everyone?" Abby suggested. "I'll treat."

Elly smiled and said, "Too late; the treat's on me today. Abby, you stay with Jim while Pastor Mike is talking with Betty Rae. I'll be back in no time." With that, Elly headed off to the hospital cafeteria.

"Have a seat, Abby," Jim said. He sat down and patted the chair next to him. She readily complied. "I've yet to thank you, young lady, for the kindness you showed Anna the other day," Jim continued. "I don't know how she would have managed to recover from her ice bath, if not for your quilt."

Abby beamed. "I was just glad I had it along," she said. "Anna is one brave little girl."

"That she is," Jim agreed, with a smile that did nothing to assuage the pain and grief Abby saw in his startlingly green eyes.

With sincere compassion, Abby asked softly, "Mr. Hunter, have the doctors told you anything yet about Davy?"

Jim shook his head sadly. "All I know is I had to sign consent papers for immediate surgery to remove the bullet," he said. "I don't even have any idea how long the procedure will take." Jim glanced at the clock on the wall, wondering when Kate and the others would finally arrive.

"I'm so sorry," said Abby. "I can't imagine what you're going through right now, but Mike and I plan to stay here with you the whole time."

"That will be a comfort," Jim told her. "And might I ask how you and the pastor happened to be there today?"

"Davy invited us," she said. "I mean, he invited Mike, and Mike invited me to go along. I didn't want to miss out on seeing the Old Ones, but had I known what was going to happen..."

Jim saw tears starting in Abby's eyes, and gave her a fatherly pat on the hand. "If you cry, Abby, you'll get me going again," he told her. Abby promptly sat up straight and put on a brave face as she dabbed the tears away with a tissue. "There, that's better," Jim said as Abby smiled at him. "Now if you think I'm being too curious, you just tell me to back off, okay? But there's something I'd like to ask."

"Is it about Mike and me?" Abby guessed correctly.

"Yes," Jim admitted. "I'll just come right out with it. Are you two dating?"

Abby's face turned bright crimson. "Yes, sir," she answered. "Today was our first date."

Jim emitted a low whistle. "You won't be forgetting this first date any time soon, I imagine," he remarked.

"No, sir," Abby confirmed. "It all started out so beautifully and magically, with Davy and the Old Ones. I pray it ends that way."

***

"Mrs. Carson?" Betty Rae looked up and saw Mike regarding her with kind, sympathetic eyes behind his round spectacles. "I'm Pastor Mike Russell, from Nantahala United Methodist Church. Would you mind if I sit down?" Betty Rae didn't utter a word, but simply motioned half-heartedly at the empty chair next to her. Mike promptly took his seat and turned to face Betty Rae, but she didn't respond in kind. Instead she resumed staring at the far wall, as if she had no company whatsoever. Her face wore a passive expression that belied the turmoil she was enduring inside. Though Betty Rae seemed on the surface to be resigned to whatever fate befell her this dreadful day, Mike was sure he glimpsed a hint of distress in her eyes. "Mrs. Carson?" Mike tried again, his voice barely audible. "Would you like me to pray with you?"

Betty Rae turned toward Mike this time, blinking her eyes as if she were seeing him for the first time. As she pondered his question in her mind, her appearance transformed from one of indifference to one of haughty indignation. "You want to pray with me?" Betty Rae snarled sarcastically. "Aren't you with Jim over there? Aren't you his preacher? What would he think about you cozying up to the enemy?"

"You're not the enemy, Mrs. Carson," Mike calmly assured her. "In fact, we just finished praying for you a few moments ago. I just thought you might need someone to pray with you."

"Think again," Betty Rae huffed angrily. "I don't believe in all that hocus-pocus prayer stuff. Never did me any good when I tried in the past, so don't think for a minute I'm going to try it again."

Mike was understandably flustered by Betty Rae's unexpected declaration and her flippant attitude, but he decided to push the envelope. "So I'm assuming by what you just stated, Mrs. Carson," he ventured, "that you and Mr. Carson don't attend church?"

"Oh, we attend church, all right," she protested. "Wouldn't be right not to. I mean, what would folks think? I just don't like all the religion garbage."

Mike pounced on this window of opportunity. "God doesn't like religion, either," he avowed.

Betty Rae's mouth flew open and her eyes grew round with disbelief. "How can you say that, you being a preacher and all?" she spluttered. "I've never heard the likes!"

"But it's true," Mike continued, undeterred. "God doesn't like religion. What He likes, what He wants from us, is relationship."

"Relationship?" Betty Rae was dumbfounded. "What does that mean?"

"It's why God sent His only Son, Jesus, to earth," Mike stated unpretentiously, "to die for our sins and restore a right relationship with the Father. It is by accepting Jesus as Lord and Savior that we come to know God as our Father, or to be even more accurate, as our Daddy, the One who loves us immeasurably as His children."

Betty Rae scowled as she mulled Mike's words over in her mind. *Daddy? How preposterous! God wants us to call Him that? It seems too simple; too good to be true. Yet this Pastor Russell seems so sure of it. I can't think why he wouldn't be telling me the truth. But I still can't wrap my head around it.* "Pastor Russell," she said flatly, her frown still in place, "I don't know what to think about what you just said. No one's ever explained it like that to me. I need time to digest it."

"You do that, Mrs. Carson," Mike said encouragingly as he stood up to go. "Now if you will excuse me…"

"Wait!" Betty Rae's command startled him. "Sit back down. I've changed my mind."

"Changed your mind?" Mike asked.

"Yes," she said as Mike caught the barest glimmer of a smile on her face. "I'll take those prayers after all."

***

Kate flew into the waiting room like a whirlwind and headed straight for Jim. Seeing her coming, Jim jumped up and met her halfway. He threw his arms around her and held her close. Kate, who had tried valiantly to hold herself together during the drive to the hospital, hung in Jim's arms like a limp rag doll and cried as if her heart would break. This sorrowful, piteous scene brought tears afresh to everyone in the room. David held Sarah as she, too, was suddenly as inconsolable as Kate. Bob, his face drawn and pale, sat down next to Elly, who had only returned with the coffee a few minutes before. They exchanged a hug and Bob asked worriedly, "Any news yet?"

"No, none," she said regretfully. "I'm thinking it could be another hour or so before we know anything more about Davy."

Bob had a concerned look on his face, but this time, it was meant for Elly. "You've had a rough week, I know," he said empathetically. "I just want you to know how sorry Susie and I are for your loss. How are you holding up, Elly?"

"As best as can be expected, I suppose," she said, smiling bravely. "There's nothing like the sorrow of another to take your mind off your own."

"You are right about that, my dear," said Bob. "May the good Lord continue to heal you and Davy both."

"Amen," Elly said.

***

"It's getting just a bit crowded in here, wouldn't you say, Reverend?" Scout observed.

"Yes, quite," said the owl. The Old Ones were finding themselves constantly displaced from their perches as more people gathered in the waiting room. "We may have to resort to sitting under the chairs instead of on top of them. Oh, how I wish we would have some good news about Davy soon!"

"You don't suppose it could be anything *but* good news, do you?" Racer inquired anxiously. "I couldn't bear it otherwise!"

"Nor could any of us," Reverend declared. "I am feeling confident the doctors will successfully complete the work I started there on the hillside.

I can't help but wonder what they made of that neat and tidy little scab on Davy's shoulder."

"Probably never saw anything like it in their lives," Scout chuckled. "Reverend, I must say, you outdid yourself today."

"Why, thank you, Scout," Reverend said with a wink. "Only the best for the Chosen One!"

"Always!" Racer said. "But what about Ronnie, Reverend? Do you think he'll pull through, too? I shudder at the thought, but then I look at Betty Rae and I feel so sorry this entire mess had to happen. Why couldn't that big lout just mind his own business and be happy with what he already had, instead of grabbing more and more from others?"

"Sadly, it is the way of the worldly, dear Racer," Reverend responded with a sigh. "And in answer to your other question, yes, I think Ronnie will make it. He may have lost the entire use of his right hand, but we will have to wait and see."

"Do you think he'll end up going to jail for shooting Davy?" Scout asked.

"Not if he goes before that judge he's got in his back pocket," Sharpeyes observed glumly. "I recall that conversation like it was yesterday."

"Be that as it may," said Reverend, "it is all far down the road. We know that at least for the time being, we've been afforded a much needed respite from Ronnie's egregious behaviors. Let us simply be thankful for that."

"Yes, we should be thankful," said Mrs. Racer, "and I know I am. But what I wish right now is that we could somehow comfort Davy's family without draining ourselves of our energies completely. Kate and Sarah are beside themselves, and it slays my heart to see them in this state."

"Hmm," Reverend said, "let me ruminate on this one for a few moments. How to comfort them? There must be a way."

"Oh, how I wish Eric was here," Mrs. Reverend lamented, "Mrs. Scout and I had a yes-no pecking system down pat with him, when we confronted the forger the other day. He would know immediately of our presence, and could ask us questions we could answer without the stress and strain of becoming visible."

"That would be perfect," Mrs. Racer agreed, "but it won't work if he doesn't show up."

"Hold on a minute!" Racer shouted so loudly they all jumped. "I just thought of something Davy told me about his mother. He thinks she has the gift to see and hear us like he does, but it's deeply buried within her. Maybe in light of the heightened awareness crisis often brings, she will be able to hear us if we address her directly."

"Could that possibly work?" Reverend wondered.

"Isn't it worth a try?" Racer said excitedly.

Reverend smiled. "Go for it," he said.

***

"I can't lose my little boy. I can't lose my little boy." Kate choked out the words between the sobs which wracking her body.

"We won't lose Davy, Kate," Jim said reassuringly, though he was just as worried as she about the outcome. "Come on, let's sit and try to calm down. What do you say?"

Kate knew Jim was right. She could hardly breathe from all her crying. She nodded her assent, and Jim led her by the hand to two empty chairs where they could sit together. As if on cue, all that were still standing did the same thing. After a few minutes, nothing remained of the weeping except some telltale sniffles and blowing of noses. Kate's eyes were swollen and her face was blotchy from crying. She leaned against Jim's shoulder and tried to keep the tears at bay, wiping her eyes each time she felt one form. The room was quiet except for the occasional murmur of subdued conversation or shared prayers. It was in a moment of absolute silence when Kate heard a voice, not louder than the most subtle of whispers, though she could tell by the faint cadence the message was urgent. She leaned forward, straining to decipher the words. She thought, too, for a moment, that she saw the wisp of a shadowy shape leaping around in front of her. Thinking it must be the blurriness of her eyes, she wiped them determinedly and stared hard.

Jim, puzzled by her sudden change in behavior, inquired, "Kate, what in the world are you doing?"

"Shhh! Don't you hear it? Don't you see the shadows?" Kate asked in a quavering voice.

Jim struggled to hear and to see what Kate was referring to, but to no avail. Then a thought struck him like a bolt from the blue. "Do you think the Old Ones are trying to communicate with you, Kate?" Jim asked excitedly. "Is that what you're hearing and seeing?"

"Oh, my goodness!" Kate exclaimed, as an overwhelming thrill coursed through her veins at the prospect. "I think you're right, honey! But I can't understand what this one is trying to tell me." *Believe, Kate, believe! Believe! Believe!*

"One of us isn't enough!" Racer announced. "Everybody come over here, quick!" The Old Ones scurried hastily to join him. "Let's chant all together, 'Davy will be well,' as loudly as we possibly can until we know Kate has heard us. Ready, set, go!"

Kate marveled at the split-second appearance of multiple shadows moving around in front of her. But what she heard made her breaking heart burst with bliss. "The Old Ones!" Kate cried, leaping ecstatically to her feet. "They're telling me Davy will be well! Davy will be well!" The whole waiting area erupted in cheers and applause. Kate collapsed onto her seat and wept sweet tears of joy.

***

Susie had taken a frightened and disconsolate Anna, with Mary and Smokey in tow, to her house once the others had departed for the hospital. Despite her own worry for Davy, Susie tried her best to remain upbeat and positive for Anna's sake.

"What would you like for lunch, Anna?" Susie asked cheerfully as she opened the refrigerator and perused its contents.

"Nothing," Anna said morosely. "I'm not hungry, Nana."

"Oh, but sweetie," Susie said, "it's been hours since you ate breakfast. Surely you could manage a bite or two."

Anna shook her head and hugged Mary and Smokey tightly as tears trickled down her cheeks. Susie knelt down and gathered Anna to her, struggling to keep her own tears at bay. "It will be all right, Anna, you'll see," she said comfortingly. "Davy has the Old Ones, remember? Do you think for one minute they would allow anything bad to happen to him?"

"I don't know," Anna said. "I used to think that, but now I'm not so sure. Nana, I'm scared."

"We all are," Susie told her, "but we can't let our fears get the best of us, can we? Davy doesn't need us thinking the worst at a time like this; your brother needs some positive thoughts and prayers."

Anna sniffled loudly. "I'll try, Nana," she said, wiping her eyes on Mary's dress.

"That's my girl," said Susie as she gave Anna a kiss on the cheek.

"But I still don't feel hungry," Anna confessed. "My tummy is all knotted up and icky feeling."

Susie suddenly had an inspiration. "Maybe if we do lunch a bit differently today, it will boost your appetite," she said happily. "How about we have a picnic in front of the television? I'll put on any show you like."

Anna's eyes grew wide. "Really? Can Mary and Smokey have a picnic with us, too?"

"Of course they can!" Susie affirmed as she stood up. "I'll fetch the old blanket Bampa and I always use for our picnics, and you can spread it out in the living room."

For the first time since she heard the horrid news about Davy, Anna smiled.

CHAPTER 23

CHANNEL TEN *NEWS AT FIVE*

Though everyone was reassured by the Old Ones' pronouncement of Davy's recovery, their anxiety grew as time ticked by and there was still no confirmation from a doctor.

"I just wish we knew how much longer Davy will be in surgery," Kate sighed. "Jim, what time was he admitted?"

"We arrived here at about eleven-fifteen," Jim said, "and Davy was rushed back straightaway. It's close to one now, so maybe we'll know something soon."

Bob was half-heartedly watching the Channel Ten *News at Noon* on the one television in the waiting room, thinking that perhaps the segment filmed earlier in the day would air. The closer the time plodded toward the stroke of one, the more his hope waned. *Maybe that Chad fellow couldn't cobble something together in time for the show. Hmm. Five minutes left in the broadcast. Not much hope, but I'll ask the receptionist to turn up the volume just in case.* Bob stood up and headed toward the receptionist's desk when he caught, out of the corner of his eye, the image of Chad Newton on the television screen.

"There it is! There it is!" Bob shouted as he pointed frantically at the TV. "Turn it up so we can hear!"

All eyes were riveted on the screen as the traumatic story of the day unfolded before them. Craig's panoramic sweep of the Old Ones was nothing short of breathtaking. The world was seeing a revelation, which up until this moment, had cautiously been shown only to a trusted few. At that distance, however, the microphone had only been able to catch Reverend's words here and there, but it was as clear as day that this magnificent creature was, indeed, speaking to the stunned group clustered in front of Ronnie's trailer. To the relief of everyone in the waiting room, Craig, panicked by the gunshots, had wildly swiveled the camera away from the tragic scene, sparing all from the agony of actually seeing Davy and Ronnie shot. Jim knew when he heard Chad's concluding remarks about the identity and condition of the victims that the hospital could expect an onslaught of media queries at any time. Kate looked at Jim worriedly. "Does this mean Davy's name will have to be released to the public?"

"I think it's inevitable, Kate," Jim said with a sigh. "Reverend couldn't be heard; people are aware of the Old Ones, but not their plight. Eventually, Davy may have to be their voice."

"Chad asked me today if I thought he would be given permission to interview Davy," said Bob. "I told him that was entirely up to you both."

"That interview won't happen any time soon, considering the circumstances," Jim said grimly. "Maybe never if Ronnie decides, after this second brush with death, to do the right thing."

"I know the names of children who are victims of a crime are released all the time," Kate admitted, "but can't you just see the three-ring circus we'll have to put up with if all comes to light?"

Jim patted Kate on the knee. "We'll just cross that bridge if and when we come to it," he said.

"Mr. Hunter?" Dr. Ray Melton, the surgeon, poked his head into the waiting room.

Jim and Kate both sprang up from their seats. "Doctor! How is Davy? Is he going to be all right?" Kate's questions tumbled agitatedly from her lips.

"You must be Davy's mother," Dr. Melton said kindly. "If you two can come with me, we can discuss your son's status privately."

"Excuse me, Dr. Melton," Jim interrupted, "but we're all family and friends here. Whatever you are going to say to us about Davy's condition, they need to hear it, too."

Dr. Melton hesitated for a moment, but seeing all the earnest, concerned faces in the room, decided to honor Jim's request. "Very well then," he said as he motioned to Jim and Kate to sit down and pulled a chair around so he could face them both. His smile heralded the news they all longed to hear. "Your Davy is one fortunate boy," Dr. Melton began. "The bullet missed a major artery in his shoulder. Had that artery been ruptured, I'm not sure we could have pulled him through. As it was, Davy lost a lot of blood. He needed a transfusion, which he's been given. Yes, it will take some time for him to heal, and he will be in quite some pain the next several days, but we will make sure he has the necessary medications to lessen it."

"How long will Davy have to stay in the hospital?" Kate inquired worriedly.

"Several days at least," Dr. Melton answered. "It will all depend upon how the healing progresses. It's a wait and see prognosis for now, but I am very intrigued and, I admit, bemused by the fact that the spot where the bullet entered Davy's shoulder had already formed a scab by the time he arrived. Was it someone here who was applying pressure to the wound?"

"I did," David spoke up, "but I can't take any credit for what you're describing, doctor. In all my years as an army medic, I never saw anything like it either."

Jim couldn't keep from grinning. Dr. Melton raised one eye-brow and looked at him quizzically. "Mr. Hunter," he said, "do you have any idea as to how this miraculous, because there's no other word to describe it, healing could have taken place?"

"Yes, I do," Jim answered, his green eyes twinkling. "And if you watch the news tonight on Channel Ten at five, I think you'll have the answer, too."

"Aha!" Dr. Melton said good-naturedly, "You have, indeed, piqued my curiosity, Mr. Hunter. I shall do just that. Now, are you two ready to see your son? He's still groggy, but hearing your voices might help him come around quicker."

"Can we come, too, doctor?" Sarah asked eagerly. "David and I are his grandparents."

"Davy is still in ICU and will be there for a while," said Dr. Melton, "so he can't have any more than two visitors at a time. Once he's in a regular room, it will be a whole different story."

***

The Old Ones, especially Reverend, reveled over Dr. Melton's inquiry into the mystical healing and Jim's enigmatic reply. "I wonder," Reverend said with a chortle, "if the doctor will actually be able to put two and two together, even if he does see us in the news report."

"There's no telling, dear," said Mrs. Reverend, "but I'm sure if he doesn't, he'll not forget the miracle he witnessed today."

"I don't know if my attempts to cease Ronnie's bleeding had the same effect," Reverend observed. "We can only hope there is another group of doctors just as perplexed and befuddled by it all."

"You better be careful, Reverend," Racer admonished him jovially. "If the doctors figure out you're behind this, they're going to try and recruit you for the hospital staff!"

"Not a chance," said Reverend. "My power, already drained at the moment, wouldn't hold up for long. Anyway, whatever would you all do without me in The Glade?"

Everyone laughed at this, and Mrs. Reverend gave him a hug. "Well, dear," she said, "I, for one, would miss you every moment. I think, too, that when Jim and Kate follow Dr. Melton to ICU, you and Racer should be the first of us to visit Davy there."

"I like the way you think, Mrs. Reverend," Racer declared happily. "Look! They're moving in that direction! Quick, Reverend, we have to slip through the door when they do!"

"I'm right with you, my friend," said Reverend. Both Old Ones hastened to the doorway and into the hallway, close on the heels of Jim and Kate.

***

Anna carefully spread out the blanket Susie had given her on the living room floor, and set Mary and Smokey together on it so they could watch television with her. "But where is the remote?" Anna wondered, her eyes darting all around. She ran to the kitchen where Susie was preparing their sandwiches.

"Nana, where's the remote?" Anna asked. "I can't find it."

"Oh, I'm sorry, sweetie," Susie said, as she glanced around at the countertops and table. "Here it is," she announced when she spied it next to the coffee pot. "Your Bampa likes to play hide-and-seek with this thing," Susie laughed. She picked it up and started for the living room with Anna trotting behind her. "I just can't train him to leave it on the television stand."

Susie pushed the power button and the Channel Ten *News at Noon* flashed on the screen.

"Ugh, news," said Anna, wrinkling her nose. "Isn't there something else?" She froze when she saw what was happening on the screen. Susie did the same. Just as their family and friends were watching the scene unfold at the hospital, Susie and Anna witnessed the overwhelming grandeur of the Old Ones, knowing with trepidation that this idyllic moment would all too soon be swept into chaos and destruction. The moment she heard the gunshots, Susie swiftly switched the channel.

"Anna," she said gently as she placed her arm around the girl's shoulder, "that is something we don't need to see. I'll find a silly cartoon or movie to cheer us up, okay?"

Anna nodded. She felt all numb inside. Her safe, small world, one that had always felt rock-solid, was crumbling around her. She felt anything but secure. Anna longed for her mother's touch. "Nana," she whispered, "I need a hug."

***

Dr. Melton escorted Kate and Jim to the ICU entrance and stopped. "Before I take you in to see Davy, you need to be prepared to see lots of tubes and hear frequent beeps from his monitors. I assure you, this is absolutely normal in this stage of recovery. The nurses are constantly checking on the patients, so know he is in good hands. They will be more than happy to answer any questions or concerns you might have."

"Thanks for the briefing, Dr. Melton," Jim said as he shook his hand. "Kate, are you ready to go in?"

"Yes," she answered. "I can't wait to see my little boy, tubes and all."

"Then let's go," said Dr. Melton. He held open the swinging door, waiting for them to enter first.

"Tubes and monitors?" Racer asked with concern. "What are those, Reverend?"

"I'm not sure," the owl answered, "but we are about to find out."

Dr. Melton led them to one of only two occupied beds in the ICU; Ronnie, Jim surmised, must be in the other one. Jim was immensely grateful they did not have to walk past him to reach Davy. He found himself hoping he would never have to lay eyes on his cousin ever again. Praying for his healing had been the right thing to do, Jim knew, but the journey to forgiveness promised to be a long and arduous trek. *"But if you do not forgive others their sins, your Father will not forgive your sins." I'll work on it, Lord. With Your help, I'll work on it.*

"Here he is," Dr. Melton said softly when they arrived at Davy's bedside. "He seems to be resting comfortably. Don't be too disappointed if Davy doesn't wake up for you just yet. He's been through quite the trauma." Jim and Kate could only nod their heads. The sight of Davy lying so small and helpless in the hospital bed, surrounded by a fortress of monitors and tangle of IV tubes, was overwhelmingly distressing to them. "I will take my leave of you then," Dr. Melton said as he shook their hands.

"Thank you, doctor, for everything you've done for Davy today," Jim said, his voice thick with emotion.

"Don't mention it," said Dr. Melton with a warm smile. "It's my job."

***

Once Dr. Melton had disappeared with Jim and Kate, Bob said, "I think it's time I step outside to give Susie a call and let her know Davy is going to be fine. I know she's worried sick—and poor Anna!"

"Good idea, Bob," said David. "Sarah, I don't know about you, but I'm starving. What say we head for the cafeteria when Bob gets back, since it will be a while before we can see Davy?"

"It's probably a good idea to keep our strength up," she agreed. Turning to Elly, Mike, and Abby, she asked, "Would you three like to join us?"

Abby and Elly assented immediately, but Mike seemed hesitant. "Aren't you hungry, Mike?" Abby asked him.

"I am," he confessed, "but if I go with you too, Mrs. Carson will be left in the waiting room alone. In light of everything that's happened, it doesn't seem to me to be the right thing to do."

"Then let me bring you back something," Abby suggested. "What would you like?"

What Mike would have liked more than anything at that moment was to have been sitting with Abby alone in a quiet, cozy restaurant, but he'd have to save that for another day.

"Any sandwich will do," he said. "No, wait. Get me anything but egg salad."

"But I thought you loved egg salad," Abby said, confused since she had witnessed Mike gleefully consume every morsel of the one she had prepared for their picnic.

"I do," Mike reassured her. "It's just that after eating your egg salad, I'm spoiled. No one else's would ever fit the bill." Abby's cheeks flushed; Elly couldn't help but notice. "I'll make it an easy order, Abby," Mike continued, pulling a twenty from his wallet and pressing it gently into her hand, "Ham and cheese on rye, mustard, no mayo."

"You got it," she said, warming him from head to toe with her smile. "But isn't twenty too much for just a sandwich?"

"Get yourself something with it, too, Abby," he said. "After all, I had planned to take you to lunch today, but as things turned out, it wasn't meant to be."

"Another time then?" Abby asked hopefully.

"Lots of other times," Mike assured her.

***

"Mrs. Carson?" Betty Rae stood up immediately when the doctor called her name. "I'm Dr. Lauren Horton," she said as he strode forward to shake her hand. "If you'll come with me, please, we can discuss your husband's condition." Betty Rae didn't like the sound of those words in the least, and her fears took a turn for the worst.

Mike, noting Betty Rae's strained and worried face, asked, "Mrs. Carson, would you like me to come with you?"

Betty Rae turned toward him, not sure if she could believe what she just heard. When she saw the sincere look on Mike's face, she knew he meant it. *Why not let him come along? I don't want to face this alone, and he's been nothing but kind to me since he got here.*

"Yes," she said decisively, "I would appreciate the company."

"And who is this young man, might I ask?" Dr. Horton queried as Mike walked toward them.

Betty Rae managed a smile. "He's my pastor," she said.

***

Racer and Reverend perched themselves at the foot of Davy's bed, their eyes round with wonder at the pulsing lights and intermittent, annoying beeps sounded by the monitors. Neither of them was comfortable when they saw the needle in the boy's arm, which seemed to be attached to a liquid-filled bag by a tube.

"Do you think the needle is hurting Davy?" Racer asked in consternation.

"Dr. Melton said Davy was being given pain medication," Reverend answered. "I would assume it is being delivered through that tube, along with the watery-looking substance. So no, I don't think our dear Chosen One is feeling any discomfort."

"Poor Davy," said Racer mournfully. "He looks so drawn and pale, not at all like his usual vivacious self. Should we join our voices with Kate's and Jim's, to try and awaken him?"

"It couldn't hurt," Reverend remarked. "There's the chance Davy, because of his unique relationship with us, will hear us before he hears them."

Racer didn't waste a second. "Davy, can you hear me? It's Racer! Reverend and I are right here with your mother and Jim. Can you wake up, Davy? Will you try?"

From the depths of induced sleep, Davy thought he heard someone speaking to him. The voice was faint and distant, but he knew it called to him.

"It's time to return, dear child." Davy heard the Good Shepherd's words distinctly. "Racer is calling for you, as is Reverend and your parents. It's time to return." Davy struggled to open his eyes, but his eyelids felt like they were covered by burdensome weights: impossible to lift. The voices encouraging him to wake up were becoming clearer. He could hear Racer. He could hear his mother. Davy tried again to force his eyes to open. They fluttered momentarily, enough for him to discern four blurry faces regarding him affectionately, and closed again.

"Oh, Jim, I think Davy's coming around!" Kate exclaimed ecstatically. "Davy, keep trying! It's time to wake up, honey. Can you do it for me? For Jim?"

"For us?" Reverend and Racer chimed in together.

"Mom?" Davy mouthed silently.

"Yes, honey, I'm right here," Kate assured him. She enfolded his hand in both of hers.

"C'mon, soldier," Jim said hearteningly, "battle through this. You've already won the war."

"Won the war?" Davy whispered. He struggled once more to open his eyes. As he did so, he was delighted to see that his vision was becoming clearer as well as his head, which had felt so fuzzy and foggy. He blinked and smiled, much to the relief of those gathered around him. "Racer and Reverend, you're here," he said softly. "I'm glad you're here. I'm glad you're safe."

"We're glad *you're* here!" Racer declared gleefully. He wished he could jump up and down on the bed, but knew that wasn't wise considering Davy's current condition.

"And safe," Reverend added. "Lad, dear Chosen One, you saved my life today. I will forever be in your debt."

"No debt," Davy mumbled feebly. He turned his head to look at Jim and his mother. He could see his mom's eyes, swollen and puffy, were now glistening with fresh tears. Jim's face appeared haggard and worn, but he wore a brave smile.

"I'm sorry I worried you both," Davy said as he felt his eyes wanting to shut again. "I love you."

"We love you, too," Mom told him, "up to the moon and back."

A smile flitted across Davy's lips as his eyelids closed. "Davy, do you need to go back to sleep?" Racer asked anxiously. Davy nodded slightly. "Tell your Mom and Jim that I will stay with you while you rest, so they won't feel badly about leaving you."

With all the effort he could muster, Davy opened his eyes again and said, "I need to sleep again. Racer will stay with me. I won't be alone." And with that, Davy slipped back into the land of healing dreams.

***

Elly and Abby followed a few paces behind the others as the group headed for the cafeteria. Even though they had just met that day, they had taken an immediate liking to one another. "It's funny, Elly," Abby remarked as they walked along. "I've only known you for a few hours, but I feel comfortable talking to you. It's like we've been friends for years. That doesn't happen to me very often."

"I feel the same way, Abby," Elly admitted. "It is truly wonderful when people hit it off right away. That was how it was when I met Eric. We fell into step with each other then and there, and haven't fallen out since."

"You mean," Abby ventured tentatively, "it was love at first sight?"

"Yes, it was," she confirmed happily. "I never believed any of that mushy stuff until the day I laid eyes on Eric." Elly cast a sideways glance at Abby. "Is that the way you felt when you met Mike?"

As she watched Abby blush six ways to Sunday, Elly knew she had hit the nail on the head. "I, I..." Abby stammered. "I didn't dare believe it, at first. Like you, I didn't think those things actually happened in real life. But meeting Mike?" Abby paused for a moment, and then asked cautiously, "Elly, can you keep a secret?"

"I certainly can," she declared. "Being a sheriff's wife has made for great training in that department."

"Okay then," Abby said with relief. "I confess: I'm totally head-over-heels in love with Mike."

"And that's a secret?" Elly asked, with an amiable chuckle. "Abby, all anyone has to do is watch the two of you together for five minutes to figure that out."

"It's that obvious?" Abby asked apprehensively.

"Yes, it is," Elly said with conviction, "very obvious. But there's another part of the equation that is just as apparent."

"What's that, Elly?"

"Pastor Mike is totally head-over-heels in love with you."

***

"Mrs. Carson," Dr. Horton began abruptly after seating Betty Rae and Mike in her office. "As you may or may not be aware, a gunshot wound to the hand can be a complicated thing to treat. In your husband's case, the bullet hit at the point where the thumb is joined to the hand and exited through the palm. There was extensive damage to the soft tissue, bone, and ligaments. We attempted to address it the best we could today, but there could be several more necessary surgeries down the road, especially if Mr. Carson is experiencing pain or difficulty in using that hand."

"But other than that, Dr. Horton," Betty Rae asked feebly, "Will Ronnie be all right?"

"He will make it, if that's what you're asking, Mrs. Carson," the doctor said rather curtly. "Mr. Carson is in ICU right now, and will probably remain there overnight, maybe longer for observation." Here Dr. Horton cleared her throat and fidgeted with the pen she was holding. "I do have a question for you though, Mrs. Carson. Were you at the scene of the shooting today?"

Betty Rae closed her eyes tightly as the horrific memories of the morning replayed unbidden in her mind. All day, she had tried to block them out. She had been moderately successful, up until now. With tears seeping from her eyelashes, she said haltingly, "Yes, doctor, I was there."

Dr. Horton leaned forward at her desk and said sympathetically, "I'm sorry, Mrs. Carson. I know this is difficult for you. But as a doctor and a scientist, there is something about your husband's injury that has me perplexed, and I was hoping you could help me with the answer."

"As in how the wound was already scabbed over?" Mike interjected.

Dr. Horton regarded him with astonishment. "Yes, exactly," she said. "How did you know?"

"It was the same for Davy, who was shot in the shoulder," Mike said. "Dr. Melton was just as baffled."

"Did he get an answer to this phenomena?" Dr. Horton inquired.

"Of sorts," Mike said with an impish grin. "Watch Channel Ten *News at Five*."

CHAPTER 24

VISITORS IN ICU

Just as Kate and Jim approached the ICU doors to depart, one swung open and there stood Betty Rae, with Mike right behind her. Jim nodded politely in their direction, but didn't say a word. Kate, though she knew none of what had transpired was Betty Rae's fault, couldn't bring herself to even acknowledge her presence. She clasped Jim's hand.

"Let's go, honey," she said as she moved toward the door.

"Wait! Please wait!" Betty Rae implored. Jim halted abruptly, pulling Kate back to his side. Betty Rae hung her head, unable to look into their eyes. "There's something I want you both to know," she said. Her voice sounded meek and uncertain, as if she feared the Hunters would miscon-strue her words. Betty Rae took a deep breath before she spoke. "I want to apologize for all that happened today," she said slowly. "It's been a night-mare for everyone, but especially for you, thinking Davy might not make it. I'm so relieved to know he's going to be fine."

When Betty Rae finished speaking, there ensued several awkward moments of silence. Neither Jim nor Kate were sure how to respond to her statement. It was Mike who stepped up and salvaged the day. "It's a relief for all of us, now that Davy is on the mend," he said. "But I don't think you have anything to apologize for, Betty Rae. None of this was your fault. I'm sure the Hunters would agree with me, am I right?" Mike gave Jim and Kate an encouraging smile.

Jim sighed. "You're right, Pastor Mike," he admitted reluctantly. "Betty Rae, we appreciate your concern for Davy, but the only person who owes us an apology is your husband. Since you are here in ICU, I'm assuming Ronnie is expected to recover from his gunshot wound?"

"Yes, he will recover," said Betty Rae, "though the doctor expects possible complications in the future."

"What sort of complications?" Jim inquired.

"At best, Ronnie's hand will require more surgery," Betty Rae answered. "At the worst..." Her voice trailed off as a sob caught in her throat.

Kate, who had been standing there stoically, was not sure whether Betty Rae was genuinely glad about Davy's impending recovery, or if she was simply relieved now that Ronnie was off the hook for possible manslaughter charges. Seeing Betty Rae's distress in this moment caused Kate to have a change of heart. *Just because she's married to Ronnie doesn't mean she's like him. And while that scoundrel has been nothing but wicked to us, maybe he really loves her and treats her well. Here she is, all alone except for Mike to be of comfort to her, when I've had so many surrounding me with their love and support.* "Betty Rae," she said softly, "if you can tell us what the greatest fears are for Ronnie's recovery, we can pray with you that they won't happen."

***

Reverend returned to the waiting room with Jim and Kate. "Where's Racer?" Mrs. Racer asked.

"He is staying with Davy," the owl informed her. "The boy woke up briefly, but is not quite ready to come around for any length of time. He needs to rest."

"When can we get in to see him?" Mrs. Reverend wondered.

"I think it's best, considering the circumstances, for all of us to return to The Glade to regain our strength," Reverend said. "We can send another round of Old Ones to take our places and to relieve Racer so he, too, can be renewed."

"And is there any word about Ronnie?" Sharp-eyes asked. "Betty Rae left the room a while back with the doctor and Pastor Mike."

"We ran into her just as she was entering ICU," Reverend answered. "It seems Ronnie will pull through, but it is possible he may lose the use of his right hand."

There were gasps of shock all around. "Well, if that's the case," Scout observed solemnly, "then maybe we need not fear Ronnie using a gun against us ever again."

"And that would be a blessing," said Mrs. Racer. "But I wouldn't put it past him to simply learn to shoot a gun with his left hand. Guns! Ugh! I've had enough of guns over the past week to last a lifetime!"

"As have we all, Mrs. Racer," Reverend confirmed. "Now what say we stand at the exit doors and wait for an opportunity to escape back to The Glade? I'm intent on building up my healing powers as quickly as I can, so I can break Davy out of this place at the earliest possible moment and give the good Dr. Melton another reason to be amazed!"

"Hear! Hear!" cried the Old Ones gleefully, as they made haste toward the exit.

***

"Where is everybody?" Kate asked quizzically as she looked around at the empty waiting room.

"My bet is they went to get a bite to eat," said Jim, "which is precisely what you and I need to do. Especially you," he added, patting Kate's abdomen gently.

"Come to think of it," Kate said as she gave Jim a hug, "now that I know Davy is going to be okay, and Racer is right there should he wake up, I actually have an appetite again. In fact, I feel famished!"

"Then let's go," said Jim with a grin. "Don't need you passing out on me, now do I?"

At that moment, Elly and Abby entered the waiting area, giggling and carrying on like two schoolgirls. "My, you both seem happy," Kate commented. She noted Elly was holding one take-out box while Abby had two in her hands.

"Is that extra box for Mike?" Kate asked.

"Yes, it is," Abby answered. "But where is he?"

"With Betty Rae in ICU," Jim told her. "I shouldn't think he'll be much longer in coming back. Now it's our turn to head to the cafeteria. If I don't take Kate right away, I'm afraid she'll steal Mike's food, she's that hungry."

Elly and Abby laughed heartily. "Stop it, Jim," Kate said playfully. "But you're right. Let's get a move on before my legs give way, and you have to put me in a wheelchair to get where we're going."

"Yes, dear," Jim said in a sing-song lilt, which made the ladies laugh even harder.

As Kate and Jim disappeared down the hall Elly turned to Abby, asking with a sly smile, "Do you think it was love at first sight for those two?"

Abby grinned. "I have no doubt," she said.

***

David, Sarah, and Bob were just finishing up their meals when they spied Jim and Kate standing in the cafeteria line. David jumped up and waved to get their attention. Jim saw him and returned the wave, adding a thumbs-up to let his father know Davy was fine.

"Well, Sarah," David said, "looks like we can visit with Davy just as soon as we're done eating."

"Oh, it will be such a joy to lay eyes on him," Sarah declared. "What a frightful day this has been!"

"You can say that again," said Bob. "I'll go in to see him after you, if that's okay?"

"Of course," Sarah told him. "I wish all three of us could go in at once, but rules are rules."

David shook his head. "I'm just so immensely thankful there's even a Davy to see, after what he went through," he said. "Bob, I still don't get exactly what Jim meant by the answer being on the news. Is he referring to the Old Ones?"

Bob grinned broadly. "That he is," he answered, "and one Old One in particular: Reverend."

"The owl?" David asked. He had been so overwhelmed by the presence of that grand gathering, and so distraught when Davy was shot; his memories of the morning were one hazy blur.

"Yes," said Bob. "Davy told us Reverend has the gift of healing. I'm one hundred percent positive he stopped the bleeding, absolutely positive."

"Well, thank the Lord he was there," said David, "because if he hadn't been?" A tear slipped from David's eye.

Sarah patted his cheek lovingly. "Now dear, let's not think about such things," she said. "Davy's fine, and all's well that ends well, right?"

"Yes, Sarah," David said as he hastily brushed the tear away. "You are correct, as usual." He forced a smile. "Bob, have I told you that Sarah here is the smartest woman I know?"

"I'm not surprised," Bob said amicably. "I feel the same way about Susie. Looks like we both married up."

"That we did," David agreed wholeheartedly. "That we did."

***

From the foot of Davy's bed, Racer watched with curiosity as a nurse studied the monitors and replaced the almost empty plastic bag with one full of some sort of liquid. Although he couldn't be sure, Racer thought perhaps this was a contraption to feed Davy, since he was unable to feed himself. It did comfort him to watch the boy sleeping as peacefully as if he was on his own cot at home. Racer wished with all his heart that they were sharing the cot right now, chatting and laughing, listening to the breeze as it caressed the leaves of the majestic oaks.

"We'll have those times again real soon, Davy, I promise," Racer said. He patted the boy's foot, lying so still beneath the covers. Davy's eyes fluttered at the squirrel's touch, and for a fleeting moment, Racer thought he would awaken; but the eyelids relaxed once again as Davy continued to breathe in the calm rhythms of deep sleep. Feeling suddenly weary himself, Racer curled up at Davy's feet. Pressing his back against them for added warmth, Racer closed his own eyes. He was snoozing contentedly within minutes.

***

Elly glanced at the clock on the wall. It was after three thirty and there was still no sign of Eric.

"I'm getting a little worried," she confessed to Mike and Abby. "I know Eric and Hoyt had a lot to tend to, with all those witnesses giving their statements, but I had no idea it would take this long."

"Do you need a ride home?" Mike asked. "I'm leaving soon to take Abby back to her house. It wouldn't be any trouble, Elly."

"Thank you, Mike," Elly said, "I appreciate it. Let me step outside and try Eric one more time on his cell phone. I won't be but a minute."

"Speaking of going home," Bob said as he stood up and stretched, "now that Davy is out of the woods, does anyone want a ride back to the farm?"

Kate spoke up. "Why don't you all go with Bob? I'm sure Anna misses you all. I'll be fine here by myself."

"Are you sure, Kate?" Jim inquired. "I'm more than willing to stay with you."

Kate patted his arm reassuringly. "I'll be fine, honey," she said. "I'm planning to spend the night here."

"No need for that, Mrs. Hunter," said Dr. Melton as he entered the room unannounced. "Since Davy's in ICU and won't be moved to a room until tomorrow, I suggest that everyone go home and get some rest. I just checked on your young man, and his vitals are doing splendidly. He even woke up briefly while I was there."

"Did he say anything?" Kate asked eagerly.

"Yes, as a matter of fact, he did," Dr. Melton answered. "He said 'Racer.' Whatever do you suppose he meant by that?"

Jim and Kate exchanged knowing smiles.

"All right, doctor," Kate said agreeably, "we'll take your advice and go home for now. I know Davy is in the best of care."

***

"They're all coming home? Mom, too?" Anna asked excitedly.

"Yes, honey," said Susie. She hung up the phone and gave the girl a big hug. "The hospital will call if anything takes a turn for the worse, but we're not going to give that a second thought. Your brother will get better and stronger every day. I just know it!"

"I know it, too," said Anna confidently. "Did you hear that, Mary and Smokey? Mom's coming home!"

***

253

"Don't worry about that ride, Mike," Elly told him when she reentered the waiting room. "Eric is on his way."

"Okay, good! Then Abby and I will be off," Mike said, as he shook hands all around as they both said their good-byes. It was then he noticed Betty Rae, still sitting all alone in the same chair she had occupied most of the day. Mike, knowing she had ridden with Ronnie in the ambulance, wondered how she was going to get home. He excused himself from the group and rejoined her.

"Mrs. Carson?" Mike asked. "Do you need a lift home? I'd be more than happy to take you."

Betty Rae regarded him gratefully. "Dr. Horton told me there was no need to stay the night either," she said as she stood up, "and I do have to tend to Buddy and Sammy. I haven't even told them about their father. Just didn't have the heart. But are you sure it's no trouble? What about your gal-friend there? You sure she doesn't mind?"

"Not in the least," Mike assured her. "If you're all set, let's be off then."

"Bob," said Kate hurriedly, "do you mind waiting a few more minutes before we leave? I really want to see Davy one more time."

"As do I," Jim chimed in.

"Of course, of course," Bob said with a smile. "He sure did look peaceful and rested when I saw him a while back. Go on, and do your hearts some good!"

***

When Eric finally arrived at the emergency room waiting area, Elly was the only one in the room. He hastened over to her.

"I'm so sorry, Elly," he said, gathering her up in a bear hug, "This whole mess took so much longer to settle than I imagined."

"I understand, honey," Elly said as she gave him a kiss. "I haven't been here by myself very long; it can't be but fifteen minutes since everyone left."

"Even Kate and Jim?" Eric asked brightly. "Well then, Davy must be doing as well as you said on the phone just now. Or," he paused thoughtfully, "there are some Old Ones around to keep him company."

Elly chuckled. "You're right on both counts," she said. "Do you want to see Davy before we go home? I've only been in once, and he was sleeping."

"Yes, of course I would," Eric assured her. "After you, beautiful."

"Here's our chance!" Mrs. Reverend exclaimed to Mrs. Racer. They had fortunately arrived at the hospital at the same time as Eric, and would now be able to relieve Racer and keep watch over Davy throughout the night. "Quick, quickly my dear!" The owl and squirrel hustled close behind Eric and Elly and scooted successfully through the swinging doors. In a matter of moments, they arrived at Davy's bedside. To their utter delight, Davy was awake and talking softly to Racer. His voice still sounded weak, but his face wore a smile.

"Well, well," said Eric jovially when he saw that Davy was alert. "This is what I've been praying for all day. How are you feeling, Davy?"

"Really sore, on my shoulder," he confessed. "I'm glad to see you, Sheriff Eric and Miss Elly. You, too, Mrs. Reverend and Mrs. Racer."

"They're here?" Elly asked in astonishment.

"Yes, and Racer is, too," Davy told her, "but they've come to give him a break. He needs to rest up in The Glade."

"The Glade you so courageously saved today, Davy," Eric said solemnly. He laid his hand on the boy's head. "I want you to know that I plan to help you protect it, and the Old Ones, in every way possible. You have my word."

"Thank you," Davy said with a sigh of relief. "The Old Ones thank you, too. They want to know if they can give each of you a hug."

"Oh, that would be a sheer delight!" Elly declared enthusiastically. As she felt the furry, whiskery embraces followed by the soft, downy feathered one, Elly couldn't help but giggle at the touch. "What miracles you are," she told the Old Ones softly.

"Yes, indeed," Eric agreed as Mrs. Reverend put her wings around him and gave him a light peck on his cheek. "You know what the Old Ones make me realize, Davy?"

"What?"

"There are miracles all around us, every day," Eric acknowledged, "if we open our eyes to see them."

***

Ronnie moaned as he opened his eyes. The pain in his right hand, though dulled by medication, still throbbed with every pulse of his heart.

He had wakened briefly when Betty Rae came to see him, but had been unable to talk. He simply didn't have the energy. Now he wished she was still here with him. *I'm thirsty. Maybe a nurse will stop by soon, and get me some crushed ice. I hope she's a cute one.* Just then he heard footsteps, which he thought were coming toward him, but they stopped at another location. Ronnie could not really determine where, hampered by the way his bed was situated. He heard voices: a child's, a man's, and a woman's. *I know those voices. I've heard them all before. But where?* Ronnie strained to listen, yet could only catch bare snippets of the conversation. He was becoming more and more frustrated by the moment. It didn't help that his bandaged hand stung and pounded. Ronnie was about to give up when suddenly the breakthrough came.

"The Glade."

The Glade! The Glade! The child must be Davy. The others? Probably Jim and Kate. Ronnie closed his eyes again. His bullet hadn't killed the boy, and for that he was grateful. *But I'm not through with you varmints yet. Not by a long shot.*

***

When Dr. Lauren Horton entered the hospital cafeteria for a much needed cup of afternoon coffee, she spied Dr. Melton sitting at a corner table sipping on his while he perused his laptop. Hastily, she poured her coffee, paid the cashier without bothering to wait for her change, and made straight for Dr. Melton. Dr. Horton sat down at the small table across from him, without asking if she could join him. Dr. Melton looked up at her over his reading glasses.

"Why, Lauren, this is quite an unexpected pleasure," he said with a wry smile. "Seeing as I'm not exactly your favorite person." The two had been engaged five years ago, when Ray Melton met another woman and crushed any hopes of their marriage. Lauren had yet to forgive him.

"There's nothing pleasurable about it, believe me," she snapped at him. "This is purely professional, I assure you."

Ray took a sip of his coffee and said, "All right then; cut to the chase."

"It's about the two patients admitted to the emergency room this morning with gunshot wounds," she said. "I understand you operated on the boy."

"I did, indeed," Ray confirmed. "What about it?"

Lauren glanced around to see who could possibly be listening and lowered her voice. "He had stopped bleeding at the site where the bullet entered, hadn't he?"

Ray put his cup down. "Yes," he said in an equally soft voice. "How did you hear about it?"

"The man whose hand I operated on had a similar mysterious stoppage," she said. "When I asked his wife who was at the scene of the shooting, she could not recount anything unusual, but her pastor knew about the scab on the boy, and said the most curious thing."

"Let me see," said Ray, rubbing his chin as he recounted Jim's enigmatic statement. "Could it be he told you to watch the news at five o'clock on Channel Ten?"

"Exactly!" Lauren asserted. "What in the world can he have possibly meant by that? Do you have a clue?"

"That's all I have," Ray replied, "same as you. I guess we'll have to catch that broadcast now, won't we?"

Lauren scowled. "Not together, we won't," she avowed as she stood up to leave.

Impulsively, Ray grabbed her arm. "It's been five years, Lauren," he stated. "When are you going to let it go?"

"Never," she hissed, yanking her arm free and stalking off in a huff, angry at herself for even coming near him in the first place. *I should have simply waited for the newscast and not have put myself anywhere near that weasel. When am I going to learn to be patient?*

***

"Chad Newton, here, reporting to you live from the Swain County Medical Center's parking lot. Behind me is the emergency room where two gunshot victims were admitted this morning, ending an otherwise miraculous and never-before seen appearance by creatures who call themselves the Old Ones with a bizarre and tragic twist."

257

The news story switched to scenes shot earlier that day and initially broadcast on the *News at Noon*. "No word yet on their identities?" Chad asked the station's summer intern, Rachel, as she came running up to him.

"They won't budge on that one," Rachel said regretfully, "but I do have an update on their conditions: stable and improving."

"Good job," Chad said, giving her a high five.

"In three, two, one," Craig warned.

"Although the full identities of the victims have yet to be released, there is good news to share with all of you who have been following this breaking story throughout the day. The hospital has just issued a statement saying that both are stable and expected to recover. Back to you, Robert and Bonita."

CHAPTER 25

ROOM 203

R efreshed and revived from their overnight stay at The Glade, Racer and Reverend arrived back at the hospital just minutes after sunrise. They encountered no problems gaining entrance; night shifts were giving way to day shifts, and a constant stream of doctors, nurses, and other hospital personnel were constantly coming and going.

"Do you think Davy's been moved to a room yet?" Racer asked.

"It might be a bit early for that," Reverend said. "I say we head for the waiting room we were in yesterday, and attempt to get into ICU."

They were just turning to go in that direction when Kate and Jim came through the doors of the main entrance and approached a large desk, behind which sat a smiling receptionist.

"How may I help you?" she asked politely.

"I'm Jim Hunter and this is my wife, Kate," said Jim. "Our boy, Davy Murray, was in ICU overnight but was supposed to be moved to a room this morning. Can you tell us if that's happened yet?"

The receptionist typed something on her computer and scanned the monitor.

"Davy Murray, Davy Murray. Yes, here he is: Room two-oh-three, second floor," she told them and pointed. "The elevators are right around the corner."

"Thank you most kindly," Jim said. He and Kate hustled toward the elevators, with an elated Racer and Reverend at their heels.

"What perfect timing!" Racer exclaimed delightedly. "Oh, I can't wait to see Davy!"

"Nor can I," Reverend assured him, chuckling as they slipped into the elevator. "What I can't wait most to see, though, is the look on Dr. Melton's face when he goes to check Davy's wound."

Racer cackled gleefully. "That will be a sight, Reverend! I'm so glad your healing powers are fully restored. With any luck, Kate and Jim will be taking Davy home this very day!"

***

A young woman in a kerchief and sunglasses, who had been sitting as near as she dared to the reception desk for over two hours, got up quickly from her chair and hastened toward the hospital doors. Once outside, she pulled her cellphone from her purse and dialed.

"Chad Newton," said the voice on the other end of the line.

"Chad, it's Rachel. Kid's last name is Murray, and his parents are Jim and Kate Hunter."

"Hunter!" Chad exclaimed. "That's the man who phoned in with the tip about the Old Ones showing up on Willow Road! Did you get the room number?"

"Room two-oh-three," said Rachel.

"Great detective work, Rachel!" Chad congratulated her. "I'll make sure the boss knows what a tremendous asset you are."

"Thanks, Chad," she said, "but this detective is bone tired. Can you let the boss know that, too, so I won't be chewed out for coming in late today?"

"Will do," he assured her as he hung up the phone and placed a call to Craig. He could tell by the cameraman's voice that he just woke up. "Wake up, Sleeping Beauty," Chad teased him. "High-tail it over to the hospital, pronto. I smell an interview."

***

Anna yawned and climbed down the loft ladder, carrying Mary and Smokey under one arm. Her grandpa was sitting at the table drinking coffee, and her grandma was frying bacon to go with their breakfast.

"Where are Mom and Jim?" Anna asked sleepily.

"At the hospital, sweetie," David answered. "Davy is being moved to another room this morning, and they wanted to see him as soon as possible. You don't mind just hanging out with your old grandpa and grandma, do you?"

Anna grinned. "Of course I don't mind," she said, "especially since Grandma is making a big Saturday breakfast, like Mom always does."

"Yes, I got my marching orders from her last night," Sarah said with a laugh. "One tires of granola and bagels; it's great to splurge once in a while, isn't it?"

There came a knock at the kitchen door. They could see it was Bob, and David motioned for him to come in. "Good morning!" Bob said cheerfully. "My, that bacon sure smells delicious, Sarah."

"Will you have breakfast with us?" Sarah invited him.

"I would, but Susie already filled up my tank," said Bob, patting his stomach. "I'm just here to do a bit of work in the garden. Would you like to lend a hand, Anna, after you've eaten?"

"I sure would, Bampa," she said. Frisky, meowing pitifully, jumped up in her lap. "Oh, no! Has he been fed yet?"

"We've fed Maggie and walked her," said David, "but we forgot all about your little Frisky. Why don't you do that now, Anna?" Anna promptly slid off the bench to fetch the kitten's bowl and his kitten chow, filled the bowl, and placed both it and Frisky on the table.

"Oh, my," Sarah observed dubiously. "Is that something your mother allows?"

"She has to," Anna replied. "If we put Frisky's food on the floor, there's a very good chance that Maggie will eat it. We don't want her to be sick again."

"God forbid!" Bob stated. "Speaking of Maggie, if you all don't mind, I'll see if she wants to come out to the garden with me."

David motioned in the direction of the porch. "When I last left her, Maggie was curled up on her bed out there."

"I'll go check," said Bob, as he strode toward the porch.

"Anna, will you set the table for us?" Sarah asked.

"Sure, Grandma," she said. She willingly set to work, making sure to set places for Mary and Smokey, too.

"Now," Anna said, as she settled them on the table, "remember to chew with your mouth closed, don't talk with your mouth full, and always use your napkin."

David had to chuckle at this. "It sounds to me, young lady," he said, "that your mother has certainly taught you good manners. As far as I'm concerned, the world can't get enough of them."

"I'm with you there," said Sarah as she spooned up eggs and grits onto their plates. "I'm so grateful both our grandchildren know how to be polite and considerate."

Anna thought for a moment, and said, "You know something? Davy and I weren't always very nice children before we came here. I mean, he was always complaining or fighting with Mom and Jim, and I whined and pouted a lot. It's just not like that anymore, and I'm glad it's not."

Sarah smiled at her granddaughter as she served up her breakfast. "And why do you think that is, Anna?"

"Don't you know, Grandma?" Anna asked in genuine disbelief. Being only eight, Anna often presumed adults knew everything and could rarely be told anything new by a child.

"No, dear, I don't," Sarah admitted as she joined them at the table and stretched out her hands for the others to hold as David said the blessing. "Are you going to tell us?"

Anna grinned from ear to ear. "It's all because of the Old Ones," she declared.

"Ah, the Old Ones!" David exclaimed. "Why am I not surprised? In that case, while we ask God's blessing over this food this morning, I say we also thank Him for each and every Old One of The Glade."

"Amen to that," Sarah readily agreed.

***

When they arrived at room 203, the door was slightly ajar. Jim knocked on it firmly.

"Just a moment," the nurse's voice sounded muffled. "We're still making the patient comfortable in his new quarters. It will only take a few more minutes."

Reverend and Racer didn't wait. The two slipped in through the crack in the door, and immediately spied Mrs. Reverend and Mrs. Racer sharing a chair in Davy's room. Their expressions were strained and anxious.

"What is it?" Racer called to them in alarm as he and the owl approached. "Isn't Davy okay?"

"He seems to be in quite a lot of pain this morning," said Mrs. Racer sadly, "he's been moaning and saying repeatedly how much his shoulder is aching."

"And it was so heart-wrenching to hear the poor child cry out when they moved him onto this new bed," Mrs. Reverend added, wiping away a tear.

"Not to worry," Reverend assured everyone with a triumphant wave of his wing. "As soon as those nurses depart, I will set things to right with our dear Chosen One."

"Your healing powers are restored?" Mrs. Reverend asked in astonishment. "Oh, my love, we couldn't hear any better news than that!"

"No, we couldn't," Mrs. Racer added with a sigh of relief. "I can't bear to see Davy suffering so."

"Nor can I," said Racer bitterly, as he caught sight of Davy's pale, stricken face lying helpless against the oversized pillow. "Reverend! Kate and Jim will be devastated if they see Davy like this. Don't wait until the nurses leave. Do something right away!"

Reverend was just as moved as Racer by the sight of Davy's distress. The owl flew to the top of the bed and perched on the metal frame just above the boy's head, a position that was conveniently out of reach of the nurses' ministrations. Taking a deep breath, Reverend prayed silently. *Creator, may Your healing power enter into mine. Breathe with me and in me that, together, we may restore Davy to perfect health.* With that, Reverend exhaled slowly and intentionally upon Davy's head. The Old Ones watched, mesmerized by the delicate mist flowing over the boy, swirling and scintillating like a thousand dew drops in the morning sun. When his breath was spent, Reverend remained where he was, head bowed in prayer and thanksgiving, his heart filled with hope.

Stephanie, the nurse who was taking Davy's blood pressure, sniffed the air, a perplexed look on her face.

"Darlene," she said to the other nurse, who was changing out the IV bag, "what's that perfume you're wearing? I've never smelled anything so enchanting in my life."

"I'm not wearing any perfume, Stephanie," Darlene said, "I was about to ask you the same question. The fragrance reminds me of honeysuckle, but it's deeper, richer. Where do you suppose it's coming from?"

"Beats me," said Stephanie, "but it sure makes me feel good all over."

"Me, too," Darlene confessed with a smile. "I can tell right now, it's going to be a fantastic day!"

***

"I wonder how much longer the nurses are going to be in there," Kate said impatiently. "I'm so anxious to see Davy, I can't stand it."

Jim put his arm around her. "I feel the same, Kate," he said comfortingly, "but we wouldn't want to rush them, would we? That wouldn't be best for Davy."

"I know," she sighed. "It's just that it was so strange, not having Davy home with us last night. I thought I'd sleep better knowing Racer was with him, but I tossed and turned all night."

"I can attest to that," Jim said. "I was pretty much awake the whole night too, but amazingly, I don't feel tired."

"Neither do I," Kate said, "but what's even more miraculous is that I didn't feel any nausea this morning. As early as we had to get up and get going, that was truly a blessing."

"I'd say so," Jim agreed, giving her a kiss on the forehead. "Maybe that's something that won't happen routinely every morning. I'd sure hate for my girl to have a rough pregnancy."

Kate smiled warmly at him and said, "Rough or not, I wouldn't trade it for the world."

Abruptly, Darlene stood in the doorway. "You must be Davy's parents," she said perceptively. "You can come on in now. He's sleeping, but his color is much better than it was when Stephanie and I first brought him here. He no longer seems to be in pain."

"Pain?" Kate asked worriedly. "But I thought he was getting medicine for that!"

"He was, and he is," Darlene assured her, as she led them into the room, "but it doesn't always alleviate all discomfort. Here's your boy."

When Kate and Jim beheld Davy lying peacefully on the bed, their relief knew no bounds. Jim pulled two chairs closer to the bed so they could sit next to their son and be the first faces he saw when he awakened. Kate reached for Davy's hand and cradled it gently in hers. "How's my brave boy this morning?" she whispered, hoping the sound of her voice would rouse Davy from slumber. Out of the corner of her eye, she thought she saw Davy's foot move beneath the covers. Kate looked directly at it, hoping to catch a repeat performance. Dimples and creases appeared in shifting rhythm on the blanket's top, but they were nowhere near Davy's feet. "Look, Jim," she gasped as she pointed. "It's the Old Ones! They are on Davy's bed!"

Jim's eyes grew wide with wonder. "Well, I'll be," he said. "You're right, Kate. I wonder how many, and which ones. Can you tell?"

Kate suddenly felt a soft, almost timid, pat on her arm. Startled, she turned to Jim. "Did you just touch me?" Kate asked in a trembling voice.

"No," said Jim, "I haven't moved."

A radiant smile flashed instantly across Kate's face. "Then it must be one of the Old Ones! They are trying to communicate with us. Am I right?" The pat came again, but this time, it was firmer and bolder. Kate detected a softness of fur and barest prick of a claw against her skin. A shiver of indescribable delight coursed down her spine. "Racer?" Kate asked hesitantly. Her finger was gently gripped by a paw that leveraged it up and down. "Yes, yes, Racer!" Kate exclaimed ecstatically. "Is Mrs. Racer here, too?" When she felt another paw resting on her arm, Kate was beside herself with joy. "Are any others here, too?"

"I can answer that one," said Jim heartily as the now familiar silkiness of Reverend's wing feathers brushed his cheek. "It's Reverend—and Mrs. Reverend," he disclosed, when he felt the ticklish touch of another wing on his shoulder.

"Is that everyone, Racer?" Kate asked, which he answered in the same way as before. "Oh, Jim, this is so exciting! We can't talk with them out loud at the moment, but we can ask them 'yes-no' questions!"

"Then I have one for them," Jim said eagerly. "Did you use your healing magic on Davy today, Reverend?" The owl placed a wing beneath

Jim's hand and moved it up and down. "Is it already at work?" Again, Reverend gave his yes handshake.

"Is it okay to wake Davy up?" Kate asked, to which Racer replied with negative, side-to-side tugs on her finger. "I see," she said. "Must he rest so the healing can take full effect?" The squirrel signaled in the affirmative.

"Well, if that's the case, Kate," said Jim, "why don't I grab us some breakfast from the cafeteria, while you stay here with Davy? He could be sleeping for most of the morning."

Upon hearing this, Racer began to vigorously pump Kate's hand. "Oh, Racer," she laughed, "You're hungry, aren't you? Jim, I think you had better bring back some heaping helpings, and not just because I'm eating for two."

***

"Eating for two?" Racer asked bewilderedly. "What in the world is Kate saying?"

"You mean you don't know?" Mrs. Racer was incredulous. "My love, 'eating for two' is an expression meaning Kate is going to have a baby."

"A baby?" Racer asked as he sported his signature grin. "Why, that's marvelous news! Davy and Anna will have a little brother or sister to play with."

"It *is* marvelous news," Mrs. Reverend concurred. "I wonder how far along Kate is?"

"If she will let me place my wing over her stomach," said Reverend, "I'm fairly certain I could make an educated guess."

"Wait a minute," Mrs. Racer intervened. "If you do that, Reverend, won't you also be able to tell if it's a boy or a girl? What if Kate and Jim would rather be surprised? Not that we would tell them, of course, but there's Davy to consider. If we all know, isn't there the off-chance that one of us, in our many conversations with our Chosen One, would, as Anna often does, spill the beans?" Here, she gave Racer a meaningful look.

"Dear me, Mrs. Racer," said Mrs. Reverend, "I hadn't thought of that. Certainly then, Reverend, we should not meddle in such things, but have respect for Kate's privacy. Goodness knows, we've been intrusive enough in the lives of humans recently."

266

"That is for certain," Reverend agreed. "We will simply allow this matter to take the course intended by our Creator."

***

As he walked the distance to the cafeteria, Jim caught bits and pieces of conversation as doctors, nurses, and visitors passed by him. That they were all chattering about the same topic didn't surprise him. The footage of the Old Ones had aired in both the five and six o'clock news hours, and they were now the talk of the town. *Or at least, the hospital. The hospital staff must be fully aware that Davy is here. I hope they have the decency to stay away from his room while he's recovering.*

Jim reached the cafeteria, which was bustling with activity, and promptly took his place in a line for hot breakfast items. Only a moment or two passed before Jim heard a familiar voice at his elbow. "Good morning, Jim."

He whirled around. "Good morning to you, Pastor Mike," Jim said as he shook his hand warmly. "What brings you to the hospital so bright and early?"

"Why, I'm here to see Davy, of course," Mike answered. "How is he doing?"

"He's sleeping quite peacefully right now," said Jim. "Kate is with him and," here, Jim signaled to Mike to lean forward so he could whisper into his ear, "so are the Reverends and the Racers."

"Aha!" Mike said with a twinkle in his eye. "That sounds to me like the very ticket Davy needs to get well."

"More perfect than you could know," Jim said affably, and glancing about, added, "What? No Abby today?"

Color rose to Mike's cheeks. "No," he said. "Abby had to work. She knew I was coming, though, so she asked me to give everyone her best."

"That's very thoughtful of her," said Jim. "She sure does seem like one fine young lady."

"Yes, yes," Mike readily agreed. "She sure is."

Jim studied Mike's face intently. He knew the look of a man head-over-heels in love; he recalled his own mirrored reflection shortly after meeting Kate. Mike, he decided, was a goner.

267

"Pastor Mike," Jim said kindly as he placed his hand on the man's shoulder, "there are lots of fish in the sea, but none of them matter once you've hooked the perfect catch. Take it from a happily married man: Reel her in."

***

Sarah was alone in the kitchen, washing up the breakfast dishes, when the phone rang.

"Goodness, gracious, it's so loud," she muttered as she hastily dried her hands on a towel and ran to pick it up. "Hello, Hunter residence."

"Hi, Sarah, it's Kate."

"Kate, honey, how's Davy?"

"Sleeping at the moment," Kate said, "but I have it on good authority that that's precisely what he needs right now."

"Yes, I'm sure he does," said Sarah. "Has the doctor been in to see him yet?"

"A nurse was just here to check on Davy, and said Dr. Melton would be starting his rounds at ten this morning," Kate informed her. "I feel certain that if he watched the evening news, Davy will be first on his list of visits."

Sarah laughed merrily. "That is, if he put two and two together as Jim hoped he would," she said.

"We'll see," Kate said. "Truly, I don't see how he couldn't—but then again, one never knows."

"Well, honey, you just keep us informed about Davy, will you? We miss that child so much."

"I will," Kate promised. "I'll call you the minute he wakes up. Oh, here's Jim with some breakfast. Sarah, I'm half-starved, so I'll hang up now. Good-bye."

"Good-bye, honey," Sarah said as she replaced the receiver on the hook. "Now to share the wonderful news with everybody." Sarah dashed for the kitchen door, flung it open, and hurried toward the garden, where David and Anna were diligently working alongside Bob. "Kate just called," she yelled enthusiastically. "Davy is coming right along, just as we hoped and prayed!"

"That's fantastic!" Bob declared. "If you don't mind, I'm going to run into the house and call Susie."

"Please do," said Sarah as she embraced both David and Anna. "We need to keep everyone in the loop."

"What does 'in the loop' mean, Grandma?" Anna asked.

"It means to inform everyone who cares about Davy when there is news to share," Sarah answered.

Immediately, Anna wiggled out of her grandmother's embrace and ran over to Mary and Smokey, whom she had seated in a lawn chair so they could watch her working in the garden. Gleefully, she scooped them up in her arms.

"Davy's doing better," she told them. "Isn't that great? What? Oh, I knew you would be. Of course! You can count on me to always keep you in the loop!"

CHAPTER 26

HOME, SAFE AND SOUND

K ate, Jim, and the Old Ones had just polished off the last morsels of eggs, grits, and bacon when Davy opened his eyes. He was immediately elated to be surrounded by the perfect company.

"Hi, everybody," Davy greeted them happily, in a voice clear and strong.

"Oh, honey, you're awake!" Kate exclaimed joyfully. She bent down to kiss him on the top of his head. "How are you feeling?"

Davy smiled broadly. "As right as rain," he declared, using one of Jim's favorite phrases. "Even my shoulder doesn't hurt any more. Look! I can move my arm!" Everyone marveled at this, a sure testament to the thoroughness of Reverend's healing power. "Oh, Reverend, Reverend," Davy said gleefully as he gave the owl a grateful hug. "Thank you for making me well again."

"It was, indeed, an honor to do so, dear lad," said Reverend. "Goodness knows, we can't bear to see you suffer, ever."

"Where's my hug?" Racer asked, his head cocked to one side and his foot tapping in mock impatience.

Davy laughed and, letting go of Reverend, embraced the squirrel warmly.

"You know I always have hugs for you, Racer," Davy assured him, "and for everyone else here," he added as he hugged Mrs. Racer, Mrs. Reverend, Kate, and Jim in turn. "Oh, it feels so good to be able to do that without any pain in my arm! It's like the whole nightmare never happened."

"And that's a blessing, son," said Jim. "It was a nightmare for all of us, but here you are, back among the living and healthier than ever."

"Reverend, you've been our angel," said Kate as her eyes brimmed with tears of joy. "If I live to be a hundred, it won't be enough time to properly thank you." Reverend reached his wing across the bed to gently stroke Kate's arm. "So soft," she said dreamily, "so soft. Thank you, Reverend."

"Now there's just one more thing, Davy," Racer said matter-of-factly. "Dr. Melton hasn't come in to check on you this morning, but no doubt he saw the news report last night, which featured all the Old Ones. He will have probably guessed that one of us had something to do with getting the bleeding to stop after you were shot. What he doesn't know is the extent to which Reverend has restored you."

"Yes," Reverend interjected. "Feel free to talk about us, myself in particular, all you want, lad, but don't let on that your scar beneath the bandage has vanished completely."

"It has?" Davy asked in amazement. "You mean he won't even be able to tell it was ever there?"

"Precisely," Reverend answered. "I'm so looking forward to the look on his face when he removes the bandage to check the wound."

"That will be priceless," Davy laughed. "I'll keep quiet, I promise."

Just then, there was a knock at the door. "Does our patient feel up to having breakfast this morning?" Stephanie asked, peeking around the corner.

Davy had been so ecstatically relieved to find himself healed, he hadn't given a thought to how hungry he was. Now as the aroma of scrambled eggs filled his nostrils, his stomach emitted a tremendous growl.

"Yes, I am hungry," Davy declared. "Thank you, nurse." The Old Ones scattered speedily off the bed as she approached.

"Are you right-handed, Davy?" Stephanie asked pleasantly as she swung the table hinged at his bedside to a position in front of him. "Because if you are, you might want to have your mom and dad help feed you, at least for now."

Careful to keep his right hand still so as to perpetuate the ruse, Davy answered. "Yes, I'm right-handed, so I'll be sure to ask for help if I need it."

"Well then, here you go, young man," Stephanie said with a wink. "Or should I call you the Chosen One?"

Davy regarded Stephanie in disbelief. "How do you know about that?"

"Everyone knows," Stephanie said with a casual wave of her hand. "I hadn't heard anything about it when I was here with you early this morning, but that's because I never watch the news. I like reality shows. But those who *do* watch the news have been talking about nothing else, leaving all of us who didn't watch feeling we'd missed the drama of a lifetime. Will you let me know if any of your friends, the Old Ones, stop by today, Davy? I'd love to meet them! Enjoy your breakfast."

"Wow—that news report sure has people talking. I wish I could have seen it," Davy said gaily. He removed the cover from his plate once Stephanie had departed, and dug in with gusto.

"I'm not so sure about that," Jim observed. "It's not real clear, but there's even some footage of the aftermath of the shooting, son. I don't think that's something you want to see."

Davy chewed his eggs thoughtfully and took a bite of bacon.

"No," he said finally, "even though I feel so much better now, I'd rather not see that part of the news report."

"I couldn't watch it either," Kate admitted. "I was traumatized enough just knowing my baby was hurt; seeing that would have added insult to injury."

"You know, it's funny, Mom," Davy said. "Any other time, I would never want to hear you call me 'your baby,' but...well, I guess it's okay, if it's just for today."

Kate laughed. "You have a deal, Davy," she confirmed.

Davy was quiet for several minutes as he concentrated on consuming his food. When he had cleaned his plate, his mother took it off the tray and Jim readjusted the table.

"Jim?" Davy asked, with a concerned look on his face. "What happened to Ronnie?"

Jim exchanged glances with Kate, took a deep breath, and said, "Not a split second after Ronnie fired his pistol, Sheriff Peabody shot him in the hand. He's here in the same hospital. Truthfully, I don't know what kind of shape he is in this morning, but I'm sure Pastor Mike will find out shortly."

"Pastor Mike?" Davy brightened. "He's here today?"

272

"Yes," Jim answered. "I ran into him in the cafeteria. He said he was here to see you. He'd planned to follow me back here to your room when he saw Betty Rae, sitting with her two boys at a corner table. Pastor Mike thought he ought to see how she was doing."

Davy's brow furrowed. "Why does Pastor Mike have to check on them? Don't they go to a different church?"

"They do, honey," said Kate, "but pastors don't limit their contacts just because someone doesn't attend their church. They serve anyone who is in need, and if you could have seen Betty Rae yesterday, you'd know exactly what I'm talking about."

"Does that mean Ronnie and I were in the emergency room at the same time?" Davy asked, his eyes wide.

"In the ICU to be more precise," Jim told him. "That's the Intensive Care Unit. But you two were nowhere near each other. Besides, as incapacitated as he was, Ronnie couldn't have caused any more harm to you, could he?"

"I guess you're right, Jim," Davy admitted. "It's just, the thought of him being there makes me shiver."

"Well, that's all behind us now," Kate said comfortingly. "Let's focus on positive things, like the doctor letting you go home today, shall we?"

Davy smiled at her.

"Okay, Mom," he said. "I'll try my best."

***

Eric and Elly were finishing up breakfast and lingering over the Old Ones' special tea when Eric announced, "I have to go into the office for a little while this morning, Elly. With all the craziness of this week, I completely forgot about mailing those boys who helped me find Edgar Mason on Monday their official deputy certificates. Don't want them thinking I let them down."

"No, we wouldn't want that," Elly said as she took another sip of tea. "I have an idea. Why don't I tag along with you, and after you're done, we could run over to the hospital and check on Davy?"

Eric grinned at her. "You've taken quite a fancy to that boy, haven't you?"

273

"How could I not?" Elly asked. "Davy's everything you could ever ask for in a child."

"I'll have to agree with you there," said Eric. "If the son Reverend has promised we'll have one day turns out to be half the young man Davy is, I'd consider us to be the most fortunate of parents."

"I second that," Elly said as she stood up to collect their plates from the table. As she reached for Eric's, she bent down to give him a kiss.

"And if our son is half the man his father is," she whispered, "he'll make some lucky lady very happy one day."

***

"Mind if I join you, Mrs. Carson?"

Betty Rae, absorbed in her coffee and cares, had not seen Mike approach her table. She smiled for the first time that morning. "Of course, Pastor," she said politely, "make yourself right at home. Boys, this is Pastor Russell. This here is my oldest, Buddy, and his brother, Sammy."

"I'm pleased to meet you," said Mike sincerely as he shook the hands of each boy in turn. Their faces, he noted, were expressionless, but there was an unmistakable glint of worry in their eyes. Mike bowed his head in silent prayer over his meal. When he was finished, he asked, "So what's the news about Mr. Carson? Will he be moved to a room today?"

Betty Rae sighed. "I'm not sure," she said softly. "The report we got this morning said Ronnie had a restless night, and that he's running a fever. I think it will be a while before the doctor even thinks about dismissing him from ICU."

"I'm very sorry to hear that," Mike said. "Is there anything I can do for you and your boys, besides praying for Mr. Carson and you all?"

"You've already done enough," Betty Rae assured him. "My boys and I, we'll get through this just fine, won't we?"

Buddy grunted his assent, but Sammy was silent. Mike knew they were much more upset than they were letting on. His mind drifted back to the time of his father's tragic death in a car accident, when Mike was just sixteen. He remembered standing beside his mother at the graveside. He'd wanted to cry his eyes out, but remained stoic and strong for her as she wept and grieved. *Maybe this is the way Buddy and Sammy are feeling, too. They fear that if they let go, their mother will fall to pieces. Poor kids! What an onerous burden to bear.*

"I'm sure you will all get through this, Mrs. Carson, if you stick together," Mike said. "But if you'd like me to escort you all to ICU when we're done with breakfast, it would be my pleasure."

"That's very kind," Betty Rae said graciously, "but I know the way." She drained her coffee and said to her boys, who had only picked lethargically at their food, "Y'all ready to go?"

Buddy and Sammy nodded and promptly got up from their seats. Mike stood up when they did and shook hands all around. When he took Betty Rae's, she grabbed his hand firmly and looked him straight in the eye.

"I'll see you tomorrow, Pastor Russell," she said, "because I plan on attending your church."

***

Dr. Ray Melton, chart in hand, was about to knock on the door to Davy's room when he heard uproarious laughter from multiple voices, a child's included, coming from it. Puzzled, he turned to Darlene, who was standing beside him.

"You told me when I called in this morning that Davy was having a rough time of it," he said. "It sure doesn't sound that way."

"No, sir, doctor," she affirmed, "it doesn't, but I haven't been in to see him since Stephanie and I were here early this morning. Could he have gotten better that quickly?"

Dr. Melton pondered this for a moment. He had already surmised from viewing last night's news story that the miraculous, mysterious creatures called Old Ones must have had something to do with the unprecedented cessation of Davy's bleeding from the gunshot wound. *Could they have done more? Is that even possible? What if the Old Ones are in the room right now? I'm not sure I like the idea of invisible beings watching and listening to me. Oh well, there's nothing for it but to forge ahead.* Dr. Melton knocked forcefully on the door in order to be heard above the din.

"It's Dr. Melton," he called as he pushed the door ajar. "May I come in?"

"By all means, doctor," Jim said. "We've been expecting you."

275

Dr. Melton, with Darlene at his heels, entered the room and was promptly introduced to Mike, Elly, and Eric. He was more relieved than he was willing to admit that no Old Ones were visible, but he had the uncanny feeling that they were close at hand. Dr. Melton then turned his attention to Davy.

"Well, well, Chosen One," he said with vigor in his voice, "you're looking mighty chipper today. I have to admit I had no idea I was operating on a celebrity yesterday."

"I'm no celebrity, Dr. Melton," Davy insisted. "I'm chosen. There's a difference." His comment evoked more laughter from the adults.

"Not according to folks around here, young man," Dr. Melton assured him. "The entire hospital is buzzing with the news of the Old Ones, but then again, you've probably already been told that."

"Yes, sir," Davy said with a grin, "and that's exactly the reaction they were hoping for."

"Really?" Dr. Melton asked curiously. "I must say, that comes as a bit of a surprise. Maybe while we're checking your progress, you can tell us more. Now, I hate to break up this merry band of family and friends, but I'm going to have to ask you to stand just outside the door while Miss Darlene and I inspect Davy's incision and take some readings."

"Sure thing, Dr. Melton," said Jim as the five adults trooped out the room. The Old Ones, being invisible, stayed put.

"Now then, Davy, first things first," said Dr. Melton. "How is the pain in your shoulder this morning?"

"There isn't any," Davy stated matter-of-factly.

Dr. Melton and Darlene exchanged looks of shock and disbelief.

"But Davy, how can that be?" Darlene asked. "You were absolutely miserable when I saw you this morning and changed out your IV feed." She glanced up at the bag and gave a startled cry. "I don't believe this, Dr. Melton. Look! Look at the bag! It's just as full as when I placed it there this morning. Davy should have needed a new one by now!"

Dr. Melton grabbed at the bag in a panic and checked the tubing that fed into Davy's hand. "There must be a blockage somewhere," he muttered as he inspected it closely.

"Tell him there is one, Davy," Reverend called. "I stopped the feed, too, because you no longer needed it."

"Dr. Melton," said Davy, "Reverend says you can take the IV out of my arm. I'll be fine without it."

"Reverend?" Dr. Melton was taken aback. "Who is Reverend?"

"The Old One with the power to heal," Davy answered. "It's because of him that I'm completely recovered."

The doctor frowned. "We'll see about that, young man," he said. "Let's inspect your incision and change out the bandage, shall we?"

"Wait for it! Wait for it!" Racer exclaimed. He jumped up and down in anticipation of the doctor's reaction.

"Oh, yes!" Reverend declared giddily. "The moment has come!"

Dr. Melton untied Davy's hospital gown at the top and noticed immediately that there was no swelling, bruising, or redness surrounding the bandage as he had expected there would be. Hands trembling, the doctor carefully peeled back the bandage. To his utter astonishment, not a trace of yesterday's incision remained. Davy's skin was as soft and unblemished as a newborn's. Dr. Melton was rendered speechless. All he could do was to stare in awe at the unfathomable miracle placed before him. As the Old Ones whooped and cheered, Davy waved at them with the hand he shouldn't have been able to move. He said, "Reverend did a good job, didn't he, Doctor?"

Dr. Melton slowly lowered Davy's gown and gripped the metal frame of the bed to steady himself.

"Darlene," he said in a hoarse, shaky whisper, "remove all the IV tubes from Davy. He's going home today."

***

When the Old Ones finally regained their composure after seeing Dr. Melton's reaction to Reverend's flawless work, they decided to join the others, waiting in the hallway while the doctor and nurse prepared Davy for his imminent departure.

"Oh, what a joy it will be to have our Davy home, safe and sound once again," said Mrs. Racer gratefully.

"You know it, sweets!" Racer exclaimed as he enthusiastically embraced her.

"Look!" Reverend shouted suddenly. He pointed a wing down the long corridor of the second floor. "Here comes that reporter, Chad, and his cameraman!"

"What in heaven's name are they doing here?" Mrs. Reverend queried.

"I can't be certain," said Reverend, "but my instincts tell me this has everything to do with Davy."

***

As Chad and Craig huffed and puffed along the hospital corridor, they spied the small crowd gathered around one of the doorways and speculated this must be Davy Murray's room. Chad hurried ahead and was out of breath by the time he reached the group.

"Which one of you is Jim Hunter?" Chad managed to wheeze.

"I am," said Jim, stepping forward as if to block the man from taking another step. "You're Chad Newton, the reporter who decided to take my news tip seriously."

"Yes, sir, that's right," said Chad as the camera-laden Craig came up alongside him. "Believe it or not, the Old Ones' story has gone national, as of today. I was hoping you'd allow me to interview Davy as a follow-up, that is, of course, if he's well enough to see anyone at the moment."

Jim's eyes narrowed. "How did you make the connection between Davy and me?" he asked suspiciously.

Flustered by this question, Chad laughed nervously. "Oh, you know we reporters are a nosy lot," he said with a dismissive wave of his hand. "It just comes with the territory."

Miffed by Chad's self-serving answer, Jim stepped toward him until their faces were mere inches away from each other. "Let's get one thing straight, Chad," he said sternly. "My family's privacy trumps your territory. There was one reason and one reason alone that I contacted you to witness and share the Old Ones' appearance with the world: To save their home. To that end, I say mission accomplished."

"And, and, and, I'm glad it has been," Chad stammered, trying desperately not to look as foolish as he felt. "It's just that an interview with Davy would be such a coup."

Eric decided it was time to intervene. "I don't think you're listening to what Mr. Hunter is telling you, Mr. Newton," he said, strolling over to stand with Jim. Even though he was out of uniform, Chad found Eric's presence to be just as daunting as it had been yesterday, when the sheriff had refused to make any comments about the tragic situation to the press. "It's clear to me that the family doesn't wish to subject Davy to any further public scrutiny. I hope you'll make the wise decision to respect their wishes."

"Oh, I don't mean to step on any toes, here, Sheriff," Chad groveled shamelessly. "I'm only doing my job, keeping the public informed, you know, giving them the entertainment they want."

"Eek!" Kate emitted an unexpected squeal, attracting everyone's attention. She seemed to be looking down at her feet; Jim suspected the Old Ones had gotten her attention, and she was trying to understand what they were saying to her. Chad and Craig watched Kate's odd behavior with befuddled looks on their faces. Having witnessed Kate's encounter with the Old Ones in the waiting area the day before, the others observed the scene nonchalantly. After a few moments, Kate looked up and smiled at the men from Channel Ten News.

"You can't speak to Davy," she said firmly, "but you can speak with his friends if you'd like."

"His friends?" Chad inquired. "I don't see any." Chad stopped, dumbfounded. His face grew pale as his eyes widened with wonder. "You mean the Old Ones? They're here?"

"Some of them," Kate answered glibly, "Four to be exact."

Craig tapped Chad on the shoulder and whispered apprehensively, "I don't know about this, Chad. It could be a trap. Maybe the Old Ones are vicious creatures after all."

"Vicious?" A melodious voice boomed out of nowhere. "The Old Ones? Perish the thought, my good man."

"What was that?" Craig screeched in alarm. His eyes darted furtively about.

"That was Reverend," Kate said with a giggle. "I believe he and the others are ready to meet you, if you are ready to roll that camera."

"He's ready! He's ready!" Chad shouted, before Craig could utter a protest.

"All right then," said Kate. "Here they are!"

279

In a twinkling, the four Old Ones appeared only a few feet away from Chad and Craig; both gasped in awe at the sight.

"Roll it, Craig! Now!" Chad ordered, as the dazed cameraman fumbled for the power button.

Reverend stepped forward. "I am Reverend," he stated solemnly as he bowed before Chad. "Mrs. Reverend is here at my left, Racer and Mrs. Racer at my right. We have agreed to be filmed once again for your viewers, because we insist that you allow our Chosen One to remain anonymous. As Jim so aptly explained just moments ago, we appeared publically yesterday for the sole purpose of thwarting plans to take our home away from us. At this time and to our knowledge, our plan has worked; we are safe once again, thanks be to our Creator."

"And who is your Creator?" Chad managed to ask shakily.

"The same as yours," Racer answered readily, his lop-sided grin sure to win the hearts and minds of the viewing audience.

"But who, or what, are you, exactly?" Chad persisted, feeling his confidence returning in the wake of Racer's appealing smile.

"Who we are and what we are is not essential knowledge," said Reverend. "Knowing we exist, however, is. Our home is a fragile one. It cannot be overrun with human occupants, or we will be no more. That is why we made our appeal yesterday. We wish to live, and to live in peace."

"So I'm assuming from what you are saying, Reverend," said Chad, "that there was someone who was threatening your existence. Can you tell our viewers who that might be?"

"It is of no consequence," said Reverend coolly. "We simply want to return to The Glade, and quietly go about our work."

"May I ask what kind of work that is?"

The four Old Ones all looked at one another and smiled. Reverend nodded to Mrs. Racer to speak first.

"Our work, that is, Racer's and mine, is to love and to serve," she said with a curtsy.

"And our work, Reverend's in a more mystical way than mine, is to heal and comfort," Mrs. Reverend declared.

"Just think, Chad," said Racer as he took a few bold steps closer to the camera. "Imagine how beautiful this world would be if you humans practiced such attributes on a regular basis."

"It would be a better world, no doubt," Chad admitted, "but there will always be some bad apples out there, like the person seeking your destruction, trying to throw a wrench into the good things others are doing."

"Yes," said Reverend, "but that should not deter us from doing what is right in the eyes of our Creator. Evil has yet to quench our spirits, and I believe in my heart and soul that mankind will at long last turn to the One who has given life and given it abundantly."

Reverend paused and blinked his eyes. The others nodded their heads.

"It seems this interview must come to an end," he said. "Our power to remain visible is waning swiftly."

"Just one more question, please," Chad begged in earnest. "If you could leave our viewers with a phrase or one word, even, that would inspire them to live the abundant life you just described, what would it be?"

"I have this one, Reverend," said Racer assuredly, and with his eyes shining brightly into the camera lens, he declared, "It's all about love and grace!"

***

Davy lay gratefully on his cot that night as Racer sat beside him, humming a low but enchanting tune.

"Are you trying to sing me to sleep?" Davy asked with a yawn.

"You could say that," Racer said, patting the boy's arm gently. "You've had a long two days, my child. You need your rest."

"That's just what the Good Shepherd said to me," Davy told him.

"You saw Him again?" Racer asked in astonishment.

"Yes," said Davy, "I was there from the time I was shot until I woke up after the surgery, at least I think I was. I know I rested there. I rested in Him."

"And that's the best rest there ever can or will be," Racer asserted. "We both know that."

"Yes, we do," Davy said with a smile. "This time when I was there, I remember asking Him if I was going to stay."

Racer planted a whiskery kiss on Davy's forehead and said gently, "That's because you were close, very close, to leaving us. You sensed it."

Davy nodded. "But the Good Shepherd told me differently. He said my life had only just begun, and that He had great plans in store for me. I wonder what they are..."

"Ah," said Racer, "those you cannot see right now, but you can trust they will be great, just as He said. Simply live your life in such a way as to honor Him, and the plans will unfold."

"That's what I intend to do," Davy affirmed. They sat in silence for the next several minutes, content in each other's company, thankful to be just where they were just at this moment. When Davy finally spoke, Racer distinctly heard a voice already heavy with impending slumber.

"Racer, will you stay with me tonight?"

"Of course, Davy," he said. "There isn't any place else I'd rather be."

"I love you, Racer," Davy mumbled. "Good night."

"I love you, too, Davy," said Racer softly, "more than you will ever know. Sweet dreams, my child, sweet dreams." Then in his incomparably melodious voice, Racer sang softly over Davy.

> *Come away, come away, come away with me*
> *To a land far beyond any ocean or sea,*
> *Where dreams begin and hope meets anew*
> *The Promise, bright as morning dew.*
> *Come away, come away, come away and see*
> *The joys awaiting you and me.*
> *For one day, all will be at rest,*
> *And in His arms, we will be blessed.*

When the last shimmering note of the song faded, giving way to the sounds of chirping crickets and the rustling leaves above, Davy opened one sleepy eye and whispered, "Racer, will you teach me to sing? Teach me to sing."

ABOUT THE AUTHOR

Martha Jane Orlando fell in love with the Nantahala Mountains of North Carolina when her husband, Danny, and she stayed there on their honeymoon.

Martha Jane is a former middle school teacher who has a son and a daughter, and two stepsons, all grown.

Aside from writing fiction, Martha Jane also pens a bi-weekly devotional blog, Meditations of my Heart, which you can visit at marthaorlando. blogspot.com. She has created a fan page which you can visit at gladetrilogy. wix.com/theglade. Your comments and feedback are warmly welcomed!

Martha Jane will be the first to tell you that her passion for writing runs second only to her passionate love for the Lord. She is blessed to help Danny lead contemporary worship each Sunday at their church, Kennesaw United Methodist, in Kennesaw, Georgia, where she resides.

www.ingramcontent.com/pod-product-compliance
Lightning Source LLC
Chambersburg PA
CBHW020233260626
47156CB00002B/663

* 9 7 8 1 9 3 9 2 8 9 8 0 3 *